Educated in Europe and Canada, Philippe van Rjndt is a former student of international and Soviet affairs, who lives in Toronto.

Also by Philippe van Rjndt:

THE TETRAMACHUS COLLECTION
BLUEPRINT

Philippe van Rjndt

The Trial of
Adolf Hitler

Futura Publications Limited

A Futura Book

First published in Great Britain by
Macdonald & Jane's Publishers in 1979

First Futura Publications edition 1980
Reprinted 1980

ISBN 0 7088 1749 1

Printed in Great Britain by
Hazell Watson & Viney Ltd,
Aylesbury, Bucks

Futura Publications Limited
110 Warner Road
Camberwell, London SE5

For Malcolm, who first thought of the idea
and
Eve, who never lost faith in it

To both for more than I can repay

Prologue One

THE DIRECTOR had been standing very still, waiting for his eyes
to accept the darkness that swathed the United Nations General
Assembly. Slowly he looked around. Above him, to the left and
right, were the glass-enclosed press and VIP booths, nudging out
from the walls like opera seats. Tomorrow, when the trial began,
two uniformed Marine guards would be stationed in each of the
booths. In the walkway behind the visitors' gallery, which, for
the duration of the proceedings, would take the overflow from
the VIP boxes, ten more sentries would be present. Cameras One
and Two were responsible for covering this area as well as providing the long shots of the court below.

The director flexed his knees, bringing his tall, lean frame down
to the point where his eyes became level with the pilot scope of
the camera. Gently, in the way a racing driver would cradle his
steering wheel, he gripped the guide lever between the pincers of
his mechanical hand, at the same time pressing his eye against
the cold plastic cap. The world below him was reduced to the
microcosm of the frame. With infinitesimal pressure on the handle, he swung the camera across the six rows of delegates' seats,
close to seven hundred in all, bathed in the subdued glow of

overhead lights; focused on the center aisle and followed it up past Camera Three to the two-tiered island. Four steps above the main floor stood the podium for guest speakers; another four above that was the platform of the Secretary-General and his deputies, set behind a marble configuration which resembled more a Roman dining table than the modern desk. Behind that, set on the wall at the level of the enclosed galleries, was the shield of the United Nations. On either side of the island rested the hooded Cameras Four and Five. A few feet from them, more uniformed Marines would take their places; the number of plain-clothes security personnel who would mingle with the delegates was unknown.

The director felt the cooled air prickle his neck. He moved back and straightened up, passing his good hand over his fore-head. His cameraman was standing beside him, ready to load the film.

"Go ahead," the director said.

He sat back, watching the youth work silently, his fingers and hands moving in swift precision over the equipment. He envied his cameraman the use of his hands; he envied him, at times, his small, circumscribed world, bounded professionally by the expertise with which he handled any photographic equipment, personally by the somewhat pathetic adoration he bestowed on his male lover. The cameraman enjoyed an existence that was egocentric to the last. There was no need to venture beyond it, to feel part of a greater whole, a nation or generation or family, any continuum in which history illuminated the future. For him, Adolf Hitler was news, an entity seized, exploited and so re-created by the excitement of the media into a creature of hermaphroditic qualities. For the youth, Hitler had never lived before and would cease to exist when network fascination with him died, as it must.

"Ready to roll. Want me to check the rest?"

The director shook his head, obliterating this intrusion on his thoughts.

There were six or seven years between himself and the camera-man—not a great number, but pivotal. For the director was obsessed by Adolf Hitler. As soon as the story broke he had had himself assigned to Hitler, using every scrap of influence, every favor owed, to be appointed coordinator of the networks' telecast of the trial. In four months he had traveled over a hundred thousand miles, conducted countless interviews with those Hitler had in some way touched since his reincarnation. He pursued his passion with a ferocity that bewildered his colleagues and inundated studio editors with hundreds of rolls of film. Yet today, on the eve of the trial, he was no closer to understanding why this was so; only that it was . . .

"Sit back and don't move!" In one motion, the director rose and brought his eye to the camera, working the focus with his good hand. He waited, listening for that sound again—the faint metallic click of a door being unlocked. When he heard it, he pressed the motor button and activated the audio system.

In the tiny frame, the director saw the door to the right of the tiered island open and an armed guard come through. He looked around the auditorium, walked a few paces to the center aisle, glanced about once more and turned back to the door, raising his arm. The camera frame swung in the same direction, picking up the second man entering. The director recognized the young defense attorney. He came to the Marine and asked him something, receiving only a nod in return. He then returned to the side of the door as another figure appeared.

He was dressed in a poorly tailored chocolate-brown suit, the jacket hanging at the shoulders, the trousers baggy. The cream shirt was set off by a dark tie—possibly black, but one couldn't be certain at this distance of thirty yards. The man walked slowly, limping noticeably, his left arm swinging loosely as though it had no feel to it. The director activated the zoom lens and focused on the face. Behind the creases that broke up the forehead and the purple-edged scar cutting across the right cheek at an angle was the unmistakable face of Adolf Hitler. The hair was cut short, as in recent photographs; the lips were pressed tightly together as though holding back pain. Between the lips and the nose there was a thick ember-gray line, the outline of a grizzled moustache.

"What's doing down there?" the cameraman whispered, leaning forward in his seat. The director swung his right arm back, the stainless-steel pincers flashing before the cameraman's eyes.

Adolf Hitler and his attorney had come before the tiered island. The attorney was standing with his back to the camera, the elon-

gated shadows of his arms slipping over the walls, pointing out
the galleries and murals. Hitler, in profile, listened, then turned
and gazed out into the darkness of the Assembly. For an instant,
he was looking directly into the lens, although in the gloom he
wouldn't be able to discern either the camera or the man behind
it. The attorney then came to the edge of the first row of seats
and swung his arm first in an arc, then up and down to indicate
height. The director strained to hear their words, but the acous-
tics were such and the voices of the two men so low that nothing
above a murmur reached the upper galleries. Not that it mattered.
The highly sensitive sound boom would record the conversation.

The camera eye followed Hitler and the attorney as they
stepped up to the left side of the Secretary-General's podium.
The director was adjusting for a wide-angle shot when his cameraman whispered,

"The door on the right!"

In a fluid motion, he swung the camera in that direction, at the
same time working the zoom lens.

They entered in single file, the West German who would be
acting as prosecutor in the lead. Following him were the five
members of the international tribunal who would sit in judgment
over Adolf Hitler. The six assembled in a rough circle on the right
side of the auditorium, looking about themselves. Only one, a
dignified elderly gentleman, continued to stare straight ahead, his
hand resting on that of the single woman of the group. It was
obvious he was blind.

A magnificently cruel and ironic mistake had been made. Hitler
and his attorney had come down to this Assembly where Hitler's
fate would be decided twenty-five years after his alleged death.
For their own reasons, the prosecutor and the members of the
bench had elected to do the same. Each party had been unaware
the other would be present. Now they were both unwittingly
caught in the battle arena, unprepared, each still ignorant of the
others' presence . . . and of the camera which was about to record their inevitable meeting.

It happened now.

The defense attorney said something to Adolf Hitler, at the
same time pointing to the speaker's podium. Slowly, testing each

step as though he did not trust the ground beneath him, Hitler mounted the island and limped to the lectern. From that vantage point he looked out across the auditorium, and with delicate, unstoppable ease his gaze came to rest on the prosecutor and the justices, who had felt his presence at the same instant.

For several seconds Adolf Hitler stared down at the tribunal, his stern expression transforming into a contemptuous smile, the entire face shining in sweat, illuminated by the powerful overhead spotlights. He motioned for his defense attorney to come around, but cut him off as the lawyer turned to address the prosecutor.

"Let them be," Hitler commanded, his voice echoing in the great arena. "Let them look upon me and wonder. Let them see me without the benefit of their rules of law, their assassins' robes and this little court in which they will perform treachery. Let them see me as a man, not defendant or accused. Well, Prosecutor—what do you think: am I not very much the man you remember from thirty years ago?"

Zooming in on the faces of the justices, the camera recorded their mesmerization. Not one eye moved from Adolf Hitler; no lips opened to protest his words. Although anger showed in the expressions of those who beheld him, it was fascination that prevailed.

The defense attorney moved to Hitler's side, and he too stood smiling down upon the group. The camera did not deceive. Faithfully it recorded the two generations of Germany, separated by thirty-five years yet so very much akin when standing side by side—the pride, the arrogance, the reveling in stature. To raise a man only a few feet above his fellows is to intoxicate him with the rare air of power. The defense attorney acknowledged as much by his expression, unashamedly. But how much more did he feel, the director wondered, standing at the side of Hitler, basking in the potency of the personality, its magnetic appeal?

The prosecutor, to whom Adolf Hitler had addressed his question, shattered the spell. Ignoring Hitler and turning to the justices, he said, "I deeply regret this coincidence and suggest we leave. There is something foul in this place now."

Hitler's eyes were burning with rage, yet he held his counsel back when he was about to retort. He watched the justices filing out the door, and then he laughed—a dry mocking laughter which rang through the Assembly, spinning round and round until it disappeared. It had been an ignoble flight, a rout from which no honor might be salvaged. When the door had closed behind the prosecutor himself, Hitler stepped down from the podium and with his attorney in his wake, shuffled through the other exit, on the left, where the Marine guard waited patiently.

The Assembly was silent.

"Jesus, did the old man shit on them! He's really something!" the cameraman giggled.

"He is, isn't he?"

At the same instant, the lights above the visitors' gallery came on, blazing down upon the camera crew. The director stepped back from his instrument and looked at the speaker standing behind him on the walkway.

He was a tall man, with the bearing of a soldier though he was in civilian dress. He appraised the crew's reaction quickly, the eyes moving over the director's face, not flinching at the sight of the mechanical hand.

"Your cameraman appears impressed by Adolf Hitler," the stranger said, his English grammatically correct but heavily accented.

The director stepped out into the aisle.

"I believe I know you," he said.

"Major Oleg Vasilievich Kuzmin, aide to Marshal Zhukov and observer for the U.S.S.R. for this trial." He looked around himself and added, "It seems all of us wished to come here today, like some soldiers who answer to that strange desire to contemplate the battlefield where they may die."

"Yes," the director murmured. "I remember you from the Secretary-General's reception. That was where we met, wasn't it?"

"Yes, Captain. You were there," Kuzmin said, looking at the bars on the director's fatigue jacket.

The director did not often wear this particular jacket, with the rank and the insignia of his former Marine regiment. Neither had he destroyed it as another might have, to rid himself of an object which rekindled hateful memories. But since the Marines were responsible for security at the U.N. during the trial, he had used evidence of his former rank, and the wound, to elicit their sympathy and unofficial cooperation.

"You fought at Khe Sanh, did you not, Captain?"

"Yes."

"It was a brave effort." Kuzmin nodded. "As one soldier to another, I salute you." He held out his hand and the director gripped it.

"I trust, Captain, you are as talented with the camera as you were with your artillery pieces. I should like very much to see that film."

"I want a private screening in an hour." The director turned to his cameraman. "Get the film through the lab and set up the sound tapes. No one from Network is to know about it."

The two men watched the cameraman empty the chambers, then bound up the stairs two at a time to the media booth where the tape recorders had been installed.

"Does he know nothing of Adolf Hitler?" Kuzmin asked, the question tinged by disbelief.

"Nothing," the director answered. "We are living in an age of action and reaction, not critical thought. We create history, not learn about it."

"That is not true of you, Captain. I was watching you film this particular piece of history. You were not the dispassionate observer. You were living every second of the experience."

They left the auditorium behind and stepped out into the lobby.

"The story of Hitler's survival began almost four months ago," the director said softly. "I was in Munich the day after the prosecutor's announcement of Hitler's surrender. For the last one hundred and twenty days I have lived with Hitler. I have read everything that has been written about him; I have hundreds of hours of tapes with those people who knew him—and still, I cannot say I know him; that having seen him today, I am any less afraid of him. His image persists. It's as though he will not die. . . ."

"I have not heard other Americans express such sentiments, but I believe you know how close they are to my own," Kuzmin murmured. "I will tell you what the circumstances were when twenty-five years ago I almost came to see Hitler, in Berlin. Another time, another place—almost, one would think, another age;

but no, when I was watching him from the booth, the years melted away."

The two men stepped out into the brilliance of an autumn day. Kuzmin pointed to a car parked by the front gates.

"I have a driver. This way we will not be disturbed."

I

Flight

April 20, 1945

THE HUNTERS had arrived at the lair, a ruin called Berlin.

To the north, in lower Pomerania, Rokossovsky's Second Byelorussian Division replenished its armor from supply trains that shuttled unceasingly between the factories of Central Russia and the front lines, honing an already fine blade.

In the south, the First Ukrainians chafed, bewildered that the final thrust upon the city had suddenly been withheld. Bitterly they lived off their nerves while Marshal Konev alternately pleaded with and cajoled Stalin to launch the attack. But Stalin had not yet decided upon which of his commanders he would bestow immortality, as leader of the assault upon the capital.

In the center, Zhukov, hero of the Battles of Moscow, Stalingrad and Kursk, brooded about the carcass of Germany, which, though bleeding, was still swollen and horribly alive. For weeks he had been probing for the right striking point, examining the beast's position in the den, seeking the openings and defenses. Three times he had submitted plans of a successful line of attack to Moscow, and all, in as many days, had been considered, then held in abeyance. Stalin remained unmoved. He would not be hurried.

At last, on the 19th of April, the Kremlin elected that Konev would take the underbelly and Rokossovsky the head. Zhukov's own divisions would move directly for the torso and heart: the Führer's bunker under the Reich Chancellery. With the selection of the hero of the Battle of Berlin, all that remained was the killing and the dying.

April 20 dawned cold and wet, the sky covered in monotonous gray streaked faintly with yellow. Gunner Oleg Vasilievich Kuzmin of the 79th Rifle Corps had slept very little that night. It had not been the ceaseless rain, pounding on the truck's canvas top, that had kept him awake; not the groans and cries of men for whom the battle continued even into the subconscious. Gunner Kuzmin had not slept because of restlessness, exhaustion and expectation. Along the thirteen hundred miles between Stalingrad and Berlin he had felt his nerves wither, die and fall away in tiny fragments. They lay in the burning streets of villages whose names he could not remember; along country roads in the Dombas Basin that were like the trails to the charnel house of Hell; in the fields of the Ukraine where blood of animals mixed with that of men; in the cities of Kiev, Minsk and Warsaw, where human time had stopped and where the human heart no longer recognized itself. In places such as these, Gunner Kuzmin's sentiments, the decency and aspirations which bound him to the human race, had been scattered, invisible seeds that would grow in a tear-filled earth to bear fruit filled with juices of bitterest memories.

When he arrived at the outskirts of Berlin, Gunner Kuzmin had been violently ill. As he surveyed the distant buildings through his field glasses, three years of cold, hunger and horror overcame him. Images of his own bestiality, times when he had matched German atrocity with his own vengeful fury, shattered his senses, as Death clapped its arm round his shoulder and pointing to the helpless, hated city, threw back its head and laughed. Such was the shattered prize to behold.

Yet it was this act of sickness which subsequently brought forth tranquillity. After he cleaned himself and rested, Gunner Kuzmin once again surveyed the city, but this time with a cold, thoughtful eye. He measured distance against velocity; tried to determine which targets would yield most damage to the surrounding area when the shells struck them, which needed only reverberations to crumble. He made a note to ask for the meteorological charts. When he had finished his calculations he reckoned his battery would completely raze the city block around the Schlesischer Station in one afternoon.

Gunner Kuzmin stumbled out of the truck and slogged his way up the muddied path to the kitchens. The cooks had not yet finished brewing the morning tea, and his first cigarette tasted harsh without the beverage.

"Take some of mine."

Gunner Kuzmin hadn't noticed the tall, heavy figure sitting at the edge of the kitchens, on a barrel stamped NAILS in German. Before him, on another barrel topped by a sheet of splintered wood, lay a bundle of maps. Kuzmin stepped over and then recognized the officer as Marshal Zhukov. He snapped to attention.

Zhukov returned the salute wearily and beckoned him to come forward.

"Where is your cup?" he demanded.

Gunner Kuzmin hastily unclipped the cup from his mess kit and held it out. The Marshal filled it with a strong lemon tea from a covered pot that stood beside the keg.

"It's probably not very warm," Zhukov said absently.

"No, Comrade General," Kuzmin exclaimed. "It's very good and hot!"

"Horseshit. Sit down, boy," Zhukov told him, pointing to another keg. "We won't get decent tea until the British meet up with us. But we do not have long to wait now."

Kuzmin set his cup down on the makeshift table and rolled the barrel over.

"Which battery?" Zhukov asked him, drawing on a cigarette, watching the light wind pick up the smoke and spin it away.

"Seventy-ninth Rifle Corps, Third Shock Army," Kuzmin answered briskly.

"The Seventy-ninth," Zhukov murmured, and looked at Kuzmin. "You've been with me a long time, boy."

"I began at Stalingrad, Comrade General."

Zhukov said nothing. The boy was one of the dozen survivors of the original Seventy-ninth he himself had formed. Holy Mother

of God . . . since Stalingrad! But it was not the Marshal's way to
ask his men personal questions. He did not feed them a false
interest. He did not care about their villages or towns, their families, wives, parents, or what the men had endured to reach this
place. In Zhukov's thinking, sentiment blurred judgment; and
over these final kilometers he would demand the very best from
his troops. He would exhort them forward by the most vicious
oaths or invocations of the Deity, for in the godlessness of war
he understood that all soldiers, even himself, called upon the
eternal strength of the Motherland and the mercy of their Creator.
He wanted the thrust into Berlin to be hard, accurate and complete. He wanted the battle done with, for he was hungry for this,
his city.

Zhukov pulled one map out from under the others and placed
two stones to hold down the ends.

"The artillery begins in one hour," he said in a harsh voice.
"The Seventy-ninth is on this rise?"

"It is, Comrade General."

"You are responsible for the Schlesischer area?"

"Yes, sir."

"And your secondary targets?"

"We are in a direct line for the Chancellery itself. With luck we
might be in range by tonight."

Zhukov shook his head and lit another cigarette off the stub of
the first.

"You will not reach the Chancellery today," he said. "Not for
a few days yet. There is more to the German than meets the eye.
He is not dead yet. But when the time comes for the Chancellery,
remember this: Use your best eyes, and go high when you aim.
Take the time to be careful. That building must crumble upon its
own foundation, burying everything beneath it. I repeat: aim
high."

"The battalion commander ordered the exact opposite, Comrade General," Kuzmin said. "A level trajectory, where possible,
guarantees more impact. The results are better."

"The commander's orders may stand for anything else but the
Chancellery," Zhukov said coldly. "I want the Chancellery de-
stroyed but not the bunker. Chip away at it, and do it with care.
I want survivors. I want them trapped until we dig them out."

Gunner Kuzmin paused and looked up at Zhukov, who was sitting in profile.

"You want . . . *him*, Comrade General?" he asked hesitantly.

Zhukov turned on him. "Say his name!" he shouted. "Do not be afraid to utter it; go on!"

"Do you want . . . Hitler?"

"Say it again, without fear!"

"Hitler! Do you want Hitler?" Kuzmin shouted.

"Do *you* want him, Gunner? Don't you want to look at the face of the man who brought this misery upon our heads?"

Zhukov's face was pinched white, the chin thrust forward, eyes burning.

"Well, Gunner?"

"Yes, Comrade General, I do."

"Then why do you still fear him, when you are here and he is cowering in his den?"

Gunner Kuzmin could not answer. He had never thought of Hitler as a living man. He was a symbol, a mythical figure who commanded vast armies and wielded terror from the air and across the earth. There was no Hitler the man—there were only his legions, the men Kuzmin had aimed his guns against, at whom he had leveled machine guns, whom he had shot in the back or stabbed with a bayonet during retreats. He had had Hitler described to him a thousand times. He had seen many caricatures and photographs; yet now he could not bring himself to believe in that image.

"Hitler . . . he is not real, Comrade General. I can't explain it . . ." Kuzmin faltered. "But I will have the building for you."

"Gunner," Zhukov said urgently. "Do not be afraid to hate a little while longer. We have earned the right to. You are sick of all this and want peace without the final drops of blood it demands. But not here and not now. That is what Hitler wants, our fatigue, or else for us to trample mindlessly over him, destroying at random. No, Gunner, I will grant him neither wish. I want him brought out of that bunker and led across the lands he has devastated. I want him to feel our grip and see our eyes. I do not want him to die without being touched by us."

Kuzmin rose and saluted, but Zhukov did not return the formality. Instead he gripped Kuzmin's hand and shook it hard.

"The attack begins in less than thirty minutes. For the Motherland!"

When Gunner Kuzmin returned to his battery, the rest of the unit
was already there. His second in command, Corporal Yavorsky,
had stacked up the shells, and the adjutant was supervising the
digging of a deeper trench around the wheels. The rain had
washed away some of the earthen foundation during the night.

Kuzmin decided not to tell the men about the change in their
orders until the guns were in range of the Reich Chancellery. It
was a foolhardy omission, for if he was hit, his second should
know of Zhukov's personal directive for the unit. But Kuzmin
did not believe he would die there, on the outskirts of Berlin. It
was not fated to happen that way. First he would carry out Zhukov's orders and live to see his duty done.

At six thirty on the morning of April 20, General Kuznetsov,
Commander of the Third Shock Army, made the final inspection
of the batteries. As he passed the guns, the first shells were
loaded into the breeches. A radioman, walking behind the general, was waiting for the signal, which he would then transmit to
the unit commanders. Three minutes later Kuznetsov barked out
the order: firing was to commence in sixty seconds. Gunner Kuzmin looked down at his watch and counted off three-quarters of
that time. He turned to his battery, clapped his hands to get the
attention of his men and swung his arm down.

Gunner Kuzmin was the first man in the Soviet Army to fire
upon the city of Berlin. Five seconds later the other forty thousand pieces let loose their power, and the earth trembled and the
heavens disappeared.

April 30, 1945

"ALL THINGS shall pass away. Nothing remains but death and
the glory of deeds."

These words were murmured and barely audible. Eva Braun,
standing only a few feet away from the speaker, was looking
down at a design on the porcelain vase filled with fresh-cut roses.

She did not appear to have heard her husband's words, for her concern was with the flowers. Where, in these days, could you still get fresh roses? And who had brought them? It couldn't have been any of the women. She knew what they thought of her; they wouldn't have considered her worthy of such a rare gift. One of the generals—Krebs or Wielding: they were gentlemen. Not once did Eva Braun consider that it might have been her husband who had arranged for the roses.

"Did you say something?" Eva Braun asked, reluctantly turning away from her flowers.

Adolf Hitler was standing with his head bowed, hands lightly clasped behind his back, a pose he assumed when he wished everyone to know he was in deep thought and should not be disturbed. Slowly he faced her and his eyes softened as he looked upon the blue-and-white polka-dot dress she was wearing, a favorite of his.

"I said"—he spoke again, deliberately—"that all things must pass. Nothing remains but death and the glory of deeds."

Eva smiled hesitantly, not knowing what to make of the words. It was increasingly difficult to understand this man who had just become her husband. His thoughts were voiced in fragments. He would begin a sentence, then stop halfway and glare at the listeners, expecting them to correctly guess its meaning.

"Do you want to finish this wine?" Hitler asked her.

Eva shook her head. The vase on the table trembled as shock waves from the shells reverberated through the concrete wall of the bunker.

"Closer; they are getting closer," Eva murmured.

Again she looked at her husband and this time did not hide her beseeching expression. They had come into this room to die, but he had insisted on a drink of champagne and a few minutes to reflect upon final thoughts. She glanced down at her watch. Only a quarter hour had gone by? She would have sworn it was more than that. Still, it was too long.

"Adolf," she whispered.

"Yes, you are right," he said tonelessly. "It is time."

He came to her and took her hand, raising it to his lips awkwardly.

"You are cold," he said. "Your skin is like gooseflesh."

"Nerves." She laughed a little too loudly. "There is nothing left to them after this constant bombardment."

"You needn't worry," he assured her. "They are still far away, very far away. They will never reach us."

Although he looked ghastly, his face pale and cheeks sunken, his eyes were clear. They were not the eyes of a dead man, nor did they carry the flame that seemed to forewarn of his raving fits. The eyes were almost content, as though for the first time he had discovered a peace, a moment unburdened by command, decision, threats of defeat, the whole terrible lie under which he had been living—the illusion of a victorious end.

Holding her hand, Adolf Hitler led his wife over to the couch and bade her sit. On the side tables were two revolvers and six capsules of potassium cyanide. He moved closer to her, and together they looked over the room chosen as their death chamber.

"It reminds me of the places where I spent so much of my life," Hitler said vaguely. "The worn rug, cabinets that are nothing but cheap reproductions, dirty prints of mediocre paintings."

She squeezed his hand.

"But we are together. That is the difference. You are not alone anymore."

"Which do you want?" he asked her suddenly. "The cyanide is very quick . . ."

At once there was a great hammering on the door, followed by the shriek of a woman and the sound of a body thrown heavily against a wall. The woman's voice rose above the shouts of the guard. Hitler walked over to the door and stood listening. The shouting died away into wretched sobbing. There was a knock on the door and the Führer opened it to find Otto Kronhausen, lieutenant of the SS and chief security officer for the bunker, standing before him.

"My Führer," Kronhausen said. He was a huge man—six and a half feet tall, with the build of a dray horse. His pale eyes looked past Hitler straight into the back wall. "Frau Goebbels insists on speaking with you."

"Is that she out there?"

"I have removed her to another room, my Führer. She was too excited to be permitted to speak with you immediately."

"What does she want?" Hitler demanded irritably.

"She believes she has a plan by which Berlin may be spared, but only if you yourself take direct command. She begs to be permitted to present this idea to you."

"Another plan! They are offering me their precious plans when it is too late, too late! We need their obedience, not idiotic speculation. Tell that stupid woman to go away. We are not to be disturbed again."

Adolf Hitler was trembling with rage. The protective aura of illusion he had so carefully woven around himself had disintegrated, and once again he was aware of the shells dropping amid the screams of debauchery that echoed through the bunker.

"That is all, Kronhausen!"

Locking the door behind him, Adolf Hitler returned to his wife's side and pressed a capsule into her hand.

"Now," he said pitilessly. "Do it now."

Eva Braun stared at the capsule and rolled it between her fingers. Her hands were sweating, and she could see the capsule leaving a residue on her skin. Beside her, Hitler was wrapping a Walther pistol in a tea towel. His expression was one of calm and quiet concentration, as though the incident at the door had never happened. Then she noticed the tightness in his mouth and recognized the struggle going on inside him, his determination to maintain a grip on death so that he would not have to think of what he was doing but could simply surrender himself to his reflexes.

"Farewell, Eva!" he said sternly. She wanted to say something to him—but whatever the words might have been, they were lost in the weak cry she uttered before shoving her fingers into her mouth. At the same instant, Hitler raised his gun to his temple. Eva Braun bit hard into the capsule and swallowed. There was only a second left to release a gurgle deep in her throat and then she died, her body in spasm, the arms flinging out and striking the water jug on the side table. When she fell against his shoulder, Adolf Hitler was squeezing the trigger.

Otto Kronhausen had heard Adolf Hitler lock the door to his private chambers from the inside. Nonetheless, before leaving to

see Magda Goebbels, the SS officer turned the outside latch as
well.

"Is he still alive?" Willi Schmidt whispered to him. Schmidt,
Hitler's personal servant, had been standing in the shadow off to
the side of the door, straining to hear the pistol shot.

"He lives," Kronhausen said curtly, and walked on. Schmidt
grimaced and tugged out another cigarette from his breast pocket.
At his feet lay almost a dozen butts.

Kronhausen continued down the corridor, jackboots echoing
off the concrete floor. Quickly he climbed the few steps connect-
ing the upper and lower bunkers, and went through the dining
passage where those who lived on the upper level took their
meals. When he reached the corridor that led to the front entrance, a storm of Furies swept out of one of the small rooms. A
naked girl collided with him, then ran in the opposite direction
shrieking in dementia. She was pursued by a half-dressed SS man
whose hands were covered with blood. Farther down the hall,
two more women were being held up against the wall and raped.
One of the brutalizers Kronhausen recognized as the wife of a
general, who had made herself a man by strapping a plastic organ
around her hips. Kronhausen paid no attention to them. He had
seen worse during these last days. In almost every one of the
sixteen small rooms that combined to form the honeycomb of the
first-level bunker, some form of depravity was being practiced
without any attempt to hide the fact. Even the doctor's office and
dispensary had become erotic theaters after the Führer's physician had departed.

Farther down the corridor, Kronhausen paused before the
open door of a larger, sparsely furnished room which served as
the unofficial gathering place of the officer corps. There was
music here, strains of Schumann which were butchered by a ru-
ined stylus and the whines of the electric generator. On the table
stood half-empty bottles of wine and spirits. There was glass on
the floor, and there were stains on the uniforms of the SS and
General Staff officers who were standing about in various stages
of drunkenness, toasting each other and recounting dirty jokes.
In a corner, an aide to General Keitel was crying uncontrollably.
Another officer walked up to him and slapped his face, but it did
no good. The officer spat upon the man and walked away. At the

other end of the room, two men were dancing, their arms about each other very tightly. When someone finally recognized Kronhausen, the security man had already noted that Goebbels wasn't in the room. As he moved off, there were shouts after him. Suddenly everyone wanted to know whether Hitler was dead.

Kronhausen walked on. Just before coming to Goebbels' apartment, he was seized by the arm by a drunken girl whose face was swollen from beating.

"I want more," she groaned at him. "More, d'you understand?"

And she began to rub both hands violently over her crotch, grinning at Kronhausen. He glanced at her arms and saw the fresh tracks of the heroin needle.

"Kronhausen! Kronhausen!"

He turned around, brushing off the girl, who collapsed on the floor. Erik Kempka, the Führer's driver, had run up behind him.

"Listen, you had better come with me," Kempka said quickly. "That son-of-a-bitch of a guard upstairs won't let me bring down the gasoline. Thinks I'm going to blow up the bunker."

"How much do you have?" Kronhausen asked him.

"About a hundred and eighty liters. I can't leave it in the back of the truck. A stray shell and that's the end of all of us."

"Take it around to the back, the entrance to the Führer's chambers."

"I told you, I can't move with it. One of your men will shoot me if I come any closer to the bunker."

"Come with me," Kronhausen told him.

They walked down to Goebbels' room, where Kronhausen asked Kempka to wait. He entered without knocking, to see Magda Goebbels sitting back in a wing chair, her husband holding a wet cloth to her forehead.

"She's fainted," Goebbels explained quickly. "Will the Führer see her?"

Kronhausen smiled faintly. "The Führer is not seeing anyone."

At the mention of the title, Magda Goebbels stirred and raised her head.

"My Führer," she groaned. "My Führer, you have come . . . to hear me."

She began to push herself out of the chair, her arms thin and spindly, the face haggard and eyes shining in brilliant madness.

"You are not the Führer!" she screamed at Kronhausen. "Joseph, you lied to me. You said—"

"Magda, you are distraught."

"You are keeping me from my Führer," she cried miserably. "In his greatest hour, when he can save all of Germany, we are surrounded by traitors. . . ."

"She is demented," Kronhausen said coldly. "Keep her away!"

Goebbels' expression turned into hatred, and for a moment he loosened his grip on his wife, who quickly leaped up at Kronhausen, screaming obscenities. The SS officer caught her by the wrist and carelessly flung her back.

"I told you to keep her still," he repeated to Goebbels, and left.

"It is like the time of the Black Death," Kempka muttered as he ran after Kronhausen. "They are all insane. What are you going to do?"

Kronhausen did not answer but kept on walking, master of the madness, enforcer of his own order.

When he reached the stairs that went up to the main entrance, he shouted for one of the guards to come down.

"Do you need anyone to help you?" he asked Kempka.

"No, there's another man in the truck."

"Let him pass to the back," Kronhausen told the guard. "And if he needs help, give it to him."

Kronhausen turned back to Kempka. "It is probably over by now. I will be bringing them up shortly."

With that, Kronhausen began his return to the lower bunker where he believed Adolf Hitler and his bride were lying dead.

Outside the door to the Führer's private chambers, Willi Schmidt was pacing nervously. Sometimes he would stop and hold his breath, trying at once to keep the turmoil of the outer corridors out of his mind and straining to hear the slightest sound in the vault. He pressed his ear to the door, and while he heard nothing, his nostrils did catch a whiff of gunpowder. It was barely perceptible, and at first Schmidt thought it might be the smoke drifting down from the other rooms, or dust from the ceiling. But no, it was the stink of cordite, Schmidt was certain.

"Thank God you've come," Schmidt whispered to Kronhausen. "It's over."

Kronhausen looked down at him, eyes narrowed.

"Smell! You can smell the gunpowder."

Kronhausen said nothing but quickly opened the first lock, then with another key undid the latch Hitler had secured from the inside. He stepped inside, beckoning Schmidt to follow, then closed up after him.

Adolf Hitler and Eva Braun were on the couch, their bodies supporting each other. Kronhausen went over and looked at the woman first. He reached under her chin and raised her head to examine the mouth. There were bits of a capsule clinging to her lips. He let the head drop. There was no need to touch the Führer. He had used both the gun and the capsules to ensure his death. There was a bloody wound above and to the right of the temple, and the remains of several capsules hung from the woolen threads of his tunic.

"Bring Goebbels at once," he ordered Schmidt. "But not his wife. I do not want to see her."

Schmidt, who had been staring at the dead couple, regained his senses and backed away toward the door. He wrenched it open and fled into the corridor.

Kronhausen did not touch anything until Goebbels arrived, followed by Artur Axmann, leader of the Hitler Youth, and Martin Bormann, Reichsleiter and Party Leader. The three men stared mutely at the bodies but did not approach them. Axmann, dressed in battle fatigues filthy from street fighting, flung out his arm in a final salute.

"Heil Hitler!"

"The gasoline is ready," Kronhausen said. "We will bring the bodies up now."

"We should tell everyone else," Goebbels muttered nervously.

Kronhausen shrugged. "That is not my responsibility. I am to oversee the destruction of the bodies."

Goebbels nodded curtly and left the room. Axmann, with tears in his eyes, bowed his head, then followed.

"Get the sheets," Kronhausen told Schmidt. The SS lieutenant lifted Eva Braun away from the Führer and carried her to the center of the room. Schmidt spread out the sheet, and Kronhausen laid the body on top. He straightened out the limbs and rolled up the sheet.

"Will you carry her up?" he asked Bormann.

Bormann nodded silently and knelt down. Grunting, he lifted the body, but its weight caused him to lose his balance and he stumbled back against the cabinet.

"It's all right!" he snapped at Kronhausen, who moved to help him. "I can manage."

"Schmidt, help the Reichsleiter," Kronhausen ordered.

While the two men maneuvered the body of Eva Braun toward the staircase leading to the rear of the Chancellery garden, Kronhausen arranged another sheet and picked up the corpse of Adolf Hitler. He laid it down gently and once more straightened the arms and legs and began to cover them.

"Stop. . . ."

The single word, though weakly uttered, carried with it the command Kronhausen recognized so well. His movements stopped instantly. He watched as Adolf Hitler's eyes fluttered open and the cold gaze rose up directly at him.

"Stop. . . ."

"My Führer!"

Adolf Hitler tried to raise his head, then groaned in pain and rolled over, exposing the wound on his temple. Kronhausen immediately lifted him forward, and Hitler vomited. He coughed and racked, and the bile poured forth onto the uniform and sheet. Kronhausen continued to hold him, oblivious to the stench and mess.

"I must not die," Hitler gasped, head bent forward. "Kronhausen, I must not die. I tried, and fate would not deliver me up. It is not my destiny to die here; do you understand?"

"Yes, my Führer," Kronhausen whispered.

"Where is Eva?"

"They are preparing her body for cremation, my Führer."

"I must not die," Hitler repeated hoarsely. "The gun, the poison, they could not kill me. It is not my destiny to die here."

Kronhausen heard shouts, followed by footsteps coming from the stairwell.

"They are coming for you," he said tightly.

"Kill someone else!" Hitler hissed. "Kill him and cover his face and burn him. Tell no one about me. Come back when it has been done."

"Lie very still," Kronhausen said. "It shall be done."

Kronhausen rose and quickly stepped over to the entrance of the staircase. He refused to think about the miracle he had just witnessed and prepared himself for what was to be done. He would kill the first man who came down those stairs, no matter who it was—Bormann, Schmidt, whoever.

It happened to be Schmidt.

Hitler's servant stepped into the room, bewildered at the mess on the supposed corpse.

"What has been going on . . . ." he began. "Kronhausen . . .?"

Like a djin rising to the command of its master, Kronhausen stepped from behind and swung down his enormous hand in a cutting motion. Schmidt did not utter a sound as his neck snapped and he crumpled to the floor. Kronhausen dragged the body next to Hitler, let it drop and helped the Führer to his feet.

"Get him out and stay with him while he burns, until the face is unrecognizable," Hitler whispered.

Kronhausen acknowledged the command and swiftly began to unbutton the Führer's filthy tunic. He managed to clean it somewhat, then struggled to move Schmidt's arms into Hitler's clothing. When that was done, he stepped into the bathroom and returned with a hot-water bottle. Using his SS dagger, he slit the thick rubber until the bottle had been cut lengthwise in two. Then he rolled the body of the servant onto the soiled cloth, quickly shot him through the temple and placed the rubber sheet over his face like a mask. He covered the head with a small pillow before wrapping up the sheet. Hitler, who had stood himself up against the wall, nodded weakly.

"Lock the other door," he said, indicating the front entrance. "And the back when you go out. No one is to enter."

Kronhausen stepped over and bolted the door. He returned to pick up the servant, lifting the body easily over his shoulder, and moved to the stairwell. He glanced back once, to see Adolf Hitler staring at him, his eyes glowing, the face glistening with sweat.

Kronhausen made his way up and kicked open the door leading

into the garden. The body of Eva Braun had been placed in a shallow trench, less than a foot deep. He kicked the door shut behind him.

"Schmidt couldn't take it," Kronhausen said. "He was ill, and I sent him away."

He laid the body next to Eva Braun's and picked up the jerry can of gasoline. Carefully he doused both corpses until they were well soaked.

"Bring me that wood over there," he ordered Kempka.

"Is that necessary?" Bormann inquired solicitously.

"For the ashes," Kronhausen replied. "There should be a mixture of ashes in case the graves are found. That will confuse the investigation."

Bormann nodded to the chauffeur, who went over to the pile of splintered boards that lay against the side of the bunker and brought over an armful. Kronhausen arranged these around and over the grave, poured on more fuel and stepped back. He soaked the top of a board in gasoline, lit it and tossed it onto the pyre. A soft flame rose; then suddenly the whole grave began to burn, sending up flames into the dusty air.

The three men watched as the wind caught the flames and carried them around the pit. The wood sputtered a little as the gasoline mixed in with the dampness, but within minutes there was a perceptible odor of burning flesh. Bormann took several steps back and looked away from the flames. As the blaze began to take hold of the bodies, Kronhausen poured on more gasoline. Through the heat he could see the face of Eva Braun melting, the flesh slowly sliding off the bone. The features of the man beside here were obscured by a mucuslike coat of blackening rubber that was running across the face. Kronhausen poured more fuel there, creating a high flame that consumed the head entirely.

No one but Kronhausen tended the fire. Kempka, who had been expecting that duty, was relieved. Bormann simply stood there, moving only when the wind shifted and carried the odor directly at him. Here, in the garden of the Chancellery, the end of the Thousand Year Reich was being solemnly celebrated in a microcosm of the fury and killing around the three men. As these two bodies burned, so did the city of Berlin, and beyond, all of Germany.

Kronhausen waited until the bodies had been reduced to bone; then he poured on a few more gallons of gasoline and turned to Kempka.

"You will take over. Do not leave here until I return. There is to be nothing but ashes."

Kempka lowered his eyes and dragged over two more cans. He was thankful that although the stench prevailed, there was nothing in the trench that could be recognized as a body.

Kronhausen returned downstairs to the bunker, locking the door behind him. The Führer was not in his chamber. Kronhausen called out softly, identifying himself. When there was no response, he entered the bedroom, discovering it empty. He proceeded into the bathroom.

Adolf Hitler was sitting slumped forward on the covered toilet, a wet towel pressed against the side of his head. He had vomited once more, as Kronhausen saw by the stains in the bathtub. He was still sweating profusely, and the eyes burned on as though in a rage.

"My Führer, it has been done," Kronhausen said. "The body has been consumed beyond visible recognition. Soon there will be nothing but ashes."

"Who was the man?"

"Schmidt."

Hitler said nothing to this but instead demanded, "Is the city still fighting?"

"It is, my Führer."

"So it is still possible to escape to the west."

"Difficult, but quite possible. The front lines are very fluid, although in the last days there has been one route used with great success."

"Good." Hitler rose, supporting himself on the washbasin. "I will tell you what happened," he said thickly. "So that only you know." He looked at Kronhausen for confirmation.

"It is understood, my Führer."

"My wife took poison. When she bit into the capsule she fell against me. At that moment I had the gun to my head. Her movement jostled my arm, and when the gun went off the bullet grazed my flesh, nothing more. I reached for the remaining capsules and swallowed four, chewing on them. I lost consciousness, but knew

I was not dead. There was a great pain in my chest and stomach.
I couldn't see anything except for blotches of color and tried to
speak but couldn't. You see what happened? The poison did not
kill me. Destiny decreed that I should not die—not here; that
there was still work to be done and my role in history had not yet
ended. In spite of the defeat brought upon me by traitors, I should
continue to live."

Kronhausen believed these words. He had seen the wound and
bits of the cyanide capsules. There had been enough poison in
those pills to put a horse to sleep. Yet the Führer lived.

Kronhausen wanted to believe in a miracle, for such acts of
Fate were closely related not only to the person of the Führer but
also to the Reich. He recalled another incident, long ago, when
poison had failed and those who would have been murderers had
been driven to proclaim the extraordinary. What Kronhausen
was thinking of was the murder of Rasputin, the mad monk who
had sat at the right hand of the Empress of Russia. Rasputin had
been lured to the home of the Grand Duke Yussoupov and there
given cakes whose batter had been generously leavened with cyanide. Rasputin had eaten enough poison to kill him several times
over. He had fainted and been presumed dead; yet when the
assassins returned with a bag in which to carry him off, Rasputin
was standing before them in vengeful fury. In the end they had to
chase the monk across the fields and at last drown him in an icy
creek.

There had never been a satisfactory explanation in that case.
Rasputin's constitution? Too much poison, so that it negated the
intended effect? A benevolent gesture from the gods? Kronhausen did not know. It was impossible to understand and therefore
a miracle.

"What does my Führer command?"

Hitler gestured at the razor lying on the stand beside the basin.

"You will shave me," he said. "And cut my hair so that it is
very short. There are civilian clothes in my room and a warm
coat. Bring them here. I will wash myself and then we leave."

"But my Führer, without the help of tanks and a company of
the best soldiers there is a great risk."

"There can be no troops or tanks—no one! What do you think
those Mongols from the East will be waiting for? Precisely that—
a sign of a breakthrough, a concentration of armor. Armor will

destroy us. No, we must move silently and quickly, without fuss; do you understand?''

"I will do my best," Kronhausen answered calmly.

"Yes, you shall. Now take some soap and shave me."

Kronhausen managed to draw some tepid water from the tap and rubbed the bar of soap with the shaving brush. His hand trembled when it came to touch Hitler's face, but he willed it to go forward, and his fingers seized the chin. He applied the lather quickly and began scraping off the stubble.

"The moustache," Hitler murmured. "Take that off completely."

Stroke by stroke the job was done, and then Kronhausen began on the hair. Soon the bathroom floor was sprinkled with irregularly cut hair, which Kronhausen later swept up and flushed down the toilet.

"Tell me, Kronhausen, how did they like my death, Bormann and the others?"

"They were grieving for you, my Führer."

"*You* might have been, Kronhausen," Hitler said. "But the others, they were thinking of how quickly to put their tails between their legs.

"Now go and arrange my clothes," Hitler told him when Kronhausen had cleaned up. "There's a first-aid kit somewhere in the front room. Take whatever medicines are left. I will need them."

Kronhausen went into the bedroom and pulled out several suits from the closet, along with shirts and sweaters. He chose the warmest of these and returned to the bathroom.

"Your clothing, my Führer."

"Bring it in."

Hitler was standing wrapped in a towel, shivering. His body was deathly white and thin.

"Hang it up on the door," he said irritably.

Kronhausen did as he was told, then returned to the sitting room and brought out the first-aid kit that lay in the bottom of a small armoire. The kit was the size of a small suitcase and contained ample quantities of morphine, ointments, bandages and vitamin pills. Everything medicinal that might be needed in an emergency had been packed—including, Kronhausen noted, two cyanide capsules. He let these remain.

There was another, smaller, case hidden away in the corner of the cabinet. Unlike the medical kit, which Kronhausen had already known about through Hitler's physician, he had no idea where this second bag had come from. Kronhausen pulled it out, surprised at its weight; opened it and stared at twenty-odd gold bars. Each ingot was only a few centimeters thick, but quite long—about twenty-seven centimeters. Kronhausen, who had thought he was privy to all secrets of the bunker, could not account for this discovery. Nonetheless, it appeared that Destiny was providing his Führer with everything needed to escape: medicine, gold for barter and a strong companion. Kronhausen locked the case and pushed it over beside the other.

When Hitler emerged from the bathroom, Kronhausen was astounded at his appearance. Even to the SS lieutenant, who was accustomed to seeing the Führer daily, he was barely recognizable: nothing remained of the proud, stern man Kronhausen knew well. Instead, Hitler looked like a clerk—an underfed, miserable little man whom life had chewed upon and spat out with contempt.

"A full change will require time," Hitler said. "For the moment this much will do." He reached inside one of his pockets and drew out a handkerchief with the initials A.H. embroidered in gold.

"I didn't expect that kind of mistake from you, Kronhausen. Put it back in the bedroom."

While Kronhausen disappeared, Hitler shuffled across the room, looking up suddenly whenever a shell exploded overhead and its reverberations penetrated the concrete. From time to time he rubbed a washcloth over his face.

"Are you certain, my Führer, that you do not want Professor Haase to come here?" Kronhausen asked him.

"What can my physician do for me but increase the risk of exposure?" Hitler demanded. "If the poison hasn't killed me now, then it will not do so. There is no need for Haase."

"Very well, my Führer," Kronhausen said. "Then we have finished here."

"Go and see what is happening outside," Hitler told him. "Get a small truck of some sort, with as much fuel as is to be found. And lock all the doors. I will be waiting here."

Kronhausen took the bags over to the door, turned around to

salute and left. The passageway was quieter now, the concrete floor strewn with bits of food, broken glass and torn clothing. As he passed by the officers' room, Kronhausen saw that only members of the General Staff remained, most of them in a stupor, lying on the floor. One had his arms stretched out toward a girl, but his eyes were staring out at Kronhausen in the manner of a zombie.

When he reached the top of the stairs, Kronhausen realized that the SS must already have abandoned their posts at the entrance to the bunker. Word of Hitler's death had spread quickly enough. So the Führer was correct, as usual: every scum for himself. Kronhausen did not see any security around the perimeter of the bunker either. He considered that that was just as well: there would be no one to witness the Führer's transfer.

Quickly Kronhausen reconnoitered the area. He spotted a military ambulance about fifty yards from the Chancellery and ran toward the vehicle, crouching low and staying in the center of the street to avoid the falling brick and stone. When he came up, Kronhausen saw that there was only a single driver. He was waiting for a unit of Tiger tanks to pass by.

"What are you carrying?" Kronhausen demanded, leaping onto the running board.

The driver was an elderly man, a member of the Home Guard.

"Children," he muttered. "I am carrying children."

"Don't move from here! I must see what you are carrying."

Kronhausen hurried around the truck and flung back the canvas. The old man had told the truth. Children. Dead children of the Hitler Youth. Boys of ten and twelve; girls of fifteen. German children thrown into the rear of a filthy ambulance like so many animal carcasses, without thought for their tender years. Kronhausen counted eight bodies; then laid back the tarpaulin and got into the seat beside the driver.

"Take the truck over there, to the side of the Chancellery."

The old man shook his head. "I must bury these children," he muttered.

"But there are more!" Kronhausen shouted at him. "Another three I took inside the bunker. We must get them as well."

The Volkssturmer gazed at Kronhausen steadily, his lips quivering. He did not know whether or not to believe this SS officer.

"Please, Father," Kronhausen pleaded. "We must hurry."

The old man nodded and threw the gears into reverse. He turned the ambulance around and guided the vehicle through the piles of rubble and shell holes, moving as close as possible to the entrance Kronhausen pointed out.

"Now help me!" Kronhausen shouted, jumping out. "We must rearrange the bodies."

The old man slowly got out and as though in a daze walked over to where Kronhausen was standing.

"We will put the bodies here for the moment." Kronhausen indicated a patch of grass beside the bunker that had escaped the shelling.

"Why?"

"Because there are those who are still alive! Now help me!"

Together the two men removed the twisted, bloodied corpses and laid them down in a ragged row, the heads all but touching the bunker. Kronhausen leaped inside the ambulance and examined what was left. All the medical equipment was gone; the blankets were torn and stained. Nonetheless, the vehicle seemed roadworthy. It ran, and Kronhausen knew there was enough gasoline. He had checked the gauge and also found three large reserve cans in the rear.

"Stay here, Father, and don't allow anyone to take the vehicle." Kronhausen said quickly. "I will bring the children up."

Kronhausen disappeared into the bunker and ran down the central corridor. There was no sound in the chambers now. Those who remained were either unconscious or dead. Kronhausen unlocked the door to the Führer's private rooms and stepped inside.

Adolf Hitler was sitting on the same couch where he had tried to commit suicide.

"Is everything ready?" he asked in a low voice, without raising his head.

"It is, my Führer."

"What kind of transport have you found?"

"An ambulance."

"If we can, we must get a few more things on the way, Kronhausen: maps, to tell us the approximate positions of the British and American forces so that we can avoid their patrols, and suitable identification for me."

"Yes, my Führer."

"Where is the vehicle?"

"To the side of the bunker. The driver was an old man, carrying dead children."

"Do we need him to get us out of Berlin?"

"No, my Führer. I know which roads are still open. We can get out of the city easily enough. Later on, when we move through occupied territory, the going will become dangerous."

"We must get to the south," Hitler said vaguely. "Is there anyone left to see us go?"

"They are all dead or drunk."

"Suitable," muttered Hitler. "You will wrap me up in a sheet, as before, and carry me over your shoulder. We must take everything this one time."

Kronhausen went into the bedroom and ripped off a sheet from the four-poster. He draped it over the Führer's head and proceeded to wrap the sheet completely around Hitler's body, taking care to cover the face twice over. Kronhausen squatted and in one motion brought his shoulder under Hitler's midriff, swinging him over. With his free hand he gripped both the medical chest and the case of gold. He kicked the door open.

Kronhausen reached the outside without incident. The ambulance driver was keeping watch over the vehicle, staring stupidly at the flames in the distance, squinting every time a shell burst. Kronhausen dropped the two cases on the ground and pushed Hitler's body into the tarpaulin, forcing it through into the rear of the ambulance. He tossed the medical bag in after it and secured the flap. The gold he took to the front and squeezed in behind the passenger seat.

"How many more are there?" the old man asked.

"No more."

"But you said there were *several* children," the Home Guard soldier protested.

"There are no more!" Kronhausen said savagely.

"Then help me get these back." The old man bent down and began to lift the legs of a dead child.

"Let me see your papers," Kronhausen demanded.

"What do you want? Help me, for the love of God; there isn't much time."

"Give me your papers, now!"

The old man dropped the child's limbs and brought out from the breast pockets of his uniform dirty, tattered pieces of identification. Kronhausen examined the Home Guard registration and identity cards. The old man was named Werner Busse; fifty-eight years old; born in Salzburg, Austria.

"All right," he said. "Let's get the kids on the truck."

The old man held out his hand. "Give me back my papers. I need them."

"You'll get them when we move off. Now hurry!"

The elderly soldier bent down once more, and that was when Kronhausen shot him, in the back of the neck. The SS officer ran back to the ambulance and lifted the flap.

"Is everything all right, my Führer?"

"It is!" a muffled voice answered. "What is keeping you?"

Kronhausen dropped the identity pieces inside. "You may find these of some use."

Then he jumped into the cab and started the engine. The escape of Adolf Hitler had reached one more stage.

A plague had fallen over the city, a pestilence in which Berlin writhed, dead yet undead, screaming in agony but also in hatred as its body was hit again and again by an opponent who was steadily working his way across to its heart.

Berlin was dying. Overhead, swirling dust covered the streets and buildings from the eye, hiding the tracing arc of shells and Katyusha rockets as they raced over and into the city, piercing, then destroying. Those buildings standing trembled and groaned, the brick and plaster and wood cracking and splintering about those who still huddled inside. The houses and cinemas, the shops and theaters, the palaces and apartment blocks stood defenseless against the onslaught, and one by one they disintegrated before the fury from the sky.

The earth trembled as though possessed by a demon demanding its freedom, and beneath the streets the arteries of the city burst apart. The subway, home of thousands of human moles sheltered there, was flooded at Friedrichstrasse. The waters burst forth from the mains and swept down upon those who lay on the platforms, their bundles and bags pressed close to their bodies, their children curled up against the walls under tattered posters of brave models who exhorted Victory. The waters carried all of them off, and no prayer from the mouths of men could have saved them. Those who attempted to flee up the ramps to the tops of the stations were also doomed, for at the moment the waters were released another artillery barrage began, and above, people were streaming from the streets into the subway. The two forces collided, and each man trampled over his brother without the slightest hesitation.

Trees splintered and broke apart in single cracks of agony, like bones snapping under the strain of a torture wheel. Between the trees, along the sidewalks and streets, rivers of fire traveled swiftly, consuming all in their path. The fires were born from the gasoline in trucks and cars, in the cavernous holds of tanks which roamed the ruins like the last of the dinosaurs. Whenever a tank was hit, the explosion shattered the dusty interior and blew it apart. What was left of the fuel then streamed out, and the fires hungrily chased after the life-giving fluid, turning the asphalt of the streets into boiling pitch.

The ambulance moved through the Tiergarten, past the area of the Zoo Station and onto Kantstrasse. Kronhausen turned left at Messedamm, which bordered on what was left of the Grunewald Forest, and made for the general direction of Wannsee. The going was very slow, along roads that were clogged by rubble, burning vehicles, destroyed guns and tanks and, always, refugees who moved like crippled phantoms among the ruins.

Adolf Hitler was lying on his back, his right hand tightly gripping the stretcher bar that was welded on the side of the ambulance. It wasn't much support, but it helped against the swaying and rocking of the vehicle. His left arm, withered and useless after the attempt on his life the previous year, was beginning to ache intolerably. But he was glad of that. By concentrating on the pain he shut out the fury of the world beyond the canvas. Slowly and deliberately he trained his mind on the damage to his body. He still felt some pain in his stomach, although it rose and diminished, and he did not know whether it was the acid in his empty stomach or the poison beginning to work its way through his intestines. Briefly relinquishing his grip on the stretcher bar, he felt the bandage around his head. Near the temple the cloth was dry—a good sign, although there was a persistent throb, which was aggravated by the shellfire. Hitler was tempted to search for the painkillers in the first-aid kit. Yet he was afraid that the combination of medicines and poison would be fatal. His life was being held by hands other than his own, and he surrendered to them, pushing back the instinct to help himself.

Hitler twisted around and worked himself forward on his stomach to lift the back of the canvas. He stared out at the destruction behind him and was spellbound by it. Just as his victories had been so complete, now in defeat he was leaving his nation in utter destruction. He who could not abide weakness; who never visited military hospitals because the crippled and wounded repelled him; who drove through conquered lands with car windows shuttered against the annihilation he had wrought so that he might not falter before the reality; who had determined which race should be reduced to extinction or slavery; who had bathed in the fury, glory and utter totality of his vision: this man now moved to the opposite extreme as he savored the ruin of his state. What drew Adolf Hitler to this landscape of human shock and misery was its utter completeness. He watched the faces of refugees as they moved down the street, carrying their pathetic bundles, their children moving ahead of them or being held tightly by the hand. They walked on quickly, stumbling, half running, never looking back at the inferno of this modern Gomorrah, victims of an avenging God.

"Do they hate me?" he muttered thickly. "Are they worthy of hating me as they loved me? Would they dare? No, they would not. It would be inconceivable for me to suffer Mussolini's fate. This rabble would not touch me, much less kill me and hang me naked from a lamppost. Just as they followed me, so now they are obeying the instinct of the herd. They are afraid and seek shelter. They know the Slavs will destroy them and so they run from the East. They smell compassion in the West, a sense of weakness which they think is a kindness. They will lie and swear they never knew me to spare themselves. It is as it should be. Without me to guide them, to force my vision and strength upon them, they return to the common drudgery of survival. But I have used them once and I will do so again."

Some of those Hitler looked out on were walking wounded. They lurched on with open wounds or lay propped against piles of rubble. Not once did Hitler consider calling to Kronhausen and stopping the ambulance. The wounded would either live or die, and it was not for him but for Fate to decide that. Adolf Hitler retied the canvas, laboriously turned his body and crawled forward toward the screen that separated the driver's cab from the rear of the ambulance.

"I am taken for a dead man," Hitler mused aloud. "Bormann and the rest believe that I am burning and there will be nothing left but ashes and later even those will be ground into dust. I will have disappeared into the earth, and from there no one will believe I might be raised. The Slavs will root through the remains, and when they find nothing they will feel cheated. They will say my death could not be proved, that I might still be living, if only to confuse their allies. But the Americans will not be interested in what Stalin says. They will be weary of the fighting. If I am dead, it will be easier to get on with the retribution and punishment."

Hitler peered through the grille and past the dusty, chipped windshield to the road ahead.

"The South is the best. It is a place I know. But I will not go so far as Munich. West of there, closer to Augsburg."

Hitler remembered the papers Kronhausen had thrown in at the last moment. He searched for them among the blankets and bandages and brought them close before his eyes.

Corporal Werner Busse. Born May 24, 1886, Salzburg. He thought, I cannot go back to Busse's hometown, where he was undoubtedly known and might still have family. But in Bavaria I could live with this identity.

The ambulance sped on, leaving the Grunewald behind, moving past the Wannsee and onto the Potsdam road. Somewhere in the distance, Hitler guessed to the east, a sudden barrage of artillery began. The shelling was so intense that the road quaked beneath the ambulance, rocking it from side to side. Hitler struggled to regain his hold on the bar and pulled himself to one side. But the bar, its fittings shaken loose, snapped back at him, and the jagged metal edge cut across his face. Hitler fell away, screaming in pain as the blood poured forth. A few seconds later he lapsed into a stupor.

Some sixty kilometers outside Berlin, Kronhausen found his opportunity. He pulled over to the side of the road and carefully nosed the car into a wagon track, driving far enough to make certain it couldn't be seen from the main thoroughfare. When he came around to the rear of the ambulance and opened the flap, the face of Adolf Hitler stared out at him, the features completely covered in blood like that of a satiated vampire.

"My Führer!" Kronhausen cried.

"What is it?" Hitler demanded hoarsely. "Why have you stopped?"

"The tank must be refilled, my Führer. Carrying gasoline in the back is dangerous. A stray shell or automatic fire . . .."

He paused, unable to take his eyes off the wounded man. "My Führer, is there anything I can—"

"Get on with it," Hitler whispered. "This place is unsafe. I can smell it."

With Kronhausen's assistance, Adolf Hitler stepped down from the ambulance. He pulled out the first-aid kit and slowly cleaned his face with alcohol. Kronhausen hesitated for a moment, thinking he might help, then swung himself inside and began moving the jerry cans.

"You are tired, Kronhausen," Hitler said, watching the SS lieutenant strip off his tunic and ease the heavy containers against the fuel duct.

"I am, my Führer; I am very tired." Kronhausen strained under his load. His eyes were bloodshot from fatigue and smoke, his uniform gray with stains and dust.

"But you must never despair, Kronhausen," Hitler muttered. "Unlike all the generals who broke their oath of fealty to me, or the cowardice shown by men I trusted without a single doubt— Goering and Himmler—you, Kronhausen, of the SS, remain faithful to me. You shall see that such dedication will have its reward!"

Kronhausen stepped back from the truck, heaving away the empty jerry can. Hitler's words penetrated his clouded mind, and some distant reflex action was touched by them. But he was too tired to carry it through—to turn and salute the leader who addressed him. It was all he could do to stand on his feet, not to mention ceremony.

May 1, 1945

As NIGHT fell, the rain returned. It came down gently on the shattered land, unheeding of the fire shells that raced up to greet it, unmoved by the curses of soldiers whose progress it impeded, unmindful of the lamentations of the refugees whose fires it extinguished. The rain held, and fighting continued through the night, but by dawn the constant rhythm of the drops had worn away men's energies, lulling them to an hour of a cold, fitful sleep while it slowly anesthetized the wounds of combat.

When the soldiers rose, they moved slowly among the litterings of spent shells and muddied gear, breathing deeply to clear their chests of the dust and smoke of yesterday. They smiled in pleasant surprise when they could taste the tobacco of their morning cigarettes. Content, they took that precious moment to bring their thoughts away from the present. This morning they did not hunger for cooked food, or consider more advantageous positions for their armor, or plan the tactics for the coming fight. Instead they gave themselves over to dreaming, to idle contemplation which removed them from the battlefield. Some thought of writing a letter home, for they were eager to share their pause and reflection. But the idea died quickly. For many there was no one left to write to, and until now they had forgotten this. Others shied away from the temptation, realizing that to attract attention to oneself before the gods would be fatal. Do not even think of family or friends; do not conjure up their faces or memories. That way the deities of War would not be jealous and those whom you loved might still be in your life when you returned home.

When you returned . . . that thought could drive away any other, destroying a man's desire to fight. The thought of return was a narcotic on such a tranquil morning. No harshness in the air, none in the heart. The thought of victory was a silent bell.

Gunner Kuzmin's battery stood poised, its guns leveled at the hollow remains of the Reich Chancellery. After two weeks of fighting and a cost of over three hundred thousand men, the city had been subdued. The Red Flag fluttered weakly in the dust and haze that covered the Chancellery dome.

Demolition crews had followed the troops and laid explosives around the entrances to the bunker. The officer in charge ordered them to hold the blasting until Zhukov himself had arrived, but then the Marshal had called up and told the captain to go ahead. He was on the way. Once the front doors had been reduced to twisted metal, the flamethrower unit moved in.

Gunner Kuzmin's battery had been advancing steadily into the city as the way ahead was cleared by troops and tanks. The unit finally emerged off Vosstrasse, to the right of the Chancellery itself. There Kuzmin had left it to his second in command, picked up a machine gun from a fallen infantryman and run to the bunker. The special NKVD unit that Zhukov had assigned to clear the bunker was about to enter. Behind the flamethrower, Kuzmin made his way down the stairs into the depths.

"Still nothing," the man ahead of him muttered. "What happened to them all?"

The unit pushed its way through the silent mausoleum, stepping over bodies sprawled across doorways. There were officers in full dress and decorations, slumped in chairs, blood still trickling from their mouths, and women, some lying peacefully in a final dignified sleep, others draped grotesquely over their consorts, capturing the instant the poison had frozen their hearts.

"Too late? No, we can't be too late!" Kuzmin cried savagely. He broke into a run, holding his gun at the ready, and made for the stairs leading to the lower bunker. He kicked open the door to what had been Hitler's private quarters, and through the other soldiers milling about he glimpsed the stains on the couch. Around him, the NKVD men were stuffing their pockets with souvenirs. Kuzmin quickly checked the other rooms, then saw the staircase leading upstairs. When the gunner emerged into the garden of the Chancellery, he almost collided with Marshal Zhukov.

Zhukov was standing over an open pit with several skeletons lying in it. The bones were charred and black, splintered, broken and raked as though with a shovel. Heat still emanated from the ditch, and the sweet smell of burnt flesh hung in the air. The

Marshal looked at Kuzmin and muttered, "Gunner, somehow I do not think that is Hitler. It would be too convenient. But we have to wait for tests. Is there anything down there?"

"I saw nothing, Comrade General," Kuzmin replied. "I went through very quickly. There were many bodies, but none that looked like . . . him."

"Come with me."

Together Kuzmin and Zhukov, with his escort, moved to the other end of the garden.

"It should be simple," the Marshal said, almost casually. "People have been cremated here, very probably Hitler among them. If so, whoever did this would have taken care to cover the evidence. But he was also hurried. Look for recently turned-up earth."

The NKVD turned up three such sites in less than a half hour. The first was dug up and revealed the carcass of a dog. The second, which Kuzmin was working on, contained ashes and chunks of bone of two, possibly three people.

"Motherfucker, son-of-a-bitch, whoremaster," Zhukov spat out bitterly. "He's dead. I can feel it in my bones he is dead. But he would rather keep us guessing!"

He turned suddenly to Kuzmin. "Who in hell is in charge of your battery?"

"The second in command," Kuzmin replied smartly.

"Then I am placing you in charge of the army detail here," Zhukov said. "You and Major Kushnevsky of the NKVD will share the command. Dig this place up, everything you see. I want it turned over until the earth yields an answer. I will send a medical unit to help out. As soon as we have the dental plates and with luck, the bastard's doctor, they will be here. Give me some flesh from this place of ghosts!"

When Zhukov left, Kuzmin organized the detail, and the digging commenced once more. Kuzmin himself arranged the bags that would hold the remains and instructed his men to be especially careful in picking up rings and other personal effects which might provide evidence as to who lay in this smoldering earth. Then he walked around the perimeter of the garden to the front and saw the bodies of eight children lying at the side of the bunker. Beside these was the corpse of an elderly man. Kuzmin pushed the body over with his boot and saw the bullet wound in the back of the neck. It appeared the man had been executed. Kuzmin searched through the clothing for identification, but found none. He wondered briefly who the old man could have been. A Home Guardsman perhaps, shot by the SS because he was fleeing; or had it simply been a stray bullet that had done him in? Kuzmin knew he could never be certain. The old man was one in thousands of whom he would know nothing, other than that they were dead.

May 2, 1945

THE VILLAGE was called Emmaus and lay in the crook of a meadow, several kilometers beyond Bayreuth.

The road had taken Kronhausen deep into the south, to the fringes of Bavaria. During the night, the light of the car's beams, reduced to tiny rectangles because the lamps had been painted over, gave him glimpses of the slow mutation of the landscape. Where, closer to Berlin, the refugees had been strewn along the road, farther along there was only the odd group of people in flight. Burnt-out tanks and troop carriers, overturned army trucks and cannon, some with the American star, littered the sides of the highway. Private vehicles, few that there were, had been abandoned because of a lack of fuel. There was also the odd assortment of bicycles and carriages, driven off the road, their owners absent, and carts with horses that had collapsed in the harness, their hooves bloody stumps. The animals had been torturously driven through city rubble without having been shod.

It was a landscape that attested to an ignoble flight. The SS lieutenant could easily picture the frightened men and women who were hiding in the forests, beyond reach of the headlights. He was certain they would have heard the ambulance's engine, but no one ventured out to stop him and ask for aid, or even to investigate. In these days, curiosity killed not only cats. Kronhausen wondered if, given a chance, he might recognize someone along this road. He thought it likely, considering the celebrities who had fled Berlin.

Although the mists still clung to the higher ground this early in the morning, below Kronhausen could see the village resting in silence. From the number of houses and buildings, he judged the population to be a few hundred, perhaps more because of the railroad station. The surrounding area, although still shrouded, smelled richly of earth. He guessed it was farmland. Kronhausen looked across the land and cursed softly that he had no binoculars nor any weapon other than his pistol. The village did not appear occupied. There were no military vehicles to be seen, nor any sentries. But Kronhausen, who hadn't seen any sign of the enemy along the route, could not believe that his good fortune would continue much longer. Still, there was little choice but to enter the village. He needed food and civilian clothing and not least, a respite from the driving.

Kronhausen parked the ambulance off the side of the road and went around to the back. He found Adolf Hitler curled up in the blankets, shivering uncontrollably.

"My Führer," Kronhausen said softly. He reached forward and gently pressed the back of his hand to Hitler's forehead. The skin was sweat-laden and raging with fever.

Hitler started, flinging out his right arm to protect himself. He stared at Kronhausen, eyes shot through with blood, the face sallow. With great difficulty he managed to raise himself on his elbow.

"My Führer," Kronhausen repeated. "There is a village below. It appears safe. I think we had best stop here, for food . . ."

"I . . . need a doctor," Hitler muttered thickly. "Bring me a doctor."

Kronhausen pulled back the canvas flap and saw that the blankets were covered with blood, crusted in patches.

"Doctor . . ." Hitler whispered. "Rest . . ."

Kronhausen rolled the Führer away from the soiled blankets and threw them out. He arranged the bedding that was left, wrapping it around the trembling man, and quickly returned to the cab. Before starting the engine, he removed his pistol and checked to see that the clip was full. Only a single cartridge was missing. With just six pieces of lead with which to defend himself and his master, Otto Kronhausen eased the car back onto the road and drove slowly toward the village.

Kronhausen's estimation of Emmaus had not been wrong. The

town had fewer than five hundred inhabitants, although this number had swelled to over seven hundred as refugees from the
bombed-out cities of the North and East fled to relatives' homes.
Many had come on the last train that had passed through Emmaus, three weeks ago. Another wave had come in the face of
the Russian advance, but of these almost all had chosen to continue farther west.

Kronhausen drove carefully, watching for any sign of enemy
troops. He turned off the main road onto a muddy track bordered
by large trees. From the surrounding forest he could smell the
damp decay of spring—a clean, pungent odor that somehow refreshed him. Then suddenly he came upon the first house. He
thought it a vision from another world, something that the war,
in its bloody embrace, had passed by completely. There was glass
in all the windows, and the bright blue paint on the beams was
fresh, unscarred by bullets or shells. By the fence grew rose-
bushes, and under the windowsills still more flowers had been
arranged in boxes. Kronhausen stared out at the sight, feeling a
mixture of relief and hatred. To have seen with his own eyes that
his country had not been totally destroyed gladdened him; at the
same time he loathed this picture of tranquillity, for it was an
offense to the suffering and destruction he had witnessed elsewhere.

The houses gradually gave way to what Kronhausen took for
the main street of Emmaus. Here the buildings appeared shab-
bier. Painting and repairs were needed and had not been attended
to. Kronhausen slowly drove past the inn; then a greengrocer's
and a butcher shop, both shuttered; then by a post office and
local militia headquarters. He noticed that there was no flag flying
from the pole in the square. He stopped briefly in front of the
apothecary's, then drove on, but there was nothing more to see.
Kronhausen turned around and brought the ambulance back to
the apothecary shop. He buttoned his tunic, unconsciously
dropped his hand on the cold leather of his holster and walked up
to the store. The door was locked. Kronhausen tried to force it,
then began to pound on the glass.

"Yes?"

Of course the man was old, of slight frame and very nervous.
He was raggedly dressed, and his dark eyes were glazed in sleep.

"Open up," Kronhausen told him curtly. "I am carrying a very sick man. We need a doctor."

"A doctor . . ." the old man started. "I don't know if I can—"

Kronhausen didn't let him finish but pushed the door hard, shoving the man aside. "Who are you?" he demanded.

"Toller," the old man stuttered nervously. "I am the apothecary."

"I told you we need a doctor," Kronhausen repeated. "Is there one in this place?"

"Yes, of course," Toller answered quickly. "But it is so early . . ."

"How long would it take to fetch him?"

"Grubber lives down the street, over the inn." Toller pointed in some vague direction.

"All right, in a moment you will bring him here. Who else has passed this way—Americans or British—and where are they now?"

"Yes, troops," Toller muttered. "The Americans are not far away, a few kilometers to the east. There was nothing for them here and they were in a hurry. They said they were going to Munich . . . and Dachau."

"When was this?"

"Two days ago."

"Is there a place I can get some clothing?"

"There is nothing left; really, nothing."

"Oh, yes, there is," Kronhausen intoned. "If you want to barter for clothing, I have things to sell. But don't hold out, because you will earn nothing but a bullet for your troubles. Take a good look at me and then get me something decent to wear. Something that fits!"

Toller looked fearfully at the massive SS man and backed away.

"I will bring the doctor first," he whispered. "Wait here. I will get whatever clothes I can."

Kronhausen watched through the window as the apothecary half ran, half stumbled across the street, jumped clumsily onto the sidewalk and continued to the inn. Kronhausen went behind the counter, rummaged through the all-but-empty drawers and found a tin with some tobacco in it. The leaf was dry, but there was plenty of paper, and he began rolling himself some cigarettes.

What distracted him was a faint rustle at the other end of the store. Under different circumstances he would have dismissed it as the movement of a cat or mice, but not in this state of exhaustion and tension. Drawing his revolver, Kronhausen stepped quickly from behind the counter and made for the door that he assumed opened onto the living quarters behind the store. In one motion he kicked it open, crouched and trained his gun on the first figure he saw.

Kronhausen faced a boy of ten or eleven—perhaps older, but it was impossible to tell, he was so spindly and undernourished.

"Is there anyone else with you?" Kronhausen called to him. But the boy stared back, his eyes, circled by large black-and-purple hollows, alive in terror and incomprehension. Only when the SS man lowered the revolver did he speak, in a voice so low and mournful that it was scarcely audible.

"No, no one here."

Kronhausen looked around the damp, miserable room: one bed and a cot set up close to the already cold fireplace; a rickety, painted-over kitchen table set with a few crusts of bread, a tin of herring and a half liter of wine. An overcoat and a child's woodsman jacket were thrown over one chair. He looked again at the boy, whose gaze had not wavered from his face, and inexplicably felt tears press against his eyes. It was as though all the horror he had created, inflicted and lived with for the last half dozen years became absolutely meaningless before this single German child, whose life had been radically altered by the war yet who would survive only to bear witness to defeat, shame and retribution.

"Are you going to shoot me the way the others shot the people?" the boy asked him.

Kronhausen replaced his gun in the holster, squatted and beckoned the boy to come to him.

"No, I promise I will not harm you. Please, don't be afraid." Still the boy did not move.

"What is your name?"

"Helmut," the child said.

"Helmut . . ." Kronhausen pressed his lips together, fumbling for the right words with which to express himself. "Helmut, I know it is difficult for you now. I know there isn't enough food and you are very unhappy. But you must remember this: we Germans have only been held back; we have not lost. No matter what you hear on the radio or from our enemies, you must continue to believe that the Führer is alive. He lives, Helmut! And soon he will return to lead us to victory. Do you understand what I am saying?"

"Yes," the boy said mechanically. "The Führer is alive and he will lead us to victory."

"Yes, you must believe that with all your heart," Kronhausen repeated eagerly.

"I believe it," Helmut Toller said in that same dead voice.

Kronhausen straightened up and wished he had something to give the boy. But he had even less than did this child. At least the boy had some food and shelter; if he was blessed with a little luck, he would also have a future. He, and thousands like him, would survive to behold the return of Adolf Hitler.

"Goodbye, Helmut," Kronhausen whispered. "You stay inside while I speak with your father."

"My grandfather," the boy corrected him tonelessly, and stared up at Kronhausen with eyes of fathomless hatred. "My parents were murdered by Allied planes, over Hamburg," he finished mechanically.

The child stepped back, his eyes always on Kronhausen, then turned and went to the window, which looked down the main street of the town. Kronhausen looked at him, wanting to say something, but words failed him and so he reached the door handle and pulled it gently toward him.

The apothecary threw open the door to the inn and pushed his way past Frau Brehm, the proprietress. Without a word he climbed the stairs as quickly as he could to Grubber's room. The doctor was standing by the window in his dressing gown, preparing to shave.

"Heinz, what in God's name?"

"SS!" Toller cried out, his chest wheezing from exertion. "SS again. He's in the store."

"How many?" Grubber asked him softly, replacing the razor on the window ledge.

"Only one. He came in an ambulance. Says there is someone inside who needs a doctor. He demanded I come and get you."

"Of course he knew I am the only physician in Emmaus," Grubber observed ironically.

The doctor stared hard at the miserable Toller, then went to the window and looked out. But the angle was too sharp for him to see the vehicle, and the street was empty.

"In the store, eh?"

"Yes," Toller whispered. "I told him to wait. For God's sake, we must do something. . . . Helmut is alone with him!"

"You're certain he is SS? Was he in uniform?"

"Full uniform."

"A fool or a fanatic," Grubber said contemptuously. "Well, thank God it's still early. There's no one about. We have to deal with him ourselves."

"But what if there are more coming?"

"What difference does that make?" Grubber turned on him. "They will be no different from the others. If there are more, then perhaps this time the town will stand up for itself and fight. But one or two, especially if the other is wounded, we can take care of."

Grubber went to his chest of drawers and from under his clothing pulled out a revolver.

"Go and tell him I am coming. Get him whatever he wants—food, gasoline, whatever. Show him we are cooperating and keep him at peace."

"He wants clothing."

"I should think he would." Grubber laughed harshly. "Tell him we have some buried away. It will take you a little while to bring it up. Now go, Toller, before he moves around and the others see him."

Grubber rinsed the razor in a basin, wiped off the soap and began dressing. He placed the revolver in the bottom of his medical bag and covered it with gauze and instruments. He wanted to kill this SS man quickly, before the villagers knew of his presence and came out from behind closed doors to deal with him in their own fashion, the fury of many falling on the helpless one. The others would not be satisfied with a quick death. They wanted a greater, more thorough revenge and would not think of the risk involved: there might well be other bands of the SS in the area, the kind of butchers who had fallen upon Emmaus seven days ago.

They had come from the east. At first the people thought the sound of heavy motor vehicles belonged to the Russians. But their relief upon seeing the SS column was a reckless sentiment. The contingent, thirty men in four vehicles, entered the village smartly. Their uniforms were clean and proper, untouched by battle, and when they jumped from the trucks, their commander organized them in precise formation. In a few moments, as though the company had designed a specific attack, the town was overtaken. Systematically the apothecaries, food stores and clothing shops were looted of what remained on the shelves. The cellars in which the townspeople had buried the last of their foodstuffs and medicines were quickly discovered and dug up. Afterward, in what the commander deemed a punishment for hoarding, the women were rounded up and the prettiest led away before the men, who were then locked up in the blacksmith's stable. While some SS men amused themselves, the rest went through the homes, plundering at random. Before they left, the commander ordered that six men be shot, those who had stupidly taken up cudgels against soldiers armed with submachine guns. Afterward, Dr. Grubber discovered that all the younger women had been raped.

At the front door of the inn, Grubber was met by Brehm. Brehm, who was also the blacksmith of Emmaus, was still very powerful for his sixty years. He did not step out of the doctor's way.

"Who is it, Klaus?" he asked softly.

"More of the same," Grubber said. "So far only one."

"Let me come with you."

"No!" Grubber stopped him. "He feels there is nothing to harm him in this town of old men. Let him keep on believing that. If we charge him, someone else may be killed. For God's sake, stay here and keep the others away!"

"I owe it to our daughter," Brehm said woodenly.

"Let him go!" his wife exclaimed. Both men turned to her and saw that she was crying silently. "Let him go, Gerd. How many times can you kill a single man?"

The doctor stepped forward and Brehm, his gaze faltering, let him pass. But the blacksmith did not close the door completely.

Dr. Grubber looked over the empty street, then walked over to where the ambulance was parked. He stopped, tempted to lift the flap.

"Get in here!"

Kronhausen stood by the open door of the apothecary shop. Grubber nodded and hurried inside. He noticed that the SS man still had his pistol in the holster. Supremely confident or merely stupid? Grubber did not care. All he had to do was be careful and not startle him. Then he could kill him without warning, without the slightest chance of defense.

"I am Dr. Grubber," he announced formally. "I was told there is a wounded man here."

Kronhausen dropped his cigarette on the floor and crushed it under his heel. The apothecary, whose instinctive cleanliness was offended even under these circumstances, winced.

"Is there a hospital here?" the SS lieutenant asked.

"No, but I can set up a room at the inn," Grubber replied.

"Don't you even have an office up there?" Kronhausen demanded.

Grubber shook his head. "There is no office. All our medical equipment was taken to Munich a long time ago. If the wound is severe I will do the best I can and God will take care of the rest. The nearest hospital that is still functioning is thirty kilometers away—if you wish to take the chance of driving. The Americans have gone there."

Kronhausen did not like the way the doctor had added the last words, as though he knew the SS officer wouldn't go near any army units.

"You look at him," Kronhausen said. "Tell me how bad the condition is. Then we will decide. But understand: I need him alive for where I'm going."

He turned to Toller.

"First you will help me carry the stretcher to the inn. Then get me that clothing and fix up a place where I can shave and bathe."

"May I ask—lieutenant, is it?—may I ask where you are going?" Grubber interrupted.

"And why would you like to know, Doctor?"

Grubber, realizing his life was in his hands, replied as sincerely as possible.

"The Americans have gone, for now. But they will return, perhaps tomorrow or the day after. They have taken the names of all the people here and will check their lists when they return. We, the townspeople, have been very helpful to special persons traveling from Munich, especially the lads who were at Dachau. We have sheltered them, provided what food and gasoline were left and hidden them when that was necessary. If you are in need of our services, I place them at your disposal. We only ask that you tell us beforehand how long you will be staying or how much you need to continue your journey."

"That is very kind of you, Doctor," Kronhausen replied with a thin smile. "If I should need to stay more than a few hours, we will talk again. In the meantime I suggest you attend to the patient."

Grubber stepped aside to let Kronhausen pass, with the apothecary hurrying after him. The doctor undid the clasp on his medical bag but held the two handles together, so that the case still appeared closed. It had taken him only a few moments to come to hate this officer with the eyes of a predator whose brutality came forth in the clipped hard voice and unfaltering arrogance. Grubber watched the two men approach the ambulance, and then he removed his revolver.

The SS officer and Toller each grasped a handle of the stretcher and pulled until Grubber could see a pair of legs sticking out from the inside of the ambulance. He wondered who the victim might be and why he was so important to the SS man. When the stretcher was all but out, Kronhausen motioned to Toller to pick up the handles at the other end. Together the two men moved across the street, Kronhausen walking with his back to Toller.

Dr. Grubber too crossed the street. He caught up to Toller and passed him, ignoring the terrified look on the apothecary's face when he saw the gun in the doctor's hand. Grubber thought it wouldn't really matter if the SS man were to turn around now. He was holding the stretcher and couldn't defend himself immediately. Grubber wanted him this way, so as to kill him as a helpless man.

When Grubber was only a few paces behind Kronhausen he

ran forward and turned to face him, raising the gun. Kronhausen, whose reflexes were numbed by exhaustion and the burden of having to remain alert, stared incredulously at the figure of an old man holding a gun at him. He was about to speak when Grubber pulled the trigger. The doctor fired all seven shots into Kronhausen. The gun bucked at each report, and when Kronhausen's body finally collapsed on the ground, it was perforated with wounds from the shoulder to the groin.

Grubber knelt down and pulled the SS man off the body lying on the stretcher. Toller, who had dropped his end as soon as the first shots were fired, was standing rock still, looking down at the tangle of horror.

"Come and help me!" Grubber shouted at him.

Together the two men rolled Kronhausen's corpse off to the side and let it lie in the dust. Grubber leaned over the man in the stretcher and ripped open the jacket.

"What if he's one . . ." Toller said weakly.

"One of them?" Grubber finished. "Appears too old for SS. He's out of uniform as well."

"There were others. Last time there were several who were older."

Grubber said nothing but unbuttoned the man's shirt. He removed it and lifted the right arm. There was no tattoo indicating the blood group, a telltale sign for an SS officer. Toller, who was searching through the pockets, produced ragged pieces of identification.

"Home Guard," he said, openly relieved. "Busse, Werner. An ambulance driver from Salzburg."

"We must get him to bed," Grubber said. "That scum was probably using him for cover. They must have been going to where he lived. Something went wrong . . . ah, we'll find out later."

He rose and looked around. The street, empty before, was slowly filling with people, most of them still wearing their nightclothes. They were watching, but only a few ventured off the sidewalk.

"Brehm!" Grubber called to the smith. "Get some more men, quickly. There is something to be done."

Brehm came forward and looked down mutely at the two bodies.

"Take this one out to the woods and bury him, somewhere where he won't be found," Grubber said gently, pointing to the SS officer's body. "Toller, help me get this Herr Busse to the inn."

Toller and Grubber placed the inert body of the man they called Busse back on the stretcher and moved off past the townspeople. No one interfered or asked any questions. No one looked back at the apothecary's to see the face of Helmut Toller pressed against the window, staring out at the horror without expression, without a single tear.

Frau Brehm let them have a room upstairs, next to the doctor's. Grubber stripped the filthy clothes from the body while Toller went downstairs for some boiled water and clean rags which would be used for bandages.

Grubber removed the bloodied cloth wrapped around the crown of the head and examined the wound. The bullet had gouged a path three centimeters long from the top of the temple to the arc of the skull. The groove of blackened skin tissue and hair and bone were crusted over with blood. Grubber cleaned this away and found that no rot had set in. Even though there were traces of ointment in the wound, it seemed incredible that it had fought off infection and even showed signs of healing. But with the wound's proximity to the left lobe and the conditions Busse must have endured over the last several days, Grubber considered the possibility of amnesia substantial. He cut up another bandage and carefully dressed the wound.

Beyond the obvious, Grubber could find little wrong with his patient. Although he was frighteningly thin, Busse obviously hadn't suffered from acute starvation. The skin was white but not sallow except in the face, and there were no signs of malnutrition, such as a distended belly. Busse's breathing was sharp and irregular, and Grubber had no explanation for this, except the possibility the man was suffering from some bronchial illness. If that was the case, there was nothing Grubber could do—not here, not now.

When Toller returned with the water, the two men gave Busse a sponge bath and dressed him in an old woolen robe with the last cover being an ancient quilt Frau Brehm contributed.

"You don't want me to bring any medicines," Toller said vaguely.

Grubber shook his head. "Let him rest. If the wound is less serious than it appears, he may be able to speak to us tomorrow. I would rather let his body heal him than resort to medicines which may not be necessary. I'll tell Lillian to come up and arrange for another bed so that she can stay in here with him. He should have someone close by if he wakes or takes a bad turn."

"What about the Americans?" Toller asked nervously. "What should we tell them?"

Grubber looked at the apothecary with contempt. "Why is it you are always so afraid?" he demanded softly. The words were cruel, for Grubber knew the answer. Toller was one of those men who drifted with whatever tide was running. In the last thirty years he had been a monarchist, a liberal democrat, then a socialist and finally a National Socialist. Now his conscience had rotted away and there was only the shell left, that of a frightened, lonely man who was never certain what people would choose to remember.

"What can you say to the Allies?" Grubber said finally. "Busse has papers. He's not a young man and certainly not SS. We don't have to offer him up to the Americans, but there is no need to hide him either. By the time they come back they will be sick of us. Too much suffering tends to blunt perception. Everything begins to run together—part of the whole monotonous gray canvas. He's of no interest to anyone; not even to us, really."

"And the ambulance?"

"I'll look after it," Grubber told him. "There may be some supplies inside. Otherwise we'll take out what we can use and dispose of the rest."

They left the inn and walked down the street to where the ambulance was parked. The few people who stood around the vehicle moved away when they saw the two men coming. Grubber got into the driver's seat, paused to check the instrument panel, then slowly drove the ambulance around the square and off to the railroad compound. He parked it out of sight behind some baggage carts and began his search.

The doctor quickly realized that the SS lieutenant had not fled without having made elementary preparations. The first-aid kit was well stocked with emergency supplies. Grubber picked up

the containers of morphine and nodded his head in silent gratitude. These and the vitamin compounds would prove invaluable,
as his own supply had dwindled away months ago. There was
also a blanket which could be used and two serviceable sheets
which needed washing. An extra stretcher was always good to
have. Grubber took all these things and piled them onto a baggage
cart. When he looked back a final time, he noticed he had overlooked two articles. The doctor reached in and picked up a boy's
shoe, what was left of it. The sole had been worn away to almost
nothing, and there were no laces. The other testimonial was a
schoolgirl's sock, once white and now resembling a rag. He took
both of these things out as well, without knowing why. He understood that they were quite useless, and yet he was unable to bring
himself to throw them away.

Grubber pushed the cart over to the front of the ambulance.
Beside the driver's seat he found an old map with a route from
Berlin penciled in. He reminded himself to ask Busse about that
when he regained consciousness. Methodically Grubber checked
under the dash and along the floorboards, not knowing what he
might be looking for but satisfying himself with the thorough
examination. He was almost convinced that except for mechanical parts the ambulance had no further value when something
came to his attention. Wedged tightly between the passenger seat
and the partition behind it was what appeared to be a large briefcase. He went around to the other door, ripped out the seat
completely and saw it was exactly that. With some effort Grubber
pulled it out and dragged the case onto the running board.

Using a jack iron, the doctor snapped the lock and pulled the
sides of the case open. The contents did not surprise him; it was
their quantity. Stuffed into the case were twenty slim gold bars.
Grubber removed one and saw that it bore no stamp. Doubtless
the others were without markings as well. Grubber had had occasion to see such ingots before. Last year, a crate of an SS
consignment from Dachau en route through Emmaus to Berlin
had broken and split on the railroad landing ramp. Then he had
seen hundreds of such bars, spilling like chunks of hard, glittering
bread.

Grubber replaced the bar and fixed the lock. He had no doubt
where this treasure came from, even though it now appeared

innocent and anonymous. Grubber had precise knowledge of Dachau and its function. Now, as he had that day on the railroad
platform, he experienced a physical revulsion. He wanted no part
of this gold.

Yet he knew that the treasure was badly needed. It could not
be eaten or used for fuel, nor was it of any medical value to him.
Yet its magic powers could buy anything that had a price, anything the village had to have.

Not that he would tell anyone else about the gold. Possibly
only Brehm, whose skills as a blacksmith might be needed to melt
the metal into smaller ingots; but certainly no one else. The gold,
Grubber thought, would be held by him alone—first at the inn,
until he could quietly hide it away in a safer place. But if others
knew, the magic would work against all of them. The townsfolk,
already dazed from mental fatigue and beaten by the continual
suffering they were undergoing, would be reduced to sheer idiocy
if they knew of this. They, his neighbors of forty years, would
become quite capable of killing him to seize the treasure which
might carry them far away from this onslaught of madness. Yet if
the treasure was rationed out, the village as a whole would survive. Supplies could be procured, and unlike the inhabitants of
other towns that were slowly starving into a cold death, the people of Emmaus would have enough food and fuel to endure, if
nothing else. Not more, but at least that.

There would be enough, Grubber thought, for Busse himself.
He who had inadvertently brought this treasure would also receive from it, anonymously, in tiny parts, when needed. Together, they would all survive, somehow.

May 4, 1945

THE RAGE had fallen upon him and held him fast in its grip. It
penetrated his exhausted sleep with fragments of thoughts and
memories, speeding them away when he tried to grasp them, or
crowding them very close, threatening him. The images, so very
lifelike and real, were of trivial things—a plate of food; Eva
dressed in her blue skirt; his dog Blondi. He tried to reach for
them, for he could hear, smell and even touch them. Yet when he

cried out, the images receded and dissolved and there was nothing but the solitary blackness, devoid of time.

Adolf Hitler passed three days with Death thus attending his bed, seated quietly beside him, ministering to his needs. Death cast a fever upon him and caused him to scream at night when fear overpowered him. But it played coyly with him, making certain his throat was dry or swollen with mucus so that the shouting, so distinctive and familiar to the German ear, would be unrecognizable as anything other than the choking sounds of a sick man.

Death waited and pondered. It could have taken this pitiful, helpless life at any moment, beginning with the instant Adolf Hitler had put the gun barrel to his head. Death had been surprised when Hitler had not been delivered up to it; then it had grown yet more curious when the poison failed. Finally it had realized that it would be obliged to pursue this man whose end had been taken for granted.

So Death had ridden with Hitler in the ambulance and lain with him when he fought against the poison in his body, curling up like a fetus, crawling from side to side in the narrow confines of the vehicle, crying out whenever a sharp turn of the wheel flung him against the hard metal. It had become fascinated with the tenacity and fortune of this man, whose will to survive was enough to sustain him, and more, to escape. Death understood that he already belonged to its legions and could never escape its grasp. Yet the knowledge that other men badly wanted Adolf Hitler alive amused Death. The idea that his body, which was quite warm, would be thought to be found in the garden of the Reich Chancellery and so create a great untruth was entertaining. But, Death reflected, it was not the first time that men had desired the extinction of another human being more desperately than did Death itself.

So Death stayed on, watching, not laying its hand over the eyes of Adolf Hitler. No one had interrupted the journey, nor had the ambulance met with mishap, because Death rode with it and its odor dissuaded its apprentices from interfering with a work the Master had reserved for itself.

Death rose and cast its shadow over the figure of the man it had decided to spare. The fever would remain, and the consumption of the body too, so that the face might become even more sallow and sunken, and so unrecognizable. Death thought there was still a likeness to the Führer, most of all in the eyes; but even if someone chanced to glimpse the similarity, he would quickly and fearfully cast away the thought as though it were a hex. The mind of Germany was turned to survival, and so this mind would protect itself from memories that threatened to cast it back to a time it was escaping from.

Besides, Death laughed softly, hadn't the radios announced many times that Adolf Hitler was dead?

Lillian Schroter was Dr. Grubber's niece, a widow of twenty-eight whose husband had survived the Eastern Front only to return and be consumed in a fire storm in Munich. A tall, lithe woman, she had a heart-shaped face framed by extraordinary magenta hair that swept about her shoulders and was complemented by fierce green eyes. In a time of defeat and abject fear that reduced men to craven caricatures such as Toller, she refused to yield anything of her dignity and self-respect, moving among the wounded and the maimed, the homeless and the hungry with extraordinary strength that belied her own loneliness and tragedy.

Lillian had come to Emmaus shortly after her husband's death in the spring of 1944, almost a year ago. The evening he had disappeared under the rubble that Maximiliansplatz had been reduced to, Lillian had joined the orderly bands of refugees that had begun moving away from the city, even though most citizens still clung to the belief that their city would endure, if by no other miracle than by the very words of the Führer. Lillian had taken no comfort in such propaganda. She had pried her husband's body from under the debris and dragged it to a shallow ditch, where she whispered a few words of prayer and carefully laid a cluster of cold, dirty flowers over his heart. She had left him this way, unburied, and walked back to their apartment, several blocks away. Quickly and judiciously she had gathered up what she could carry and departed, leaving her door open. Let whoever needed the place use it; they might find the shelter and warmth comforting even if only for a little while.

On the Autobahn she had discovered a surprising number of people. Some were driving private cars, making liberal use of their horns. Others were packed into trucks, and still others used bicycles. The least fortunate were the single women who walked with bundles hanging over their shoulders from poles. No one wore clothing that wasn't burnt, giving off an acrid smell; all walked in desperate silence, trying to stifle the horror of the fire storms, to blot out the flaming images of their family and friends whom the horror had embraced with a pitiless hand. Lillian counted herself more fortunate than most of the others. She at least had somewhere to go, but what charity did the homeless have to look forward to?

Lillian had arrived at her uncle's four days after leaving Munich; reverted to the use of her maiden name, Grubber, and looked about for whatever pieces of a new life she could find.

Today was the third day of her watch over this patient whose name was Busse. Lillian had slept in the same room as he; even though she could have taken the room opposite, she had chosen to remain close by. She had been trained as a stenographer but in the course of the year had become a very competent nurse—for which Dr. Grubber was grateful, since the woman who had worked for him had left for Hamburg. Lillian considered she owed it to this man, who had suffered so much during his flight, to remain by his side.

Adolf Hitler stirred and rubbed his hand across his forehead. When Lillian came over and laid a cool cloth against his skin, there was a slight smile on his lips.

"You're better today," she said softly. "I can tell. You slept without waking last night."

She always spoke to him, not knowing whether he heard or not. She thought that if he could hear her but was unable to tell her so, her voice might at least reassure him. She wished he might open his eyes so that there might be some hint of his understanding.

Adolf Hitler could have shown her he was conscious, but he continued the sham. He had come out of his tormented sleep some twelve hours after his arrival at Emmaus. He did not remember if it had been dawn or dusk, only that the room was full of golden orange light.

Lying perfectly still, he had squinted, opening his eyes just a little, and seen a woman standing by the window folding cloths, her hands working quickly, the lips pressed together in concentration. In the sunlight she was transformed into a figure of almost inconceivable beauty and comfort. Where had she come from, to stand before him in the tranquillity of this hour, so far removed from the horror of his memory and pain of his body? Was she German? Fear closed Hitler's eyes as footsteps approached the door.

"His name must be Busse," the man was saying. "I can't find any other identification on the vehicle. He came from Berlin in that ambulance."

"Where do you think he was going?" the girl said.

"Busse's home is in Salzburg. The SS officer who was driving needed him for one reason or another—to mark the last stages of the route; to use as a hostage; God alone knows. Anything is possible."

"But he isn't SS."

"No, Home Guardsman."

"And the SS man?"

"Dead," the man said abruptly. "Dead and buried."

Hitler had strained to hear more, but the voices subsided into whispers. With great concentration Hitler closed his eyes and summoned back the thoughts their words had stirred. Kronhausen, the blond giant, carrying him out of the bunker into the ambulance. The drive . . . he recalled the faces of the refugees as the ambulance bullied them off the road, their expressions drawn in defeat. There was the smell of gasoline in the back of the car, and there were the stops Kronhausen had made to refill the tanks. That had been the last time Hitler remembered seeing him, he was quite certain.

So Kronhausen had arrived in this . . . town? Or was it only a village? He had arrived and someone had killed him. The people here. They had dared to kill an officer of the SS? Hitler was angered by the thought and considered what might be done to punish such an injustice. It was then that his mind snapped back at him. It called him a fool and sternly told him to thank Destiny.

Kronhausen had been killed, murdered—what difference did it make? He would have had to die soon enough, because he was the only witness to the fact that the Führer lived. So whoever had killed him had spared Hitler the need to commit this act, and he himself had been taken in because the people believed he was someone named Busse, a victim of the SS, a Volksstürmer. That was very good, to have been taken for another so readily; very good, as long as he was careful. . . .

Then the powers of concentration had failed him and quickly blackness had descended. But his subconscious, awake and in command, was protecting him now. That night, Lillian had not heard him cry out at all. But neither had she discovered that the man she knew as Busse was watching her the next morning, when her back was turned, and listening to her conversations with Grubber. He was pushing back the uncertainty of where he was and in whose hands, working against the fear which at times had overwhelmed him and grown into panic until this, the third day, when he chose to rise from his half-death.

Adolf Hitler opened his eyes, and the girl, when she turned around, was startled.

"You're awake!" she cried.

He nodded feebly but said nothing.

"I'll get the doctor."

"No!" Adolf Hitler, struggling to bring his arm out from under the covers, motioned her back.

"No, first you must tell me where I am," he said quickly, breathing hard in an effort to get the words out. "Tell me where I am and how—"

"You are in the village of Emmaus," she answered kindly. "My name is Lillian, and my uncle is the doctor who has been looking after you."

"Emmaus . . ." Hitler muttered. "I do not know it."

"Near Munich."

"The SS officer," Hitler whispered. "Where is the SS man?"

"He has gone. You don't have to worry; really you don't."

"No, you don't understand," Hitler said, very much agitated. "He wanted to go to my town. He threatened me . . ."

"The SS man is dead," Lillian said flatly. "Please, Herr Busse, it is all over with. You don't have to worry anymore."

Lillian removed the cloth and stood up. "Let me fetch my uncle. Just lie still and don't worry. You are safe here with us."

When she left, Adolf Hitler lay back and stared at the ceiling. It is all over with, she had said. Of course; how could it have been otherwise? Yet whatever he was able to recall of the bunker and of the men who had been with him in the last days seemed to belong to another age. It had all happened, yes, but in a different time; not the past, but in another plane.

Hitler thought about this. Since leaving the bunker he had suffered for the first time in two decades. He had entered the hall of Death and faced the silence of eternity without flinching, prepared to render up his life, eager to place himself upon the faggots whose flames would then transport his soul to the kingdom of warriors where he would dwell for all eternity. He had confronted Death and he had mastered it, and in the end Death had given him back his life.

Then against all odds, Kronhausen had brought him out of a city that no longer existed. Through the slaughter he had been driven, like a charmed being, untouchable by flame or metal. He had been thrown into a wasteland ruled by Death, yet he had emerged unscathed—this in spite of his total helplessness.

The desperate flight and the pain he had endured throughout had served to break the illusion he had lived with in the bunker. For weeks he had dwelt fifty feet under the earth, plotting, issuing commands and organizing his armies while not daring to believe the bloodied reports filtering in from above. When the radio receiver had gone, the last communication with the outside reality had disappeared, and he had been left to sit alone in the silence of the fetid air that choked his lungs and stifled his thoughts.

His act of survival had dispelled the illusion. The brief glimpses of burning streets and swollen bodies had forced upon him a picture of the truth he had been unwilling to acknowledge, a truth he had heard about only in whispers, since his entourage did not speak to him directly. He had touched the suffering, and it had in turn inflicted itself upon him. Now he could accept it, and the fantasies of victory disappeared into the poisoned sky. The dreams off which he had fed were scarcely recognizable. He looked upon them as an observer, as one who has no stake in the outcome, nor the slightest interest in where they might lead. He could measure the failure of his task but at the same time absolve himself of responsibility for it, for the failure was incomplete so long as he lived. Those who thought themselves victors would never be able to claim their reward legitimately without his death.

Adolf Hitler closed his eyes and breathed as deeply as possible. His heart was beating much too quickly. He would have to slow himself, to rein his thoughts before they threatened to engulf him. Through the chaos that continually broke over his mind, he perceived that he would have to anchor himself on the idea that he had survived. Although the twin pillars of his character, infernal pride and tempestuous arrogance, which had fueled his actions for decades, both rebelled at the threat of subservience, the instinct of survival overrode them. It said he must be a different man now, that he *was* a different man—broken, alone, a victim. Such was the persona that would ensure his continued existence, and he must not rail against it. Only by looking through its eyes would he be able to endure, to endure and see what it was his rule had passed to.

Grubber entered, preceded by Lillian, who was carrying a mug of steaming liquid. She set it down carefully on the windowsill and turned to the man called Busse.

"How are you?" Grubber asked quietly.

"Don't know," Hitler rasped, the words barely intelligible. "Confused."

"That will pass," Grubber told him. "You can stay here as long as need be. There is nothing to worry about. Think of getting better; that is all you have to do."

"The Allies . . ."

"You are in the American zone. Oh, there are some French, but they came and went. The Americans will return, but there is no need to think of them. They are not interested in people like us.

"Lillian," Grubber said, turning to her, "would you bring me some gauze from the cabinet downstairs?"

When his niece left, Grubber pulled back the bedding and examined Hitler.

"I want you to start eating," he said. "You are very weak."

"Just sleep," Hitler muttered. "Rest . . ."

"You came from Berlin?" Grubber asked him.

"Yes, Berlin."

"You were very lucky."

"The SS man. I showed him the route. I knew the roads beyond the Russian lines. I was driving an ambulance filled with dead children . . ."

"Don't think about that," Grubber said softly. "Forget the SS and Berlin. It is over with, finished, and you have survived. Anyone who survives in this age is a living miracle."

"I have nothing," Hitler said. "Nothing to give you."

Grubber looked down at this broken wreck of a man and shook his head.

"You have given us something," he said. "One day, when you are better, I will show you. You, Herr Busse, have saved us."

Grubber replaced his instruments and took the cup from the windowsill. Putting his arm round Hitler's shoulder, he raised him up. The soup was thin, but it had bits of fat and was hot. Hitler sipped it slowly, thinking how good it was.

"Day by day you will get better," Grubber was saying. "Do not think ahead. Do not think of anything but yourself. The madness is subsiding. Soon we will be free to look for whatever good has survived this age. But not now; not for some time yet."

Prologue Two

THE HAZE of blue smoke had settled along the low ceiling of the screening room, its thickness all the more apparent when the projection was completed and the soft overhead lights came on.

Kuzmin, who had long ago taken off his jacket, gently ground out his American cigarette in an ashtray filled with stubs, his own and those of the director's filterless Gauloises.

"You truly are a sorcerer," he said. "The film you shot this afternoon would have been effective even without the dialogue. But you captured that too—every nuance, every hesitation—the surprise and outrage perfectly matching the words and the expressions of those who spoke them. A piece of history, imprinted forever."

The director said nothing. He did not judge his work to be good or bad; to him it was simply there, existing. The opinions of others seldom touched him. He was satisfied, and that was enough.

"Will you pass the footage to your company?" Kuzmin asked him. "It is quite a coup to show Hitler in the General Assembly prior to his actual appearance."

"I think I'll keep it for myself," the director said slowly. "I

suppose the news people would love to break into network pro-
gramming with a special, but . . . no, the more I think about it
the less I like it. The piece may or may not be history, but it's not
their kind of news."

He switched on the intercom that connected him to the projec-
tionist.

"Give me that Emmaus reel.

"I wish I had footage of what you were describing—the last
hours of Berlin, the discovery of the bodies," he murmured to
Kuzmin. "They must exist in your war archives. You have the
best but never show it. And Christ, if we had even a photo or two
of the flight . . ."

The director let his breath whistle out through his teeth.

"There is something that will interest you," he said. "Some
footage I managed to dig up in Munich. The quality is dirt poor.
The photographer was an amateur—first-year student in some
technical school. He thought the annual spring festival in Emmaus would be an interesting subject to do, but he had no idea
what he was on to."

"How did you come by the film?"

"I got to him before anyone else; purchased the negative and
the only print in return for a two-year contract with our Frankfurt
office. The kid lost on the deal."

Kuzmin said nothing but lit another cigarette and settled back
as the lights dimmed.

"I know of the Emmaus festival," he said softly. "It is not
very different from others held in Bavaria at that time of year.
Sometimes they would show us films of them before we left for
the front, just so there could be no mistaking what kind of men
we would face." .

II
Walpurgis Night

In Germany, the worlds of the sacred and profane draw closer and closer together until, in April, they touch and flow into each other. Here the sorrowful rites of Easter are preceded, or in some districts, followed, by the pagan rituals of Walpurgis Night—a homage paid to all that is dark, superstitious and eternally mysterious in the human imagination.

Every village has its variation of the Night, which honors the woodland fairies; the spirits of the rivers and lakes; the silent but omnipresent gods, protectors of the dark mountains which remain their kingdom. In Emmaus the rite took place on the evening of the day following Easter Monday, a tradition born in the shades of time. The festival had endured wars and famines, plagues and reversals of fortune, yet every year it was revivified—except for 1944 and 1945, when there was no food for the feast tables nor were there young men to wear the satyr costumes in which they would seduce the forest maidens and water nymphs. The musicians' instruments lay silent, tarnished from neglect, their players lying dead in the fields across the breadth of Europe, from Dieppe to Stalingrad. The theme of the festival— a jubilant celebration of the life force in which the opaque workings of Nature were briefly revealed to men—could not be given substance.

Two and one half decades had passed. The village of Emmaus,

like others throughout the land, had replenished itself. Each year, the festival had regained more of its depth and pageantry; the voices of its singers had become stronger, more vibrant, the antics of the dancers wilder, performed with greater abandon. Tonight, the greatest of all the Walpurgis Night revelries since the war would take place. The evening was a warm one, a cloudless night strewn with stars. The moon, still pale and cold, like a winter moon, would fill out as the hours passed, bathing the merrymakers with its invisible magic. Tonight, in the center of an age that had grown disdainful of the mysteries of its land, the past would reach out for the present as a spirit primitive and awesome was given its due.

The man called Werner Busse was walking along the empty main street of the village, idly reading the names of the various shops as though his were a benign proprietary interest. He was an old man now, the gray-and-white hair a sparse covering on the freckled scalp. He limped noticeably and seemingly in pain, although he never carried a walking stick; the left arm hung useless at his side, a detriment to his balance. The heels of his specially designed boots echoed off the cobblestones. At the end of the street, he stopped and looked first to the right, where his home stood, and, beside it, a very successful gardening center, then to the left, at the house of Dr. Grubber.

The woman beside him stared mutely at the small house with its gaily painted flower boxes and crossed herself.

"It is difficult to imagine him lying there," Busse said, his voice stern and direct as though he were annoyed by the death. "I believed he would outlive us all."

"I should have buried him," the woman murmured. "It was madness to wait because of the festival."

"You are wrong, Lillian," he answered her. "I know you have never enjoyed the feasts—why I can't understand—but to have held the funeral today would have destroyed the spirit of the holiday."

Lillian Grubber, delicate and lovely in her maturing years, ran a palm across the front of her long peasant skirt.

"For me to wear flowers in my hair yet a black armband for his death, to watch people who owe so much to him carry on in

. . . in some pagan rite while he lies there, alone, uncared for. . . . *that* is what I cannot bear.''

"You have never had much respect for tradition," Busse said shortly. "I would have thought you would appreciate its importance to our people."

Lillian Grubber looked at him and said, "In the Germans tradition can be a terrible thing, a weakness and vice. It is something we should have learned by now."

The door of Dr. Grubber's home opened and a shaft of light broke across the sidewalk onto the street. A young man stepped out and, after making certain the house was locked, stuffed his hands deep into his pockets and came toward the couple. He leaned forward, kissed Lillian on the cheek and nodded to Busse.

"I'm all right," he said gruffly, looking away from Lillian, who had taken his arm. "I had my time with him. It is all over. Let's get on to the festival."

"Helmut, are you sure you wish to go—"

"Yes, I am!"

Lillian dropped her hand and moved away from her foster son as he walked on ahead of her, his shoulders hunched forward against the inoffensive night wind.

It had been almost a year but seemed only yesterday that he had come home to Emmaus, a prominent attorney who had conquered the challenges of the great city of Hamburg. His practice there had brought him success but not wisdom, flattery but not friendship, sycophancy from his peers but nothing of substance to share. He was a man to whom things came too easily; whatever he touched grew and prospered, and it was so until the day his conscience rebelled at the consequences of some of his acts, when he finally understood that he destroyed as many lives with his talent as he saved.

Helmut Toller had come home, to rest and reflect in the house into which Lillian had brought him almost twenty-five years ago when his grandfather, the apothecary Toller, had died. An orphan, he was naturally taken in by Dr. Grubber and Lillian, who had been closest to his grandfather. Lillian had never had children of her own and so lavished all of a mother's love upon him. Now she was struck by the depth of the metamorphosis; for he had come back, of necessity, a changed man.

The shy, uncertain, yet vibrantly alive youth (she still thought of him as a boy) had returned a man too old for his thirty-five years, his thoughts held in check behind a veil of sadness, his voice hardened by his understanding of the world, a vision hurting and unapproachable, and she despaired for him because he would allow no one to lead him to a different light, just as tonight his sorrow at Grubber's death was translated into anger, a desire for solitude which repelled attempts to reach out to him.

They had left the darkened town behind and were walking along a road that led to the meadows of one of the district farms. There, according to the traditions of the village, the people would feast, the tables shared equally by human beings, satyrs and nymphs. In the distance Lillian could hear the faint notes of a horn gliding softly through the woodland, merging with the cacophony rendered up by crickets, tree frogs and night birds. She shuddered and, in spite of herself, stepped closer to Werner Busse. Up ahead, the broad shoulders of her foster son weaved in the darkness, sometimes disappearing altogether when the shadows of the trees fell upon him.

Lillian walked beside Busse, falling into his slow, short step, listening to his labored, at times rasping, breathing. His condition, enfeebled by geriatric infirmities and deteriorating rapidly as his strength fell away, reminded her of the first time she had seen him, twenty-five years before. Neither she nor her uncle had thought Busse would live more than a few days. Weakened by what must have been a devastating journey, anemic, with a raging fever that drained the last of his reserves, he had seemed inevitably destined for death. Yet the hours had lengthened to days and the days to weeks. Every evening, unless she was needed elsewhere, she was at his bedside, whispering to him as he screamed and sweated through his rages, holding him in her arms when he would whimper and cry out at the phantoms of his swirling imagination. At first she took no notice of his words, but after a time, when she would come into his room and he was conscious, he would be staring balefully at her, his dark eyes suspicious, often looking to see if anyone was with her.

Lillian began to listen carefully to his ramblings; but by late summer they had become more infrequent, and they finally stopped altogether. The man who called himself Werner Busse was healed as best he could be. Yet in his convalescence he brought on a different kind of sickness upon Emmaus, and Lillian watched first in fascination, then in growing horror as he proceeded to spread his influence over the village.

The gold.

If she had had any say in the matter, Lillian would have counseled her uncle, Dr. Grubber, not to mention the gold to Busse. But her uncle was a man of principle: true, the gold had been the booty of the fleeing SS officer; yet it was because of Busse's condition that the ambulance had stopped in Emmaus. Therefore he was indirectly responsible for the gold's being here and should be consulted as to its disposal.

With the help of only one other person, the blacksmith Brehm, the gold was melted down into very small bars and, over a period of two months, moved to Switzerland a little at a time. Brehm acted as courier; the signature at the bank was that of Werner Busse. On the return trip, Brehm carried back medical supplies and black-market Red Cross ration coupons. Werner Busse concerned himself with their disbursement, while Dr. Grubber extended his practice to the areas around Emmaus, there now being enough medicine to go around. Thinking back, Lillian could almost believe that matters were being guided by divine intervention. At least, that was how she viewed it for the period of limbo into which their lives had passed in 1945.

When the Americans discovered Dachau, their righteous fury knew few bounds. It was not enough for them to prod the townsfolk of Dachau through the concentration camp; the net spread farther, far enough to include Emmaus. In what the citizens considered an act of insanity, wasting precious gasoline to ferry farmers, women and children forth and back, the Americans had villagers go through the camp, even inside the crematoria, before the first ration cards were handed out. Those who refused to enter the lager were prodded or dragged through and on the way out handed a reduced ration. American bread tasted very hard that winter. Yet few had any alternative: to starve did nothing for one's pride. Yet dignity had its own hunger. Werner Busse knew this very well.

Werner Busse adroitly parlayed the fate of Emmaus into his outstretched hands. Discreetly, he established himself as the center of the illicit distribution of the Red Cross coupons. He gave cards to one family, asking them to share their provisions with relatives or neighbors, then a week later bestowed a card on the recipients of the charity with instructions to share *their* food and fuel. This way no one family would appear too often at the Army distribution offices; no one would become suspect. The method was taken as Solomonic in its wisdom; Lillian came to perceive it as a clever way to maintain maximum dependence and garner everlasting gratitude. Yet people ate; they had fuel and enough medicine, which rumor credited to Werner Busse as well. There was no one to whom she could voice her suspicions of Busse's motives; even if she did, what could she impugn? Those who were recipients of his generosity had nothing to give him in return and knew as much. They took, and prayed that such a miracle might pass their way once more.

Two winters passed, the second more severe, but by that time a kind of normality had returned to the community. As well as feeding the people, the supplementary ration cards created a sense of self-pride. No longer did they bow and scrape before the conqueror—who, as it happened, had softened his grip in a need for allies. To take from one of their own inspired the townspeople to greater efforts at self-sufficiency, and their attention turned to enterprise—to the rebuilding of the small hardware store, to setting up an undertaking concern, to establishing of a modern bakery.

What Heinz Nordhoff did to resurrect the crumbling Volkswagen concern and the site of its production, Wolfsburg, Werner Busse accomplished for Emmaus. He was amenable to the bourgeois aspirations of his people; encouraged them to voice their dreams and confide in him. When one aspiring merchant dared to raise the subject of finance for his pet enterprise—a simple scrap-metal depot—Busse guaranteed its funding. The necessary capital arrived within the fortnight. A dream had become reality; the floodgates were open.

Within a few months Busse underwrote financing for three dozen enterprises. The money was never secured from him personally; it found its way to Emmaus through the Skrip Bank of Zurich, which held thousands of tiny gold bars in Busse's account, collateral against the loans which regularly crossed the borders. No one inquired into the reasons behind the Skrip

Bank's willingness to lend; no one dared to speculate on Werner Busse's connections with that institution. There was no reason for such rude curiosity. One had only to present a reasonable plan to Busse; it would be approved, and shortly thereafter, his word would be borne out to have been as good . . . as gold.

As a result of his position as broker, Werner Busse was constantly being offered partnerships. He took none, asking only that the loan be repaid in regular installments at the given interest rate of two and a quarter percent. No one quibbled over the figure, and no one had the means or the inclination to discover that Werner Busse was in fact a moneylender, earning one-half percent over the bank interest on every transaction. Even Grubber himself required money to build his clinic; he received it as quickly as anyone else, at precisely the same rate.

But in all of this, who was the man known as Werner Busse? He had various identities which were bestowed upon him by others: the good Samaritan who had discovered and shared a means by which his countrymen had regained their pride and rebuilt their community; the partial cripple who returned, so he said, to his first passion—gardening—and who slowly, with his own hands, built his own enterprise, a small but very prosperous greenhouse and gardening center; the agnostic who never attended the Catholic services in the church whose coffers he replenished; an employer fair to his employees, even the schoolboys working for him in the summer. Lillian had no doubt that if Emmaus were to elect a modern-day saint the unanimous choice would be Werner Busse. Yet, curiously, he always refused to serve on town councils or participate in politics. He went out of his way to avoid these and was known to disassociate himself from polemics. It was, Lillian thought, as if he were afraid of the subject.

Lillian Grubber was one of the few who were not indebted to Busse and so could view him critically. Therefore the question: who was Werner Busse? Sometimes, when she was in his company, he suddenly became translucent, and a gesture, a phrase spoken too gutturally with the wrong emphasis on a word, a nervous tic or a particular stance would illuminate what might be the inner man. In such a moment, she glimpsed a figure standing in the distance, his profile defined by a flash of lightning, then blending with the night. Recognition was impossible, yet the fear within her stirred.

"I said he was a great man in his own right. Lillian, are you listening?"

She turned around, startled.

"Yes, yes, of course."

"I like to think of his death as coming at a very symbolic time, when we celebrate Walpurgis Night. A time of decay and ultimate rebirth."

"As is Easter," Lillian said quietly.

"Yes, that too. But the true spirit, to which we adhere in our hearts, is not the Christian ritual but the pagan. I have always maintained this."

"My uncle was a doctor," Lillian said stubbornly. "He did not think superstition a healthy thing."

"I know," Werner Busse answered thoughtfully. "That was one area of disagreement between us."

They walked on a way in silence before Busse said, "Here we have three generations of Germans: myself and Grubber, you, and Helmut. I always believed it would be so; that the Germans, through discipline and will, would rise once more."

Again the lightning, the glimpse and uneasiness rising like a wisp of smoke. . . . But Busse was oblivious to her scrutinizing gaze.

"Strange," Busse continued, "I never felt this sense of loss at anyone else's death. But I did not truly believe Grubber would die. Death surrounded him constantly; he was always in its midst and so I must have felt he was immune to it. . . .

"Ah, here we are. Such a magnificent sight!"

The road had taken them to the top of one of the hills that circled the meadow. Helmut Toller, whose long strides easily outdistanced theirs, had disappeared. He had taken the short route, a wagon track that broke with the road and cut across the field to the meadow.

Lillian had to concede that Werner Busse was right: the scene was spectacular. In the meadow, four large fires were burning, the pyres set up in the pattern of a diamond. Upon each lay the split carcasses of pigs tended to by a cook. The aroma, mixing with the night sweetness from the fields and forest, was tantalizing. Away from the flames, long tables had been arranged, with torches set along the sides and ends. On these roughhewn boards lay a repast of monumental proportions: a dozen varieties of cold meats; marinated onions and green tomatoes, spiced with bay leaves, cloves and thyme; potatoes høt and cold; sharp sour cabbage and sweet pickled beets. There were pitchers for the beer and small casks of wine, already tapped, their liquids flowing. And around all this milled the two thousand people, the citizenry of Emmaus—God-fearing, hardworking, sober folk whose night had come.

Busse and Lillian stayed on the road, following it right around the hill and down toward the neck of the meadow, where the gloom of the forest was pierced by yellow-orange light. The first shouts greeted their arrival, and suddenly, from all sides, the dancers appeared.

Although she had expected them, Lillian was nevertheless startled and involuntarily grasped Busse's arm. To her this was the most hideous aspect of the ritual—the dance of the satyrs and nymphs. They came upon her from the brush and from behind the trees, their heads covered by grotesque masks of stags, the antlers bobbing and weaving in the light. Some of the men had stripped and wore only deerskin to cover their intimate parts, their hands transformed into hooves. Rivulets of sweat bathed their shoulders and bare arms, and when they threw their heads back she could see the shining necks, the muscles stretched taut.

They were all around her now, pressing against her, their antlers brushing her hair as they stamped the earth, clawing the darkness with their hooves, the groans and snorts of animals coming from the mouths of men. She turned to Busse, a desperate smile on her lips to hold back the fear. But the satyrs had sensed it, jeering and crowding her, forming a wall through which she couldn't pass.

"Werner!" she screamed at once.

Busse laughed at her. He shook off her grasp and waved to the satyrs, swinging his arm, urging them, shouting, "Hé! Hé!" They roared back their approval and parted before him. Some girls, dressed in diaphanous robes, brought up the torches, handing them out to the satyrs who now lined the path to the feast tables.

With the faggots held out at arm's length above their heads, they formed a canopy of light, the aroma of the wood and entwined brush fragrant like incense. As Busse and Lillian entered the meadow, silence fell upon their pagan regiment. Then the music of a horn, not a trumpet or bugle but one carved from wood, underlined by the lilting sound of a flute, drifted over the assembly. As they passed the ranks, those behind them took up the chant, at first only a faint whisper but building rhythmically to its crescendo.

"Busse . . . Busse . . . Werner Busse!"

From the head of the column there leaped a figure of mountainous proportions with the largest mask Lillian had ever seen. The eyes of the creature were red like fresh coals, the antlers so wide that she did not believe the man within the beast could hold them up. But he did more. Flinging out his muscled arms, he squatted and bade two nymphs come to him. They ran up, and in one motion he swept them from the ground and set them on his shoulders. Rising, he turned his great head first to one, who kissed the mask, then to the second, who embraced it passionately. The satyr threw back his head and roared in pleasure, satisfied with the tribute. Turning slowly, he presented the others with his treasure, and all the assembly shouted back their approval.

The chanting was taken up again. Werner Busse and Lillian were led to the first table and seated. As the woodland creatures crowded about them, thrusting earthen goblets filled with cold white wine at them, one satyr with the mask of a faun leaped onto the table and in a terrible cry demanded silence. It was given at once: this was the prince of the festival, the ruler of all the forest for that night.

"Bring her here!" the faun commanded, pointing to a lovely black-haired girl in flowing white robes. Instantly the nymphs responded, giggling and pushing the girl ahead. The prince had chosen his princess.

"And him!"

No one touched Werner Busse. Men rolled up two kegs and set them upright to form steps, and slowly he went from these to the seats of the table and onto the table itself. The faun embraced him, then the girl, and ordered that the torches be brought forward and that all the people gather together.

Hundreds of people, their ranks sprinkled with torches held aloft, drew closer and closer to where the three figures stood on the table. As if obeying some ancient instinct, the crowds thickened in the center of the meadows, shadows leaping out into the night as they passed the gigantic fires: the older men in the rough dress of farmers or woodsmen; the women in flowing peasant robes with embroidered jackets; the small children straggling along, their costumes torn askew in playfulness.

When they were all pressed together in a rough circle, the faun slowly removed his mask and held it aloft, the signal for all satyrs to do likewise. Helmut Toller, prince of the festival, moved closer to Busse and held the mask over the old man's head. There was total silence.

"The benefactor of the festival!" he roared out. "We will all drink to the benefactor!"

A thousand hands rose into the night sky as though to pull down the stars. Drops of white wine splashed from the cups, sparkling in the torchlight, the heavy mead of ancient chieftains.

"I salute you," Toller cried out, and drank from his cup.

"We salute you!" the assembly roared back. "We salute you!"

Lillian, who had managed to climb onto the table, was sitting at her foster son's feet, her gaze fixed by the sight that spread out before her. Through the raised arms she could see the shining faces of men and women, uplifted toward the magnetic figure of Werner Busse, who beheld them calmly, as though he were removed from them, had no need to acknowledge their homage. She watched as ordinary people who, in daily life, seldom raised their voices, expressed opinions in a matter-of-fact way, went on with their lives without a hint of deeper passions poured forth their undiluted adulation upon this man, chosen from all people by all people as "benefactor"—not mayor, councilman, priest or policeman but benefactor, the custodian of the spirit of the village, a title more meaningful than any temporal one.

And so it had happened again this year. The spectacle revolted her; she felt anger at the pathetic way in which emotions were strewn naked before the feet of the cripple she had helped nurse back to life so many years ago. But when she looked up to Busse, Lillian beheld a sight that froze her heart. Standing side by side with him was Helmut; and Busse, with one arm on Toller's shoulder, was presenting him to the crowd, drawing their applause away from himself onto her foster son. Even though there wasn't any physical likeness, an unmistakable resemblance surrounded them. As they stood with feet apart, bodies held erect against wind, faces turning slowly over the multitude, she could sense Busse taking possession of Helmut Toller, imbuing him with his spirit, which made the young man's eyes cruel and conceited, which twisted his lips in arrogance and transformed him from the pagan faun to the terrible beast whose visage adorned the Biblical shield of the Apocalypse.

She watched as Helmut, captive in the spell of the old man, looked at him and shouted through the din, "It is different this night! It is different!" Werner Busse smiled, his eyes holding those of Toller. He reached over and brought the young man's arm down so that he might take the mask from his hands. Busse held it aloft, displaying it to the crowd, and shouted, "The Prince of the Feast!"

The crowd roared back the salute. Lillian stared at the obscene mask and at the man who was clutching it. The image of Werner Busse receded and the translucent man emerged. The years spun away to a past time, three decades ago, when she had watched another man, possessed, as Werner Busse was now possessed, by the spirit of a Germany far more ancient than memory could recall. He who had held it then believed in his vision, in his ability to penetrate the darkness of the past and recall to his service the old gods whose swords had not grown dull in jewel-encrusted scabbards. He had looked out onto the multitudes as Busse did now, a symbol of pagan authority. The image of such a figure pierced her memory, and she shrank before it. Her reason screamed at her that Busse could not be this man, but instinct stoked her terror.

Lillian could stand it no longer. Sliding from the table, she plunged into the crowd, her arms pushing away the mass of flesh which sucked her into itself like a mindless amoeba. With a furious energy born of fear and revulsion, she continued to pummel her way through, oblivious to the grunts and curses around her, to the blows that fell upon her body. She heard a great cry go up, as if a beast had roared in its den. But she dared not look back for fear she might be transfixed, like Lot's wife by the vision of a burning Gomorrah. Then Helmut, her foster son, flung his mask high into the air, the signal that the revelry might begin.

There was no rest for the earth that night, nor did the star-encrusted sky ever regain its tranquillity. Human time had ceased to exist, and another measurement, not of this earth, overtook the revelers, bearing them away upon their music, their wine, the debauchery which long ago had been transformed from a rite of festival lords into an orgiastic pageant of self-indulgence.

Helmut Toller awoke when the dew still lay heavy upon the fields and the mists were rolling across the silent waters of the lake. He groaned, rolled over in the straw and rose, shaking himself like a dog. He stared down stupidly at the girl beside whom he had lain, his princess of the night. Her black hair was tangled and filled with bits of straw and grass, the cheeks a cold marble color and the lips tinged with purple as though she had just come from a cold swim. He covered her as best he could with his leather jacket and stepped over her, hearing the joints in his knees and thighs crack.

The scene around him resembled a battlefield. The fires were still smoldering, but only the occasional flame burst through the charred embers. The pyres were smoking from the wetness. Across the meadow, across the grass near the fires, huddled side by side against the trees or sprawled across the tops of tables whose remains of food now littered the earth were the bodies of the revelers. Helmut could see only a few hundred, those around him, for the mist hid the rest. As he walked around and over them he heard a fitful cry from a sleeper or the grunts and snoring of those who lay deep in the cocoon of drunkenness. He passed men and women lying in a clutching embrace half naked, and others frozen in the act of copulation as though some invisible ash from a volcano had petrified their position for eternity. He walked on, to the lake's edge, and there knelt down and washed himself, feeling the leaden weight of fatigue dissolve in the cold, fresh water.

"I am glad to see someone has the presence of mind to get up."

Helmut Toller rose slowly to his feet and turned, wiping his face with his bare forearm. Before him stood Werner Busse, dressed as he had been last night, even the tie in place. He was wearing a heavy woolen coat. Toller could not guess if Busse had returned from a warm sleep in his own bed or if he had stayed in the meadow. Only the red, glowing eyes, usually so lackluster, suggested he might never have left the festival.

"Well, my prince, you see what has become of your subjects," Busse said.

"The prince is in none too much better condition," Toller answered, his voice still thick, the tongue dry and rough.

"Walk with me," Busse told him. "There is some coffee, brought down by those who left."

As Toller fell into unsteady step beside Werner Busse, the thought of coffee suddenly led him to remember.

"Where is Lillian?" he asked Busse. "Have you seen her?"

"Lillian never stays for the festival," Busse answered in a neutral tone. "Over the years she has made her disapproval of the whole affair, I might even say revulsion, quite clear. No, she left early," he repeated, "before the feast."

Toller was silent for a moment, then said, "I should have stayed with her. It was unfair of me to leave her alone. You are right, of course: she doesn't like it. She's never told me why, though."

"Lillian does not understand the significance of such things," Werner Busse said shortly. "To her, it is all madness—she used that word once. A throwback, she called it, to barbarism."

"But why?"

"Because it reminds her of the Reich years, a time she would rather forget."

"I don't see it that way at all," Toller said. "A holiday, a festival, simply that. Christ knows, there's reason enough to celebrate; such tremendous things have happened to us Germans. We're proud once more. Traditions are part of our pride."

They reached the table where a large pot of coffee was being kept warm on a brazier with a grille across the coals. Ernestine Hassell, Busse's housekeeper of many years' standing, poured out a large mug for Toller and handed it to him, along with a hot wet towel to cleanse his face.

"There are those, still, who do not understand what happened thirty-five years ago. They never remember the victories, the euphoria of becoming Germans again, the pride of the race. They think only of the defeat, what they have suffered—Lillian is such a person."

"I don't mind her eccentricities," Toller said slowly. "It's only that it's easy to tell she is unhappy. It bothers me tremendously."

"I understand that," Busse said, cutting him off, "but you must think of your own sentiments. Did you not say to me last night that there was a different feeling to the festival, something you have never before experienced?"

"There was a magic, a spirit which I could almost reach out and grasp," Toller said, holding his cup with both hands.

Helmut Toller and Werner Busse began walking toward the wagon track which would lead them to the road.

"Tonight," Toller said, "it was as though my entire personal history had coalesced, the scattered pieces all drifted together and formed a coherent whole. . . . Do you know what I mean?"

"I believe so, but you might explain a little more."

"My grandfather, for instance. As a child I remember his taking me to Nazi rallies and feasts such as this one. It was such a glorious time; he seemed so happy, full of life and strength then. It was when the war took a turn for the worse and it was obvious Germany would lose that the periods of black depression came over him, became more frequent and lasted longer as conditions deteriorated. By the time he died, in late 1945, I loathed him because he was so weak and insignificant, because he bowed and scraped and begged until there was nothing left that might be recognized as manhood. I remember I never cried for his passing. How could I, when all he left to me was a legacy of hopelessness and fear, intertwined—the fear of inheriting nothing more than the hopelessness he had allowed to kill him?

"It was that fear which drove me to Lillian," Helmut Toller murmured. "Not love, although that came later, but fear. For a time I believed I survived—not physically, but mentally—because their house held no despair. They appeared immune to misery around them, as though hidden away somewhere there were a knowledge, a belief that upheld them, something more powerful than politics, economics and the like. One day—I was fifteen at the time—after I had returned from school and told

Lillian what the headmaster had said about Dachau, that only criminals who had sabotaged the war effort had been kept there, I discovered what that belief was.

"She didn't allow me to return to school the next day. Instead we drove to Dachau and spent several hours at the camp. We saw everything—the lectures, the films, the crematoria and barracks, everything. Then she turned to me and said, 'This, this whole camp, represents what Germany was under Adolf Hitler. You are horrified by what you see, and so you should be, for Dachau is the most repugnant example of what one man can do to another, what Germans did not only to helpless foreigners but to other Germans as well. No, Helmut, you must not look away. Too many of us have already done that. We looked away while innocents were being slaughtered, and now you are being told lies about this in school. After today, you will know, when some-one speaks of this period, if he is lying!'

"On the way home, in the car, I said to her, 'But it wasn't my fault. Why should I be punished for it!' And she answered, 'No one will punish you, Helmut. But those who suffered will always see you as a German and they will remember Dachau and blame you because you belong to the people who allowed it to exist. So you must, as you grow older, work as hard as you can to restore the pride of your country. You cannot hate those who may not forgive us; rather, work to show them that there is another face of Germany, one that can live in peace with others, can respect them for what they are, is willing to help them, because, Helmut, all men are brothers. We cannot live any other way.'

"That was the foundation of Lillian's house—made not of politics or self-interest but of an understanding of what had happened and what must be done as recompense. There was no despair but hope for and faith in ourselves, that we were much more than the silhouettes Dachau had cast on us."

Helmut Toller lit a cigarette and snapped the match in two before dropping it to the ground.

"So I was given a reason to hope; yet that same conversation, which opened up my love for Lillian and old Grubber, irrevocably damned my grandfather. For what had he been if not one of those who had turned away, and whose guilt in the end had overwhelmed them? At that point I erased all memory of him and gave myself over to Lillian and let her guide me as to how a man should live; and perhaps if I had not taken up the study of law, I would have become a different man."

"Why is that?" Busse asked him.

"The first indication that something had changed came during my second year. You must remember that eight or nine years had gone by. I began to sit in on war-crimes trials when I wasn't in class. The longer I watched charges of genocide and mass murder being leveled at old, broken men, the more absurd the proceedings appeared. The bigger the death statistics put forth by the prosecution, the greater my incredulity. To me it seemed an exercise in the grotesque, especially with the high number of acquittals. For the first time in almost a decade I began to doubt the validity of my hatred for my grandfather, whom I had included among all those guilty of our so-called 'national shame.'

"The other turning point came after five years of practice. I arrived in Hamburg a complete unknown; yet within fourteen months I had not only made a substantial amount of money but gained, within the legal society, a reputation as a tough, astute tactician. In subsequent years the accolades multiplied and with them, the volume and importance of the cases that were being brought to me. But when Hans Bayer Weiss, the industrial magnate, approached me to defend his daughter, I suddenly realized I might have gone too far too quickly. You may remember the case.

"Erika Weiss was charged with murdering five people—three children, all less than ten years old, and their parents. After a drunken spree through the Hamburg nightclubs, she had driven her father's mammoth Rolls-Royce into—or more correctly, over—the Volkswagen that was carrying the family. The charge against her was negligent homicide.

"I was familiar with the incident through the newspapers, which gave it full coverage. When Hans Bayer Weiss appeared before me, there was nothing he could say that I hadn't known already. Except his proposition: if I could practice my legal magic for Weiss, there was, quite literally, no end to the rewards that would be mine.

"I really didn't have to think about the offer, knowing that at best I might obtain a lesser sentence for the girl but one that nevertheless carried several years of prison.

"To my surprise, Weiss did not seem put out. It was obvious, he told me, that I had misunderstood him. Then, very precisely, as though he were peeling apart a stalk of celery strand by strand, Hans Bayer Weiss listed all the cases I had been involved in where guilt or innocence hadn't been the issue at all, but rather the preservation of some higher interest. In a soft, unhurried tone—I remember it so well!—he spoke of a dubious real estate deal that I had preserved from being called criminal; of an actor's involvement with an underage girl who, it might be charitably put, was persuaded to change her testimony when I kept her on the stand for three days running; of the pilot of the national airline whose income was supplemented by heroin smuggling but who was freed after the prosecution walked into an invisible trap I had set, causing a mistrial.

"This was the magic Hans Bayer Weiss was referring to—to be retained on the largest case I had yet been offered. The magnate, a foremost predator of the jungle, was not interested in buying justice. Only a victory.

"I remember that for a time I had said nothing. As Weiss's voice led me through the gallery of names and faces, I relived the proceedings in the courtroom, and watched my own performance. What Weiss was saying was true: I *had* exonerated the guilty by my talent. I had taken on the cases because there was a challenge in them, and once I achieved total victory in the first— not a mere reduction in the charge—anything less could not suffice thereafter. As for justice, I really did not concern myself with that. I spoke for the accused, a human being who had placed his life in my hands. Justice, or what passed for it, was represented by the opposing side. That oftentimes that side could not measure up to my ability was unfortunate. In the courtroom, justice, like the accused, took its chances; well represented, it triumphed; otherwise, it was the loser.

"I told Weiss I would telephone him the next day, but never did. That evening I drank myself sick, while pondering the details of previous cases. In their sordidness was reflected, I felt, my own condition, and the brilliance of my arguments now struck me, like an actor caught unprepared in the spotlight, as cold and devious. The audience was no longer applauding. They were murmuring, 'Liar! Liar! Liar!'

"Within the week I had given away the cases left over and

informed the senior partners, by letter, that I was taking a leave of absence. In the end, it seemed to have made no difference to the Weiss case: Erika Weiss had been released on bail pending trial set for late in the year.

"So you see," Helmut Toller said, "somewhere in the force of circumstances, the ideal Lillian had instilled within me had died. And just as before, when I was an orphan, I returned to Emmaus to try to gain some sanctuary, to find a place where I might rest and try to discover where it was that I had abandoned what I believed were the things I lived by. But I couldn't. Lillian was unable to help—partly, I suppose, because I wouldn't allow her to. . . ."

"But you said last night was different," Werner Busse prompted softly.

"Yes, it was," Toller agreed. "Hans Bayer Weiss, in making his proposition, showed me power I had never seen before. I became frightened and retreated here, where I had sanctuary. But last night showed me I could never come home again. There was an intoxication in the air, the music and dance which made me believe that unlike my grandfather, who was afraid to truly believe or commit himself to anything, I had to be stronger. I had to look at those depths, explore them, master them! It is no good any longer to turn a blind eye on that which tempts me more than anything else in the world."

"And that is?"

"The power I felt when I practiced law. Its beauty and terror, the way it felt in my hands, like the wand of Merlin . . ."

As he listened to these final words, Werner Busse knew that something had taken place, a movement for which he had waited twenty-five years, which he at times had despaired would never come to pass. Each year for a quarter century he had anticipated the return of the spirit, the manifestation of its will.

"This night is different!"

So Helmut Toller had spoken. And so it was for him, Busse, since he had at last glimpsed the ferment that lay behind the pale faces of the German people. In one moment he had witnessed the yearnings which, like gray embers, needed only to be carefully stirred to leap into flame. He had touched the psyche of his nation and in return had been overwhelmed by its torrential response.

Werner Busse knew Toller had felt the power flow from the crowd into his outstretched hands. He now knew the sensation of being chosen to represent, yet still stand above, a people. His ears rang with their exhortations and approval, their demands and their tributes. He had tasted the power; his mouth would learn to hunger for it, and when the hunger became insatiable, no one, not even those he professed to love, would be able to stand against him.

When they reached the road, Werner Busse tried to hurry along as best he could. Because of the shrubbery that grew along the path, his trousers were wet from the knee down. In an hour the flesh would turn an ugly gray and the bone begin to ache in protest. Yet he believed that this day he might withstand any pain, for as he had perceived a pivotal point in Toller's life, so he recognized that the balance had shifted in his own.

The death of Dr. Grubber had shaken Werner Busse. Although bound by the secret of the gold, the two men had been more acquaintances than true friends—for the aloof personality of Busse did not permit camaraderie, much less intimacy. Yet there was a strong sense of their relationship. With Grubber gone, there remained few people of Busse's generation in Emmaus, and in spite of himself, he had to admit the loss.

But as so often happened in his life, the balance was quickly redressed. For Werner Busse remembered another death, another time when all he had created was slowly being destroyed. "All things shall pass away. Nothing remains but death and the glory of deeds."

Those had been the words he had uttered a quarter century ago. He had been so right in that observation, more so than he knew at the time. For Death still remained, and the glory of deeds he had witnessed again last evening.

In speaking to Helmut Toller, Busse was reflecting aloud on what he had seen at the festival. The spirit had been so very familiar. He had felt its precursors in the years during the subjugation and shame; had seen the sudden manifestations, as quick and bright as the flash of a salamander's tail, in a pamphlet, a meeting of the Old Guard, a historian's revisionism. The spirit lived; it had subsided, but nonetheless it still lived. At the height of the festival he had felt as though he could embrace it once more, let it loose beyond Emmaus, into the German cities which were great metropolises again, and still farther beyond, into the swollen bellies of Europe.

But he was an old man and recognized himself as such. Although seized by the vision, he could not translate it into a tangible form. That task would have to be left to younger men, purified of their parents' guilt: men like Helmut Toller. But there was still the last role for him to play, the role that would breathe life into the vision. With Grubber's death and Toller's ascendancy, Werner Busse understood exactly what it was he had waited twenty-five years to do.

III

Surrender

THE MAN walking along the platform to the exit of the Munich railroad station was the sort who attracted attention followed immediately by embarrassment. The right side of his face was lacerated by a deep scar, from the top of the cheekbone through to the tip of the jaw. Although Grubber had several times put forward the idea of plastic surgery, the suggestion had never been taken up.

Naturally the familiar moustache never grew again, and the telltale cowlick disappeared under the careful attention of a barber he visited punctually twice a month. But the barber's meticulousness could not cover the streak of pink flesh, smooth, curved and pulsating from the veins surrounding it, that separated itself from the hairline, the hair roots having been burned away permanently by the passage of the bullet.

The final grotesque touch came in the contrast between the pudgy, overweight body and the left arm, which remained now as then withered and emaciated. That he was a cripple and ugly caused strangers to look away from him rather than at him. He was never put out by this. In fact, he took pride in his disfigurement, which was better than any disguise and afforded him free movement among people without causing suspicion.

The man crossed the length of the station, walking carefully over the stone floor, followed by a porter with a cart for the two bags. When he reached the station lockers he inserted a coin, pulled out the key and asked the porter to place the larger of the two bags inside. After trying the door several times to ensure that it was properly locked, he tipped the porter, retrieved his briefcase in his good hand and continued to the exit.

Upon reaching the taxi rank, he scanned the men behind the wheels and let two cars take on other fares before stepping forward. He could not abide young drivers whose obvious contempt for their means of livelihood extended to their passengers.

"And where will you be going, sir?"

The elderly driver in a workaday uniform—shiny black suit, tie and visored cap—had placed the man's briefcase up in front and had taken his place behind the wheel.

"The Office of the Public Prosecutor of Bavaria," the man said formally. "That is on Spassartstrasse."

As always, the Public Prosecutor was immaculately attired: tweed jacket, freshly starched shirt and plaid tie. The most striking feature about his dress was the elegant hand-crafted shoes.

Dr. Hans Kleemann was a man of sixty-five, tall and scholarly in appearance, with a freckled balding crown rimmed with gray wisps of hair, a large, prominent forehead and soft brown eyes flecked with green. His face appeared undernourished, given the prominence of the nose and slanting cheeks, yet it was marked by dignity and an authority tempered by compassion.

He had just finished reading the morning papers and was about to open his appointment book when his secretary entered. She carried in her hand a neatly folded note and laid it on the desk.

"There is a gentleman outside," she informed him, in a tone that told Kleemann she was put out. "His name is Busse and he insists he made an appointment to see you today. The arrangements, he claims, were made a very long time ago. I"—she added emphatically—"can find no such entry in my book."

She stood back, waiting for the prosecutor's confirmation of her statement. But Hans Kleemann did not turn to his calendar. Instead, he read the note and looked up at her.

"Kindly show him in, Marthe. And if there is nothing urgent, see that we are not disturbed."

To signal her discontent, the secretary did not announce the caller when she brought him in. Nor did this man called Busse speak at once. He shuffled over to the desk, his body bent to one side from the weight of the briefcase, which he deposited beside the wing chair. Without being asked, he settled himself opposite the desk and watched as Kleemann, who had risen upon his entrance, also sat down.

"Perhaps," the man began, "we can talk about your helping me."

Then he broke off and looked around himself.

Kleemann's office, he noted, was both spartan and secretive. There were four filing cabinets, the old sort with sliding drawers, painted a dull green and showing traces of rust around the edges. These were all closed. The desk, of nondescript government issue, was bare of any papers. A crystal ashtray in the shape of a sea horse, a fresh pad of yellow legal-size notepaper and a selection of pens were all that lay on the ink blotter. The only personal effect was a rack of aromatic briars, of various woods and descriptions.

"In keeping with a man of your stature and reputation, Doctor, I expected more appropriate quarters," he said.

Hans Kleemann thought the man sitting before him was accustomed to making such blatant, even rude, comments. The authority he had noted in Busse's first words had not disappeared, and he recognized it as an authority accustomed to control.

"I am sorry you find the surroundings wanting," Kleemann answered. "To me they make little difference."

"Aha!" The man laughed suddenly. It was a sharp, staccato exclamation which startled Kleemann. "Well spoken, Herr Doktor. But remember: there is a point at which humility becomes pride."

Kleemann ignored the man's rudeness.

"What is it I can do for you?" he asked civilly.

"We are here to speak of war crimes," the man said easily. "The investigation of which is part of the responsibilities of your office and one that, according to your reputation, you pursue very assiduously. Tell me, Herr Doktor, do you think that after so many years, it is fair to keep after these men you call war criminals?"

"I imagine that depends on whether one feels more affinity with the Old Testament than with the New. To favor Yahweh, the God of vengeance and justice, over the love and mercy of Jesus Christ."

"And the prophets of the Old Testament have more appeal for you?"

"I believe," Hans Kleemann said quietly, "that certain acts are not affected by the passage of time. These—mass murder, wanton cruelty and the continuous systematic infliction of pain leading to death and genocide—are beyond exculpation. The fact that a man has not paid for his actions in twenty-five years does not lessen the intrinsic character of that action, nor does it affect his association with the crime. The blood may have dried on the hands, but it has not been washed away."

"Obviously not too many people share your viewpoint," the man remarked. "Officially, that is. This office is understaffed, pathetically so, and the courts are very slow to move against so-called war criminals—to say nothing of the noncooperation you receive from German police forces."

"One does what one can."

"For how long, Dr. Kleemann?"

"For as long as one feels it necessary."

The man paused for a moment, looking thoughtfully at the prosecutor.

"Tell me, why are you being so kind in putting up with me?"

"You have something to tell me, Herr Busse. You are very cautious, but understandably so. Any man who has written me a note asking whether I remember the significance of the date April 30, 1945, is touching a sensitive subject. It is a day that has a number of malign contexts. For example, the ancient Feast of Beltane, one of the most powerful rites of the Satanist calendar, is held then, the climax of Walpurgis Night. April thirtieth is also the date assigned to the death of Adolf Hitler. . . ."

"I somehow feel," the prosecutor speculated, "that you are not here on behalf of a victim. You come from the pale, from those whom I seek; I am wondering what it is you have brought me and why."

"I have not been wasting your time," the man said stiffly, "although your tone implies that. What I have to say is true."

"I believe you."

"My name is not Busse."

"I see."

"I am Adolf Hitler, Führer of the Third Reich."

Hans Kleemann was certain he detected the glint of pride in the eyes of the man who called himself Adolf Hitler. Although what he had stated sounded preposterous, Kleemann sensed an undertone of truth to the words. He found it difficult to raise his eyes and look at the man again. The cripple had kindled a wisp of fear inside him, the faint curl of smoke that precedes an uncontrollable blaze.

"You allege that you are Adolf Hitler," Kleemann began slowly, but Hitler cut him off immediately.

"I allege nothing! I am the Reichsführer. And you should do better than pretend that you do not believe me. It is quite clear that you do."

"I find your contention quite incredible," Kleemann said mildly. "And for the moment it remains only that—an allegation, without proof or substance."

"Ah, the tiresome burden of proof!" Hitler exclaimed. "You shall have it. I brought it with me."

He kicked the briefcase with his left foot.

"But, Dr. Kleemann, tell me this: do you not feel instinctively—and you must admit that instinct is important in your work—that I am who I say I am?"

Kleemann looked at Hitler without wavering. He forced himself to stare into the face of this elderly man and mentally strip away the layers of sunken flesh until he could find the image he was searching for. Yes, it is possible, he thought. But after twenty-five years, visual identification could hardly be exact.

"There is a resemblance," Hans Kleemann said carefully.

"So your eye does not lie, although it would very much like to," Hitler said with satisfaction. "It is a very curious thing about human nature: whenever people think they see something distasteful or repugnant, the eye immediately obliges and alters the perception. Then, presto—they do not see it at all!

"Tell me something else," Hitler continued, his tone confident. "Has anyone else ever come into this office claiming to be me?"

"Why should anyone have done that? Who would want to claim such a thing?"

"Then why have I done so? This is not a joke or some charade—it is the truth!"

"I see you are becoming disgusted by these proceedings." Hitler laughed suddenly. "What is happening, Dr. Kleemann—are you truly coming round to believe me?"

It might be exactly that, Kleemann thought helplessly.

"And if so, what will you do with me?" Hitler demanded.

"May I see your passport?"

From the inside breast pocket of his jacket, Adolf Hitler brought out a fat leather billfold, the leather smooth and cracked from age. When he opened it, Kleemann saw that both halves were crammed with folded pieces of paper, notes and stubs. From the bottom of one side, Hitler extracted the passport and laid it out on the desk.

"Werner Busse, born in Salzburg, 1886," Kleemann read aloud. "Place of residence, Emmaus, Bavaria." He examined the passport carefully.

"Genuine."

"Why shouldn't it be?"

"And you have been living in Emmaus for the last twenty-five years?"

"Exactly."

"What is your occupation?"

"I am the proprietor of a gardening center. Where you buy bulbs and saplings, tools for the garden, manure, that sort of thing. I also have a very good greenhouse for flowers."

"I see," Kleemann said. "May I keep the passport?"

"Of course. I have no more use for it."

The prosecutor stared at the sharp black-and-white photograph.

"You are wavering again, Dr. Kleemann." Hitler smiled at him, the scar deepening around the ridges of his mouth. "Like a metronome you go from this side to that—believing me, not believing me. So what shall it be? If you do not believe me, I have arranged for an attorney in Zurich to distribute certain sealed records—duplicates of the contents of my briefcase—at this time tomorrow. These will be sent to international journals, to the television and radio stations and, of course, to Israel . . . unless I call and say that that will be unnecessary."

"Who is your attorney?"

"Ernst Fischer."

Hans Kleemann depressed a button on the intercom and said to his secretary, "Marthe, please confirm for me that there is an attorney by the name of Ernst Fischer practicing in Zurich. No, I don't wish to speak with him—not yet."

Kleemann turned to Hitler, who was observing him with evident satisfaction.

"Have you arrangements to stay in Munich?"

"No. I assume you will attend to that."

Kleemann said nothing, and changed tack.

"What of your affairs in Emmaus?"

"The business will take care of itself for the time being. I have excellent people to staff it. As for later, arrangements have been made and can be modified if need be."

"Obviously you have planned for some contingency. What would that be?"

"The investigation you will undertake, of course. Surely you will verify all the documents I have brought you."

"You are very eager for that to begin. Why?"

"And the corollary to the question is, why should I have given myself up to you in the first place—is that not right?"

"It is."

"Dr. Kleemann, I believe you are still suffering from shock," Hitler commented with the slightest disdain. "As inured as you think you are—and with all the research into war crimes you have done, all the intricate and, for you, unpleasant details you must consider—you still cannot grasp the magnitude of the moment that history has fated you to witness. And why is this? Because I am no longer considered a man but someone superhuman. A myth. In the minds of everyone but the most paranoid Jew, I am dead. The others—Eichmann, Mengele, and others of that ilk—do not have my aura. Because they are—were, excuse me—only subordinates. Important ones, to judge by the attention they have received in popular history, but underlings nonetheless—most of whose names, I might add, I never knew. I, on the other hand, am the supreme leader. I am Adolf Hitler.

"Consider your own reaction. The implications of knowing that Adolf Hitler is alive are in themselves of tremendous significance. They would trigger the greatest manhunt in history. The Jewish bloodhounds have proved themselves very capable. But here, sitting before you, is the Führer—quite alive, as you cannot doubt, although with not much natural time left to him. The average man would be dumbfounded. His reaction would in fact, and you must not take offense, be very much like yours. He would not want to believe that such a thing was possible. A chase after an elusive shadow can be scoffed at because the mind believes not in the man but in the myth.

"I must confess that you disappoint me. I would have expected a more detached and professional observation."

"You have no fear, have you?" Hans Kleemann said softly. "For twenty-five years you have lived in the country you destroyed. There is nothing inside you—no soul, no remorse, no need for forgiveness."

"I would have considered a quarter century wasted had it been spent in contemplation of what you speak of," Hitler said contemptuously. "Do you think I would have allowed myself such an indecency?"

"Then, why now? Why twenty-five years to the day after your alleged death?"

"The exact details of my decision are too copious to be discussed at the moment," Hitler said pompously. "But I shall tell you that it began with the death of a friend three weeks ago. This gentleman was my contemporary; I had known him every day of the last twenty-five years. He was the closest person to me on this earth, although at a distance it would have appeared we were only acquaintances. At no time did he know my identity, nor did I ever give him reason to suspect that I was anyone but what my papers read. I can also say that I was his closest friend. And as is so often the case, his death led me to a realization that I too had better concern myself with time.

"You understand that time—or my second life, as I prefer to call it—began for me in May of 1945. The destruction of the city I had restructured after my own image should have been paralleled by my own death. But because I had lived through death, I chose to close my first life, the years that ended with the gathering of power and my stepping forward into history.

"My second life, then, was peopled by men of flesh and blood, not the ghosts or shadows of those who once served me. Here I lived and worked among people who believed me to be someone else, who hadn't the slightest suspicion of whose hand it was they shook or at whose table they shared a meal. It was a life in which I prospered, and that was, at most times, one of contentment, yet one whose frailty became evident with Grubber's death."

"Dr. Grubber was this acquaintance," Kleemann interrupted.

"Yes," Hitler said impatiently, as though the detail were unimportant. "You needn't worry about names. In due course you shall have all of them.

"It was the recognition of my own mortality that first led me to think about coming back before the world. But I hadn't realized then just how my subconscious had laid the foundation for such an action, that I had already worked out why and how I was going to go about this.

"You see, Dr. Kleemann, as soon as I realized that I would die, possibly tomorrow or perhaps not for years yet, I asked myself what, if anything, was to be gained from destroying this second life I had built up over a quarter century. And I arrived at some interesting conclusions.

"Since you are a German and were present during the rule of National Socialism, you may understand. In my last talks with Martin Bormann I said to him that it would be unimaginable for me to continue to live in a defeated Germany. That was why suicide was mandatory. Death seemed a minor inconvenience when compared with the humiliation and anguish I would have had to bear being brought to trial by the Allies. At the same meeting I recall telling Bormann of my vision of the postwar world: how Germany, hacked to pieces, would be divided between the Americans and the Russians, each maintaining and nourishing a sphere of influence; how these two giants would rule the world before the silent masses of Africa and Asia rose to claim their due. In spite of all that has been written about my state of mind, I was quite rational and cogent when the need arose.

"Because Fate decreed it, I survived and became part of this much-vaunted new age, blending myself into the texture and mood of the so-called German democracy. Needless to say, I had only contempt for the manner in which Germany regained her position of strength. Adenauer catered too much to the past, to that ignominious 'national shame' designed to pacify the conquerors. He did not recognize the strength he commanded. However, that is slowly being rectified. A new spirit is passing over this age. We Germans have had enough of groveling, of having the past spat back into our faces. I can assure you that my generation and a good part of the following one are pleased to see that the virtues I gave to Germany forty years ago—virtues of pure blood, strength through pride and belief in victory—these are the very same to which the rest of the world is tending and which it will soon embrace.

"The British, the Americans and the French came as noble victors, pure in thought and deed. But slowly over the years we see the hatred each has for the Indian, the black and the Asiatic, the Arab and the Jew. Yes, even the Jew, much revered after the war, has multiplied with such alacrity and force that he too is no longer an endangered species but a mere pest.

"Therefore I understood that the time was auspicious for my coming forward from the shadows. I could not win the race against death and wait for others to unequivocally accept my principles. But I could, for the children of the German nation, the second postwar generation, commit an action that would rewrite history, that would rekindle the faith I had instilled in the blood of their parents and grandparents."

"You believe that they would listen to you?" Hans Kleemann asked incredulously.

"Kleemann, I do not have to tell you that the psyche of a nation does not change—it cannot change—within the space of a single generation. You know that, and in fact I believe it is the basis of your reason for undertaking the kind of work you have chosen. And you are right! I do not expect the German people to embrace me as they once did, but I know—I can feel—that I shall make their blood rise once more.

"I shall also punish some of them. I shall make them pay for the lies they have told their children and the shame with which

they have burdened them. Because their children will see me as
an old man who has had the courage to come before the world
and challenge its conception of Adolf Hitler!''

''That would be a most heinous outrage to perpetrate against
your people!'' Hans Kleemann shouted. ''How could you think
they will believe you?''

''Oh, they shall, Dr. Kleemann, they shall.'' Adolf Hitler
smiled. ''For I come not to lead but to inspire, to fill the clothing
of the myth with my flesh and blood. The very fabrications and
distortions that have been fed to the world for a quarter century
will now work for me, not against me. You will watch as that rich
harvest of my seed matures in the coming generations!''

These words wove a web of promise and unreality around the
prosecutor, binding him to the power they carried. He was swept
back in time, back to stand in the presence of the Führer. The
words were born of a vision, and in them the vision became
reality—repugnant, but strong, confident, with the power of will
behind them, and so they were also enticing. That this partially
crippled old man could still practice such potent magic frightened
Hans Kleemann. He had few doubts that the man sitting opposite
him was indeed Adolf Hitler.

''Have you had any contact with the Nazi groups organized
after the war—the ODESSA or Kameradenwerk?'' Kleemann
asked at once.

''No,'' Hitler answered shortly. ''I avoided them altogether.
Do not misunderstand me: I regard them as keepers of the faith,
men who have retained the principles they swore to uphold, and
so they will be the vanguard of the new National Socialism. But
for all of that, their security has not been the best, eh? Look at
what happened to Eichmann. Or Mengele, for that matter. I had
no wish to hide myself away in the jungles of South America: I
have always detested warm climates; and there, in spite of
the best of intentions, word would have got out that I was still
alive.

''No, I have watched the activities of ODESSA and the other
groups quite carefully, but have never participated or reentered
to claim the leadership. My men will have their roles to play.
They will stand behind me when I come forward to challenge the
precepts of so-called justice, when I come before the Jews and

once more watch them quake. It will be quite the thing to try me, will it not, Dr. Kleemann?"

"Perhaps the trial will not be public," Kleemann answered harshly. "Quite possibly it will be held *in camera*."

"You are a fool grasping at straws," Hitler rebuked him. "Do you believe I haven't considered such a maneuver? I have taken pains to know you, Prosecutor. Believe me, you were a careful choice; and you, in a desire to protect men from me, would work for a secret trial. Of course, you might be under great pressure from this pack of squeamish fools who govern us today, for they too would fear me and try to hide me. But think of the legalities involved! I must have a defense attorney. He in turn would bring witnesses in my behalf. The prosecution would also have to abide by the rules of a democratic court. Very soon all the security arrangements would be in shambles.

"Even if such a conspiratorial trial could be designed, I have guaranteed its destruction. You know about Fischer and the papers I have left behind. Well, Dr. Kleemann, the Swiss are a notoriously reliable people, and I have no doubt Fischer will act on my instructions, present or future. I think you understand the nature of your position now."

Kleemann found Adolf Hitler's gaze, filled with malignant glee and malice, unbearable. He shivered and closed his eyes.

"It is the heart, is it not Herr Doktor?" Adolf Hitler said softly. "Do not be surprised. I can tell by the color of your skin, how pale and tight it is. Above all, the sweat."

Kleemann made no attempt to hide his condition. But that this man could have diagnosed his ailment so quickly astonished him. Perhaps . . .

"No, Doctor, I do not suffer from it myself."

Kleemann pressed a handkerchief to his forehead and settled himself. It was imperative that he take command of this surrealistic discussion.

"I should like to see what you have brought: the evidence, as you call it."

"By all means, Doctor. It is all here." Adolf Hitler tapped his briefcase.

"I shall return in a moment."

The Public Prosecutor of Bavaria rose and went into his secretary's office. In a quiet, deliberate voice he asked her to tell his callers that he was not in the office today. Only if a Minister telephoned should he be interrupted. In addition, he was prescribing security status for his visitor and whatever discussions the secretary might hear. Under no circumstances was she to mention Werner Busse to anyone.

The secretary, who had served Kleemann for fifteen years, understood implicitly, asking only that she be allowed to call him on the intercom once an hour, for her own peace of mind. She then handed him a slip of paper. The prosecutor looked down thoughtfully at the address of Ernst Fischer. It belonged to one of Zurich's most fashionable districts. Obviously Adolf Hitler dealt with only the best representatives. He pocketed the paper and asked her to send up his two detectives, the Farben brothers. They might not be needed immediately, but the prosecutor wished them to be available. They were also to bring a fingerprint kit.

His reading lasted two hours. All the while, the man who called himself Adolf Hitler sat in the chair opposite, scarcely moving. There were moments when Hans Kleemann, engrossed by the words, forgot his presence. Then he would glance up and see Hitler looking at him, watching with black, pitiless eyes, his scarred face devoid of expression. The silence of the office was broken only, punctually on the hour, by calls from the secretary, to which Kleemann replied in a monosyllable.

"I assume, Dr. Kleemann, that you are satisfied with all this."

Adolf Hitler's voice had lost none of its arrogance. Nor, so it seemed, had his endurance diminished. If he felt any tension, he did not express it.

Kleemann surveyed the papers and files that cluttered his desk. There were a physician's reports and dental charts and X-rays, certificates for a driver's license and photocopies of the passport forms. There was also a copy of the Questionnaire, an interrogation sheet that the Allies had passed out among the German citizenry at the end of the war and that had been designed to surface active Nazis in the bureaucracy and civil service. But by far the most fascinating and illuminating work was the one done in Hitler's own hand: his diary. Begun in late 1947, the writing recounted his deliverance from Berlin, the conva-

lescence in Emmaus, his gradual acceptance by its people and
his rise to prosperity. But more, it revealed a train of thought
that could be traced back unerringly to an earlier work, *Mein
Kampf*.

Whoever this man was, he had structured his evidence carefully, using the Questionnaire and other bureaucratic data as
foundation, then adding the diary, which allegedly only he could
have written in such detail, for the personal touch. To finish off,
there were the dental plates, which would confirm or refute all
else that he had said. The prosecutor wondered why there hadn't
been any mention of fingerprints.

Although the Questionnaire and most of the other papers belonged to a man called Werner Busse, the key pieces—the dental
plates and physician's reports—would, when verified, constitute
proof, one way or the other, that the man sitting before him was
or was not Adolf Hitler. The final evidence would be the matching
of the fingerprints.

"The details are impressive," Kleemann said. "On the face of
it, we know a great deal about a man called Werner Busse, who
died in Berlin in April of 1945. You say that you took on his
identity as yours and proceeded to hold it until this day. Then
there are the dental charts and medical data which you say are
your own, as well as the many pages of notes on the personal
details Adolf Hitler would have known of, since they concerned
him directly—names, dates, places of births, deaths and bap-
tisms. Unfortunately, I recognize everything on this sheet. The
sources are generally available to the public, and with patience
and research anyone could have compiled this dossier. However,
there are the dental plates. . . .

"The names you have given us, the people in Emmaus—I assume they are all legitimate and can be called forth."

"Oh, yes, of course." Hitler sat back and regarded the Public
Prosecutor severely. "Will you tell me, then, Herr Doktor: am I
under arrest?"

"No. No warrant has been issued; nor can it be issued—because you are legally dead. I would therefore ask you to abide
with the arrangements I will make for you; that is, a kind of
protective custody."

"By all means. As long as you understand that from time to

time I require medical attention. Dr. Grubber informed me some time ago that the prostate gland is functioning badly on occasion."

"We will see to it that you have everything you require."

"And where am I to be held?"

"I haven't decided yet," Kleemann answered. "You can appreciate that the location must be carefully chosen."

"Very well. But you can tell me this: are you ready to believe that I am the Führer of the Third Reich?"

Kleemann had been anticipating the question, but in spite of himself he wished to answer in the affirmative. He recognized the gut feeling which compelled him to believe.

"I can find no fault in your story, nor any discrepancies," he said quietly. "But there are, as I have said, a number of details still to be taken care of."

"Ah, you are postponing the inevitable!" Hitler shouted at him. "Tell me, Doctor," he added slyly, "what is it you cannot accept about me, eh?"

"There are a number of things which perplex me," Kleemann admitted cautiously. "The one which interests me most and which, in terms of the importance of the investigation is almost irrelevant, is this: do you not care for those people, whom you refer to repeatedly in your journal—Dr. Grubber; his niece, Lillian; Helmut Toller, grandson of the apothecary, and others— with whom you have shared twenty-five years? Do you feel so little for them that you are willing to disrupt their lives, to fill them with horror and revulsion?"

"Those things pale before the final task I have set myself," Adolf Hitler stated coldly. "If you think that for a single moment during these twenty-five years I have lost sight of my mission, that mission I had embarked upon *fifty years* ago, you are very much mistaken."

Hans Kleemann lowered his eyes and turned away. He was engulfed by a feeling of nausea which had been growing since the moment the interview had begun. But he dared not show emotion before this man who would consider it a sign of weakness, indecision, fallibility.

"Why did you choose to come to me?" Kleemann asked suddenly, as though the question had just occurred to him. But in his heart he was asking, What crime or sin have I committed that I should have to bear this evil in the twilight of my life?

"That is obvious, is it not?" Hitler said. "You are an eminent jurist, member of a legal family of long standing, author of noted tracts on criminal law and politically in good odor. There isn't the slightest stain on your past. You are the most prominent and the most potent of all war-crimes investigators.

"If I had gone to other offices, assuming I had been able to deal with a man as intelligent as yourself, then the chances are that I would never be tried, but instead helped out of the country. Or looked after in a different way. Be honest, Herr Doktor: there aren't many prosecutors who are keen on war-crimes prosecution."

"To our shame, there are not."

"Ah, but you are a moral man, are you not?" Adolf Hitler said delicately. "You must settle accounts with your conscience or else it will not let you rest. Yet admit it: I *do* tempt you. Perhaps you see me as your Mephistopheles. But then again, you are not noted for heroic vision.

"It is all too obvious what you feel for me—the contempt, the revulsion, the hatred. But you are still my worthiest opponent. In dealing with me you will have the eyes of the world upon you also, yet you appear to have the ascetic's benign indifference to fame. You know that recognition adds nothing to those elements you consider important in a man. But perhaps, hidden away in the past, is a dormant desire for revenge, against those who have impeded your work, who tolerate you, respect you, but who inwardly fear and vilify you. . . . Ah, we shall see!

"And within this desire, does there not lie a second, greater temptation? Whether or not to engage me in this struggle? For a struggle it shall be. You are a worthy opponent, and every drop of sweat and blood I extract from you will be precious to me and give me the greatest pleasure. You have already grasped some of the ramifications of my existence; given time, you will understand more. You perceive that we shall be doing battle for the minds of men. Not only here in Germany, where the conflict will be the most brutal and where I shall achieve total victory, but throughout the world.

"There! Does that not appeal to your vanity? Or will you say to me that in all 'good conscience' you stand opposite me because, being the man you are, you can do nothing else?

"We shall see," Hitler repeated softly. "And a third temptation shall be placed before you. When you face it you will know that we understand each other perfectly."

The hypnotic spell was broken by these last words. Hans Kleemann said very deliberately, "That is where you are mistaken."

Both of them wore three-piece suits, tailored to camouflage their powerful frames, evidenced only by large, thick hands; both had the family's true blond hair and watery, expressionless blue eyes. They were young men in their early thirties. Although there was two years' difference in their ages, they were often mistaken for twins, so closely did one resemble the other.

The Farben brothers were detectives who worked solely for Hans Kleemann. They had begun their careers in Berlin but after two years had requested a transfer to Ludwigsburg, the seat of war-crimes documentation and investigation in Germany. Having an independent income and being related, however vaguely, to the famous chemical clan of I. G. Farben, the brothers could afford to disregard police politics and remain aloof from the usual scramble for advancement. They had done one war-crimes investigation in Berlin and discovered that ferreting out phantoms was infinitely more challenging and rewarding than galloping after ordinary criminals. From that time on they had looked upon themselves as historical detectives whose quarry was made of equal parts of notoriety and elusiveness.

The Farben brothers had undertaken three investigations for Hans Kleemann, each one completed successfully. The Public Prosecutor of Bavaria had been impressed with their work to the point of asking them down to Munich and offering them an exclusive position in his office. The brothers, who respected Hans Kleemann without reservation, accepted, and from that day became not only his investigators but his silent guardians as well, never too far away from this man who was unloved most of all in his own country.

"Have you the fingerprint kit?" Kleemann asked them.

The younger of the two, Gerd Farben, held up a leather case the size of a jewelry box.

"Whom do we have?" he asked.

The prosecutor took them aside and explained what he wanted done. The man inside his office, who might or might not be Adolf Hitler, was to be fingerprinted, then taken to Kleemann's country home in Frischen. The house was situated on a lake, well away from other property, so privacy was assured. Their stay would be indefinite, and security had thus far been absolute. They were to see that it remained so and that their charge did not communicate with the outside world.

When Kleemann finished, he looked from one brother to the other, waiting for questions. But there were none. Their understanding of the magnitude of this responsibility showed in the steady hard gaze of their eyes.

"And what do you propose to do with these paraphernalia?" Hitler demanded as Gerd Farben arranged the pieces of the fingerprint kit on Kleemann's desk.

"The dental plates you have brought me can be checked against those on our records," Kleemann told him. "With a correlation of fingerprints we will have absolute proof of your identity."

"Would you mind stepping over here?" Gerd Farben asked politely.

Hitler did not rise from his chair.

"There is no record of my fingerprints," Hitler said coldly. "Everything was destroyed."

"That is not quite true," the prosecutor answered. "Now, if you will cooperate with me—"

"I tell you I saw to it that the records of my imprisonment were removed from the files—on my express order to Himmler!"

"Will you cooperate or not?" Kleemann demanded. "Or has all this been so much wasted time?"

"Very well, Prosecutor," Hitler murmured. He rose and limped to where the younger Farben was waiting, a small ink-stained roller in his hand.

"You are sure," Hitler said to Kleemann. "And you do not need this to prove it."

Kleemann did not reply but nodded to the detective. Carefully Gerd Farben inked Hitler's right hand, then took the bony, veined fingers one by one and pressed their tips against the paper. Adolf Hitler smiled as the midnight-blue whorls appeared before him. It was a minor humiliation, he thought; he would get his own back many times over.

Wednesday evening was Dr. Kleemann's night to take dinner, followed by billiards and small talk, at his club. Tonight, however, he felt he could not face the other members, or even the few friends he had there. He had no appetite for dinner, and his attention would wander from the conversation. Such uncharacteristic behavior would be noted, and speculation would begin as to what tantalizing "case" had caused it. It was better not to make an appearance.

Although the decision was made, Kleemann regretted it. The club was a source of mild recreation and relaxation for him in the city. As he walked to his apartment, he found it odd that stepping out of habit should trouble him so much.

Still, he reasoned, it was not by any means without precedent. Childless, he had lived alone since his thirty-third year, when his wife had been killed in a train wreck outside Stuttgart and shortly thereafter he himself had had to quit his post as judge in that city. That was 1936, half of which he had spent in prison for refusing to apply the new racial laws of the Reich. He had then emigrated to Denmark but had been arrested once more in 1940. Several months later, with the help of the Danish underground, Hans Kleemann had made his way to Sweden, where he had stayed for the duration of the war.

The apartment was small—only four rooms including the bathroom—but it was clean and well lighted. Two windows facing the street provided a view of the zoo. The Public Prosecutor stepped into the living room, removed his jacket and poured himself a glass of dry sherry. Settling down behind his ancient desk, he lit a pipe and drew on it gently, watching the bluish-white smoke drift over the wing chairs toward the library cabinets.

What had happened today, the entry into his life of a man long thought dead, long wished dead, threatened to destroy everything to which he had devoted himself over the last twenty years. As custodian of the new German conscience, Hans Kleemann understood how his countrymen would behold the reincarnation of

Adolf Hitler. He had both conducted and sat in on enough war-crimes trials to know that the Germans turned their faces from the past, desperate to obliterate it. The images that were pushed before their eyes during such proceedings hurt and shamed, embarrassed and angered, and like children, they shut their eyes, hoping that when they looked out again the image would have disappeared. But this reaction came in the bright light of prosperity, of confidence in oneself and pride in the rebirth of a nation. In the psyche lay darker things, shadows that grew tall and memories that festered in resentment and a drive for true retribution—memories which recalled a time when fear had been the foundation of respect. It was these shadows Hans Kleemann would be challenging, and he understood that he would stand before them alone.

Adolf Hitler was pleased with the arrangements. He was particularly appreciative of the bed,. which was Kleemann's own and which, as befitted a man getting on in years, had a firm mattress. Adolf Hitler thought he should sleep very comfortably tonight.

He leafed through the pages he had written in the last hour, of the events that had happened that day, and closed the notebook. Then he began to undress, laying out the clothes on a chair behind the desk. After he had washed, he carefully broke a pill in half, a mild sedative, and went to bed.

As he lay back, Adolf Hitler felt completely satisfied with what the day had brought him. He had surrendered to a formidable opponent and in the surrender had achieved a twofold victory: he was convinced that Kleemann believed who he was and that this belief had brought fear. The first rock was rolling down a mountainside, soon to shake loose other, bigger stones and eventually to produce a landslide which would bury everything in the valley below. He was that rock, and Germany the valley. He would bury it with his presence, and out of the rubble there would rise a new monument to his greatness, a memorial built to the glorification of his vision. This was a dream Adolf Hitler believed he would mold into reality.

The little sleep Hans Kleemann managed that night was filled with horror and nightmares, and he was relieved when the last of the monstrous visions finally flung him from the dark pit into consciousness.

He rose with the first light, at half past five, and dressed quickly. Picking up the briefcase he had placed by the door the evening before, he let himself out and within a half hour was driving through the outskirts of Munich. He arrived in the town of Landsberg am Lech shortly before seven o'clock.

It was here, in the prison of the same name, that in 1924 Adolf Hitler had been briefly incarcerated for his role in the abortive Munich Putsch. Although all records of the Führer's stay were supposed to have been destroyed upon his assumption of power, one copy had been inadvertently preserved. The file itself contained no information that wasn't known to the Public Prosecutor, but within it there was a single paper that was the key to any investigation Hans Kleemann could launch against Adolf Hitler. It was the definitive proof that the man who had come to him yesterday was the Führer: a fingerprint sheet, taken by the German police almost half a century ago.

Adolf Hitler had, in all likelihood, issued Himmler the order to have the prints destroyed. But Himmler had not executed it. A sly provincial policeman, Himmler had accumulated vast dossiers not only on his peers—Goering, Gestapo chief Mueller, Goebbels and Hess—but on his master as well. Self-preservation founded on information—the smallest details to the grossest but most secret facts—was the hallmark of his mentality. But in 1945, when those archives had been sequestered by U.S. intelligence, Hitler was presumed dead. His file was plundered for security information, copies made and the original returned to the BND, the postwar German security service, which, in keeping with regulations, deposited the various documents in their proper nesting places. The fingerprint chart belonged to the prison in Landsberg am Lech, and so it was returned there, to remain a historical curiosity.

The lieutenant governor of the prison and a guard led Kleemann to the archives, which, to his surprise, were not in the basement but in a clean modern room in the new annex of the prison. The records were kept by years and cross-indexed by names of inmates. Under "1924" in the "H" section he found the reference to Adolf Hitler and pulled the file. Without bothering with the rest of the dossier, he removed the fingerprint sheet and from his briefcase brought out another sheet, on which were the prints of Hitler, a.k.a. Werner Busse, taken yesterday. He laid out both on the table and compared them under the magnifying glass he had brought with him. There was no discrepancy.

Hans Kleemann stepped back from the table, regarding the two sheets. Slowly he removed a handkerchief from his pocket and wiped away the sweat that fear and anticipation had brought on. The distance between Busse and Hitler had shrunk to the point at which the two images were touching each other, on the verge of overlapping. Like the dream dissolving into reality as one slowly awakes, the prosecutor felt the warmth of ignorance slip away to be replaced by the light of knowledge, its brilliance brought on by terror. He could no longer not believe. The axis on which his world had spun shifted, and nothing, nothing would ever be the same again. Not even the past. Of that he was certain, for his hand trembled as he reached for the bell that would summon the guard.

Hans Kleemann returned to Munich and went directly to the Records Room of the Ministry. From his own cache of files, accumulated over a quarter century, he removed the dossier on the "July Plot," the abortive attempt on Hitler's life in 1944. Again there was only one detail he was seeking.

The Public Prosecutor brought out the X-rays and dental charts made by Dr. Morell, Hitler's personal physician, while the Führer was recovering from the bomb blast. The photograph of the skull confirmed that there had been no brain damage as a result of the explosion, but Morell, being a thorough diagnostician, had also taken prints of the lower jaw. It was this chart which Hans Kleemann matched up against the X-rays Hitler had brought with him, displaying the structure of the present-day dental work.

At first, the results confused him. There were obvious discrepancies between the two plates. Puzzled, Kleemann examined each one very carefully. Then suddenly he struck the table with his palm. Of course! The plates Hitler had brought him had been taken only last year. Between 1945 and the present day there had been much dental work carried out. Kleemann looked at the old plate again and checked the bridgework against that of the new.

If one eliminated the work done over the years, what remained matched perfectly against the original plate.

Hans Kleemann placed the Morell X-ray alongside the fingerprint chart from Landsberg am Lech, deposited the file in his case and left the Records Room. He would tell Adolf Hitler of his conclusions in person, in Frischen tomorrow.

From the way they were sitting on the veranda, their chairs angled toward the screen door, a stool with coffee cups and a plate of biscuits between them, one might have thought them old friends. The late-afternoon sunlight was shot through with a blue haze from Kleemann's pipe, and the wind threaded the smoke around the porch, finally sweeping it across the lawn. Adolf Hitler found the aroma pleasing, although he himself did not smoke. He pushed himself up on his good arm and reached over for the lukewarm coffee.

"Did I not say it wouldn't take long to verify my claim?" he asked lightly, and shifted in the chair so that the sun might warm the ravages of his face.

"You did," Kleemann answered him.

"And what will you do now, Public Prosecutor?"

Hans Kleemann had concluded that if he allowed himself and his strength to be fragmented by indecision, he could never deal with Adolf Hitler. He had, at the very least, to be bold and as sure as his opponent.

"I have the critical pieces of evidence," he said slowly. "According to the law, I should write out a formal letter of arrest and issue an indictment. You would then be given over to the Federal Police."

"Yes, that is what you *should* do," Adolf Hitler answered swiftly. "But what *will* you do?"

"I will take some time—a week, perhaps more—and investigate the possibility of your being tried by an international tribunal instead of a German court."

Adolf Hitler replaced his coffee cup on the stool and laughed in his sharp, staccato tone. "I insist," he said, "on the most public forum possible, because of the propaganda value it holds for me; and you will see to it that I have it, because you do not trust our Germans to try me at all. You are catching up with me, Public Prosecutor. You surely are!"

At nine o'clock the same evening, in Bonn, Hans Kleemann called upon Dieter Wolff, justice for life of the Federal Constitutional Court. Wolff's housekeeper showed him in and guided Kleemann to the study, where Wolff was waiting.

"So, Hans, you are keeping late hours these days!"

Dieter Wolff was an imposing, robust man with the gait of a woodsman. Even though he was in his sixtieth year he remained physically strong and was the most tireless justice on the Court, with a reputation for detesting sloth and ambivalence. Nor was he beyond bullying the other justices to sit until a decision had been reached. Although only one of the twenty-four justices on the Court, Dieter Wolff virtually ruled the bench.

"You take this."

He handed Kleemann a large cut-crystal glass of amber liquid.

"The best malt whisky the Scots can produce—sent specially for me."

Kleemann smiled and accepted. He raised his glass to the toast he knew Wolff would propose.

"To the hangman, God rest his soul!"

"The hangman," Kleemann murmured.

Wolff refused to say where the toast had originated. But he often repeated to both confreres and students that in the dispensing of justice one must consider the ultimate penalty that a man might pay, and after that weigh all other punishments against it. Only when you understood the supreme verdict could you appreciate the role of mercy and temperance in the final decision.

"So, Hans, what is on your mind, then?" Wolff asked directly. "By your quietness I know that something is stewing in that cranium of yours."

"It is a delicate matter," Hans Kleemann said. "Not to be spoken of outside this room."

"As are so many of your concerns," Wolff said dryly. "And this leads me to think it pertains to your queer little Office of War Crimes rather than to the usual Ministry claptrap. But I see you are waiting for me to swear myself to secrecy. Well, so be it!"

"Thank you, Dieter," Hans Kleemann said.

Then he proceeded directly.

"Adolf Hitler is alive-and in my custody. He wishes to be tried."

Dieter Wolff laughed. He laughed so hard that his great head was thrown back and the liquor in his glass spilled over the edges of his cut-crystal glass and dribbled over his enormous fingers.

"Is there an end to this joke?" he asked finally, wiping tears from his eyes.

"Oh, yes, certainly. But I do not know it yet. I beg of you, Dieter, to let me finish."

Dieter Wolff became silent and regarded his friend carefully. He simply nodded and said not a word for the next forty-five minutes as Hans Kleemann recounted the story he had to tell.

"Although I know the answers, I must have the words from your mouth," Wolff said. "Are you satisfied that the fingerprints and dental plates are of the same man—that is, Adolf Hitler?"

"I am."

"Then you understand also that you have violated this man's legal rights by detaining him without counsel."

"I do not believe so. His confinement is voluntary, and he has agreed to waive, in written form, the need for counsel until such time as we are to proceed with a trial."

Dieter Wolff splashed more whisky into his glass, offering the decanter to Kleemann, who refused.

"And you have no doubt formulated some plan, eh?"

"On the surface, the matter appears simple enough," Kleemann said. "Hitler wishes to be tried and I am willing to oblige him. But I do not propose to do so in Germany. That is where I need your advice."

Wolff nodded. "Proceed."

"Adolf Hitler has been living her for a quarter century as Werner Busse, German citizen. He has been participating in elections, drawing a veteran's pension, paying taxes—in short, conducting himself as a citizen. Given this, would Bonn be inclined to set up another Nuremberg and try him on German soil?"

"No," Dieter Wolff said flatly. "That would be the last thing they would want. Never forget that in judicial and political memories, Nuremberg remains the epitome of foreign imposition of foreign justice. Never mind whether such a vehicle was necessary or not, effective or ineffective, just or unjust: it existed, and that alone was cause enough for humiliation. Even a proposal for the reconstitution of a Nuremberg court would infuriate the public, accustomed as it is to the belief that Germans manage the affairs of the German state. And can you imagine the kind of inflammatory issue you would be handing the Nationalists?''

"Would the government be willing to waive its right to try him and advise the High Federal Court dealing with criminal matters to do the same?''

"I believe so. I say this even though the government would be denying Adolf Hitler the protection it guarantees him under Article Sixteen of the Basic Code—that no one who is a German citizen may be extradited to stand trial for war crimes. The Chancellor would have to think long and hard before setting such a precedent as to allow Hitler to be tried in an external forum.''

"His dilemma will in part be resolved by Hitler, who wants just such an external international arena,'' Hans Kleemann countered. He paused, then pressed on.

"Assuming there would be no fuss in the High Court, what would the Federal Constitutional Court's stance be?''

"The same.''

"Very well. Do you, then, think a German justice should be part of the international tribunal that would eventually try Adolf Hitler?''

"If you could find one who would be willing, yes. Come to think of it, it would be a terrible thing not to have one. But''— Dieter Wolff held up his glass—"now that I can see where you are going, let me ask you a question or two: Has the government been informed?''

"No.''

"Have you informed anyone else of Hitler's existence?''

"Only my investigators.''

"But you mentioned an international tribunal—they won't all be German nationals?''

"No.''

"I thought as much. My good friend, I must inform you that you not only are guilty of conspiracy within your office but also are tempting treason charges, since this collusion will extend beyond the German border.''

"If you were in my position and held my conviction, would you act any differently?"

Dieter Wolff set down his glass and flexed his great fingers, the knuckles slowly becoming red.

"You have acted correctly and wrongly both at once," he said. "It is no secret that the stance of the Attorney-General is somewhere to the right of Attila the Hun. An exemplary figure of law and order, Jaunich has support not only within the party but also across the country. The public demands tough and decisive action in dealing with extremists, and he gives it to them. Of course, no one discerns any difference between such suppression and the actions of forty years ago when another lot were going around breaking the heads of socialists, Communists and anarchists. Interestingly enough, our public can't make the connection between a denial of rights to the Baader-Meinhof lunatics and a possible future extension of the same principle to those who simply have different views from those of the majority. And Jaunich doesn't want them to. This is the kind of man you would have had to deal with had you kept within the letter of the law. From your perspective there is every reason for you not to have gone to him."

"There is also something else," Kleemann interrupted. "The Attorney-General was a card-carrying Nazi. This minor fact, completely forgotten these days, would be dredged up as soon as a public announcement concerning Hitler's existence was made. The press would make hay of it and the obvious question would be asked: how could the highest legal officer in the land be able to bring his former leader, a man he had sworn to obey, to trial?"

"No, I hadn't forgotten that small item, Hans," Dieter Wolff assured him. "That is another area where you have acted correctly. The Attorney-General would be too compromised to act. However, that does not let you off so easily: the fact remains you could have *consulted* him, and he, with every authority, *could have claimed the case as his own*, to deal with it as he saw fit."

"Then there would be no case at all," Kleemann said thinly.

"There is a distinct possibility of that." Wolff nodded his great head. "Now let me ask you this: why do you think a trial, an international trial at that, is at all necessary? Why should Hitler be paraded throughout the streets of Germany and the world like some French aristocrat on his way to the guillotine?"

"What would you prefer—a secret trial?"

"You must have thought of that, Hans," Wolff said quietly. Then he abruptly broke off this train of thought and asked, "Where is he now?"

"In my country home, guarded by two detectives who are completely trustworthy."

"And aside from them, the only other people who know that you have him are those in your office?"

"No. Only the Farben brothers."

"Then why, while it is still possible, do you not kill him?"

The question struck Hans Kleemann with such force that he uttered a low moan, as though a hand had reached into his chest and wrenched his heart. He now understood what Adolf Hitler had meant by the third temptation.

"Not once did that thought ever cross my mind. Not for a single instant!"

"Good God, Hans, do you think everyone has such a perfect sense of justice as to be able to recognize Adolf Hitler for what he is—the reincarnation of a nightmare we have been trying to wake ourselves from for the last twenty-five years?"

"Are we Germans so very frail that we cannot look upon something like Hitler?"

"Yes, we *are* that fragile!" Dieter Wolff retorted. "Don't you realize that Hitler has surrendered because he knows that? Hans, you are assuming that a sense of justice will prevail. That is not the case at all. Listen to me. You know better than to think that one more act of castigation will help us. The Germans are inured to it. They have had too much of the past shoved into their mouths for too long. By giving them Hitler you will be giving them a demon they would like to believe has been exorcised. But if they see he is not, they will again plunge into their pathetic act of breast-beating, navel examining and pathos. They will resent having Hitler thrust upon them like that. And this resentment could well cause them to embrace him again."

"Am I right in thinking that you believe Hitler's death would serve two purposes?" Hans Kleemann said pointedly. "First, that it would spare the government tremendous embarrassment and second, that it would never bring forth the hidden feelings of allegiance some Germans still feel for Hitler?"

"That is exactly what I am saying," Dieter Wolff cried. "Kill him and get it over with. Spare yourself the agony of having to circumvent the government at every step and save everything that *you* have been building for the last quarter century. If I didn't know you better, Hans, I would say there is an element of revenge in all of this."

Is there that? Hans Kleemann wondered. Do I know so little about myself that the obvious could have escaped me entirely?

"It's no good, Dieter, for us, the German people, to go on thinking that we can live forever in this illusion—the good German, the industrious German, the jolly, the-past-is-forgotten-let's-all-be-brothers German. How long can we live with this lie when every day we give credence to it? By that I mean our *real* attitude toward the past, our true concern with those who have shamed us, or ostensibly shamed us. How dare we take pride in our justice and concern for human values when our constitution declares that a war criminal, who is German and who has committed atrocities beyond the national boundaries, may not be extradited to stand trial?

"To play the hurt and the innocent, the penitent and the reprieved while in the blood we believe we are not guilty, that we have nothing to repent and are doing so merely to play along with the opinion of others—this cannot last forever. The major issue of bringing Hitler to trial is not to have the German character examined once more. It is simply to carry out justice, and that in itself should be enough. That in the passing of justice other factors will arise, that we may inadvertently bring forward a new dimension of the German personality, or rather, cast the light upon one that has been hovering in the shadows—so be it. Sooner or later we will have to deal with that dimension. Better to look at it now, while there is still time to truly understand it."

"You expect too much of people," Wolff reiterated. "There is nothing more to say than that. You are the Samson who might bring down the tower that is Germany. I would ask you to consider whether that tower, every brick of it, is so evil that the whole is worthy of destruction. Do so carefully, Hans, because once you begin, you will not be able to rest until there is rubble at your feet. Then it will be too late. We will not be able to rebuild from the same stones. And if you do not care about yourself, then consider those who will be touched by the destruction.''

"I am very much afraid for myself," Hans Kleemann said. "But if I were to move away from this path of bringing Hitler before the world, I would be shirking my duty as a jurist and my conscience as a man. There will be no personal victory for me, Dieter; I think you can see that. On the contrary, my life will be very hard afterward. Not only will I be vilified by my own people, but I must also hold out against those whose lives I will have irrevocably altered. And I cannot tell you now which is the more important: the sparing of individual pain or the carriage of justice. How to weigh one against the other, and with what measure? I do not know. But I would not be able to live with myself if I took the gun and placed it against Hitler's head.

"We understand so very little of evil, Dieter, yet we are fascinated by it because it is opaque and tantalizing—much more so than good. That is why we often succumb to it. When we wake— if we wake—we cannot comprehend what it is we have done wrong. That is what has happened to Germany. Hitler is evil personified. Let him come forward and tempt us all. Let this be the yardstick of our strengths and weaknesses; and yes, let us dare to look at the results, for only they are the measure of what we truly are.''

Dieter Wolff sighed, nodding his head. "So be it. There is nothing to be done about changing your mind, so we might as well get on with it. Is there anything else you want of me?"

"Would you be willing to serve as the German justice on an international tribunal?"

Dieter Wolff looked at him thoughtfully, with the eye of a hangman measuring his victim for the noose.

"I would have made certain of my place on such a bench," Wolff said with grim satisfaction. "Even if you hadn't asked me."

It was an evening in Paris which made one think that spring would not follow into summer but had, instead, chosen to roll back into winter. In the fog-laden air, which reached deep into one's chest, one could almost make out the ice crystals when passing under street lamps. The streets were slippery, and couples had the excuse to cling to each other with fierce tenacity. It was the kind of Paris Hans Kleemann loved most—cold, melancholy and faintly tragic.

Almost twenty-four hours after having met with Dieter Wolff he arrived at the Meurice, shortly after dinner. While his bags were sent up to the room, he asked the switchboard to call the Soviet legal delegation, which was also staying here for the duration of an international jurists' conference, and inform Justice Morozov that the Public Prosecutor of Bavaria was here to see him. Kleemann had made the appointment with Morozov's secretary from Munich.

Hans Kleemann was in the process of unpacking when the return call came through. Morozov, said the secretary, would be pleased to meet with him in the Maritime Lounge in a half hour.

Ivan Morozov was a surprisingly young man to hold the position he did. No more than fifty-five, he was short, slender and trim to the point of being dapper. The effect was heightened by his dress, which was a brazen choice of 1920s style: charcoal gray wide-stripe suit, suspenders, oleander shirt and red cravat. His hair, perhaps too black for a man of his age, was slicked down, emphasizing the smooth oval face in which the lips were mere creases but the nose as prominent as Pinocchio's. He greeted Kleemann in passable French, but the conversation continued in German.

"I am honored that you should take the trouble to call on me, Dr. Kleemann," Morozov said formally. "It has been a long time since we last raised glasses."

"The Hague," Kleemann answered faintly. "It was at The Hague during the laws of extradition conference."

"So it was," Morozov agreed. "Although the discussion about political exiles lasted only a short time; then we managed to become entangled in greater issues. Human rights, I think it was."

Morozov's obsidian eyes flashed at Kleemann. The legal systems of the two men might be centuries apart in development and their ideologies beyond hope of reconciliation, yet they had met on the neutral ground of international law and recognized each other not as representatives of competing systems but as men who shared a common bond: a concern for a justice that was not born of, nor whose precepts were dictated by, politicians.

A waiter was summoned and the order given. Morozov settled

back with one of the long Russian papirosi and looked directly at Kleemann, knowing that the prosecutor had not sought him out to make small talk. The prosecutor waited until they had been served.

"In the last several days," Hans Kleemann began, "there has been an extraordinary development in a certain war-crimes case, one that has never come to public attention before. I have a man in custody who we all believe died in 1945. Until a week ago, this has been accepted as given. I can tell you now that I am certain that the individual being held in West Germany is Adolf Hitler."

Morozov's reaction was infinitesimal. It consisted of stopping the movement of his hand, with brandy balloon, toward his mouth.

"Do you realize, my dear Kleemann, what it is you are telling me?" he inquired.

"I do."

"And you are certain, beyond all doubt, that the man is Hitler?"

"Absolutely."

Morozov was at once tempted to ask how this certainty had been arrived at, but refrained. There would be time enough for details.

"I take it there has been no announcement of the arrest," he murmured.

"No, not yet."

Morozov set down his balloon and brought his fingertips together in a fastidious manner. "It would appear," he said, "that there is some conspiracy involved. Is there?"

"The West German Government has not yet been informed of my . . . ah, discovery," Kleemann told him. "I do not wish to make any announcement until I have consulted with several members of the international judiciary, yourself included. This is a very delicate case whose technicalities must be arranged, as best as possible, *beforehand*."

"So that the strong arm of politics does not meddle," Morozov finished for him. "I can understand that. And I would like to reassure you, Dr. Kleemann, that you have just provided me with the soundest reason for keeping silence. I assume you have definite plans for Hitler—It is still difficult to believe this!—and if any government, including mine, were to be informed of his existence and arrest, well, we of the poor judiciary would soon find ourselves overwhelmed with 'priorities.' "

"Exactly," Kleemann replied.

"Very well. Where, then, is all this leading?"

"It is my belief," Hans Kleemann said softly, "that Adolf Hitler must be tried. I also think that it would be inappropriate to do so in West Germany, for reasons that you must be familiar with."

"You will have no argument there," Morozov said.

"In your opinion, would it be legally feasible to try Adolf Hitler before a court of the world, a tribunal comprising members of the world judiciary, who are citizens of the powers that were represented in Nuremberg?"

Morozov finished his brandy in one draft and drew slowly on his cigarette.

"The suggestion is not only sound but sensible," he said, intertwining his long, carefully manicured fingers. "In fact, it may be the only true satisfactory solution. We in the Soviet Union would have our reasons for trying Adolf Hitler. The Israelis, I am certain, would also find the challenge most interesting. I believe an international tribunal, on the Nuremberg model, would satisfy everyone, myself included. After all, a squabble as to which nations merit the greater portion of Hitler's carcass would be unseemly."

"I realize," Hans Kleemann said, "that you cannot speak for your government. But can you speculate as to whether such a vehicle would be acceptable to the Soviet Union?"

"Let us be honest. There is no love lost between Moscow and Bonn. There will not be for a long time to come. Deeper still, as long as there is an East and West Germany, the wound that lies between the Soviet Union and the German people will never heal. Our stances are therefore ones of mutual hostility tempered by a pragmatic appreciation of modern-day realities, manifestations of which may be found in trade agreements, cultural exchanges and so on.

"But if you are asking me whether there is a propaganda victory for the Soviet Union in this affair, I must answer yes. Although you haven't yet told me where it was you discovered Hitler."

"In West Germany."

"There you have it." Morozov shrugged. "The temptation to stoke the editorial fires. However, if it is shown that there is a plan to include the Soviet Union in the passing of judgment on Adolf Hitler, then I believe the words may be tempered somewhat. I also believe the leadership, in its curious fashion, will be pleased to cooperate. I would remind them that you asked our opinion and for our cooperation at a time, now, when you were not at all obligated to do so. This is evidence of goodwill shown in a common cause. We are receptive to things like that."

"In that case," Kleemann pursued, "would you consent to being a member of such a tribunal?"

Morozov nodded, his lips pressing together so as to become almost invisible. "I would; but the decision of the final representative must lie with the Politburo."

"Would you agree to the United Nations as the venue?"

"Considering the lack of isolated lands in which to hold a trial, yes, I would think New York would be the logical place," Morozov said dryly. "I assume you have already consulted with American liaison."

"No, you are the first to be told."

"Thank you."

Without warning, Morozov threw back his head and laughed with such uncharacteristic abandon that several people sitting a few tables away looked over.

"Forgive me, Kleemann," Morozov gasped, bringing out his handkerchief. "It was that heretical ideologist Koestler who postulated that laughter is a relief of tension. He was quite right after all."

Morozov wiped his eyes and lips, and Kleemann noticed a faint line of perspiration breaking out on the top of his forehead.

"I was observing you sitting there," Morozov went on, "looking at me as though I had ice in my veins. I confess to you that since the instant you mentioned Hitler's name I have been trying to control my heart. I didn't know whether to laugh or cry. Laughing, I suppose, may have been rude, but better than crying, which would have been misinterpreted.

"You know, Kleemann, what Hitler means to a Russian?"

"I have an idea, yes, but not one that can do any justice to that sentiment."

"I was twenty-one years old when Operation Barbarossa, the invasion of Russia, took place. For the next five years I saw nothing of my family. Every year, I would hear that a few more friends were dead. Every week I would lose two or three comrades whose faces, in the space of a few days, had become more familiar to me than those of my loved ones. And the terrible part about it was that one never knew whether this nightmare would ever end. It seemed to me that man had suddenly found himself in a perpetual-motion machine, a vehicle of continual slaughter and savagery. One of our poets described it as mankind sucked into one of the levels of Dante's Inferno, where the sinners have no choice but to kill and kill and kill again, where there is never any lack of an enemy, no end in sight.

"That is what it was like for me, to be flung into the most pitiful abyss I could ever have imagined. In those days we did not think of blaming a specific individual. I remember looking down at corpses as we took a town and quickly went through it. The Germans, like us, were all different: some had brown hair; others blond; some were skinny as poles; others couldn't have run to save their lives. I asked myself, who was behind it all? Who was it who had ordered these men to march?

"In Nuremberg some of those who had issued the commands were tried. But the supreme leader was missing. I confess to you that reading the Nuremberg transcripts, I was struck by the emptiness created by Hitler's absence. For myself, he was more alive than any of the other defendants, perhaps because they were such a pitiful lot, perhaps because everyone knew they would die—or should have died. But their master was not present and they were incomplete without him, in the courtroom as much as they would have been in the war councils. That is why I believed we were cheated at Nuremberg. That was the first instance. After that, of course, even the guilty were accepted into the victorious ranks. . . ."

Ivan Morozov shivered, as though throwing off some vile insect that had crept onto him.

"Your investigation is in its embryonic stage. There is much to do. If something should happen that would deny the world Adolf Hitler in the box, it would be a tragedy of monumental proportions. Only by bringing this evil forth can we banish it forever. If

I can be of any assistance to you, in whatever way, call upon me. I expect to be here in Paris for the week and then will be returning home to Moscow. I can be reached either at my office or at home at almost any hour. I trust you still have my telephone number."

"Thank you very much, yes," Hans Kleemann said quietly. "As soon as I have spoken with the others, I will contact you."

Morozov rose and took Hans Kleemann's hand in both of his.

"You exhibit an understanding about your conscience that few men ever do," he said. "Be proud of your task and take strength from it. I commend you for it."

The El Al flight left Paris at seven thirty, precisely one hour late. Hans Kleemann took his dinner immediately and then slept. He did not stir until the stewardess nudged him four and a half hours later, when the plane touched down at Lod.

Etta Kirsch was a woman who had aged delicately, the years deepening and accenting the beauty that lay in the sculptured face, wide violet eyes and smooth, almost silken hair. She received Hans Kleemann in her apartment, a spartan living space which lacked the charm one would have expected its occupant to bestow upon it. But the apartment was, as she later explained to her friend, only a place to rest her head when the court was in session. Otherwise she lived in the country, on a kibbutz south of the Golan.

"Are you very tired, Hans?" she asked, bringing out a tray of fruit.

"Yes," he confessed. "But there is still much left to do."

"Eat some fruit. It will cleanse your mouth. Then I will bring you tea."

She sat opposite him, on a woven-straw chair, hands folded on the lap of her silk kimono, and watched as Hans Kleemann ate a peach, carefully cutting it up into pieces. She noticed that his fingers shook ever so lightly when he held the knife and wondered what it was that could be so important for the Public Prosecutor to have come to her, so quietly, so desperately. She rose and brought out the tea.

When she was sipping her second cup, Etta Kirsch said, "It is obvious you have been under considerable strain, Hans. Was it necessary for you to come so quickly? You know I would have set aside any time you wanted."

Hans Kleemann looked at her and nodded faintly.

"I think you had better sleep now. We can talk in the morning."

"No. By tomorrow I must be on my way back."

She sighed and shook her head in helpless reproach. "I confess I was surprised by your call," Etta Kirsch said, as though she had reached out for a memory and were now holding it close, looking at it after many years had gone by.

"We are old friends, yet you wouldn't tell me anything over the telephone. So I have tried not to speculate too much. But I know your work and I can guess what you've found."

Hans Kleemann replaced his cup and sat forward, covering his face with his hands, the fingers massaging his eyes. When he looked out at her, she could see the red imprints from the fingers on his face.

"I have Adolf Hitler in custody. He is alive and I have him."

The words were spoken quietly, almost woodenly, as though saying them was too great an effort.

Etta Kirsch started. He saw her mouth open and heard an involuntary cry escape her. One hand clutched at the other, the long fingernails digging into the flesh of the palm.

"Can it be?" she whispered. "Is such a thing possible?"

"It is true," Hans Kleemann replied. And he explained to her everything that had happened, taking care not to leave out the smallest detail. As he spoke, Etta Kirsch regained her composure and listened intently.

"I agree completely," she said slowly. "An international tribunal is really the only mechanism capable of passing sentence on a man such as Hitler."

"There is one other possibility," Hans Kleemann said. "Would the State of Israel wish to try Adolf Hitler here, in Jerusalem?"

Etta Kirsch looked up at him, her eyes liquid in sorrow.

"You understand, Hans, that for some the temptation to bring Hitler here would be very strong. There are several reasons, the first being the irony of retribution—that Hitler should be tried in a land he never wished to exist, by a people he did his best to exterminate from the face of the earth. He would be weak here, and we, strong. That is the way some of us would want it: the survivor passing judgment over the exterminator, now the vanquished.

"The second point is this: The State of Israel, despite appearances, is a vulnerable entity. With threats all around us, we withdraw into ourselves and see only the tactical problems: how to deal with the Arabs, how to keep our defense budget within some reasonable proportions, how to curry favor with America without appearing a beggar. Juxtaposed against these are the internal difficulties—labor strikes, political disputes, the general hardship of the economy. These are the everyday realities people are faced with and which take a tremendous toll of our strength, psyche and judgment. There is little time or volition left to regard the moral foundations of our land.

"I can foresee tremendous political and ethical benefits stemming from Hitler's trial in Jerusalem. It would bring the Jews to a confrontation of the evil which once wished to destroy them and which, contrary to belief, is still alive and probably flourishing. This confrontation would act in the same manner as lightning when it strikes two pieces of metal: it would awaken and fuse Israel. The concept of survival would be removed from the everyday and placed upon a higher plane, the survival of a people.

"For these reasons I feel that some of us, perhaps many, would accept responsibility for trying Hitler."

"There is also the other side," Kleemann said. "The vicious reopening of wounds. I remember the terrible weeping at the Eichmann trial and how memories were torn apart, revealing every anguish that the survivors would have wished to forget."

"That is true. But Eichmann's trial was an event which, although brutal, brought us face to face with a piece of our own history."

"Would you, then, press for Adolf Hitler to be brought to Jerusalem?"

"In spite of the arguments presented, no." She held up her hand. "Do not be surprised. You know I have a penchant for playing devil's advocate.

"I am not a native Israeli," Etta Kirsch went on. "I was born in Manhattan, educated there, and my first husband was the scion of a liquor empire. My second was a painter, a survivor of Belsen. So I have lived in both worlds, the one untouched by the Holocaust and another that bears perpetual witness to it. In some respects this has helped me to achieve balanced judgment.

"I believe that Adolf Hitler should not be tried here. It is, in the long run, more important for Israel that he be tried by the world rather than by the Jews. His crimes, as I have said, might be particular to the Jews, but they embrace all of mankind. So we must show that the force Hitler unleashed can be directed against anyone, that the evil he engenders can infect anyone.

"Let us be honest: if the Jews were to try him, the world would think that a guilty verdict was inevitable and punishment inescapable. You mentioned Eichmann and the tearing open of wounds. That hurt was magnified by the innuendos and outright accusations that Israel had violated the national sovereignty of Argentina by kidnapping him only to bring him before a kangaroo court where the death verdict was a foregone conclusion. Very few thought to ask themselves why, if that was the case, we had laid ourselves open to so much pain, so many tears, so much terror when a single bullet could have avoided it all. I would not wish to have to answer that again, not in Israel. Nor do I want Jews to bear the exclusive privilege of creating a martyr for modern Hitlerites and fascists of all strains. That is not why Israel was founded, not why we continue to exist."

Etta Kirsch paused, and rubbed her arms as though she were suddenly cold. But her voice lost none of its clarity.

"There is another reason, perhaps more esoteric but nonetheless valid in my view. The land of Israel was built after a tremendous destruction of our people. It is, in many ways, a pure land which has brought forth children who belong to a different period of Jewish history than did their parents. These children, although carrying in their blood the remembrance of the Holocaust, were untouched by it. I believe this land they dwell in, defend with their blood and cultivate for their children would be defiled by the presence of Adolf Hitler.

"I would therefore argue no, do not bring Hitler here. Let us try him before the world. Let humanity look upon him for what he is: a living example of inhumanity."

"Would you, then, be willing to sit on a tribunal?"

"Yes, I would."

"And would you support this decision before your government?"

"I would." Etta Kirsch rose and came over to Hans Kleemann and placed both her hands on his shoulders.

"You are so tired," she whispered. "What you have come here to do has been done. Now go and rest. There is a bed for you in the other room. Tomorrow, before you leave, we can talk a little more."

"You are so very calm about it all," he murmured.

"No." Etta Kirsch smiled wanly. "You do not feel my heart or see my thoughts racing through my mind. There are so many things to be done that I'm afraid something might happen and this trial will never come to pass. You see, I have some way to go before I come to terms with the horror of it all."

For the first time in two days, Hans Kleemann had had a full night's sleep, but that was not enough to return vitality to his eyes or lift the weariness from his bones. He had arrived in New York to learn that Justice Thomas Worthington had left the city and was spending the weekend at a lodge named Topnotch, in Vermont. In his note, the Justice had apologized for the inconvenience but added that he expected the Public Prosecutor to come up. This way, Worthington went on, they would be free to discuss matters without any interruption.

It took Hans Kleemann over three hours to get from the city to Topnotch, traveling by air and then a rented car. But in spite of the fact that he had been en route for eleven hours, the prosecutor insisted on speaking to Worthington that evening. The two men spent an undisturbed forty-five minutes together in front of the fireplace in the Buttertub Lounge.

In the early morning in the mountains of northern Vermont, when the mist rises from the ground, it leaves the grass laden with a dew that, for only a few moments, remains frozen. As the sun ascends over the mountains, the mist lifts to the tops of the trees, where it clings stubbornly until the sun, a majestic orange globe, slowly feeds the sky with heat and bears away the tissue of the fog as imperceptibly as the hand of a magician might make silk scarves disappear.

"God's country," Thomas Worthington murmured as he stood on the small rise that overlooked the valley where the inn's horses were being exercised. The mist was still evident over the Green Mountains, but beneath, along the riding trails, the spring greenery was coming to life, the gentle wind blowing a scent-laden moisture across the fields.

"I come up here, oh, every couple of months. It's especially good now, before the season starts. But then, it's not too bad when the clutter sets in either. You can meet some interesting people."

Worthington looked at Hans Kleemann and smiled sympathetically.

"Feel like a walk?"

"Badly. Too many hours in airplanes."

Worthington clapped him on the shoulder, and together they descended to the road, crossed it and made their way down across the streams that provided the trout for the inn's table.

Thomas Worthington walked quickly, in long steps, swinging his arms and occasionally kicking at some stones or small branches on the ground. He was a man of intense nervous energy, and his actions were rapid—in striking contrast to the deliberation of his speech, a characteristic that had lulled almost two generations of attorneys into believing that Worthington never listened to their arguments. Inevitably there came a time when either the defense or the prosecution had its knuckles rapped for trying to slip an illegal maneuver past him.

But it was this same measured, reasoned method of thought which had kept Worthington on the right hand of three Presidents for whom he had acted as ambassador extraordinary. Pragmatism and common sense were inherent in his New England gentry heritage; the responsibilities of civic duty and public service were never shirked in his family. Each generation had made its contribution and passed on the fruits of its experience—diplomatic, legal and financial—to the next. Over the years there had been few domestic or international events that a Worthington had not engendered, molded or participated in.

If there was a single flaw in such an admirable lineage and

career record, Hans Kleemann thought it would lie in the way
Thomas Worthington had been taught to interpret the law: on the
strict legal letter, with little allowance for mitigating circumstances or compassion. It was seldom the business of the court
to rule on the wisdom of a law passed by Congress or any other
legislature. The duty lay exclusively in the application of the
statute. If the law was worded incorrectly, the prosecutor
thought, even the most vicious of tyrants might escape punishment through its interpretation. Still, Worthington's stature, his
reputation for fairness and toughness, and his rapport with the
current President would make him by far the most potent representative the United States could send to the tribunal.

"Well, I tell you, I've been thinking about what we talked
about last night," Worthington said. He stopped and wiped the
sweat off his pale, freckled forehead.

Again Worthington lapsed into silence, and Hans Kleemann
had to wait until they were almost across the meadow and walking upstream before the justice spoke again.

"I like your idea of holding the trial outside Germany," he said
abruptly. "Let me throw out some possible venues and you tell
me what you think of them.

"First there is the International Court of Justice, part of the
U.N., which sits at The Hague. There are fifteen justices on the
Court, representing the major legal systems of the world. Now,
the jurisdiction of the Court covers all questions that member
states may put forth. Generally the Bench deals with violation of
borders, trade agreements, the rights of nationals operating
within a foreign territory and so on. Also, the Security Council
and the General Assembly can ask the Court for an opinion on a
strictly legal interpretation of a given action. The key point here,
if I remember rightly, is that a *state*, not an individual, must
present the case for arbitration. In this instance, I doubt very
much whether the Bonn Government would, even with pressure
on it, give Hitler over to the Court. It would simply raise the
issue of national sovereignty and declare that the Court has no
business dealing with one of its nationals when domestic courts
could conceivably do the job themselves."

"That would be the principal argument," Kleemann agreed.
"But cannot the United States or the Soviet Union or Israel bring

the action before the Court and demand that Hitler be placed within its jurisdiction?"

"Each of those states could do that; however, the Bonn Government need not answer them. The Court's ruling is not binding on the parties who brought the question before it in the first place. Out of the many disputes The Hague has seen, only a handful have been actually settled; that is, the principals involved have agreed to abide by the Court's verdict.

"There is also the composition of the Court," Worthington continued. "Some of the justices currently sitting on it are representatives of states that did not exist during Hitler's time. I personally would be in favor of having a tribunal composed of the two major powers which actually participated in the Nuremberg Trials—that is, the United States and the Soviet Union—with the inclusion of Israel, which I view as both inevitable and necessary."

"There is something else I see coming out in your argument," Hans Kleemann said. "The matter would be dragged out over a number of years. From my understanding of the Hague Court, although it is not pressed with too much work, it nonetheless moves at a very slow pace."

"That's a charitable way of putting it," Worthington said dryly. "One would think the issue of whether Hitler is guilty or not would be clear-cut, but I assure you, and you probably know this from experience, fifteen judicial opinions are one hell of a kettle of fish."

"What is the alternative?"

"I considered the possibility of the International Law Commission, which is basically a law-forming institution, codifying rather than legislating. It came to mind because the principles of law that it articulated in 1949 were recognized in the Charter and Judgment of the Nuremberg Tribunal. But in this case we are dealing with twenty-five legalists, and once they had codified the charges against Hitler, the matter would still have to go before some body with the power to hand down a sentence."

"So we are left with nothing but the Nuremberg precedent," Hans Kleemann said. "Unless we count the Russell International War Crimes Tribunal."

"The Nuremberg precedent is good enough," Worthington

stated. "In composition—representatives from the United States, the U.S.S.R., England and France—it was a small, cohesive body with enough legal intelligence to arrive at decisions and small enough to implement those decisions without undue haggling. It was, as I have said, recognized by the United Nations. Lord Bertrand Russell's tribunal, staged with Sartre in Stockholm, on the other hand, was more of a propaganda affair. Although in my heart I agreed with their indictment of American actions in Vietnam, I thought their case was based entirely on prosecution, the judgment a foregone conclusion in the absence of any defendants. Such was not the case in Nuremberg."

"What would it take to resurrect the Nuremberg principle?"

"Basically, an agreement between the two major powers who were represented at the time, us and the Russians," Worthington said. "In fact, as I was thinking last night, a reconvening of the Tribunal, modified, would be most appropriate.

"In Adolf Hitler we have what might be called the missing link, the figure ultimately responsible for World War Two and whose spirit pervaded Nuremberg although he himself was not present."

"If that could be done," Hans Kleemann murmured, "if we could bring together a body such as the Nuremberg Tribunal, and present it as a continuation of the old Tribunal rather than a new animal, then we also have a legal precedent within which to work.

"What would the United States position be, do you think?"

Worthington laughed bitterly. "This Administration isn't known for its special concerns about justice. In fact, its record in this area is pitiful. However, this may well be to our advantage. The President and his Attorney-General would very much like to bolster their flagging images. One way of doing this would be to appear proponents of the kind of trial we have in mind. It would all be good copy for them, and who knows?—perhaps we might use the clout. A cynical approach on my part, I grant you, but if you haven't any objections, I will knock on the Oval Office door."

"I'm afraid we can't be particular about our handmaidens," Kleemann answered. "It's a *quid pro quo* I can live with."

The two men began walking up the slow incline that led to the road and beyond that, to the inn. When they reached the terrace, Thomas Worthington guided the Public Prosecutor into the almost empty dining room, where he ordered the house suggestion of pancakes with Canadian bacon and local maple syrup for both of them.

With his customary concentration, Worthington abandoned the conversation in favor of breakfast, and they ate in silence until the second cup of coffee was served. Hans Kleemann rekindled the conversation over cigars.

"We have discussed the technical points of the case. Have you any personal ideas about it?"

Worthington drained his coffee and replenished his cup from the pot left at the table.

"The trial is possible," he said softly. "Possible and necessary. But I also see a dilemma between the necessary and the actual. You see, the Nuremberg Trials were needed in their time, and they were possible because of the circumstances and conditions in postwar Germany. It would have been unthinkable to walk through Germany following the war, through the open doors of Dachau, Buchenwald and Auschwitz, and not be moved to a desire for retribution. Such sentiment was all well and good for a little while—a year, perhaps—until international politics entered the picture.

"Suddenly our Germans, in the Western zone, appeared slightly less guilty because of the Soviet threat. The American military looked around and saw forty Russian divisions stretched across Eastern Europe and decided that new allies were needed. Where were they to be found? In the Germans. The politicians watched as Soviet domination of Czech, Hungarian, Rumanian and Polish governments became complete, and they asked themselves where the line would have to be drawn. In Germany, of course.

"But one cannot win the hearts and minds of a defeated people when one is actively pursuing their leaders. So after the major figures like Goering, Jodl and Kaltenbrunner were disposed of, the investigations were played down. It became more important to show the Germans that we were not a vicious race bent on revenge, but humanitarian conquerors who were doing everything to help them back to their feet.

"We had seized the moment to initiate and dispense, perhaps for the first time in history, a humanitarian justice, and at the last moment we shied away from it because an ostensibly larger, more important issue—the security of the West—came out of the woodwork and overruled us.''

"Do you think this can happen if we put Hitler in the dock?'' Kleemann inquired softly.

"If everything goes as you plan, I can't see political interference winning out,'' Worthington said. "There will probably be attempts made to stop the proceedings, but as I've mentioned before, I believe the President would give us his support, which will go a long way toward quashing whatever arguments the Bonn Government might have against holding the trial. No, that's not it at all.

"What I fear,'' Worthington said sadly, "is that no one will really care. We think of the present and the future as though they had no relation to the past, moments that have never existed before and will never exist again. We do not understand that the present and the future are only the past, happening over and over again.''

"I wish to speak with an attorney! Repeatedly I have told this to your men, and each time they have refused to allow me even to approach the telephone. I would have thought, Prosecutor, that your hounds would have been better trained!''

Adolf Hitler was standing over Kleemann, who, slumped in a chair, stared at him with vacant, weary eyes.

The tirade had begun the moment Kleemann had entered the study of his country home. Born of a power beyond the prosecutor's comprehension, Hitler's words had seized him and held him fast in their fury. While Kleemann sat, Hitler paced about the room like a man possessed, the heel of his good leg smashing down upon the floorboards, his gestures, cutting and vicious, slashing open a path in which the harsh, guttural words followed. Swathed in a mantle of power that blurred the scarred, distorted features of the man and covered his physical deformity by terror, Hitler raged over him.

Hans Kleemann had scarcely arrived back in his office in Munich when the Farben brothers had telephoned with an urgent summons. He had driven to his home feeling stale and numb, the fruits of his travels hard and tasteless in his mouth. And his home, he discovered, had been overtaken by madness.

"I have asked you a question!" Hitler spat at him. He stood a few feet away, one arm flung across his chest as it gripped the other withered, emaciated limb.

"You have asked many questions," Hans Kleemann replied in a weary, hollow tone. "Why do you go on, knowing what it is we agreed to?—that you would remain incommunicado until I returned. I said I would be away for a week; it has been less than that."

"Then you have been successful!" Hitler shouted. "There will be an international tribunal."

"There is the *possibility*," Kleemann said sharply. "Nothing more."

"Do not tease me, Kleemann," Hitler retorted. "You are so cautious a man that even when you suggest something, one may take it for granted. I knew this would happen, that you would succeed. That is why I want my lawyer brought here. Now. Today."

I should kill you, Hans Kleemann thought, staring down at his hands. If he lifted them off his lap, the fingers would start shaking, so he did not move. Each time I witness the enormity of your evil, I am further enticed. I should kill you and be done with it. You knew long ago whom you wanted as your defense lawyer. It might have been years ago that the choice was made; and did you select him as you did me—carefully, after much deliberation?

But the thought of another human being's coming between himself and Adolf Hitler gave the prosecutor hope. He would no longer be alone before this infernal presence; and suddenly he craved to know the name of this companion who, although he might speak for Hitler, was, after all, a man, a comrade in law.

Hans Kleemann rose and faced Hitler.

"Whom do you want?" he demanded softly. When Hitler spoke the name, he at once laughed at the expression of horror that came over the prosecutor's face.

He was younger than even Hans Kleemann had expected. The high cheekbones, clipped beard and moustache contrasted sharply with the wide gray eyes which, framed in gold-rimmed spectacles, refused to age. Yet Kleemann knew him to be an intelligent and patient man, who preferred to follow common sense and intuition rather than regulations and accepted practice. His impertinence tended to stubbornness, yet not once had he heard that it had been without cause. Kleemann had also been told of a vicious streak in him, an unerring instinct to strike at the jugular. This quality he had witnessed.

The prosecutor had heard of Helmut Toller several years before, from colleagues whom he had defeated in the courtroom. He had been sufficiently curious to take the time to see Toller's performances for himself. The impression he had walked away with was a powerful one.

Helmut Toller had learned, and practiced, the cardinal rule of the court: preparation is all. But not only was his research clear, concise and thorough; its exposition was fired by imagination. When the occasion warranted, philosophic interpretation was mined from the arguments; at other times, the interpretation of statutes was so novel that the objections of the prosecution were reduced to pathetic attempts to forestall an inevitable end.

But this brilliance was often unleashed without consideration of either argumentative overkill or the feelings of the witness on the stand. It appeared to Kleemann that Toller was completely insensitive to the emotions of those he cross-examined, that their own discomfort or, on one occasion, total breakdown did not touch him in the least. Although charity was not the mainstay of any criminal lawyer, its lack, in Toller's instance, had led the prosecutor to wonder at the degree of the man's human empathy. He had also heard of his involvement in some unsavory cases which Toller had won only because of the prosecution's errors, not because of the innocence of his clients.

Nonetheless, Kleemann had been appalled that Hitler should choose such a young man, no matter what his qualifications. He had been expecting an august personality, flamboyant, with a sense of theater. There were a number of such attorneys in Germany, although Hitler could as easily have procured the services of an internationally known American or Swiss. But he had chosen Toller. Because, as the prosecutor now considered, Toller came from Emmaus, he was probably sympathetic to Hitler through his association with Dr. Grubber; but above all, Toller, an exemplary figure of the New Germany, was young. Hitler did not want the old or the foreign or the tainted. Each had his drawback. He wanted the young. . . .

"Herr Doktor, it is a privilege to meet you," Helmut Toller said formally, taking Kleemann's hand and bowing.

Kleemann said nothing but gestured for the young man to sit. They were alone in Kleemann's study with only a single lamp, on the desk, to dispel the darkness.

"I am sorry to have called you out at such an hour," the Public Prosecutor apologized. "Nonetheless, I am glad you came."

"Was it necessary to send a detective to fetch me?" Toller asked.

"I am afraid so. You will understand in a little while."

"I wish to see Herr Busse as soon as possible," Toller stated. "The letter your man gave me was disturbing, to say the least."

"Then let me put your fears to rest," Hans Kleemann said. "Herr Busse, as you call him, is here and is quite well. But before he joins us, I should like to put several questions to you."

"I see no reason why not," Toller answered.

"Your former practice has been principally in criminal law, has it not?"

"Yes. I have spent four years in criminal practice in Hamburg and Frankfurt."

"Your fame has preceded you," Hans Kleemann said. "You have an enviable reputation for such a young man."

"Thank you, Doctor."

"May I ask whether you have, at any time, acted in the capacity of legal counsel to Herr Busse?"

"No, I have not. As you doubtless know, Herr Busse operates a gardening center in Emmaus. To the best of my knowledge, any legal work that has been done has been connected with that enterprise. I believe he also retains a counsel in Zurich. Whether any personal details, such as a will, are also handled by this firm I don't know."

"I see. Then would you know of any reason why Werner Busse would wish to specify that you come, in your capacity as a criminal lawyer, rather than his business attorney or even a representative from Zurich?"

"No, I do not."

Hans Kleemann looked at the young man and believed his words. As Hitler had done with him, he used the same practice on Toller: surprise and paralyze the quarry. Give no warning before the strike.

"You implied a moment ago, Herr Doktor, that Werner Busse was 'known' to you under that name. What did you mean by that?" Toller asked coolly. It was time to take the offensive, to discover what it was this august man wanted of him.

Kleemann hesitated, then answered.

" 'Werner Busse' is not his real name. The man who has been living in Emmaus for the last twenty-five years is in fact Adolf Hitler."

At first, there was no reaction from the young man. The prosecutor almost believed that Helmut Toller did not find any revelation in his words, so complete was his equanimity: as though he had known. . . .

"Dr. Kleemann, I must take exception to such a statement!" Helmut Toller answered at last, the words hard and cold.

"And why is that? It is, after all, the truth."

Both Kleemann and Toller turned in the direction of the speaker and saw Adolf Hitler standing there. He was dressed in the same gray suit he had worn when Kleemann had returned to his home, but appeared refreshed from his sleep.

Helmut Toller rose immediately and offered his own seat.

"Thank you, Helmut. Please do not be shocked by anything you hear. Undoubtedly the Public Prosecutor will present the facts clearly and without prejudice. Then you and I will have our own discussion."

Adolf Hitler seated himself and looked around as though he were waiting for a performance to begin.

"I must first tell you, Herr Toller, that this entire matter—your coming here under such circumstances and your possible involvement in this affair—is repugnant to me," Kleemann said coldly. "However, this is a most unusual case and I have had no choice in your being included. I must impose upon you the secrecy that surrounds this matter and ask you to agree not to speak to anyone about it. Do you so agree?"

Instinctively, Toller looked at Hitler, who nodded.

"Very well, I abide by your request—for the time being," Toller answered.

"I shall begin," Kleemann said, "by giving you a brief résumé of events thus far. You may then consult privately with the detainee.

"The man known as Werner Busse called at the War Crimes Office last week. He presented himself to me as Adolf Hitler and brought with him documentation which supported that contention. The evidence has been verified, and supplementary material adds weight to his statement. I repeat: the man sitting beside you is not Werner Busse but Adolf Hitler.

"The reasons why Adolf Hitler has surrendered after living in anonymity for so long and without fear of being unmasked or arrested will be explained by him; suffice it to say that his surrender was voluntary. The same day he agreed to be placed in protective custody and has been staying here ever since. Until now he has not asked to see an attorney.

"During this period, further investigation has been carried out by myself only. The others in Germany who know of Hitler's existence are the two detectives who are responsible for his safety. You have now been added to the list.

"I do not know what it is that Hitler hopes you will do. I assume he will ask you to act as his defense attorney. However, until he does so formally and you accept, I will say nothing more about the technicalities of the trial."

"At that point you will tell me who, *outside of Germany*, has been told of Hitler's existence?" Toller countered.

The prosecutor acknowledged the astute point with a nod.

"Yes, of course."

Hans Kleemann rose and looked at Helmut Toller.

"Forgive me for bringing this upon your head," he said. "It was agreed between the accused and me that he would have access to any representation he wished. You were his choice."

Kleemann walked to the door, opened it, but before leaving, added, "I will wait outside until you have finished your conference. Then, if I may, I should like to speak with you once more."

With Kleemann's departure, a silence lay heavy in the twilight shadows of the study. Voices Toller had not heard before now became faintly audible: somewhere in the house, the Farben

brothers were speaking, their words a blur by the time they
reached him, punctuated only by sharp exclamations. Were they
having an argument or playing cards? Outside, the sounds of the
lake crept through the cracks in the windowsills: the splash of
waters pushed up over the rock . . . a medley of trees and shrubs
bending with the wind . . . a solitary cry of a bird calling out like
a clarion to the night.

"You look well, Helmut. I hope I haven't taken your attention
from anything important."

Hitler's words broke the trance, and Helmut Toller had to face
the presence of the other man.

"No . . . not at all. Herr Busse—"

"The name is Adolf Hitler; you will address me by it."

Toller opened his mouth to speak, but choked on the words.
He could not bring himself to say that name.

"What is the matter, Helmut? Does a change of a name alter
the man you have known for so long?"

The words struck Toller as though they had been physically
hurled at him. His memory was sent spinning back to every detail
about a man he knew as Werner Busse, a man whom he loved
and admired, whom he thought of as a relative. There was nothing wrong or ugly about these images. They were ones he wished
to remember. He tried to think about Adolf Hitler, but his mind
was blank. He could not conjure up a single image.

"Quite frankly, I am disappointed in your reaction, Helmut,"
Adolf Hitler stated. "I think I overestimated your ability to deal
with such a matter. Therefore, it might be best for you to leave."

As Hitler turned away, Toller whispered, "No! Please, I just
needed a moment to collect myself. . . ."

"And why is that?" Hitler demanded coldly. "Am I suddenly
such a monster that you cannot look at me?"

"Herr Busse . . . excuse me. No, Herr Hitler . . ."

Again he could not go on.

"That is my name!" Hitler shouted at him. "Say it! Go on, say
it!"

"Herr Hitler . . ."

"Yes, I am no longer the Führer. I am now Everyman: Herr
Hitler!" And he laughed as though such an idea were both ap-
pealing and contemptible.

"Herr Hitler, I ask you to forgive my behavior," Helmut Toller said, clearing his throat. "You can understand my surprise, the shock of . . . of hearing this. But if you were to explain . . . what is happening, I will listen."

"Good," Hitler said flatly. "My reason for asking you here is quite simple. I have surrendered to Hans Kleemann because I wish to be tried. That being the case, I have need of an excellent defense attorney. If you so agree, that person will be you."

"You have surrendered?" Helmut Toller demanded, struggling to put the act into some context.

"For twenty-five years my name has been blasphemed," Hitler said, seizing Toller's question. "I have been vilified; all manner of lies have been propagated about me. I am no longer in the best of health and fear that there isn't much time left to me. Therefore I wish to reveal myself and be given the chance to prove my innocence before my death.

"I do not believe Kleemann has drawn up a formal indictment, but I think you can guess which crimes I will be charged with—waging of aggression, acts of violence against humanity, genocide . . ."

"You wish to challenge history," Helmut murmured. "It is history that has drawn up the indictment against you."

"And that is wrong!" Hitler shouted. "For twenty-five years I have lived with the lies poured upon my head. I have endured and suffered, and now I wish to confront my accusers. I want them to come out from behind their words and look me in the face and substantiate every piece of garbage that has been heaped upon me!"

"Out of all the attorneys you might have contacted, why did you choose me?" Toller broke in. "I have only a few years' experience. There are others, much better than I . . ."

"I can be honest with you," Hitler replied, his voice softening. "You are my choice because you said to me on Walpurgis Night, 'It is different this night!' Certainly I could pick any lawyer closer to my generation and he would understand perhaps more clearly what it is I am fighting for. But I wish for *you* to understand. It is more important for me that your generation have my story brought forward by one of their own. For if you believe me, so shall they!"

Adolf Hitler rose and came before the young man. As he stood over him, he saw the stricken face of Helmut Toller, a grief brought on by helplessness and ignorance, and in both he could read his victory.

"By summoning you here I have affected the course of your life," Hitler said, emphasizing each word. "I have changed it beyond anything you might have imagined. I have done so because I need your help. Because I saw, on that night, the spirit move within you.

"Forty years ago, there was a tremendous revolution in our country. Forty years ago we created a land for all Germans to live in and partake of. Because of our will, we became the envy of those hapless creatures we called our neighbors. That I led a war to protect and extend our sovereignty is true; but what the world has come to see in that war is a lie. We killed and were killed; we conquered and in turn were conquered; but we endured. Now it is time once again to go forward in dignity and pride.

"Dignity and pride," Hitler intoned softly. "The last feeble images an old man can conjure up. Yet for me, a man without a country, anonymous, embraced only by hatred, they are all that is left. This one last time, I must come before the nation I led and ask it to remember me. I must have my trial before the hearts and minds of Germany.

"I could tell you, Helmut, of the great things—the honors and attention—that would come to you as a result of defending me. But I offer you more than that: I give you the choice to touch the soul of Germany, to place your hand upon her breast and feel your heart beat in unison with hers. Your generation has been ignorant about me. I ask you: let me lead you through a time few understand better than I. Let me take you back across the years so that you too may feel and touch the earth from which you sprang."

The bird cried out again, this time three or four times, its echo spreading across the waters. It was a desperate cry, Helmut Toller thought, with no one to answer the creature.

"My foster mother . . ." Helmut Toller murmured. "What about her? You know how she loathes anything or anyone touched by Nazism . . . and that she had tried to pass such a feeling on to me. Am I now to stand against her? Do I not owe her some sort of consideration for all she has done for me, an orphan?"

"There I cannot give you any guidance," Hitler pronounced. "I understand what you feel for her. That she will despise me when she learns who I am is true, and her hatred will be shown to you. You alone can decide whether I am worthy of defending— at the expense of Lillian Grubber, your foster mother . . . as you say."

"I would need some time to make a decision," Toller said quietly.

"I must ask you for one before you leave here. I know Kleemann will demand the same."

"I do not need much time."

Without another word, Helmut Toller rose and took his leave. He went into the hallway and saw the Public Prosecutor standing there with the detectives.

"I wish to be alone," Toller said, addressing only Kleemann. He did not wait for an answer but grabbed his coat and stepped out into the darkness.

He walked without direction and was stopped only by the fence that bounded the prosecutor's property. His trouser legs became soaked with moisture from the grass and underbrush, and his boots filthy from the mud and wet earth. In spite of the wind, he threw off his coat and draped it across the fence and turned around. Franz Farben was not to be seen, but Toller knew he was there, in the darkness, for he had caught glimpses of his lantern.

Helmut Toller stared out into the black fields that lay like soft velvet beyond the fence and farther, to the wooded shores of the lake, where the trees pierced the sky, random streaks of black on a midnight-blue canvas. The solitude and stillness rested lightly on his soul and for the briefest moment relieved him of the weight he was carrying and the decision that would add to his burden.

"I could not have been more wrong," Helmut Toller murmured to himself, aloud. "God help me, but I couldn't have!"

Only a few weeks ago he had walked away from the aftermath

of the Emmaus festival with Werner Busse—no, Adolf Hitler!—at his side. What had been his words? . . . "The pieces of my life have coalesced . . . the fragments have all come together. . . ."

He had known nothing then, had been as ignorant and myopic as he had remained until an hour ago. It was so easy, in hindsight, to see the pattern; to be frightened because the obvious had seemed invisible.

Suddenly he was a child again, the young boy staring out the dirty window at the street where his father and the SS officer were carrying a stretcher between them and Dr. Grubber walking behind them. His ears rang with the sounds of gunfire, the officer heaving and collapsing to his knees as Grubber fired at him . . . again and again . . . just as earlier the SS had lined up some villagers against the walls and shot them. And then there were the women, screaming in the barn . . .

"The Führer is alive. . . . He is alive and will lead us to victory!"

Those had been almost the final words the SS officer had spoken to him. He had repeated them mechanically, as his father had taught him, without conviction. What feeling could have been demanded of a shivering, stunned child who had been touched by horror and so paralyzed of all feeling? Perhaps that too was why he had never imagined that the old man on the stretcher could have been Adolf Hitler. . . .

Yet he should have. Many times he had run errands for Dr. Grubber, and sometimes these had taken him into the room where the stranger lay. But there had been no recognition, only a vague uneasy suspicion that all was not right. . . . How could he have explained to others feelings he himself did not understand?

And Lillian. Hadn't she felt that same suspicion and lived with it week after week, year after year? She must have. It was the only reasonable explanation for her coolness toward Busse, the persistent attempts to keep young Helmut from having much to do with Busse even though the old man had been a frequent visitor, a friend of Dr. Grubber's. Toller remembered that he had resented her for this, for he had come to enjoy Busse's unexpected calls. The old man had never failed to bring a small present; he had always had the time to speak with the boy about school, his friends, sports. . . .

Finally, Walpurgis Night: the singing, dancing and feasting; the adoration of the crowds for Busse and the mesmerization he had cast upon them. Oh, yes, there was always the logical explanation! The character of such a holiday is always exotic, libidinous and fueled by drink. The frenzied devotion shown the Prince of the Feast and the "benefactor" could be taken only as the exaggeration of an already existing respect. Such rational thinking could dissuade a man from perceiving what had really happened, the truth that lay just under the veneer of reason.

Helmut Toller picked up his coat off the fence and began to walk. Having come to terms with the extremity of his myopia, he felt calmer. He now accepted the fact that Werner Busse was Adolf Hitler, although shades of incredulity still flitted over his reason. They made progress to the next step no easier: what to do with this knowledge.

The attorney in him knew that such a case—the defense of a man long thought dead yet so reviled even in memory—came only once in a lifetime. Adolf Hitler could have had his pick of any one of the twelve most prestigious criminal lawyers in the country; more, a host of foreign barristers of international repute would have undertaken to defend him. No matter how ugly or ignominious the substance of the trial might be, to participate in it would be to achieve the pinnacle of one's career. No, the problem lay elsewhere; in a single person; in Lillian.

By taking on this case, Helmut Toller understood he would spiritually murder the one woman who cared for him more than anyone else in the world, the woman who had always comforted him and provided shelter and solace when he needed them. The distrust she had for Werner Busse would explode into blind fury, hatred and horror when she learned of his true identity. And then she would do all in her power to protect Helmut from this creature, while at the same time trying to destroy it.

And what was Adolf Hitler to him? More myth than man. On the one hand, for decades the most feared and hated statue in Mme. Tussaud's wax museum; the subject of countless historical works, some apologetic, some damning; the shadowy figure who stood in the far corner of every courtroom that held a war-crimes trial. Helmut Toller did not hate this legend that postwar Germany had grown up with. His reading on Hitler was far from extensive, but sufficient to satisfy his curiosity and allow him to form a neutral opinion. Not that this was unusual: the Germany of Adenauer had been too preoccupied with the practice of miracles, economic and otherwise. It took one's mind away from the war, the camps, the killing of the Jews. . . .

And against this neutrality weighed the last factor. For Helmut Toller, the figure of Adolf Hitler was inextricably bound to that of Werner Busse, the "benefactor" of Emmaus who, over a quarter century, had never done harm to anyone, who had lived as a charitable, decent human being and had made a place for himself in Toller's affection and respect. . . .

The rain began to fall once more, in soft tiny drops, like a fine mist. Toller turned his face toward the sky, feeling the cool water wash over his tired eyes.

The power of the law . . . its majesty and terror . . . the wand of Merlin . . .

These were other words he had spoken to Werner Busse on that gray dawn after Walpurgis Night. These were the words he recognized and admitted as being the truth about what he believed. They acknowledged that he had tried to come home, tried and failed. Now there seemed to be only one choice to be made: make the commitment his grandfather had never had the strength to make, much less maintain; to plunge into the depths of the power Hans Bayer Weiss had shown him and which Adolf Hitler would help him explore, call his own.

He did not know how long he remained standing there oblivious to the rain and the cold wind which drew in from the east. Only when the detective Farben came up to him did the reverie dissolve.

"Perhaps, sir, you would consider returning to the house," Farben said. "It is unwise to stand out here like this."

Helmut Toller looked at him and pursed his lips.

"Yes, you are quite right. It is time to confer with my client."

"I assume you have chosen," Adolf Hitler stated when they were alone. He was sitting perfectly still behind Kleemann's desk, the brown, veined fingers intertwined.

"Are you giving me sole custody of this case?" Toller asked him.

"I am."

"I have the power to consult or retain any other counsel that might be needed as well as hire research assistants?"

"Of course."

"Are there adequate funds available to sustain a case that may last some time?"

"Certainly. There is more than you know of."

"Then I accept," Toller said quietly.

Adolf Hitler rose and limped over to the young man.

"You may now look upon yourself as the architect of a new history," he said. "Which you will build and which will live forever in the memory of our country. You cannot understand the importance of this moment, but you shall. And you will live to see all that grows from it."

It was midnight, and the single lamp on the desk continued to burn, although the light flickered erratically from time to time, sizzling when it did so. Again there were only two men in the study.

We are like actors in a surrealistic tableau, Toller thought. Each of us has his time with the other and then must leave before the third comes on.

He looked at the Public Prosecutor, who was sitting in the same chair Adolf Hitler had occupied only a few minutes earlier. As he entered the room, Hans Kleemann had instinctively moved toward the desk. The realization of who had sat there, the sense of the warmth of Hitler's body, stopped him, yet he succumbed to weariness and sat down.

"So you have decided to take it on," Kleemann said. It was a statement, not a question.

"Yes."

"Why?"

The pain in his question and the sorrow of the red, swollen eyes moved Toller to pity. Yet it was not a charitable compassion that he felt, but a sense of power the strong carry over the weak.

"You decided quickly. I would give you more time if you wish."

"One could weigh the balances forever," Toller answered softly, "and still never be certain."

"Is this not such a tremendous choice that it merits careful thought?"

"With no disrespect, Dr. Kleemann, I could turn the question back to you: how quickly did *you* choose, considering all that you have to lose?"

"I am an older man. Whatever it is I have to live with, it will not be for very long. That is not the case with you."

"If you think I do not understand what it is you are trying to do for me, you are wrong," Toller said. "But please do not try to save me—even from myself."

Kleemann nodded and drew a deep breath.

"Very well, colleague. Let us discuss a few points and then Farben will take you home."

Hans Kleemann withdrew a sheet of paper from his breast pocket and consulted it.

"I trust you are satisfied that my office has not denied the detainee any of his basic rights?"

"I am," Helmut Toller replied. "To date, I take no issue with your arrangements."

"Have you, for example, considered the matter of venue?"

"I am not certain what it is you have in mind on that count."

"The stature of a man such as Hitler would dictate his being tried by an international tribunal, on the Nuremberg model," Hans Kleemann said.

"Article Sixteen of the Basic Law forbids the extradition of a German national to stand trial in a foreign country," Toller replied. "Furthermore, there is no nation which can legally demand his extradition, since Adolf Hitler has committed no crimes outside the borders of the German state as it existed between 1933 and 1945. It is also highly questionable whether in fact any crimes were committed by him during this period within Germany."

"My understanding of Hitler's desire for a trial was to have the broadest possible venue. Am I to understand that he has changed his mind on this matter?" Kleemann retorted.

"I will advise Herr Hitler not to settle for any particular venue until such time as the terms and conditions of the location have been agreed upon."

"Very well," Kleemann continued. "I would then ask you to consider the following. I have contacted several persons who may form the nucleus of the tribunal. Do you agree that these four people—Morozov of the Soviet Union, Thomas Worthington of the United States, Etta Kirsch of Israel and Dieter Wolff of West Germany—would be qualified to sit in judgment on Adolf Hitler?"

Helmut Toller considered the names put forth. Without exception he was familiar with them and he would have had to say he could not have selected more prestigious and experienced people himself. That evaluation extended even to Morozov, a man who retained Toller's respect while at the same time representing a political system the German loathed. Yes, Kleemann had chosen well. There would be no need for a subsequent inquiry on his part. But he wouldn't show his satisfaction. On the contrary, reserve was called for.

"I have no quarrel with their qualifications," Toller answered. "But have you considered the reactions of the British and French, represented at Nuremberg but not on this tribunal? Both might take offense."

"So would half a dozen other nations—Holland, Denmark, any of the East European satellites. I felt I had to draw a tight circumference to keep the bench membership from expanding indefinitely. As it stands, the major interests and legal systems are represented: Germany, for Hitler, in law, belongs to her; Israel, which has an undisputed right to sit in judgment; the same for the Soviet Union. America, with her position in the world, would provide the underpinning as she did in Nuremberg."

"Fair enough," Toller commented. "The simpler the better."

"And you see no conflict of interest in the proposed judiciary?"

"That is another question altogether."

"Would you at least agree that your client would receive as fair a trial in their court as he would in any in Germany?" Kleemann asked irritably.

"You know yourself that that is not necessarily the case," Helmut Toller said. "The element of psychological support would be missing abroad. In fact, the atmosphere, depending on venue, might be definitely hostile. I must therefore have substantial guarantees that my client's case would not be prejudiced in such an instance."

"And what would those guarantees be?"

"That the trial be held in such a place as to allow the largest possible collection of media personnel who would report all the facts of the proceedings. I do not wish *in camera* proceedings."

"This is acceptable to me. But you understand that such arrangements are not within my jurisdiction to arrange."

"I am certain, Dr. Kleemann, that such details can be looked after by your office, considering the efficient way in which you have operated thus far."

The prosecutor let the remark pass.

"As I have mentioned, all matters pertaining to this case have thus far been handled in secrecy. I believe the time has come to do away with that. If you are amenable, I will speak to the Chancellor tomorrow and inform him that we have Adolf Hitler in custody."

"Again I agree that the government should be told at the first opportunity, and I feel I should be present when you make the announcement," Toller answered.

"I would also arrange for a formal public announcement at the same time."

"I would wish to read that release before it goes out," Toller said. "I have no objections to it in principle."

"Do you, then, have any questions on the indictment itself?"

Toller paused and picked up the single legal-size sheet from the prosecutor's desk. He read it aloud.

" 'Prepared by the Office of the Public Prosecutor of Bavaria, this twelfth day of May.

" 'Initial Indictment.

" 'The defendant, Adolf Hitler, former Führer of the Third Reich, also known as Werner Busse, citizen of Emmaus, West Germany, is hereby charged by this office on the following counts:

" 'A: *Crimes Against Peace*

" 'The planning, preparing and execution of acts leading to aggression, contrary to treaties, agreements and assurances formed under international law.

" 'B: *War Crimes*

" 'The violation of accepted rules of conduct during wartime. These violations shall include transgressions carried out not only by the military whose supreme commander was the accused against military forces of another state, but acts perpetrated by the military, secret police and other executive organizations (SS and SD) against civilian populations both in the Reich and in conquered territories.

" 'C: *Crimes Against Humanity*

" 'Such crimes comprise mass extermination, enslavement, deportation and genocide against civilian populations.' "

Toller replaced the paper.

"There will be little change, I trust, in the formal indictment."

"I am prepared to stay within those three categories," Kleemann answered. "The words are few, but every one of them weighs more than the thousands of pages that have been written in the course of war-crimes proceedings.

"And that, I think, is all I have to say for the moment," he concluded.

"There is the matter of Herr Hitler's confinement," Toller said. "Unless you believe other arrangements should be made, I propose that he remain where he is—as long, of course, as there is no inconvenience to you."

"Security is more than adequate and the location virtually unknown. He will be perfectly safe here."

"I trust you have informed your people of my coming visits," Toller said. "I will be here quite often from now on."

"I wish," Kleemann said, looking into his eyes, "that I could say I will be happy to see you."

The next morning the prosecutor telephoned Bonn and was told by the Chancellor's secretary that the head of the West German Government would be arriving in Munich for a party meeting. Further calls determined that the Chancellor was staying at the Bayerischer Hof hotel. Before the day was out Hans Kleemann managed to speak with the Chancellor himself and was granted a meeting at eleven o'clock that evening after the Chancellor had finished his social affairs.

The Chancellor of West Germany was a tired man—not only because of the hours endured at the conference and dinner, the boredom of listening to too many pathetic speeches, but also from the fatigue of his office.

Three years ago he had taken the reins of the party and led it to its first majority victory. Proclaimed as one of the shrewdest politicians West Germany had produced since the war, the Chancellor reveled in his accomplishments, which seemed to have no end. His public record within the country could bear any scrutiny. It was, as always happened, events outside of Germany that took their toll of his popularity and finally his own health and the aggressiveness that was dependent on it. The instability of world currencies, student activism, a bloated defense budget all left the country's economy in the doldrums, although still many cuts above the sick men of Europe, Italy and Great Britain. But the economic miracle was over with, and the electorate realized the Chancellor too had clay feet. His reward was the reduction of his majority from twelve seats to one, and the opposition sniping at his heels.

So far from being buoyed by the evening's festivities, the Chancellor saw them for what they were: a necessary showing of the flag which probably could not be counted on to add one voter to his side. And as for the industrial barons who supported him, the Chancellor thought them rather myopic: they demanded his presence at regular intervals so that they might heap their complaints upon his shoulders. Never once did any one of them thank him for the years that had seen their ascendancy. More, more—everyone always wanted more. . . .

The Chancellor knew Kleemann by reputation and had met him three or four times at official functions. When the prosecutor was shown into the suite, the Chancellor decided to make short work of him and get some much-needed sleep.

"Ah, Dr. Kleemann, come in, come in. A pleasure to see you again."

The brave words could not mask the doughy gray complexion

that had settled over the Chancellor's features, and the camaraderie behind them was leaden with fatigue.

"It was very good of you to receive me at this hour," Kleemann said quietly. "Had it been any other matter I would not have disturbed you."

He almost regretted his coming now, for he knew the Chancellor would not rest that night, not after what he was about to hear. The Chancellor was above all other things a political animal, and his instinct of danger was already roused by Kleemann's controlled tone.

"Would you care for something . . . coffee?"

"Thank you, no. Although later on perhaps a small drink would do."

"Well, then, you had better get on with it."

The Chancellor settled down on a divan and looked up at the man standing before him.

"My office has in its custody a man who claims to be Adolf Hitler. After extensive checks we are satisfied that he is in fact the former Führer."

The Chancellor looked up at the prosecutor and said sourly, "It is a poor joke, Kleemann, especially at this time of night."

"If it were a joke, Chancellor, I would not be here," Kleemann replied evenly. "If the Chancellor desires to see the proof, I have it with me."

The Chancellor looked him up and down and said, "Please proceed."

Over the next half hour, Kleemann carefully led the Chancellor through the circumstances of the last days, supplementing his monologue with photographs and papers, of which the most important were the fingerprint comparisons and dental plates. When he had finished, the Chancellor had given up trying to appear rested and was sitting slumped forward, his head bowed.

"Who would have believed it?" he asked incredulously. "After all these years . . . Who in Christ's name would have believed it?"

"Very soon the whole world will believe it, Chancellor," Kleemann said. "When we place Adolf Hitler on trial."

"You propose to try him?"

"Does the Chancellor have an alternative view?"

"Do you realize what this sort of trial will do to the country?" the Chancellor hissed. "We have more important things to do than dredge up the past, especially at a time like this."

"Do you have another idea in mind?" Kleemann repeated patiently.

"Yes: that we keep the matter quiet until I've had a chance to speak to the Cabinet."

"I mentioned the security involved, Chancellor," Kleemann said. "Do you believe it will be preserved once you mention Hitler's existence to your people?"

"Why should you doubt it?" the Chancellor challenged.

"I do not doubt anything. I merely pose a question. I believe the Chancellor is aware that there are certain individuals or groups who would be rather pleased if this man were to be done away with before a trial."

"A trial, a trial!" the Chancellor shouted. "Why are you so insistent on this trial?"

"Because the indictment has already been drawn up and Adolf Hitler has retained counsel," Kleemann said. "Furthermore, I have arranged for a press conference to be held tomorrow at which time I will announce that Hitler is in my custody.

"And," Kleemann continued relentlessly, "I have discussed the feasibility of such a trial with four eminent international jurists and they are in agreement not only that must Hitler be tried but that he should be brought before an international tribunal."

The Chancellor did not speak immediately. He rose and went over to the sideboard, where he made himself a stiff drink of English whisky.

"If I am to understand you correctly, Kleemann, you have already broached this subject with people outside the country," the Chancellor intoned.

"That is correct."

"Why did you so choose to overreach your authority?"

"I did not believe I was going beyond the bounds of my authority," Kleemann answered. "As prosecutor I felt it well within my limits to seek out an international opinion on several points concerning the trial of Adolf Hitler."

"And what were these points on which you felt you needed embellishment?" The Chancellor's anger was showing through his words, harsh and clipped.

"First, whether or not it would be feasible to try Hitler before an international tribunal. As I've already mentioned, I think he is not in the category of the ordinary criminal. He is a former head of state, and no court in modern times has been convened to deal with such a circumstance. Secondly, his acts—or rather, their consequences—touched not only Germany but the whole of Europe, Russia and America. In my view it was important to establish whether or not the world community would be prepared to bear the responsibility of sitting in judgment.

"Then, if it was the opinion of these four justices that Hitler could be judged by a universal tribunal, what would the mechanisms be? The questions of venue, selection of justices, indictments all come into play here."

"I see. And how have you contrived to get around Article Sixteen of the Basic Code?"

"Certainly West Germany may turn to the Federal Constitutional Court and ask that Hitler be kept here in Germany under the act which prohibits the deportation of a war criminal to stand trial in a foreign country. However, Chancellor, I think you will agree that the issues are somewhat more involved than those of, say, the Kleist case. It is quite possible the Federal Court would be more than willing to let Hitler be tried in New York, for example, at the United Nations, rather than have justice dispensed within a country he once ruled."

"I do not have the benefit of the Attorney-General's opinion," the Chancellor said curtly, "but I believe you have in fact exceeded your mandate. There has not been a single war-crimes hearing conducted outside of West Germany since the Eichmann fiasco."

"There hasn't been a criminal of this magnitude apprehended either," Kleemann countered. "Actually, the Eichmann case probably comes closest for comparison. You will remember, Chancellor, that West Germany had every right to insist that Eichmann, by virtue of his being a German citizen, be returned to his country to stand trial. The Israelis believed, quite rightly in my view, that his crimes transcended national borders, both physically and morally. The thought of the crimes may have originated within Germany, but their execution was spread over the whole of Europe. West Germany reconsidered her position and did not press for extradition."

"You are offering me every consideration for treating this as a *fait accompli*," the Chancellor said. "Everything you have said indicates that you've thought out a course for this affair and have already guaranteed certain results—namely, that Hitler will be exposed to the public. I ask you again: why?"

Hans Kleemann permitted himself to take a drink from the sideboard without bothering to ask the Chancellor's permission. He tasted his brandy slowly, then set it down before speaking.

"Our recent record of dealing with war crimes is at best pitiful," Kleemann said quietly. "We have held trials against men and women who committed atrocities in Auschwitz and Majdanek, and we have turned them from expositions of tragedies to farces by allowing them to drag on and on through every letter of the German legal alphabet, by tolerating the abuse of witnesses by our own prosecutors. Further, we have not pressured any of the countries holding known criminals into returning them to us to stand trial. The most notorious example of this is that of Rajakowtisch, Eichmann's deputy in Holland, who now lives in Austria. It is a known fact as well that in some of the police forces in West Germany there exists a policy of not acting upon leads that could lead to the apprehension of former Nazis.

"So our judicial machinery and enforcement cadres are not exactly brilliant in the execution of their duties in this regard.

"It is also known, Chancellor," Kleemann pressed on, "that under your government the activities of the rightist elements in the political arena have increased substantially. Even Brandt had to write to you that it was a national shame that the Nazi emblem could be seen at meeting halls, that some of the hateful literature which filled the Third Reich was once again being touted in the streets as the cure for our political and economic ailments. In our schools we have lied to our children by our refusal to discuss that period of our history. What understanding have we given them? What forewarnings have we taught them to recognize? None. Nothing at all.

"For these reasons, Chancellor, I chose to use my full judicial powers, acting to the letter of the law."

The Chancellor remained silent for a moment, then rose and paced slowly over the thick carpet of the suite.

"We have met, what—two, three times?" he said, as though

thinking aloud. "But I know your reputation. Your office has prosecuted war criminals, within your jurisdiction of Bavaria, with singular passion. But you yourself have never taken the limelight; you have never set yourself to be what your reputation has made you: a custodian of some vague moral values in this country.

"Yes, Kleemann, you are correct in thinking that I am not so very much interested in the doling out of retribution for events that happened twenty-five years ago. I think it would be fair to say that our government after the war could not afford a thorough 'cleaning' policy, if I can call it that. We had to get on with the job of rebuilding this country. We needed—and even the Allies saw this—men of experience who could do the job and whose past relationships with the Nazi regime had to be, if at all possible, dismissed.

"There were many factors involved here. The obligation of the new government was to the people, to give them whatever shelter, fuel and food could be scrounged, to get them back on their feet. You were here; you remember. What does justice mean to a man with an empty stomach and no bread to fill it, or to a woman who watches helplessly as her children starve or die of disease? Justice will not put bread into their mouths or cover them from the winter. So accommodations had to be made. Whatever the Third Reich was, one cannot deny that in its ranks were to be found some of the greatest organizational minds in the country. And these people were needed.

"There was also the fact that a people, any people, are generally loath to prosecute their own kind before the victor. It was not the German people but foreigners who arranged Nuremberg. It was their justice, not ours, that prevailed. That this was necessary I cannot quarrel with. But its necessity does not take away from the psychological fact that the German people saw their own kind being brought to some kind of tribunal which had no Germans on the bench and which, quite frankly, appeared so prejudiced that any concept of fairness was nonexistent. What the people saw was Germans being hounded by foreigners, and so, since blood is thicker than water, a certain sympathy prevailed for the accused. This hasn't changed. It has, in recent years, grown even more acute.

"Yet, there are those among us who purport to be the custodi-
ans of our moral heritage. You are one such person. And I think
that is right. You are necessary to the country in the same way
that music and poetry and art are all necessary. They provide a
certain enlightenment, offer an image of what might be instead of
dwelling on what is. But there are times when your vision and my
practical considerations come into conflict. This is one such
time."

The Chancellor poured himself more whisky and drank it
quickly.

"It is my opinion that the matter of Adolf Hitler and the dispensing of justice could have been handled in an entirely different
manner. To be honest, a short, quick trial could have been arranged, here in Germany, a sentence handed down and carried
out. That would have been that. The public would have been
intrigued for a few days, but as we've seen with the trials of the
student left and, on the other side, the camp trials, public attention is very lax. One must, after all, get on with living.

"But you obviously believe that judgment upon Adolf Hitler is
far too important a moral event to be passed over so easily.
Therefore, you have taken advantage of every letter of the law
and—let us be frank—have extended your mandate to the point
at which you are blackmailing me and my government. Please, no
righteous indignation. It does not become you, and I am not
concerned with hearing the legal grounds on which you have
acted. The fact remains that you have, and that now I must answer you.

"Very well—make your announcement and see what comes of
it. Put your petition before the Federal Constitutional Court to
have Hitler tried at the United Nations and see what it says. But
remember one thing: if I find that the political wind has changed
direction and that my government is going to suffer because of
your actions, I will come down very hard on you, Kleemann. Just
as you have used the letter of the law, so I will find every comma
and colon to make certain that *I* do what the public wants, not its
self-appointed custodian. If I come out of all this as a champion
of freedom and justice, I will take the tributes and you will get
nothing. If I am going to be hurt, then I shall see to it that my
losses are minimal, regardless of what I might have to do. And

you know, Kleemann, that when it comes to political self-preservation, I too have a reputation as a survivor.

"And now, I think there is nothing more to be said. I will listen
for your announcement tomorrow. Very shortly thereafter you
will hear from me as to where we stand."

The Chancellor turned his back on the prosecutor and went
into the bedroom, slamming the door behind him. Hans Kleemann looked after him, drained his brandy and set the glass on
the sideboard. Anger and disgust welled up in him as the Chancellor's words echoed in his mind, spinning forth their implications. He had not dared to believe he would be given political
support; but had it been so wrong of him to expect understanding—and with it, a neutral stance by the Chancellor? Now there
was nothing to sustain him but the strength of his own commitment; yet the loneliness of his task had already begun to eat away
at that.

IV

Trial

THEY SHALL BEAT THEIR SWORDS INTO PLOWSHARES AND
THEIR SPEARS INTO PRUNING HOOKS; NATION SHALL NOT LIFT
SWORD AGAINST NATION, NEITHER SHALL THEY LEARN WAR
ANY MORE.

HE WAS standing in the central path of the rose garden, facing the
General Assembly Building, upon whose marble face these words
were etched. The heat of the summer had suddenly fled New
York in the first days of September, leaving the city, hushed and
tranquil this Labor Day weekend, to the cool winds that traveled
from the ocean up along the East River, pushing away the layers
of sticky warmth to where they were lost in the already changing
colors of the Massachusetts peaks.

Former Gunner Oleg Vasilievich Kuzmin of the Seventy-ninth
Rifle Corps read the motto of the United Nations once more,
moving his lips as he did so. His knowledge of English was quite
good for one who had learned the language only four or five years
ago, although he was not quite certain of the adjective "pruning"
and made a note to look it up in his pocket *Webster's*.

As is the habit of most visitors whose stay in a foreign city is
lengthy, Kuzmin had sought out a place where he felt comfortable
and to which he might retreat when the pace and sheer physical
mass of New York overwhelmed him. He had chosen the rose

garden of the United Nations for the calm that lay upon it and its proximity to his hotel, although, in some hours, the sound of traffic along First Avenue traveled even as far as the river. Still, he enjoyed walking among the thousands of roses, listening to the crunch of gravel beneath his boots and taking in the exotic scents which cleansed the air of the fumes and odor of the street and the river.

Kuzmin, now a major in the Second Rocketry Division, could still remember, and would do so for the rest of his life, the unexpected telephone call from Zhukov, who had not forgotten the young gunner at the Berlin bunker, and how the two of them had searched for Hitler's remains. Twenty-five years later Zhukov had been told that the Führer, not his bones or ashes, had at last been found. Appointed by the Politburo as the Soviet Union's official observer at the trial, Zhukov had called upon Kuzmin to accompany him. The two of them had arrived together with Ivan Morozov, who would represent their country on the Bench.

In the interim, Kuzmin had studied every article he could find about the trial in both the Soviet and Western newspapers, so that he might not only understand the constitution and procedure of the Court but be able to monitor the world's reaction to this phenomenon. He was intensely proud that one of his countrymen would serve on the Tribunal, and his presence offset, however slightly, the suspicions he had about the choice of prosecutor, the German, Kleemann.

Kuzmin saw Kleemann frequently. Either coincidence or a similar need for quietness brought the prosecutor to the rose garden almost every afternoon. Sometimes the two men walked only a few feet apart, separated by the bushes, but never did they acknowledge each other. Kuzmin, in civilian clothes, appeared as just another tourist, and Kleemann, hands behind his back and head bowed, seldom paid any attention to whoever might be around him.

Kuzmin looked toward the doors of the General Assembly Building and reckoned it must be half past one or thereabouts. This was the time the prosecutor always appeared on the plaza; but today he did not come into the garden. He remained standing in the court, looking out onto the East River, a solitary figure rendered irrelevant by the magnificence of the architecture around him—seemingly so small, so impotent. Perhaps, on the eve of the trial, even the roses were no longer sweet to him.

Of all seasons, autumn was the one Hans Kleemann loved most. It was a time when the soul, tired of its summer wanderings, began to draw back into itself and prepare for the winter of meditation. Autumn was the season of decay and finally death, but a living death crystallized in the snows of winter, under which the metamorphosis continued, silent, invisible. It was a time for a man to reflect upon his life, the chance to pause and look back over the road he had traveled, this year or all the years of his life.

But there had been little time for reflection for Hans Kleemann. The three months of June, July and August, during which he would gather together his strength in the long, slow summer days, had been denied to him.

Driven and obsessed by his vision of having the trial become a reality, Kleemann had abandoned the calm, measured pace of his former existence. His hours at his desk, where he waded through countless pages of research material, were without end. The distinction between day and night blurred as he labored on until the early hours of the morning and often slept at midday. With the aid of only two assistants, he proceeded to accumulate a formidable reservoir of knowledge, from which he carefully selected the most salient facts upon which to build his case. Given his expertise in the field of war crimes, he could have done without such a gargantuan effort, yet he had sworn to leave nothing to chance, to use perhaps one-tenth of his storehouse of facts but to have the remainder at his fingertips in case it should be needed.

The prosecutor's mood, dictated by the pulse of action, gave way to impatience and short temper. He demanded almost as much of his staff as he did of himself, urging them on, correcting and expanding their efforts; it appeared he remained oblivious to their mutterings of dissatisfaction and frequent outbursts of anger when cooperation from other departments of the Attorney-General's office was not forthcoming. Wolff had warned him to expect recalcitrance from Jaunich, the Minister.

But it was not the demands of his task that alone accounted for his temper. In those moments, before sleep, when he lay with

eyes open and temples throbbing from the thoughts which continued to fill his already crammed mind, the prosecutor felt the cold
fingers of loneliness and despair reaching out for him. In moments
of self-pity, he asked why he was giving so much of himself only
to receive so little in return, to be faced with such antagonism
and contempt from the majority of his colleagues. And although
each time he pulled back from despair and rediscovered the worth
his mission held, he was left with a feeling of sadness. The road
ahead was still long, and he had started on it, so it seemed, such
a long time ago.

The afternoon of the day Hans Kleemann held his press conference, the West German Government had added its official seal
to the news of Adolf Hitler's existence. The same evening, the
President of the United States, by personal envoy, had sent a
letter to the Chancellor. In addition to the congratulations, the
President spoke of the feasibility of holding the trial of Adolf
Hitler at the United Nations, although the suggestion was so
carefully worded that the Chancellor could not interpret it as a
demand and so take offense. Worthington had worked his influence silently and imperceptibly.

The following day the Soviet Union had added its voice for an
international tribunal. This announcement, sober in tone and devoid of any propaganda against West Germany, took Bonn by
surprise. The Chancellor had expected a vitriolic diatribe from
the Soviets, filled with accusations of West German complicity in
hiding Adolf Hitler from the world for a quarter century. Instead,
the Soviet Foreign Minister (in person) delivered the congratulations of his nation and an expression of its earnest desire to see
the Führer of the Third Reich tried by a tribunal that would include a Soviet justice.

So the Chancellor of West Germany had nowhere to turn,
flanked as his choices of action were by East and West. Before
his Cabinet, who recognized the pressure politics involved, he
was impotent, but with the public, which remained ignorant of
the background details, he could not only save face but perhaps
gain stature.

Two days after Kleemann had brought Adolf Hitler before the
world, the Chancellor of West Germany spoke to his people.
Because of the extraordinary nature of the accused, he said, the

West German Government would find it appropriate that the man known as Adolf Hitler be given over for trial before an international body of jurists. However, West Germany requested three conditions in return for rendering up Adolf Hitler, who, as a German national, under Article Sixteen of the Basic Law could not be extradited to stand trial beyond his country's borders. These were:

1. That West Germany be represented on the international bench by one of its own jurists.
2. That the prosecution be headed and conducted principally if not wholly by Dr. Hans Kleemann.
3. That the State of Israel, which might feel it had a particular interest in the person of Adolf Hitler, be represented on the bench by one jurist.

These points, which came to be known as the Bonn Declaration, were unanimously endorsed by the other three states. Within hours of the Chancellor's announcement, the Justices were named: Thomas Worthington for the United States; Ivan Morozov for the Soviet Union; Etta Kirsch for the State of Israel; Dieter Wolff for West Germany.

This done, the Chancellor took his political revenge against Kleemann. The Attorney-General of West Germany spoke of his government's satisfaction with the reception the Bonn Declaration received. To demonstrate the gravity with which West Germany was treating this matter, the Cabinet had agreed to free Dr. Hans Kleemann of all responsibilities deriving from his post as Public Prosecutor of Bavaria. His duties would be passed on to a subordinate so that Kleemann might devote all his energies to the forthcoming trial. In that one stroke, seemingly generous and misleadingly temporary, the Chancellor had put to death the legal career of Hans Kleemann.

He had known it would come, but still the suddenness and silence of political Coventry left him bewildered. It was only afterward, in the weeks that followed, that he understood into how many fragments his life had been shattered. He saw them in the guarded conversations that ceased altogether when he approached colleagues in the hall; in the cold, smirking eyes of the junior who now held the title that had once been his; in his club, where small talk with his peers became strained, often curdling into silence which sat heavily between the members, causing embarrassment, uncertainty metamorphosing into resentment. The trial was never a subject of discussion at the club; conversely, one could not speak to Kleemann without being conscious of it. So there was silence first and then nothing at all as Hans Kleemann gave up his treasured evenings at the club.

He had become a leper in a society that paradoxically was itself infected, yet believed itself perfectly healthy. Hans Kleemann understood that among his people he was the voice and conscience of a past that they were loath to speak of. In spite of themselves, they were not through with it. In the eyes and voices of the young defenders of those accused of the atrocities at the Majdanek concentration camp, he witnessed the triumph of daring over caution. These men and women, between thirty and forty years old, were defending people a generation older than themselves. Until this day they had labored behind the curtain of shame, because that was what the world had decreed the actions of their clients to be—ignoble beyond all comprehension. With the emergence of Hitler, the shame no longer existed, and in its place a new form of an ancient arrogance came into being.

"Let us deal with the past," one young attorney had stated emphatically after the acquittal of an SS guard, "as a period of *German* history to be examined and evaluated by *Germans*."

Yes, the sons and daughters of his generation wished to throw out the sentences passed upon the heads of their fathers by foreigners who had ruled the bench at Nuremberg. They wished to open the crypt once more and drag out the dusty old bones and rearrange them in a different order. To give them a proper, honorable burial.

And as the sons proceeded to do this, their elders became hostile to Hans Kleemann; though one of them, he walked in his own land holding the sword against his own people. The past that they taught their sons to believe was "not so bad" was heinous in his eyes. Since this was so, what could be his opinion of them?

It was inevitable that such sentiments lead to threats upon his life. After three telephone calls and dozens of obscene letters,

Kleemann reluctantly accepted the Farben brothers' insistence that they escort him wherever he went. But he pitied and was ashamed for the unknown hands who perverted their love of Germany into hate. He did not know how many people such hands represented, but that they spoke in their own brutal eloquence for more than just themselves he was certain. He had seen the faces of the others in Emmaus.

There had been no need for him to go personally to Emmaus. Some town records, dealing with Hitler's ownership of property and his bank accounts, had been subpoenaed by the prosecutor's office. His assistants had taken the statements of the mayor and councilmen; other townspeople who were particularly familiar with the public life of "Werner Busse" had been questioned, their observations carefully noted and then double-checked and cross-referenced.

In spite of the sullen reaction of the Emmaus citizenry, the process had taken all of two days. After the official inquiries were complete, the Farben brothers moved in and with characteristic thoroughness unearthed the less pleasant secrets. But the bribery, petty theft, mild extortion in the form of palm greasing and several hitherto unheard-of abortions bore no relation whatsoever to Werner Busse or his enterprise. Such information would be of no significance to the prosecutor, this much he had made clear. He realized that in his defense Helmut Toller would wax eloquent on Hitler's stature in and contribution to the community. But if Kleemann were obliged to challenge the credibility of a defense witness, he would do so in the context of his relationship to Hitler, not on indiscretions that were just so much dirty linen.

Nonetheless, Hans Kleemann drove to Emmaus in the last week of August. By going, he was answering to his own curiosity, that part of him which very much wanted to see the place where Adolf Hitler had dwelt for twenty-five years. In part he was also seeking the reason why the arrest and forthcoming trial had earned him so much hatred. He wanted, if possible, to speak to some of those who had known Hitler. Although he knew so much about the man, Hans Kleemann did not understand the fundamental spirit that moved him. He had not ferreted out that fatal attraction which Hitler exercised at will. He did not, the prosecutor admitted, truly know the man he wished so much to condemn.

He arrived at midmorning, left his car in the square and mixed into the pedestrian traffic that was gathering about the vegetable stalls, the butcher and pastry shops and the fish market. Hans Kleemann walked the length of the square and soon found himself opposite the greenhouse which still belonged to Adolf Hitler. Business was brisk. The parking lot was filled with small trucks and cars with their trunks open. Five or six teen-age boys were loading twenty-kilo bags of fertilizer into vans or strapping down blue spruces, their roots tied up in burlap sacks, on the tops of cars. From inside the gardening center, a foreman was shouting about a consignment of shovels that had never arrived. Two buildings and a little house to the side of the greenhouse, the result of twenty-five years of labor . . . so innocent, so removed from the man . . .

A woman appeared at the door of the house. Plump, with a matronly bun and hair net, she had started to go across to the greenhouse when she noticed the prosecutor, standing in the center of all the activity. She stopped, squinted at him and began to walk toward him, a helpful smile on her face. It vanished when she came within a few feet of him. Hans Kleemann knew her from photographs as Ernestine Hassell, Hitler's housekeeper; she also recognized him—as the enemy, the intruder and slanderer.

The housekeeper looked upon him without fear, her fat lips twisting in contempt as she deliberated as to what to do. Ernestine Hassell took a few steps backward, her eyes ever on Kleemann, then turned and hurried into the house. The prosecutor was certain that within a quarter hour all of Emmaus would know of his presence.

He walked back the way he had come. When he reached his car, he thought of leaving then and there. Obviously nothing was to be gained by staying. Yet he was unsatisfied, and so the prosecutor elected to stay until the townspeople received word that he was here, if others, as Ernestine Hassell had, did not recognize him first. He speculated as to what their reaction would be.

Walking across to a café, Hans Kleemann took an empty table that looked out onto the square, ordered a café crème and asked the proprietor for a box of matches. As his pipe grew hot, he waved away the blue smoke into the chatter of conversations of housewives and the workingmen taking their midmorning pause. The sunlight streaming through the windows pleasantly warmed his face, and he listened to the cries from the street and its markets.

When she entered, all talk ceased at once, and that was what drew his attention. She was regarded not so much with hostility as with incomprehension and a hint of anger, as though she had done them all a wrong, had acted in an unseemly fashion, bringing shame upon herself and them. And in their eyes, she had. Lillian Grubber had refused to sign the town petition calling for a dismissal of charges against Adolf Hitler. Standing just behind the door, she searched for an empty table; but there were none, nor was anyone already at a table offering her a chair. Finally her gaze met that of Hans Kleemann. He rose, drawing back a seat for her. She smiled briefly, acknowledging his courtesy, but her eyes were a reflection of her surprise, for she recognized him, as he did her.

"I would like a café crème as well," Lillian Grubber told the proprietor, who was observing her sullenly. She turned to the prosecutor and said, "You are very kind, Doctor."

The talk in the café picked up again, low at first as speculation about Fräulein Grubber's cavalier was chewed upon, then more animatedly as someone mentioned seeing this same man on television . . . making an announcement about Adolf Hitler. . . .

"You *are* Hans Kleemann?" Lillian said in a low voice.

He looked at her sunburned cheeks and the little bit of peeling skin across the delicate forehead and answered, "Yes."

"Somehow I had expected to see you sooner than this," she said, watching him as he sat down and speaking as though nothing had happened.

"Your people were here a few weeks ago—isn't that right?"

"Yes, but there was no need for me to come here, not then. And now least of all."

"The investigation must be complete. Helmut—" She caught herself at the mention of her foster son.

"That's all right," Kleemann told her. "I know. He has finished his work and is in New York."

He looked at her as she stirred her coffee absently.

"If you like, I will leave."

"No, please don't!" The green eyes flashed up to catch and hold his own.

"Don't go; there is no need to," she repeated.

A silence came between them, made of embarrassment and the realization that an intimacy had been created out of the hostility around them.

"Do they hate you?" Hans Kleemann asked her at once.

"Hate?" She considered the word he had used. Could it be something as strong as hate? Lillian had not thought of her ostracism as based on hate. Yet where did contempt end and hatred begin?

"You may be right," she said at last. "I am not acting at all like the foster mother of a local hero."

And there was bitterness in her voice—toward herself, Helmut or the townspeople, he didn't know which.

"Yes, he certainly has become a celebrity," Kleemann murmured.

"Hey, Willi," someone called out to the proprietor. "Why don't you let some air in here? The place stinks all of a sudden!"

Amid the coarse laughter, one of the women called out, "They come in trying to look for dirt, but all they find is their own!"

"Tell him to get the hell out, Willi. Tell them both!"

Hans Kleemann rose and addressed the proprietor. "If we are causing you embarrassment we will leave," he said levelly, but the anger was apparent under his words. "However, if not then we ask to be left in peace. We still have, in this country, a law to protect people from slander."

It was the mention of the law that brought silence. Whatever malice was aching to slip off their tongues was held in check by *the law*, an entity this stranger represented, controlled and wielded. It did not shrink their loathing for him, but their fear silenced them.

Hans Kleemann was still looking at the proprietor, waiting for a reply.

"You paid for your coffees," he said with mock graciousness. "Please enjoy them."

Hans Kleemann returned to his table.

"I must apologize for them," Lillian said in a voice that deliberately carried across the café. "It is the first time I have seen a stranger treated with such discourtesy. A shame."

The words were a challenge to the hecklers, but none picked up the gauntlet. Hans Kleemann was about to speak when Lillian pressed his hand with her own.

"Do you think Helmut will win?" she asked him suddenly. "Do you believe there is any possibility of that?"

He considered the question, aware that ears had pricked up at the next table.

"No, he shall not vindicate Adolf Hitler," the prosecutor said. "I will not permit him to do that."

"I am glad!" Lillian whispered. "You see, everyone believes he *will* win, that there is no question of it."

"But why—why do they believe that?"

"Werner Busse . . . Adolf Hitler is one of their own. To take him away, to try him before foreigners is to bring back the images of Nuremberg and the Occupation. It is a return to the shame and defeat which has been all but forgotten."

"Is there no understanding of who Hitler is? Or that he surrendered and wanted to be tried by an international tribunal?"

"Oh, on the surface everyone knows that. But knowing and accepting are two different things. There are also the pride and stubbornness, the willingness to believe that words had been put into his mouth, the belief that we take care of our own affairs—if compelled to. Hitler has outraged no one here. Quite the contrary: he is loved, and a threat to him is taken as a threat to the community. In defending him, they are protecting themselves."

"But you do not see it that way."

"I? No, and I have paid the price." Lillian laughed at once. "Do you know, I don't think I've had a civil word addressed to me since refusing to sign that petition."

Kleemann had heard of the petition distributed in Emmaus in support of Adolf Hitler. His staff had dissected it, back-checking all the names that appeared on it, and had kept him abreast of similar expressions of public opinion throughout Germany and the world.

"May I ask why you didn't sign it?"

"Helmut is wrong in what he's doing," Lillian said simply.

"He does not understand it—any more than he truly understood the reasons for his coming back to Emmaus. But he is wrong, and one day, God willing, he will realize it. Even if it will be too late . . . to change what he will have done."

"Fräulein Grubber . . ."

"Won't you call me Lillian?"

"Thank you. Lillian—can you tell me, do you know why Helmut is doing this?"

"That is not why you came to Emmaus, Herr Kleemann."

"No, and I didn't come to persuade him to drop the case or to save him either," Kleemann snapped. "I came to understand why . . . if I can."

Looking at him, she thought Hans Kleemann a handsome man even though his years now hung heavily on him, had aged him more than they had a right to.

"I have tried to understand," she said. "But he knew I would not, and so he left Emmaus after telling me of his decision—you know, after he met with Hitler at your home. I haven't heard from him in two months. The best I can do is read the papers and listen to the news—to know from them where my son is!"

Kleemann nodded as though he had expected Helmut Toller to act in precisely this fashion. It was only a small, very small indication of the callousness he had perceived in him.

"At first I thought his behavior resulted from his revitalized fame," said Lillian. "But then I realized the issue was far deeper than that. We could not discuss Adolf Hitler without Helmut's working himself up into a rage. Hitler wasn't a mere client, even a particular client. In Helmut's mind he seemed to have been elevated to the status of an untouchable, a venerable old man who had been wronged and slandered and who had to be protected, by brutality if necessary."

"I assume there was plenty of support in the town for such a reaction."

"More than enough. I had the feeling that a transfer of authority was taking place, Hitler passing on his position in Emmaus to Helmut, the heir apparent."

She smiled wanly.

"It was no contest, really. I couldn't expect my feelings and opinions to influence him, not here in his home where everyone was supporting him."

"I am very sorry," Hans Kleemann said to her.

"And I regret that you have traveled all this way to learn nothing. These people won't talk to you. Not that you expected them to. I'm sure you're aware of the reception your representatives received. Yours has been worse. Their anger has grown, and you are the one being held responsible for it."

They sipped their cold coffees, and Lillian smoked a cigarette, inhaling in long, slow drafts. Gradually the café emptied as the workingmen returned to their stalls and delivery vans and the women gathered together their morning shopping. They went out of their way to avoid passing by the prosecutor's table, and they left in silence that spoke volumes.

"Is there any way I might help you?" Lillian asked him.

Hans Kleemann shook his head.

"The offer is very generous, but no, I must decline it."

"Because you think I would suffer more for helping you than I am suffering already?"

"That is part of it."

"You will need someone to rebut the petition," Lillian told him. "You are obligated to show the world another face of Germany, that which has not forgotten. You will need me, Hans Kleemann."

Yes, she was right, he thought. He did need her, more for himself than against Helmut Toller. But he did not tell her so.

"Thank you," he said softly. "I will remember your offer. But I will not take advantage of it unless I am sure it's needed.

"What will you do when this is all over?" he asked her. "Will you be able to stay? Will they forgive you?"

"No," she answered. "I am beyond redemption in their eyes. Nor do I wish to stay here much longer. I will do exactly what you must do after you have won."

Pushing her chair back, Lillian rose and picked up her handbag.

"You must look out for yourself now," she said. "I will meet you again when, as you say, it is all over with."

She left him without his having said goodbye, and in some strange way he felt comforted by that.

After nine weeks the investigation was complete. The final copies of Kleemann's presentation were drafted, and those who had helped him received his thanks at a small dinner party he gave before leaving for New York. As his secretary cleared his office of the innumerable volumes that had accumulated in the course of the research, the prosecutor made last calls to witnesses whom he wished to be ready to appear should he need them. Then he read over his opening remarks, once more examined the structure of his prosecution and, finding no fault, quietly departed from Munich on the last day of August. He would return to Germany only after the trial was through; and then, after arranging his affairs, he would leave it forever.

He looked upon the four bronze portals, a gift from Canada, with their bas reliefs of justice, peace, truth and fraternity. For a moment he hesitated, not knowing which door to choose. The United States Marine guard, who knew him by sight, came up to ask what was the matter. Kleemann shook his head, and the young serviceman, in full battle dress, held open the door of fraternity. Kleemann thanked him and walked through.

The United Nations had been closed to the public since the beginning of the week. Only those with special badges, changed daily, could enter and leave, passing through the cordon established by the First Marine Battalion. On orders from the President, the detail responsible for security at the U.N. was in combat readiness, supplementing the city police and FBI, who would keep First Avenue clear of demonstrators. The harbor police and a Navy unit continuously patrolled the East River. The Chief Executive's wish was simple and to the point: the trial was not to be interfered with or interrupted by any person, any group, no matter how righteous their cause might be.

He came here now, to the silent magnificence of the great cool halls adorned with masterpieces of the arts of a hundred different cultures, so that in peace he could feel the passion for his task expand to embrace all of mankind. This place, removed from the city by stone walls, chain-link fences and security posts, was his retreat of solitude, into which he entered to cleanse himself and make ready. The silence and repose spoke of higher affairs that might be carried on here, matters pertaining not only to the international community but to the international conscience as well.

It was not very often, Kleemann thought, that men could infuse an object with dignified purpose. Too often that which had been designed to serve noble ends became cheapened, and the spirit that made it great and the words that gave the spirit substance sounded hollow because of all the lies that were whispered in these halls. He did not know whether such would be the fate of this trial. He would do all in his power to save it from being corrupted. But before the arena saw battle, he wanted to know what it had been like in peace.

Walking into the massive silence of the General Assembly, going down the center aisle, with the delegates' seats on either side and above, the media and spectator booths enclosed in tinted glass, Hans Kleemann felt the spirit of purpose move him once more: to show all men that there exists an evil for which no statute of limitations may be invoked and that justice, if the word is to have any meaning, must be administered as remedy. For a moment, only an instant on the clock of History, Kleemann prayed that the attention of the world would be on this splendid auditorium. If he had only that fraction of time, he was certain he could infuse the true meaning of what was about to happen into the hearts of all who listened. And those who listened, he was certain, would never be the same again. That they would forget much of what they were to hear, and that later memory would distort what they remembered, was true. But he believed that if ever again they were confronted with an evil the like of which he would unveil before them, their hearts would beat faster in fear and they would recognize the danger that had come over them.

Evil, Kleemann believed, was not obliged to struggle for the mind of man. It was already latent within it, waiting only to be nourished. The understanding of this evil, or what might be called good, was always on the offensive, trying to gain a foothold in man's imagination so that it might contribute to and guide his actions.

This was why he had not acted as Dieter Wolff had once suggested: kill Hitler, at the first possible opportunity. Wolff and the others who would gather here were judges. They accepted death as a tool, if it was so justified. Hans Kleemann saw his responsibility not in the formation and passing of a sentence, but in the development of arguments that would make that sentence right.

In spite of all that had been written of the deeds of Adolf Hitler, Hans Kleemann believed the argument for his death still had to be articulated before the sentence was passed. If he had murdered Adolf Hitler, he would have become no better than his victim. He would have shown Hitler that the conscience of a single man had not moved one millimeter beyond that point at which Hitler had infected it.

In spite of the fact that he was shivering from the cool air, the prosecutor found his forehead bathed in sweat. He mopped it carefully with a handkerchief, then moved back up the center aisle of the auditorium. Perhaps tonight, he would be spared the demons and nightmares that plagued his dreams, for quietness and peace had been what he needed.

Tomorrow, it would all begin.

It had rained early on that same morning, and the earth was damp and soft. The brown needles of the pine trees clung to his heels as he walked along the path broken through the woods. Sometimes he would brush at a branch or against a clump of ferns, and the moisture on the leaves would spray against his hands and clothing. There was the smell of decay in the forest, the pungent odor of the earth slowly turning over, revitalizing itself from all that had fallen upon it. It was a good smell, he thought, and it reminded him of the days at the Eagle's Nest, when he had had all the mountains of southern Germany and Austria to call his own.

Adolf Hitler limped slowly along this forest lane, taking care not to trip over the roots of trees that sometimes rose from the earth. Ahead of him he could hear the crackling and swishing progress of his first escort, a German-speaking American military policeman assigned to him since his arrival from Germany, courtesy of the U.S. Air Force, at this National Guard camp on Long Island. Behind him there wasn't a sound, although he knew that one of the Farben brothers was following. Unlike Hans Kleemann, Adolf Hitler was very well satisfied with the way events had unfolded, although he never mentioned this to anyone and steadily maintained a stern, unrepentant expression.

It had all begun after the press conference Hans Kleemann had held the afternoon following his interview with the Chancellor.

The next day, Helmut Toller brought in a dozen newspapers from around the world. Without exception the headlines spoke of Adolf Hitler—his survival, his surrender and the trial that would inevitably follow. Hitler, still residing in the comfort of Kleemann's country home, read the German reports very carefully, some several times over; and when he had finished, he laughed.

"You see, Helmut, there is no one baying after my blood. No German would do that."

Helmut Toller pointed out that the leading dailies were quite unanimous in their opinion—that Hitler must be tried by the International Tribunal and that Germans must be prepared to accept what sentence was handed down. The Führer shook his head.

"Of course they would say that! They are obligated to. But do you find the same kind of ranting in the provincial papers? No! Intellectuals always find it convenient to kick at the carcass. It is the little man who will decide whether I live or die—no one else but he."

Toller could not fault the analysis. The newspapers and broadcasts from the smaller towns either were underplaying the whole affair or had come out with editorials deploring the government's action, some even going so far as to demand clemency for Hitler. In the following days, Toller discovered the reason. He had opened a temporary office in Munich, and it was there that the "representatives" somehow discovered him.

The first men were lawyers like himself. Some, because of their reputations, he recognized on sight. These came usually at night and spoke in low, confidential tones about the wishes of their always anonymous clients to contribute to the Führer's defense. That these benefactors could not show themselves was understandable, was it not?—given the as yet unresolved political situation surrounding Hitler; but nonetheless, they believed a contribution had to be made. It was invariably cash—crisp, fresh small-denomination notes in large amounts. Only Erik Bendt, the Hamburg financier, disclaimed anonymity. As he departed, he assured Toller that his door was always open to him, the only condition being that he should pass through it discreetly.

Adolf Hitler expressed neither surprise nor gratitude at the approach or the contributions of these men.

"They realize their debt to me," he said. "Take their money

and use it however you feel is necessary. But do not trust them. Remember, they always stand in the shadows, cowards who contribute so as to cover all eventualities, to be able to say later on that they stood by my side. They will not follow unless I succeed in vindicating myself. Above all, Helmut, wait for the little people."

As the days passed, the "little people" made themselves known. By this time, Toller understood that his police escort, a Munich detective, was the conduit through which contact with his office was made and clandestine appointments arranged. The detective seldom spoke of these things; he preferred to leave handwritten notes on Toller's desk, stating that this or that person would be coming at an appointed hour and advising the lawyer to spare him some time.

And they came. Representatives of Wehrmacht veterans' groups which still celebrated, through feasts and reunions, "the good old days." After them, the editors of right-wing newspapers bearing "unsolicited money" that had been sent to their offices. The piles of stained, crumpled bills, workingmen's money, accumulated in Toller's safety-deposit box. In three weeks, over half a million marks, about two hundred and fifty thousand dollars, had been collected.

Adolf Hitler reached the end of the forest path and stepped out into the open space before the lake that bordered the National Guard compound. The sky was covered in diaphanous clouds, and the gray waters lapped and gurgled at the bank, wearing into the soil beneath the bullrushes. There was the noise of a stone hitting water, and when he turned, Hitler saw the American MP trying to skim flat stones along the surface of the lake.

There had, of course, been the counterdemonstrations. In Berlin and Frankfurt, even Munich, the leftist university students had formed marches and parades protesting the government's refusal to assume responsibility in the Hitler affair. Asked what they wanted, the students demanded that Hitler be tried in Germany by the people upon whose heads he had brought infamy. When the Attorney-General categorically refused to reconsider the government's position, the rioting had begun. Some reports stated that the police did not intervene until it became obvious the students would be beaten senseless by rightist gangs who were out at every gathering. Other witnesses claimed the police had used unnecessary force in dealing with defenseless people. There had been one particularly ugly affair when a group of students took refuge in a synagogue in Munich. A service was in progress, and although the police did not follow them in, the rightists did. In a few minutes smoke could be seen coming out through the shattered windows. When the final count was taken, forty people had to be hospitalized. Of those forty, three, one Jew and two Christians, died. The synagogue had been gutted.

Helmut Toller reported each incident to Hitler; every time, Hitler only nodded and smiled. Like a tribal sorcerer of the Dark Ages, Hitler had only to put his hand here and pestilence would erupt; lay his eyes there, and blood would flow. But all the while he did not have to come before those who did his bidding. To Toller, such command and power was beyond anything he had ever witnessed. It reduced political influence and financial strength to mere trifles, for he recognized that Hitler was able to coax the most potent of all forces from a man: the will to act as Hitler wished. It was a genius which fascinated Toller, and the memory of its potency on Walpurgis Night dispelled the fear that sometimes rose within him.

The audacity of Hitler's sympathizers grew to the point at which they demanded that a delegation of German people be permitted to see him. The government would not yield, but the crowds received their wish nonetheless. Prior to leaving for the United States, Adolf Hitler was moved from Kleemann's country house back to Munich to be officially served with the indictment. There wasn't any legal need for such an act, since his representative could have conveyed the papers to him. But on the Attorney-General's insistence, the full letter of the law was applied: Hitler had been arrested in Munich, and that was where the indictment would be read to him.

The journey and destination were to be kept secret; but again someone within the police force had broken security. When the automobile entourage reached the Ministry of Justice, the officials found over three thousand people gathered in the square and more rushing in from every side. The roar of the crowd, the cheers, broken by a few obscenities, still rang in his ears, and it did not subside even when he was inside the building. No glass, concrete or steel could drown out the hysteria that filled the streets.

In that one moment, Adolf Hitler admitted to himself he had been tempted. The surging of the crowd fed back upon him his own magic, and the magic seized him, making him hunger for more. But he took hold of himself and remembered that in those voices he had the victory he desired. This was only the beginning of his rise, his rebirth; he was certain of it.

Suddenly Adolf Hitler turned to the American MP and asked him, "What time do we leave for New York?"

"Tomorrow," the soldier answered, not looking at him. "In the morning."

"Surely you do not propose to move me back and forth between here and the city every day!"

"You'll have a place at the U.N. as long as the trial lasts. Believe me, no one wants to touch you any more than is necessary."

"Tell me, what would you think if I am found innocent of all charges?"

The soldier, a professional in his middle years, stared at Hitler and answered softly, "I lost my father in the Ardennes. Mister, if the court doesn't do the job, I or someone like me will."

The American MP was astonished when Hitler, after looking him up and down, demanded, "And it is men of *your* sentiment who are to sit in judgment upon *me?*"

"Would the delegates of this Assembly rise for the International Tribunal of Justice."

The Secretary-General of the United Nations, speaking from the podium at the far end of the hall, set the example by leaving his customary seat in order to move down to the table that had been arranged for him at the foot of the center aisle and stand beside it. Almost in unison the six hundred and twenty-six representatives to the U.N. General Assembly rose, their eyes on the small door in the left corner of the auditorium through which the Court would enter.

But there was one formality to come which took all of them, except the Secretary-General, who had been notified beforehand, by surprise. On his signal, a sheet of clear plastic measuring fifty feet across in a gentle arc and fifteen feet high was lowered from the ceiling of the auditorium. It hovered over the floor, then touched down lightly, completely encircling the area of the podium, where the justices would sit, the witness stand, directly beneath it, and the two tables arranged for the prosecution and defense.

"Ladies and gentlemen." The Secretary-General took the microphone from his table and turned to the Assembly. "Ladies and gentlemen, there is no need for concern. At the request of the member states conducting this trial, I have permitted an extension of our usual security procedures. Before you, you see Samson's Shield, a device designed for the protection of the President of the United States. It is able to withstand bullets and even small rockets and will serve to protect the Court while it is in session. The Assembly will hear all proceedings through the microphones behind the shield. I am certain that after a time the members will forget that it is even there."

These last words were spoken halfheartedly, for not even the Secretary-General believed them. Who, even if he hadn't witnessed it himself, could forget Eichmann in the glass booth of the Jerusalem court? But the times had changed, the Secretary-General reflected. It was not so much Hitler whom the shield would protect but the jurists and, above all, the prosecutor. Insulated from the outside world by this Assembly and separated from the Assembly itself by the flat plastic, the participants of the trial would play out their roles like actors of the Middle Ages, weaving their words and gestures in total quarantine.

One of the cameramen, following the director's order, rolled his instrument right up to the shield, working his lens as he did so. From his Marine colleagues, the director had learned late last evening of the additional security measure. He had managed to get inside the General Assembly two hours ago to change all the lenses.

Hans Kleemann, gowned in black, was the first to enter the arena. As soon as he was through the door, he stopped, dazzled by the ring of lights that had been arranged for the cameras. He moved to his appointed desk, set halfway between the shield and the witness stand, to the left of the podium; stacked the papers and turned around. For an instant he was frightened by the thousands of somber eyes peering down at him. Self-consciously, he shielded his vision and looked up at the public galleries. In the first row of the glass-enclosed booth, he recognized the President of the United States and, several seats across, Marshal Zhukov, representing the Soviet Union. But West Germany was not represented by her Chancellor. Instead, Hans Kleeman could make out the sharp, badgerlike features of the Foreign Minister, who sat unmoving, eyes fixed on Kleemann. The look he passed on to the prosecutor was one almost of a personal enmity, as though Hans Kleemann were guilty of placing him in an embarrassing, untenable position. The Foreign Minister, Kleemann was certain, would not let him forget his presence.

Helmut Toller's entrance was markedly different. Walking in long, purposeful steps, he carried himself with the confidence of the challenger, not the challenged. He too was wearing the black gown, and it lent dignity to his youth. Before going to his desk, Toller came to where Kleemann was standing and said, "No matter what the outcome, it will have been a great honor to face you."

The prosecutor looked up at him, his anger shot through with sadness. He believed Toller's words to be sincere, yet he had made a thorough study of his courtroom methods. Toller always presented his respects to the opposition; in some instances, the ploy made his ruthlessness surprising. He was tempted to ask if Toller was trying to catch him off balance, but held back. Toller, receiving no answer, shrugged and returned to his table.

They came in single file, with Etta Kirsch leading. There was an involuntary murmur from the delegates as the second jurist appeared, walking very close behind her, his hand resting lightly on her shoulder. This man, wearing his robes by unmistakable long custom, as though he had been meant from birth to bear them, took Etta Kirsch's arm and allowed himself to be directed to his seat on the podium. The jurist was Sir Adrian Potter—the fifth member of the Tribunal, which had elected him its president, and a man who had lived for half a century in the special world of those without sight.

Sir Adrian had not been asked to join the Tribunal until midsummer, when the German Attorney-General suggested that four jurists was a bad number to have on any bench. What, he queried solicitously, would happen if there was a difference of opinion on the final verdict—two for acquittal and two against! Although Ivan Morozov thought the question ridiculous, he agreed with the others of the Tribunal that the addition of one other justice would remove that infinitesimal chance of indecision. Equally, the agreement on Sir Adrian was unanimous. Although handicapped, the Englishman was a jurist of international repute, holder of numerous judicial posts in the United Kingdom, former judge on the International Court at The Hague, and a man whose infirmity was balanced by a phenomenal memory. There could be no doubt as to his impartiality or his qualification for the position of President.

The others—Ivan Morozov, Thomas Worthington and Dieter Wolff—followed after Sir Adrian. When all were settled on the podium, the microphones as well as the simultaneous-translation units were activated, and Sir Adrian's quiet voice spoke out to the world.

"Would all be seated."

Etta Kirsch glanced over at the court reporter, whose tape recorders were already in operation. The man indicated he was ready.

"Bring in the accused," Sir Adrian called.

Adolf Hitler, followed by a Marine in parade dress, came through a door to the left of the podium, opposite the side from which all others had entered the court. Limping visibly, his head held high, he moved across to where Toller stood, his eyes surveying the packed audience, then turning and staring directly into the television cameras. Finally, he looked up at the galleries, squinting against the lights. Slowly, one by one, he let his gaze rest in turn on the world leaders who had assembled to see him, and to each he sent the thought: In watching me, you are watching a part of yourself. He then looked at each of the justices as though this would be his only chance to do so and he wished to imprint their faces on his memory forever. To Hans Kleemann, he gave only a passing glance without any scrutiny, and only a hint of a smile pressed on his lips.

Finally Adolf Hitler came to stand by his counsel. The Marine took his place behind the defense table, his hands held smartly at the small of his back.

"The accused will be seated."

"What kind of charade is this?" Hitler demanded of Toller. He either was unaware or did not care that his microphone carried his words not only to the Bench but to the Assembly and television cameras as well.

"This man is blind! What competence has he to sit in judgment on me?"

"Silence," Sir Adrian intoned.

Helmut Toller rose to his feet and addressed the Bench.

"The accused was not informed that your Lordship had been elected President of the Court," he stated, but without the slightest hint of an apology. "I am responsible for the omission and the reaction on the part of the accused."

"Have you any questions as to my qualification?" Sir Adrian demanded.

"None, your Lordship."

"Then I presume the accused is of the same opinion."

"He is, your Lordship."

"An apology would be in order," Ivan Morozov interjected sharply.

To which Hitler smiled grimly and shook his head.

"You may sit, Counselor," Sir Adrian intoned softly. "And bear in mind that we will tolerate no improper behavior here, particularly slander and other derogatory remarks."

He sat almost motionless, with his hands spread before him, palms down, the sightless eyes staring calmly out into the darkness as though he were beholding some mystery of creation.

"I will now make the opening statement for the Court, after which the prosecution shall proceed with the indictment."

"The constitution of this, the International Tribunal of Justice, is based not, as it may first appear, on the Nuremberg Principle, elucidated in 1946," Adrian Potter began. "The roots of this juridical body can be traced back through the centuries, even millennia, to that first council at which Reason humbled Power and the first stirring for Justice overruled the hunger of Force.

"Although composed of only five persons representing as many national states and cultures, this Tribunal speaks for all of those nations represented by this United Nations Assembly. I say this because it is my belief that the essential legitimacy of this Court lies not so much in precedent as it does in the collective conscience of mankind.

"There are those who will argue that my preceding statement is in no way founded upon reality. It cannot be, since the jurists of the Tribunal represent basically the Western nations, with no voices from the cultures of Asia or Africa. To such a challenge I may reply as follows: through his acts, Adolf Hitler and the Nazi Germany he led were a phenomenon particular to Western Europe. Even though the seeds of this extraordinary event were scattered across the globe, it is, I believe, the responsibility of those whom his actions touched in a most direct fashion to sit in judgment upon him.

"The legitimacy of this Tribunal has not been contested by the defense or, to date, by any other third party. Nonetheless, it would be proper and correct for the Court to state the basis upon which its jurisdiction is founded.

"The grounds of legitimacy in the case of the Nuremberg court lay within the governing authority of the Four Powers which occupied Germany and in the fundamental right of such an authority to administer the law. While this Court sees itself as a descendant of Nuremberg, it is nonetheless different in several respects.

"As a sovereign state, the Federal Republic of Germany had, under international law, the right to refuse to have one of its citizens tried by a foreign body. The fact that the Federal Republic assented to surrender this individual to the custody of this Court endows this body with not only jurisdiction but powers as well. In the same manner that a state, recognized and accepted by the international community, may formulate and enforce its laws, so too a court, one recognized by those who wish to come before it, becomes a *living* entity with full judicial powers. Therefore, while this Tribunal is not responsible to any one state, in the strict definition of the word 'state,' it is recognized by sovereign nations. Proof of this recognition is reflected in the constitution of the Bench, which is made up of a number of nationalities.

"I would now like to state as clearly as possible the principles of this Court so that all may understand the compass of these hearings.

"Our fundamental premise rests on the belief that any person who commits an act constituting a crime under international law is liable to punishment whether or not such an act is considered an offense under the laws of his own nation. Further, the responsibility for such a transgression may not be evaded if the accused has been head of state during its commission, or if his role was one of complicity and not initiation. In this case of war crimes, the Bench has taken painstaking measures to ensure that the accused has fully understood the indictment against him and has been rendered legal representation of his choice. The work of the Bench seems to me to have been adequate in both regards, and it is the Court's belief that the foundation has been established for the most important element of these proceedings: a fair trial for the accused, based on the facts of the charges laid against him, governed by the procedure enunciated in the Nuremberg Court. Insofar as this Court is, in effect, an extraordinary body, gathered for this one sitting only, the rules of evidence may, to observers with judicial experience, appear inconsistent with common practice. The Bench wishes to state for the record that deviations from procedural norms have been carefully instituted and only after consultation with and agreement of counsel for both prosecution and defense. This point applies especially to the prosecution's right to examine the defendant without his first having been called to testify by his own attorney; conversely, the defendant may, upon consideration, refuse to answer those prosecution questions he considers may lead to self-incrimination.

"Finally, I cannot emphasize too strongly that it is for the carriage of justice, not retribution or automatic punishment, that we have convened this Court, and such carriage we guarantee.

"It is on these precepts that the Tribunal is founded," Sir Adrian said. "The power to consider the actions of the accused within the framework are bestowed upon it by the Bonn Declaration.

"Initially the Declaration issued by the West German Government agreed only that the accused be tried outside his country of residence. However, the said government has since agreed to the following amendment: that the Tribunal has full powers to render a verdict in this case and that such a verdict both is binding and permits no appeal.

"It is also within the authority of this Tribunal to order the exact method by which punishment, if any, shall be administered and by what jurisdiction."

Sir Adrian paused and stared out at the Assembly in the serenity of the blind.

"This Court," he intoned softly, "is all too aware of the responsibility it has undertaken. May we, its members, find the strength and temperance within ourselves to act as persons of conscience and good judgment, always remembering that we sit in the sight of the Lord."

The awesome purport of Sir Adrian's address cast a terrible silence over the Assembly, but Adolf Hitler removed his translation earphones and said mockingly to Toller, "Is there a sixth jurist we knew nothing of?"

"The prosecution shall now make its opening remarks and introduce the indictment."

Hans Kleemann pressed his palms against the table and, leaning heavily on them, rose. He pinched the bridge of his nose between thumb and forefinger, pushing his glasses closer to his eyes. For a moment, Kleemann looked around himself—at the Bench, at the table of the accused and further to the Assembly beyond the shield. He felt like a skier poised on the precipice of a mountain run.

"His Lordship has spoken of the magnitude of the task," Hans Kleemann said slowly.

"I cannot recall when in history a man's crimes have been better known, or more intimately explored; his motives more minutely scrutinized; his subordinates and accomplices more universally condemned. Nor, as in the case of Nuremberg, was justice ever left more undone when he who was responsible for the destruction of his nation and the infliction of unspeakable pain upon the world remained undiscovered and so escaped judgment. I ask the Court and all those who are listening to erase the twenty-five years that separate this hour from the final ones of the Third Reich. Re-create the image of all the destruction as if it were happening today; only then will you truly understand what it is that is at stake here.

"The poet Goethe said of my own people, 'It is the German destiny to make everything difficult'; and it was a constrained set of circumstances in which the German people found themselves after the First Great War. In a shattered land, the human spirit was deflated: self-respect, hope, compassion, sound judgment lay in ruins.

"The conditions of life in Weimar Germany forced aside any objective considerations of right and wrong, good and evil. There weren't enough good men, strong and diligent, to guide the nation through its post–Great War experiment in democracy, to sustain a viable economy and stable government. Nor, perhaps most tragically, were there safeguards in the constitution to prevent a convicted criminal such as Hitler, who had organized the abortive 1924 Munich Putsch, from manipulating his way into power. In a helpless land, Hitler used the currency of despair to establish the image of himself as savior of the people. He accomplished this because he recognized that what the German of that time wished for was decisiveness; an action—right or wrong—that would reflect strength instead of indecision, passion in place of despair.

"So, on the seizing of power in 1933, a gruesome act accomplished over the myopia of the dying President Hindenburg, this man created a title, that of Führer, and with it a principle: the Führerprinzip. In one stroke, a people who had believed in nothing were suddenly endowed with a godhead, who created his own high priests, who in turn nurtured a crowd of the faithful. The hierarchy was established; one had only to wait a little before it would, through *orders*, become a living, vibrant mechanism.

"One can state with certainty that had the hierarchy not been created, and more important, had the Führerprinzip not been established, the orders themselves would never have come into being.

"This is precisely where the guilt of Adolf Hitler lies, a culpability and complicity he cannot deny or turn away from: as godhead of a new, terrifying religion; as head of state, he alone manipulated the course of Germany. It was in his mind that the conceptions were born: they became reality through the willingness of his minions to obey. If Adolf Hitler has any defense, it lies in the stupidity and myopia of the world at that time. He presented it with *Mein Kampf*, whose words could lead nowhere but to the gas chambers; and the world, to its eternal shame, ignored them."

Hans Kleemann returned to his table and passed his hand over the stack of dossiers and papers.

"Let no one be deceived by this small collection of documents which is the basis of the prosecution's arguments," Kleemann warned. "The magnitude of our task would seem to dictate an equal representation of information and evidence. Yet is this necessary?"

He picked up one sheet of paper and began to read:

"The prosecution has called for an indictment on three counts:

" *'One:* The willful waging of aggression.

" *'Two:* War crimes relevant to battlefield conduct.

" *'Three:* Crimes against humanity.'

"Each count shall be represented by a single example, illuminated by others if need be. It is the prosecution's belief that whether a man has committed one crime of a given magnitude or many, the penalty he must pay is no different. One life or twenty million, justice can be done only once. But it must be done."

Hans Kleemann had finished and now he sat down, breathing hard as though he had been relieved of some tremendous burden. The pulse of his blood sang in his ears, and he could hear the echo of his words reverberate around him. His presentation had been strong—he could feel that; but as was his nature, he wondered if any one point might have been amplified, or if he had overlooked an opportunity to augment his case. He did not think so.

"The Court will now hear the statements of the defense," Sir Adrian declared.

Toller did not rise at once. From his seat, he looked up at the face of each justice; he then whispered something to Adolf Hitler. When he finally spoke, his voice was hard and opaque, that of an angry man.

"Dr. Kleemann has spoken most eloquently," Toller said, with the faintest trace of sarcasm. "And I could not agree with him more: this trial represents the single most important judicial event of the century, perhaps the millennium. But I must differ with my august colleague as to *why* it carries such significance.

"The prosecutor has spoken of reexamining the alleged guilt of Adolf Hitler, a process he believes will reiterate the verdict that history has passed. I say he is wrong. The object of these proceedings is to present the world with a new understanding of just who this man called Hitler is. So while I agree that there will be reexamination, I state that the object of the trial is to relieve

Adolf Hitler of the guilt placed upon him by default, to lift the veil of misinterpretation that has lain across the eyes of two generations.

"Interpretation—or rather, reinterpretation," Toller asserted, "is the essence of this trial. The prosecution has given us one idea, its particular vision, of what Germany was like in the twenties and thirties. I wish to compliment Dr. Kleemann on his exposition; but the conclusions it reached were, I fear, quite misleading and, in some instances, altogether erroneous. For instance: Dr. Kleemann posits that after the ignominy of defeat in the First World War, followed by the severe sanctions the victors imposed on Germany, and then the Great Depression, a spiritual vacuum was created within Germany. A time of hardship, fear and bitterness. But one cannot blithely go on to say that, presto! into this emptiness Fate placed Adolf Hitler. There was, after all," Helmut Toller said in a silken tone, "the glorious Weimar Republic. To understand his ascendancy to this position one must glance back to see what authority he legally replaced—not, as the prosecution would have us believe, usurped.

"It will be remembered that the German people, after the Great War, forced Wilhelm the Second to abdicate and take refuge in Holland. In place of the Imperial Reich, there came, for the first time, a democratic form of government in Germany.

"And this government was to last a full fourteen years!" Helmut Toller shouted at once. "Fourteen years is a large vacuum, is it not? Quite enough time to worsen an already bad situation!

"Consider, if you will, these factors. There were at least five parties vying for the electorate's vote—not to mention the anarchists and Communists, who were doing their best to interfere with everyone concerned. The result of proportional representation was the impossibility of electing any single party to the Reichstag. This resulted, in turn, in coalitions, which dissolved whenever a crisis occurred. The upshot was this: at a time when the German people were desperate for a government, there was none! And because of this oversight, there was no one to speak for Germany when the Versailles Treaty brought down its fist upon a nation already prostrate. No statesman arose to mention that such a treaty was infamous in its contents and, morally, contrary to the spirit of Woodrow Wilson's Fourteen Points and the principles of the League of Nations—of which, I must add, Germany was a member. No legalist challenged the ignoble Article 231 of the Treaty which placed *all* the blame for the war upon Germany. No Finance Minister ever explained to an already penniless population why they would have to pay whatever reparations the Allies decreed, the sum to be set at some future date. No general came forward, even as a gesture, when in 1923, on the pretext of a minor default in payments, the French Army chose to humiliate Germany by occupying the Ruhr.

"Yes, there was a vacuum in Germany, compounded by sorrow and tragedy, and for the thousands who died in it, that was all there ever was!"

Helmut Toller pushed his fingers through his thick hair, leaving the impression of a man confronted and confused by stupidity.

"Dr. Kleemann has insinuated that Adolf Hitler became leader of the German Republic not only by default but in a ghoulish manner. This is politically inaccurate. Article 48 of the Weimar Constitution provided an emergency clause which permitted the Chancellor to suspend civil law and, in its place, impose martial order when faced with possible insurrection. Given the severe economic conditions of the early thirties, and the memory of the brief Communist domination of Bavaria in 1918–1919, Adolf Hitler, in his legitimate assumption of power in 1933 endorsed by President Hindenburg, acted well within the letter of the constitution and in accordance with the spirit in which it had been written—that is, one which had in mind the security and safety of the country.

"There is no question not only that as of July 31, 1932, when the National Socialist Party drew 37 percent of the popular vote, Adolf Hitler was the leader of the strongest, democratically elected party, but also that he was, for all intents and purposes, a legitimate head of state. It is for acts committed in that capacity, between the years 1939 and 1945, that he is being tried, a quarter century after the events. I should like to state at this juncture that it is the defense's intention to plead not guilty to each count of the indictment.

"It will be demonstrated that it is impossible for the Court to return anything but a verdict of innocence because Adolf Hitler, as was the case with the Emperor of Japan, may not be held

responsible for the acts of his subordinates. The Court will remember that at the conclusion of hostilities in the Far East, the
prevailing political opinion was that Emperor Hirohito, as the
physical embodiment of Japan's imperial war policy, could have
been held responsible for encouraging, fostering and finally directing the war policies of his nation. Yet the Emperor was never
tried, even though there was allegedly ample evidence of his complicity. If, a quarter century ago, the Emperor of Japan was ex-
empt from retribution, it is inconceivable that any kind of judicial
action be taken against Adolf Hitler.

"Secondly, the defense will demonstrate that Adolf Hitler has,
for the last twenty-five years, conducted himself in the manner of
a model citizen, one who not only is respected in Germany, but
would be welcome in any country in the civilized world. We shall
also show that such respect is tangible, in the form of testimonials
the defense has gathered from witnesses who have known Adolf
Hitler for this time. In short, it is one of the major responsibilities
of the defense to shatter forever the monstrous image which popular imagination has woven of Adolf Hitler and which may prejudice these proceedings."

Helmut Toller came directly before the judicial podium and
looked into the face of each jurist.

"We shall," he concluded softly, "rewrite history in the days
to come and, to borrow from Pushkin, we shall show who is right
and who is wrong in *this* furious age."

Morozov was the final man Toller confronted. He saw the terrible anger in the Russian's eyes as the words of the great Slavic
poet were thrown at him.

There was silence as Helmut Toller returned to his table. He
glanced at Adolf Hitler, but the impassive features betrayed neither satisfaction with nor objection to the manner in which the
lawyer had presented the issues.

The President of the Court was speaking.

"I thank both the prosecution and the defense for their statements concerning their respective positions.

"I am told that the time is half past one in the afternoon.
Because of this, I would suggest the Court recess until tomorrow
morning so that the expositions concerning the first indictment
may be undertaken with a view to concluding them the same
day."

As Sir Adrian rose from his seat, so the entire Assembly came to its feet and watched as the inhabitants of the world behind the shield made their way out.

He had seen crowds like this only at the May Day Parades in Moscow. Major Kuzmin had come out of the General Assembly Building and was standing on the plaza facing the street. Beyond the elegantly crafted iron fence were thousands of people, an immovable force which had caused all traffic to cease along First Avenue. Along the perimeter of the U.N. compound scores of police in riot dress had lined up, although the crowd made no attempt to penetrate the international territory.

Holding one hand at his brow against the brilliance of the sun, Kuzmin recognized the majority of them as Jews. Held aloft in the crowd were many flags of Israel and placards, in Hebrew and English, demanding death for the exterminator. Yet for all the passion he felt streaming from the people, they were strangely silent. Moving closer, Kuzmin looked down upon the faces, vacant, sorrowful, indignant or bewildered, that stared back at him.

"Where is he?" a woman screamed at him. "Where is the murderer? Show him to us!"

She struggled free of the crowd and ran at the cordon. Two of the police grabbed her and, picking her off the ground, marched her back. The woman was still screaming, her head twisted in Kuzmin's direction, although he was certain she couldn't see him. The sight brought back vicious memories to Kuzmin, when, after a village had been liberated, whatever townspeople had survived had (using only their bare hands) turned on the fleeing Nazi soldiers and dismembered them.

That would be the simplest and most honest form of justice, Kuzmin thought. Give him over to those whose lives he mangled and walk away.

Kuzmin raised his hand as though this would show the woman that he understood her wish. But she had disappeared and he could no longer pick her out of the crowd.

"The prosecution calls upon Adolf Hitler to take the stand!"

He rose, supporting himself by the table with his good arm,

then limped across the carpeting and took his seat in the comfortable chair in the witness box. Calmly Adolf Hitler looked out
over the Assembly once again, passing his gaze over it like a
feudal lord surveying his vassals. He could sense the anticipation
in faces that were turned on him, in the eyes that urgently sought
his. After a silence of a quarter century, the world was once more
awaiting his words.

"I must ask you to stand while the oath is being administered,"
Hans Kleemann admonished him.

"A man's word is different whether he is seated or standing?"
Adolf Hitler queried. But he rose nonetheless.

"Which Bible would you prefer?" Sir Adrian asked him.

"Neither. My oath is sufficient."

"Do you so give it and swear to reply truthfully to any and all
questions put to you?"

"Yes, yes!" Hitler snapped impatiently.

"The prosecution is satisfied that such a declaration is binding
upon the accused," Kleemann said, addressing the Bench. "In
the interest of saving time and ensuring an orderly progression I
am prepared to carry on."

"The Bench will consider the accused bound," Sir Adrian intoned. "Proceed."

"You are Adolf Hitler, Führer of what was known as the Third
Reich."

"Yes."

"The name you have lived under for the last twenty-five years
is Werner Busse."

"Yes."

"And the facts listed as supplemental information to the indictment—where you have resided, your occupation and so on—are
all correct?"

"Yes."

"On August 2, 1934, you proclaimed yourself, upon the demise
of President Hindenburg, head of state and commander-in-chief
of the armed forces in addition to your current post at the time,
leader of the National Socialist Party?"

"Yes."

"And did you not require that all members of the armed forces
swear the following allegiance: 'Before God I swear this sacred

oath: that I will render unconditional allegiance to Adolf Hitler, the Führer of the German Reich and people, Supreme Commander of the Armed Forces, and as a brave soldier will at all times be ready to lay down my life in fulfillment of this oath'?''

"Many took the oath, and for a time, all lived by it," Adolf Hitler said softly. "It wasn't until the last days that the cancer of betrayal set in. Even then it was not evident in the common soldier."

"You therefore do not dispute that all social, political and military matters had yours as the final voice."

"That was the Führerprinzip," Hitler stated, not without pride. "Previously, responsibility resided in the highest offices and represented the power of the anonymous electorate. Now authority went from above to below, and through our system of Gauleiters, Kreisleiters and Blockleiters, information on the people's reactions to such authority returned to the top."

"Therefore, the ultimate responsibility for all acts committed by your subordinates would rest with you."

"Objection!" Toller was on his feet. "The only actions of a subordinate for which a superior may be assigned responsibility are those in which direct orders were issued. Even then, there is a possibility that directives had been misinterpreted by the lesser rank."

"Would you agree with your counsel's objection?" the prosecutor demanded of Hitler.

"What is it you are really asking, Kleemann?" Hitler asked him slyly.

"The acts of your subordinates—from Goering through to Frank, Eichmann and the lowliest SS corporal in Belsen—would have been founded on one of two things or both: an exact written or oral command or an exact interpretation of a veiled command, whose meaning was quite clear if not stated in so many words?"

"The prosecution should make up its mind as to what the question is!" Toller shouted.

"Prosecutor, I understand what it is you are groping for," Hitler said mildly. "You had only to say it, you know. Yes, there are two methods by which to issue a command, explicit and implied. But I must say you are wrong about the chain of command's reaching that far down the ranks."

"But did you not just say that more often than not it was the members of that rank, the soldiers who had taken their oath to you, who carried out your orders most completely?" Kleemann challenged.

"Yes." Hitler shrugged.

"So you agree, then: whether or not action was taken in accordance with certain meanings you gave to words, in the end it was you, and you alone, who held the power to issue commands in the Third Reich?"

"Yes."

"And you find no quarrel with Goering's statement that so long as you were the Führer of Germany, you alone determined the conduct and leadership of the war?"

"That is correct."

"And for the internal social policies of Germany which were later applied in conquered territories?"

"I am not clear as to your meaning."

"Euthanasia; the establishment of concentration camps."

"Ah yes, that tiresome question of the camps . . ."

"Again I must protest!" Toller said vehemently. "I assume the prosecution is dealing in sequence with the points of the indictment. What went on in Germany internally before and during the war has nothing to do with the alleged waging of aggression!"

"It has everything to do with it!" Hans Kleemann thundered at him. "How, in the name of reason, can you argue that the establishment of the Gestapo and SS was not the initial experiment from which methods and techniques would evolve to be later used throughout Europe? How can you believe that the model concentration camps of Dachau and Theresienstadt were not forerunners of the Eastern death camps?"

"The defense appeals to the Bench to put an end to this spectacle," Toller said coldly. "This is no arena in which to discuss the internal policies of what had once been a free nation. It is a breach of state sovereignty to challenge the domestic workings of any country!"

Hans Kleemann reacted to the words as though they had struck him physically.

"I will forgo further mention of this apparently objectionable issue," he said bitterly, "until such time as we have concluded the first two counts of the indictment."

He turned back to Hitler.

"On November 5, 1937, you summoned six generals of the High Command—three of whom, I might add, you would replace in a matter of days—and discussed with them the German need for 'Lebensraum'—living space."

"Yes."

"You also stated that Germany would have to move against Czechoslovakia and Austria sometime in the period between 1943 and 1945, when the Reich military strength would be a deterrent against French and British forces."

"Ah, let me correct you. That was my first schedule. I later decided that 1938 would be a more auspicious time."

"But we can establish November 5, 1937, as the date on which you, and you alone, decided to implement a policy of aggression."

"Aggression," Hitler murmured. "In my view it was liberation. You must remember, Prosecutor, that there was a substantial German population in both countries, a kinship of the blood which transcended mere politics. As leader of the German peoples, I had a responsibility for those living beyond the frontiers of the Reich, and I exercised my power as concerned this responsibility just as the French defended their precious settlers in Algeria two decades later."

"Austria and Czechoslovakia were sovereign nations," Kleemann reminded him. "Your counsel has gone to great lengths to demonstrate how wrong interference in a nation's business is. Are you suggesting that there may be an exception?"

"When members of your race are living in a different land, the idea of sovereignty extends into that land."

Kleemann did not press the issue with Hitler. His point had been made, and he was satisfied; but he reiterated his conclusion for the Court.

"It is clear, then, that the defendant was solely responsible for the birth of the idea of aggression against two states which posed no threat to the Reich and whose denial of sovereignty was an act calculated months before the event. On November 5, 1937, Adolf

Hitler conspired with members of the General Staff to break international law; on March 12, 1938, when the forces of Germany swept into Austria, a physical violation of that law, which guaranteed the borders of Austria, occurred.

"And next it was the turn of the Czechoslovaks," he shouted at Hitler.

"Prosecutor, do not raise your voice to me," Hitler said coldly. "It is obvious you understand nothing of contemporary history. On May 21, 1938, the Czechoslovak government partially mobilized its armed forces. There was no choice but for me to react immediately to protect the rights of Sudeten Germans living in that country."

"Again using the excuse of an extension of German sovereignty?" Kleemann retorted.

"I should like to bring to the Court's attention . . ." Toller, standing, head bowed and shaking slowly, a picture of the provincial schoolmaster before a truant child, appealed to the Bench. "I *must* point out that in 1938, there were three major powers that held mutual-assistance pacts with Czechoslovakia: Great Britain, France and the Soviet Union. The first two, represented by Neville Chamberlain and Édouard Daladier, respectively, counseled the Czech government of Dr. Beneš to yield the Sudetenland. It was obvious that both parties believed Czechoslovakia was not a country worth going to war over. The second admission made by these two figures, although tacit, was that Adolf Hitler was not incorrect in voicing his concern over the Sudeten Germans. This recognition by two major powers of Germany's right to care for its people beyond the frontier would argue in favor of what Adolf Hitler has been stating all this time: a natural extension of national sovereignty. If any proof of such recognition is needed, we have only to glance at the Agreement of September 29, 1938, signed by the three countries mentioned, plus Italy.

"Now, as to the position of the Soviet Union, in spite of its mutual-assistance pact with Czechoslovakia, it abstained from entering the discussions.

"I must therefore submit that there was no aggression in the case of Czechoslovakia; and if the prosecutor wishes to pursue this questioning and insinuation—*three decades after the event*—

then so long as one man, Adolf Hitler, is being tried on this particular count, I shall have to charge Great Britain, France and Italy with conspiracy in this alleged action."

Yes, of course, Kleemann thought. Accuse three other parties, tie their acts to that of the accused—and if one attempts to prove the innocence of the three, then it is impossible for the fourth to be guilty!

"But if the defense contends that other parties must share the blame for the partitioning of Czechoslovakia," Kleemann reasoned, "it certainly cannot contest the fact that the troops, tanks and armored divisions that poured into Czechoslovakia at three fifteen on the morning of March 15, 1939, were those of the German Army."

He walked to his table and picked up a sheet of paper from which he read: " 'It is my intention to smash Czechoslovakia by military action in the immediate future without provocation, unless an unavoidable development of political conditions inside Czechoslovakia forces the issue or political events in Europe create a favorable opportunity that may never recur.'

"Further, in the case of Poland, does the accused deny that on August 22, 1939, he said, in a speech to members of his General Staff: 'The destruction of Poland stands in the foreground. The aim is the elimination of her fighting forces. I shall give a propagandist cause for starting the war. Never mind whether it is plausible or not . . .'?

"Well it was not plausible, but enough to push the world into war! On August 31, 1939, a half dozen prisoners from a concentration camp were drugged, dressed in uniforms of the Polish Army and shot near the Gleiwitz transmitter station. Claiming that that installation had been attacked by Polish regulars, Adolf Hitler ordered the invasion of Poland!

"Honored jurists, I feel that the essential question is this: does Adolf Hitler deny that at his command and instigation, Nazi Germany was led into a series of aggressive acts of war? Can he disclaim sole responsibility for issuing the commands that initiated each campaign? In short, is it not obvious that he is the very embodiment of war, unchallenged and undisputed?"

Adolf Hitler stared at Hans Kleemann with open contempt, angered by the incredible gulf between their perceptions and his actions, actions that to this day he believed right, beyond criticism and reproach.

"Prosecutor," he declared, "do you not know that since the beginning of time, war has been an instrument of man, a tool for him to employ in his dealings with other men?

"As head of the Third Reich, I used violence to haul my nation from that pit into which the rest of Europe had thrown it. I sought to unite my people in the same manner as the English continue to do in Ireland, or as the French attempted in Algeria. I ask you, Prosecutor: where does my sin differ from theirs? On this count, aggression, why am I presumed more guilty than they surely are?"

Suddenly everything seemed terribly still to Kleemann, as though this examination of Hitler were taking place not in a vast assembly but back in Germany, on the porch of his country home. Kleemann looked up at the Bench and saw each face, save that of the blind man, looking down upon Hitler. He turned and, in the world beyond the shield, witnessed the same phenomenon: all eyes were upon Hitler, and all present were silent, as though what Hitler had said, in a voice so quiet, so rational and persuasive, had impressed or shamed them. Was it only he, who stood inches from the man, who could recognize the malicious glee that burned in those fathomless eyes?

Hans Kleemann gathered together his strength and set out to shatter this spell. "The essence of my argument," he said in a dangerous soft tone, "recalls the Court's enunciation of its basic premise that a man may not escape the consequences of his actions. While you saw your goal, that of uniting the German people through acts of aggression, as a just cause, the upshot of your ambition proved to be destructive. You not only destroyed tens of millions of people by your thirst born of vengeance, but condemned your own nation to everlasting shame."

Adolf Hitler rose and leaned forward, about to answer back, when the prosecutor cut him off.

"The witness may leave the box," Kleemann instructed him. "But he remains under his own oath nonetheless."

Startled and angered by the prosecutor's curt dismissal, Hitler looked across at Helmut Toller, but he was motioning him to step down. For a moment it appeared Hitler would refuse, standing and staring balefully at the back of Hans Kleemann. "You may step down," Etta Kirsch repeated. Hitler turned on her with a furious expression, but slowly he made his way down the steps from the witness box and returned to the defense table.

"The prosecution calls upon Gerhard Stephanus!"

A murmur swelled among the delegates of the Assembly. The name was not unfamiliar to most of them, but they asked themselves if it was possible for the prosecutor to bring forward the Stephanus almost all had heard of, but whom very few had ever seen.

The door opened and a short gentleman, no more than five feet six inches, came into the court. He walked briskly, with a military step and an authority that appeared inbred rather than acquired. Beneath the dark prescription glasses, which covered part of his eyebrows and descended almost to his cheeks, lay a thick iron-gray moustache, clipped neatly above the upper lip. As a result of the glasses there was nothing distinguishable about his features other than the few broken veins along the side of the nose; similarly, the gray suit he wore allowed him to blend into his surroundings, making him almost invisible. It was both a fitting entrance and a fitting effect for the man regarded as the world's former leading spymaster.

Stephanus took the stand and responded in a very soft tone when the oath was administered to him. All the while he was staring in the direction of Adolf Hitler. Whether he was looking directly at his former commander-in-chief was impossible to tell; only the telltale shadow of a smile offered an enticing clue as to his thoughts.

"Would you state your full name and rank," Kleemann asked him shortly.

"Gerhard Stephanus, major-general, retired."

"Your occupation?"

"Until three months ago I was director of the West German Security Service, the BND."

"How long had you been in that position?"

"Twenty-three and a half years—since the Service was established after the war."

"You were its founder?"

"I was."

"And prior to that? What was your position during the war?"

"Director of Intelligence, General Staff Operations Sections, responsible for Foreign Armies East—the intelligence organ designed to gather and evaluate information on Soviet offensives."

"But this posting came only in 1942. What was your position in 1935?"

"That year marked my entry into General Staff Command. I held the rank of major."

"And in 1936?"

"My work was brought to the attention of Colonel-General Franz Halder, Chief of Staff of the army. In the fall of that year I became his chief aide."

"How would you describe your duties at that time?"

"They were those of a soldier—to plan and prepare for war."

"Your association with Halder brought you into direct contact with Adolf Hitler?"

"Yes, on several occasions I had the privilege of presenting briefs to the Führer."

"I would ask you to describe to this court the meeting between Hitler and the Chief of Staff on December 13, 1939, three months after Neville Chamberlain's visit to Munich."

"Yes, very well."

Stephanus paused for a moment, as though organizing his thoughts, then began.

"I remember that particular meeting quite clearly. It took place in the War Office, in Chief of Staff Herder's suite and not, as was usually the case, at the Reichschancellery. It was also extraordinary because Hitler brought with him Himmler, Goering, Minister of Propaganda Goebbels and Chief of the SS Heydrich; normally Hitler preferred to deal with the military by himself.

"When Hitler entered, Herder and I had already laid out the various maps and dossiers that had been requested. The meeting, we had been told, should deal in generalities, an overview of the military capabilities and positions of the various European powers. Neither Herder nor I expected very much to come out of such a conference; both of us believed Hitler merely wanted another briefing, just to keep his hand in with the armed forces. You see, he was always conscious of the fact that his responsibilities took him away from the military sphere, and while he enjoyed politics, the army remained his first love.

"He was in good spirits that morning. He came over to Herder and addressed him by his first name, then turned to me and did the same. There was no standing on ceremony on this occasion. Hitler removed his cap, straightened his military tunic and walked over to the magnificent windows which overlooked the street. I don't know whom it was he saw on Unter den Linden, but Hitler smiled and waved.

" 'You have such a beautiful office,' he said, turning to Herder. 'It is better than mine. More sunlight, a better view. How did you manage it?'

"This was one very rare occasion on which Herder was at a loss for words. He had started to answer when Hitler came over, slapped him on the back and said he shouldn't worry, Hitler had no designs on it. He laughed, and Himmler laughed also; finally Goebbels and Goering as well. Herder just shook his head in incomprehension; no one had seen Hitler behave in such a garrulous, easy manner before.

"He sat down behind Herder's elegant Empire desk and with the General's silver letter knife beckoned all of us to come forward. Himmler was told to bring over the maps Herder had arranged on the other table—which he did, but they were all topsy-turvy by the time he had finished. Hitler poked at them with the knife, then looked up at Herder.

" 'So far what I have seen here,' he said—he tapped the maps—'has been translated well out there'—and he looked out the window.

"Hitler—I recall this very distinctly—was speaking in a low, almost funereal tone, again out of keeping with his character, since he tended to become very vociferous where military affairs were concerned.

" 'The military,' he continued, 'has distinguished itself in the task I set before it—namely, by the bringing together of all Germans into the Greater Reich. The SS and Gestapo have done equally well in uprooting Bolshevism and international Jewry on our sacred soil. This battle shall continue until we are completely victorious and not a single polluter is left within our borders.

Now I see our nation as standing on the verge of yet another challenge, far grander than any we have yet had to face.

" 'I believe, my dear General, that the time has come for the great German armies to smash Europe open like the rotten fruit it is!' Hitler concluded.

"I could tell that Herder was shocked by the force of such words, but he maintained absolute control; unless one knew him well, as I did, one could have said there was no reaction whatsoever. Yet it was clear to me that Herder, whose intelligence sources stretched into Hitler's personal office and normally forewarned him of what Hitler might say, was taken aback. He had hoped, as we all did, that the expansionist policies would stop after Czechoslovakia, or Danzig. It seemed to us that Hitler had accomplished his goal: the rearmament of Germany and achievement of economic stability. We also believed, because of Italy's Ethiopian adventure, that he understood the feeble nature of his allies. But that was not the case at all. He was heady with the elation of easy success; and—it must be admitted—so were many on the General Staff.

"Herder considered Hitler's question for what seemed a very long time. From time to time he would look at the others in the room in an abstract way, as though looking through them. He then rose, and cutting a most impressive figure, he said, 'The armies, my Führer, shall march where you say they shall march.'

"It was the subtlest yet also the most eloquent capitulation. You see, Hitler now had his anvil."

Gerhard Stephanus permitted himself the semblance of a smile, a faint creasing of the lips; but because of the glasses, which hid the truth expressed in the eyes, the gesture was lost on most.

"After Herder had said this, the meeting got down to order. We all moved over to the larger desk, and this time the maps were handled in a different fashion—as a soldier would treat them: cleanly, with respect. As Europe was spread out before us, Hitler pointed—or rather, jabbed—at various countries, as a butcher might jab at pork. He put questions to Herder: Was he certain that the Poles did not have a Trojan horse, in the form of a highly mechanized army, hidden away somewhere? Could he guarantee that the thrust through Belgium and the Netherlands would ensure passage into France, or should the Maginot Line be bombed first, to give the army another operating flank? Could the Panzer divisions under Guderian burst through French defenses, at the same time inflicting such casualties and damage that it would be impossible for the French to regroup and re-form? To these interrogatives, Hitler expected and received detailed answers from Herder. He also put a number of questions about military intelligence matters to me and appeared satisfied with what I told him.

"The meeting lasted perhaps four hours or a little longer . . . four hours to dismember Europe as one would a carcass. I could almost smell the blood that would soon flow. There could be no question in anyone's mind what it was Hitler was proposing: it was, quite simply, the most total war Europe had ever known."

"Did Goering or any of the others make significant contributions to the discussions?" the prosecutor asked him.

"Oh, Goering made some noises about the invincibility of the Luftwaffe," Stephanus responded with a shrug. "But he was always going on about his precious air fleet. Himmler and Heydrich said nothing at all; Goebbels interrupted once or twice with queries about propaganda matters. He was chafing at the bit to announce the invasion—any invasion: it didn't matter!"

"In your mind, did this meeting reveal anything about Hitler's intentions of which you had been ignorant before?"

"The details were brought out into the open. We in the military had never believed, not in our hearts, that we had been rearmed simply to march about parade grounds. That was not the German way. We had all heard the rumors about expansionism; we had our own intelligence on the subject. But that meeting marked the first time that I knew exactly what it was Hitler intended and how he was going about attaining his objective. War was his tool, and he had elected to use it."

"Thank you, General Stephanus," Hans Kleemann said.

Turning to address the Court, the prosecutor stated, "Such a charge has been substantiated by the testimony of former General Stephanus, and his expertise on the matter is not in doubt. I repeat: no matter what the motive, the fact of the matter is that Adolf Hitler, willfully and with premeditation, contravened international law, and he not only is guilty of complicity in this action but is totally responsible for its inception."

As Hans Kleemann walked back to his desk, the Soviet jurist Morozov inquired, "Does defense counsel wish to question the witness?"

"I would ask the witness to remain seated," Helmut Toller said. "I may have need of him."

Toller rose and approached the stand, but he did not address Gerhard Stephanus directly.

"I should like," he opened, "to deal with the fundamental point: that aggressive war was never a crime under international law. The Kellogg-Briand Pact of 1928 delineated no boundary between aggression and self-defense. As for the League of Nations, on a number of occasions when one member of the League was engaged in hostilities with another, the League did no more than condemn such a set of circumstances. Never did it believe an international tribunal should be arranged to try the politicians and generals leading the contenders. The United Nations, following in the footsteps of its predecessor, has no authority to bring together such a juridical instrumentality. Therefore we are not dealing with the intentions of an international body, and must base ourselves in fact: that the Third Reich under the leadership of Adolf Hitler committed no known crime in international law when its armies annexed Austria and Czechoslovakia and repelled the Polish attack.

"*Nulla poena sine lege.* This is the operative principle: no punishment without a penal law in force at the time of the commission of the act. It would be, in terms of existing laws, impossible to punish a head of state or condemn the behavior of a nation strictly on *post facto* law. From time immemorial in the courts of the civilized world this dictum has been honored and obeyed.

"Furthermore, it cannot be forgotten, as Adolf Hitler has mentioned, that the Third Reich was scarcely the only nation acting in an offensive manner. Aside from the complicity of the French and British in German action, there is the issue of the Soviet Union.

"We forget the Russo-Finnish conflict in the winter of 1939–1940, in which the Soviet Union, citing the concept of sovereignty, disregarded the objections of the League in regard to this adventure. Even though the League's condemnation was unanimous, no statesman came forward with the suggestion that the Soviet leadership who instigated the hostilities should be brought before any international tribunal and tried for alleged acts of aggression. It must therefore follow that one nation cannot be punished for the same acts which another nation committed free of any culpability. One cannot presume to try the leader of one nation while at the same time, because of shifting alliances, choosing to overlook identical acts of another leader."

Helmut Toller looked up composedly at the Court and continued.

"There is one other principle I wish to bring to the Court's attention: that an individual cannot bear guilt for acts of state. It must be remembered that whenever we speak of aggression, we refer to it in terms of *the Reich's* aggression, not that of Adolf Hitler, Hermann Goering, Himmler or the obscure Corporal Schmidt, the everyday soldier. No one man, even if he is head of state, may be held responsible for the actions of that state. When the prosecution links together Adolf Hitler and the Third Reich, and states that the actions of one are the responsibility of the other, it is moving against the essential concept of state sovereignty, for the actions of a state, an entity in itself, may not be so joined to those of an individual.

"I recall here the quandary of the Israeli court when faced with this very issue in the Eichmann case. The question then—and it has not been satisfactorily resolved—was whether Eichmann had ever committed a single war crime *with his own hand*—that is to say, as an individual man, as opposed to a state functionary. In a most dubious manner the prosecution dredged up an account whereby Eichmann had been personally involved in the death of a thirteen-year-old Jewish youth. In so doing, it linked that one crime to Eichmann's actions as head of Section 4 B IV of the SS, the department of the so-called Final Solution.

"But I believe the most adamant refusal to link together the acts of a head of state with those of the state itself was shown by General Douglas MacArthur at the conclusion of the Pacific war.

"During the Yamashita trial it was demonstrated that Emperor Hirohito had actively participated in the conspiracy to expand Japan's political and economic boundaries through force.

"In spite of his knowledge, MacArthur never once thought of trying the Emperor of Japan for war crimes.

"If the logic of the prosecution were allowed to stand, it would follow that the Emperor Hirohito, alive today, would have to be summoned here before this Tribunal and take his place beside Adolf Hitler. But has such a thing been contemplated? No. Because if it had, then how could the prosecution explain that *now*, and not twenty-five years ago, would be the right time to try Hirohito? Dr. Kleemann has stated that there are crimes whose nature is not diminished with the passage of time. To follow his logic, this must mean that although ample evidence is available to prove Hirohito was directing the policies of his nation to a similar degree as Adolf Hitler in Germany, such leadership must have been devoid of any criminal intent or consequence.

"The object of the defense in this trial is not only to refute the charges of the prosecution but to redress the popular opinion held of the accused. To this end, I state that if for a quarter century the Emperor of Japan has not been held responsible for any actions in the period 1940–1945, then it is impossible to charge another head of state, Adolf Hitler, with culpability for similar actions."

Helmut Toller stepped over to the desk, picked up a buff manila file, opened it and read quickly. He tossed it down and came back to the witness box where Gerhard Stephanus was sitting. He appeared not to have moved at all during Toller's address.

"Your father was Walther Stephanus, commander of the Nineteenth Thuringian Field Artillery Regiment in the First War, was he not?"

"Yes, that is correct."

"And on your mother's side of the family, the van Vaernewycks, Flemish aristocrats, there was also a strong military heritage?"

"Yes."

"And you married, in 1931, Anna von Seydlitz-Kurbach, whose family distinguished itself in the regiments of Frederick the Great?"

"She is my wife, yes."

"Tell me, then, former General Stephanus," Toller said, grinding out the words, "are you, to the best of your knowledge, the only traitor in your exemplary family?"

Toller was standing directly before Stephanus, hands in his trouser pockets, eyes staring hard as though trying to break through Stephanus' dark glasses.

"I have asked you a question, Stephanus," Toller repeated softly.

"And I find it unworthy of any answer," Stephanus replied.

"Herr Toller," Dieter Wolff declared, barely concealing his contempt, "seldom have I witnessed an exhibition of such viciousness in a court of law. This Bench demands you offer the witness an apology, at once!"

"For stating the truth?" Toller challenged him. "This man is a traitor to his state and I can prove this on his own record!"

"I must ask the Court to strike such slanderous remarks from the transcripts," Hans Kleemann enjoined. "Not only has the integrity of the witness been sullied but that of the Court also."

"Counselor," Sir Adrian intoned, "this Court insists on a retraction of your comments. Once that has been given, you may proceed—but I caution you, not one slur, not one inadmissible suggestion, or I shall hold you in contempt of court. You have been duly warned!"

In the standoff, it appeared that Toller would not yield, but suddenly he smiled. "My apologies to the Bench, and to the witness." Immediately he was back on Stephanus.

"Can you tell this Court what impelled you to testify?"

"I am an authority on military intelligence during the Reich period. Having been very close to those in authority and, as I have said, attended a number of meetings with the Führer himself, I am eminently qualified as a witness."

"But in the past, when you were the director of the BND, and even upon leaving it, you maintained strict security and anonymity about your person. Why should you choose to cooperate with the prosecution now and reveal yourself to the public?"

"There is no personal gain for me in any of this, if that's what you're implying," Stephanus answered quietly. "I was induced to come forward because Herr Doktor Kleemann convinced me of the importance of my testimony. I also admit that I harbored a great deal of curiosity to see Adolf Hitler once more, a desire to at last state publicly the impressions the General Staff had of him. The fact that he survived fascinates me; in all my years in intelligence I never believed that could be possible."

"Well, at least we understand your noble motives," Toller observed. "I would like to take you back in time—for some background, you understand.

"The so-called July Plot of 1944 against the life of the Führer—were you privy to it?"

"Not directly."

"Explain, please!"

"I knew there was tremendous dissatisfaction in the General Staff over the manner in which Hitler had taken command of the war and the manner in which he was exercising that command. My intelligence at the time did not dismiss an attempt to remove him from office by a show of arms, which might result in his death."

"Did you know that such a 'show of arms,' as you call it, was in the offing in July of 1944?"

"It would have taken only the most elementary deduction to arrive at the conclusion that if a move was to be made against Hitler, it would have to come about in that summer. My own analysis concluded that autumn of 1944 was the final season in which a peace could still be negotiated with the Allies. After that it was simply a matter of time before their revenge fell upon Germany."

"Did your 'intelligence' indicate the major leaders of the conspiracy?"

"Some of them. Although my information was based exclusively on oral communication and independent analysis."

"Did you not report these—rumors, let us call them—to the Gestapo?"

"No, I did not."

"And why was that?"

"As I have said, there was nothing concrete to report. I was not about to slander my commanding officers on hearsay evidence. The results would have been unthinkable."

"More so than the bombing of the Führer's chambers?" Toller demanded. "More horrible than his possible death?"

"In my estimation, yes," Stephanus said. "After all, Germany still needed her army commanders, more so than a demagogue."

"And in your eyes was this not a treasonable position to take?—to stand by and watch as the conspiracy attained its climax?"

"I was not part of the conspiracy. I had no definite foreknowledge of it."

"But it was said of you, by Canaris, I believe, that if Stephanus had undertaken to lead the plot it would surely have succeeded, so meticulous was his organization and execution."

"That is neither here nor there," Stephanus answered disdainfully. "I did nothing."

"Oh, that is precisely the point, my dear former General," Toller intoned. "In abdicating responsibility, in not voicing your suspicions to the Gestapo and, on the other hand, watching as the plot failed, you did nothing, as you said. So what does that do for your idea of loyalty—to whom, and in what fashion?"

Stephanus was about to answer, but Helmut Toller could not be stopped at this point.

"I would ask you, Stephanus, to think back once more, to a time when you did act and again, in the view of any officer, treasonably so. On April 9, 1945, the Führer personally dismissed you as head of the intelligence unit known as Foreign Armies East."

"Yes, he did. My replacement was Wessel."

"Can you tell this court whether you handed over the command completely to Wessel?"

"I did."

"But you had microfilmed the entire contents of FAE's files, had you not?"

"Yes."

"And this cache was *not* given to Wessel?"

"No."

"In fact, General, you left Berlin with, I believe it was, forty strongboxes of highly classified microfilm, all having to do with your department's intelligence on the Soviet Union."

"That is correct."

"You therefore disobeyed a direct command from the Führer to pass on total control of your operations to Wessel."

"The Führer did not consider that such valuable intelligence might be destroyed in the Battle of Berlin," Stephanus said, "as was subsequently the case. I believed my individual judgment was correct in moving the microfilm to safety."

"Ah, but for whose safety, General?" Toller sneered. "Not

the Reich's, surely. For you the war was over. It was time to
think of one's own hide, never mind nobility or those outmoded
concepts of loyalty and obedience.

"General Stephanus, you and select officers from your staff
moved to the Lake Spitzing region of Bavaria in late April. You
buried the cases of film for safekeeping and waited as the Americans moved in, occupied and established control. When their
G-2 intelligence officers had set up a Bavarian office, you surrendered—you and your men—and you subsequently used the forty
crates of intelligence to barter your way out of a POW camp.
Now, that was your final act of treason was it not, General: the
passing of state secrets to the enemy, using the intelligence to
save yourself? That was it, wasn't it?"

Stephanus looked up at the young man and touched the dark
glasses with his fingertips. For a moment it seemed he might
remove them.

"Yes, you are correct," he said, speaking out to the hushed
Assembly. "In late April 1945, there was no longer a German
Reich; there was no government worthy of the title. There was
nothing. I perceived that if even a little of German intelligence
was to survive, it would have to be organized, hidden and finally
used as a barter tool. I also perceived that the camaraderie between the Americans and the Soviets would be short-lived. When
the Americans came to recognize the true face of Stalin, they
would need, badly so, all the intelligence available. I could provide them with the best information in the world—in return for
their alliance with a new Germany.

"You see, Herr Toller, the matter was really quite simple:
either I participate in the destruction of Germany, which to me
made no sense, or I plan for the resurgence of Germany, which I
then believed was inevitable. You tell me whether Adolf Hitler
could have survived if all had chosen destruction, so that he
would be here this day defending himself. You think about that,
Toller, and tell me."

"I have only one comment upon your actions and how they
reflect upon the man," Toller spat back. "By your admission you
are an opportunist, whose loyalty is derived from what you perceive as being best for yourself. I therefore do not believe that
your testimony as to the events of December 13, 1938, has any

validity for this court. There is no manner in which to substantiate your claim as to what passed between the Führer and Chief of Staff Herder. There is no one even to act as witness to the fact that *you* ever attended such a meeting—''

"The Führer will answer that," Stephanus said.

Toller wheeled around and shouted, "Very well, I ask Adolf Hitler to rise and comment on Stephanus' question!"

"Such procedure is illegal," Morozov spoke up immediately. "The accused must wait to take the stand if—" But Adolf Hitler stood up behind his table and looked directly at Stephanus.

"You are a traitor, Stephanus," he said in a low voice. "I want you to hear that from my lips—the words of the man you had sworn to obey!"

Then to the Bench, in a harsh, final tone, "I disclaim everything he says! There was never any such meeting between myself and Herder. Never! Never!"

"What was the reaction of the Assembly to the defense's statement?"

Marshal Zhukov, bundled in several blankets and sitting propped up against the headboard of his bed, regarded Kuzmin as the Major stared out the window onto the bustle around the entrance to the Hotel Pierre, where a delegation of ebullient Texas oilmen was attempting to quit the premises. Zhukov had been unable to attend the day's session on strict orders from his physician, who had scolded him that without care his cold would certainly progress into pneumonia. The doctor wanted no part of that.

"So what was it?" he demanded.

"I don't know whether I was more disgusted than angry or vice versa," Kuzmin murmured. He lit a cigarette and carefully blew the smoke away from Zhukov, up toward the oval molding on the ceiling.

"The comments from the West were to be expected; most of the delegates felt that Kleemann had scored hard and well. They did not, however, discount Toller's defense completely. No one can rule without guilt: that was the main thrust of Toller's argument, and its impact wasn't lost."

"All right, so he had them contemplating their navels! What else?"

"The Africans seemed rather sympathetic to Hitler," Kuzmin commented. "Something we might keep in mind for the future. I passed through several of their groups and managed to hear what was said—a tight-lipped bunch, by the way: they hushed up when they noticed me. I think their sentiment falls into two categories. One side will say it's all the colonial white problem, which has nothing to do with them. In a way, this faction is right: many of the black states didn't even exist as nations during the war. Others sympathize with Hitler, picturing him as some knight errant doing battle with the capitalist exploiters. Most Arabs are of the same mind—because of the anti-Jewish element—but they're keeping their opinions to themselves."

"What about the Orientals?"

"They're playing it very close to the chest except for the Japanese, who are furious and very much embarrassed by that reference to their emperor."

Zhukov grunted and unwrapped a mentholated cough drop, which he then popped into his mouth.

"Another thing," Kuzmin added. "The South American states, aside from those closely aligned with the United States, such as Venezuela, have come out in support of Hitler."

"Big surprise!" Zhukov spat out, inadvertently setting his teeth on the drop and cracking it. "They're fascist to the bone down there. Perhaps by tomorrow I can get back. In the meantime, keep listening, Kuzmin; God only knows what filth this trial will uncover."

The prosecutor had chosen his only witness to the second indictment with great care. From the thousands of accounts he had read and listened to over two decades—the testimonies of war from men and women still alive—the prosecutor had remembered this particular one and in the quiet month of August, when Paris was abandoned by her citizens, he had traveled there and spoken with the man and persuaded him to relive his nightmare before the world.

Lev Veznarod was at this time fifty-four years old. He had

lived in Paris since 1946, one of the few fortunates who, having fought both with the partisans and in the Red Army, had not been repatriated to the Soviet Union, and subsequently cast into the labor camps, in the spring of 1945. Veznarod had made his way into the French sector of what was left of Germany, where he had been interrogated by a sympathetic counterintelligence officer and issued papers to cross the frontier into France. Had Veznarod been an ordinary soldier instead of the leader of a guerrilla unit, it is doubtful that the French would have been so kind; but then the image of Resistance appealed to the Gallic imagination.

Unlike other refugees who tried to improve their alien status by publishing accounts of their deeds, Veznarod had kept the details of his war years to himself. In the small engineering firm where he worked as a draftsman, he was regarded as a withdrawn man, a foreigner who belonged to no fraternal organizations dedicated to keeping memories of the war alive nor appeared interested in sharing his accounts with others. It was generally agreed among his co-workers that Veznarod had no politics. No one knew that Veznarod had broken his vow of silence once, on the tenth anniversary of the Allied victory in Europe. That spring he had traveled to Munich and given a deposition to the Public Prosecutor against an SS major on trial for the slaughter of the inhabitants of three villages in the Ukraine. No one had asked Veznarod to come forward. He had read about the proceedings in a Paris newspaper and taken a week's sick leave.

Hans Kleemann was sitting on the arm of a Scandinavian easy chair, contemplating the brilliant colors of the Bo Beskow mural that partitioned the Dag Hammarskjold Library of the United Nations. Opposite him, Veznarod was staring vacantly at the city skyline smoking an aromatic French cigarette. He was not a particularly impressive man. A job behind the desk had covered his thick-muscled body with fat and, given his short stature, this made him appear chunky. Yet the face had never recovered from the years of deprivation. It remained lean, with a prominent nose and large ears that were accented by the crew cut Veznarod favored. No, Kleemann thought, there was nothing extraordinary about him, not as long as he remained silent. Only when Veznarod began to speak, his voice commencing in a low monotone but building quickly as the words took possession of him, did he

come into his own. He had a gift so rare in men, especially witnesses: to be able to recount a story and have that story come to
life before those who listened. The cadence of his voice would
rise and fall, and the words he uttered became a living organism,
vibrant, passionate, yet also melancholy and sorrowful. But he
did not exaggerate or embellish; the horror of the truth spoke
eloquently enough for itself.

"We must go now, no?" Veznarod asked him, carefully putting
out his cigarette.

Hans Kleemann rose with him, and together they walked to the
door that opened into the court. "Do not be afraid of him," the
prosecutor said. "Or of his defense counsel. There is nothing
they can do."

Veznarod shrugged and opened the door. Kleemann had no
way of knowing if the words had comforted him at all.

"The prosecution will now deal with the second count of the
indictment: inhumane behavior on the part of the accused relating
to battlefield conduct."

"So he did dredge up that Slav." Hitler muttered to Toller, all
the while watching as the Court administered the oath to Veznarod.

"I don't believe it matters," Toller said softly. A Frenchman,
a Norwegian or even a Pole would have been difficult to deal
with. But a Russian! I wonder if Kleemann knows he is offering
me his head on a platter! What could a Russian, having served in
Stalin's army, know of humane conduct?"

"Would you give us your full name, please," Kleemann asked.

"Lev Matveich Veznarod."

"Your residence and occupation?"

"I have lived in the suburb of Neuilly in Paris since December
of 1946 and have been employed as a draftsman at Beauchamp et
Fils since early 1947."

"But by birth you are Russian?"

"Yes," Veznarod said. "I was born in the village of Rovno in
the Ukraine in 1922."

"You were nineteen years old when the invasion of Russia,
known as Operation Barbarossa, was undertaken in the spring of
1941."

"Yes. At the time of the invasion I was in the Reserve Front. However, my unit was transferred to the Active Front in the last days of June. Subsequently Marshal Budenny was unable to halt the German offensive in the south and Kiev was taken, with the loss of almost two-thirds of a million troops. I was one of the few who managed to escape the encirclement."

"What were your circumstances then?"

"I had been wounded—not seriously, but enough to require medical attention for a short period of time. It was my extraordinary fortune to find refuge in the town of Kupai, some forty kilometers southeast of Kiev."

"Would you now relate what happened to you there."

"Kupai was truly a blessed town," Veznarod said gently. "It had, at most, three thousand inhabitants, yet so many churches! So many because it was, according to legend, in Kupai that the Virgin appeared a hundred and fifty years ago. Now, in 1941, there occurred yet another miracle.

"The people had all heard of the scorched-earth policy the Nazis were pursuing as they swept through the countryside. Rumors of the extermination commandos, the Einsatzgruppen, were also rampant, and we, the soldiers who had been closest to the fighting, had no choice but to confirm them. Yet the most fearsome thing was that there was nowhere to flee. At first the people all were prepared to leave, taking what they could and burning the rest—their homes, the farms and storehouses, yes, even the churches—so that the destruction would not be done by German hands. Then the first reports of those who had tried to make their way east filtered back: Kupai was surrounded. The enemy hadn't yet come upon it, but the SS armored divisions were all around. The town was like an island of refuge in a sea of blood, at least for a little while. I don't think there was one person who didn't believe that very soon we too would perish.

"The first troops arrived three days after I did. Although many did not know it, Kupai was fortunate in having regular Wehrmacht soldiers in addition to the SS unit. We could sense the tension between the conquerors almost at once.

"Major Ritter of the SS reveled in his nickname, 'The Torch,' with good reason: he moved through the land like a sheet of fire that devoured everything in its path. Whatever his flamethrowers did not consume the Einsatzgruppen had for themselves, and after them, there was nothing. On the other hand, Lieutenant-Colonel Weber was a soldier of the old school. A man of tremendous stature, both physically and ethically, he made it clear that he held Ritter in contempt and abided him only because of orders from the High Command.

"While Ritter was proceeding with his head count to see how many Jews and other 'undesirables'—the Russian wounded, for example—he might have to burn, Weber rounded up the leaders of the village and assured them of his protection as long as they complied with his orders. In the fashion of a true commander he then turned to the welfare of his men, setting up a hospital compound, checking rations and ammunition, and so on. After that was done, he asked if there was an experienced radio operator among those in the sick ward. His own man had been killed in the fighting, and until a suitable replacement could be found he had need of someone who not only was skilled but also understood German. I came forward and, after a quick interrogation, was given the post.

"It may have been this very action which set the tragic events in motion. When he learned of my appointment, Ritter was livid. I remember him screaming at Weber that it was unheard of to spare any prisoners during the Blitzkrieg. Weber retorted that perhaps there wasn't any reason for wholesale execution. Ritter, I think, could not believe what he had heard, for he asked Weber to repeat himself, and when the Lieutenant-Colonel refused, Ritter cursed him, shouting that he was contravening the Führer's orders and that he, Ritter, would report as much to Hitler himself. This, I must add, was not an idle threat; it became known very quickly that Ritter had met the Führer on a number of occasions and had been personally decorated by him for his work in France. Ritter finished his harangue by stating that he would do as he wished in his particular region of authority and that if Weber tried to stop him, he would have the SS place him under arrest. However, Weber stood his ground and made it clear that Kupai was under his authority, no one else's.

"Not long after the Germans arrived, a sense of order was imposed on the town. Things were done at specific hours, with the military having priority, of course. Thus at six o'clock in the morning it was the SS corps that arrived to bathe in the pool lying at the foot of a waterfall in one of the many glens that ringed the town. The Wehrmacht soldiers had been given the less scenic place up the stream before it reached the gorge. This area had also been designated for the exercise of prisoners, which took place in the evenings, often just before the troops themselves retired. Since all of our men were wounded in one way or another, only a dozen or so ever left the hospital. But the option to walk was always given by Weber, who maintained strict adherence to the Geneva Protocols on the treatment of prisoners.

"My own regimen was to rise early, often before daybreak, and get to sleep immediately after supper. Weber was a vigorous man who preferred to get on the airwaves before the other commanders. Not only was there no traffic then, but also he wanted to know the results of the night's fighting in the region as quickly as possible, information to which he attached the greatest importance. As a result, I often breakfasted with him, alone, in his tent. I was in the middle of sending a message to the commander of Strike Force North when the explosions began.

"For some reason neither I nor Weber at first seemed to take notice of them. He finished his sentence and only then looked about, perplexed but not alarmed. It is possible, I suppose, that we were both so inured to explosions that calm rather than panic prevailed. Until the screaming.

"Weber's tent was at least a hundred yards from the waterfall. But neither the distance nor the sound of the waterfall could mute the terrible cries that we heard. The next moment I found myself staggering along with him, trying to keep up as best I could as Weber ran among the soldiers who were also converging. The explosions would not stop.

"When we arrived at the edge of the slope, a terrible horror awaited us. All along the bank one could see twisted bodies lying like crumpled dolls, as though broken and tossed down by some malicious giant child. In the early-morning fog, through which moved the heavier smoke of gunpowder, we saw a leg here; an arm there; the torso of a man decapitated, the chest ripped open. In the middle of this beautiful wood, we had come upon a sacrificial altar for the Germans—a sight more horrifying to them than to me, because it was their own who were butchered there in a manner and circumstance the SS used on the civilian population.

"When Ritter ran up, he quite literally went insane. Scrambling down the embankment, he crawled his way from corpse to corpse, picking up pieces of the bodies, holding them before his eyes, then placing them next to what else there was of the remains, as though trying to reconstruct them. All the while he was moaning, 'My boys! My boys! Look what they have done to them!'

"I cannot tell you how long we stood on the embankment, listening to the inhuman shrieks of the wounded while farther below, the stream continued to flow over rocks and fall away into the gorge. I don't think anyone moved, nor was any order given, until Ritter had climbed, on all fours, from the bank. He was like a monster, covered with the primeval slime in which he lived, dripping of the blood he feasted upon. He staggered to his feet before Weber and clamped his hands on the other's shoulder.

" 'You see what they have done?' he hissed. 'You see what they did to my boys? Now I shall begin killing! I shall kill them all! I will call Hitler and he will tell me to shoot everybody!'

"Ritter reached for his gun, and then Weber flung him off. Ritter slipped and, screaming, slid down the embankment into the corpses. That was how we left him, tangled among the dead, screaming and crying for his men.

"It did not take Weber very long to determine what had happened by the waterfall. Sometime in the night, a series of mines had been planted along the embankment at the exact place where the SS descended to bathe. But the charges hadn't been set in the conventional manner—that is, to explode as soon as a man stepped on the device. Instead there was a delayed action, so that the entire SS unit might walk into the field and, when the charges went off, no one could run away; they would all be trapped in the middle of the field. The carnage would be complete.

"When we were back in his tent, Weber turned to me and asked if I knew who had been responsible. I said I did not, and he shook his head, murmuring that he believed me and he thanked God it had not happened to *his* soldiers. The implication was clear: the partisans who had set the mines could as easily have planted them in the place where the Wehrmacht soldiers bathed. Instead they chose to kill the SS. Weber understood this.

Nonetheless, it was a senseless and needless gesture, which awaited Ritter's reaction. Ritter, everyone knew, would not be cheated of his revenge.

"He reappeared one hour later. The change in him was unbelievable. Immaculately attired in a fresh uniform, he showed remarkable self-control; yet in his eyes I could see that his was the discipline of a fanatic: that in himself there was an ongoing struggle of will, between the beast who would have enjoyed tearing my throat open and the soulless machine that had already plotted every aspect of my death. For the moment he chose not to recognize my existence. Turning to Weber, Ritter formally demanded to know whether the High Command both on the Eastern Front and in Berlin had been informed of the incident at Kupai, to which Weber replied that this had been done. He then asked me whether the radio channels were open. I said they were. He instructed me to raise Berlin once more. In a few minutes Ritter was speaking with Berlin communications, ordering them to pass us through directly to the Führer, who was, at the time, at the Eagle's Nest, his retreat in Berchtesgaden.

"In all, I believe we waited an hour before Hitler returned our signal. In that time neither Ritter nor Weber left the tent, although Weber had many duties to carry out. I sincerely believe he thought that if he were to leave me alone with Ritter, the SS major would find a pretext upon which to shoot me.

"Then all at once the transmission began from Bavaria and I heard the unmistakable voice of Adolf Hitler. This was confirmed by Ritter, who addressed the speaker as Führer and quickly gave out the details of the massacre. For a moment I thought that our communications had collapsed, for there was no reply on the other end. Then Hitler began shouting at us, demanding how such a thing could have befallen his best troops and what Ritter proposed to do. Ritter answered that hostages should be shot as an example, and Hitler immediately agreed. Ritter then added that he had had to contact Hitler himself because some local commanders and even members of the High Command were refusing to grant SS leaders clear autonomy in dealing with such situations. This made Hitler even more furious. He shouted at Ritter to brush away any obstructions and report any interference in SS affairs directly to him. As for the present circumstances, Ritter was to take ten lives for every one SS man killed. Hitler finished by stating that he wanted a very clear example of the results of treachery made to the Russians. Ritter could shoot whomever he wished.

"It was all too obvious where, as of that moment, the authority in Kupai resided. No sooner had transmission been completed than Ritter ordered me to return to the prisoners' compound. To his credit, Weber protested immediately, and Ritter, with the silken voice of a psychopath, asked him whether it was necessary to speak with Hitler once more, this time on Weber's account. The Lieutenant-Colonel had no choice, and he himself escorted me back to the compound.

"I had no doubt that I and my comrades would never see the end of that day. The explosions had been heard around the entire town, so word of the events passed among us very quickly. The women who had been allowed to bring the prisoners food had told them what had happened. When I entered, they fell upon me begging me to tell them the SS' plans. A man can bear the realization that he is to die, yet the uncertainty of when can reduce him to despair. But there was nothing to be done. I knew only that Ritter would exact the most pernicious revenge and its nature would be too horrible, and therefore impossible, to predict.

"But we learned of its first manifestation early in the afternoon. It was soon enough.

"Ritter had gathered together a large number of town women and sent them to dig across the field from the prisoners' compound. I estimated that there were several hundred; later I learned that the exact number was four hundred and thirty. As they toiled it became obvious that a grave was being prepared. We saw them clamber out at the end, and the work did not require more than two hours to complete.

"The women were shunted to one side and guarded by many SS men, which we thought unusual. Then several trucks arrived and a large number of salt blocks were thrown out. The women set about breaking these into pieces the size of small rocks. Throughout all this there was total silence around us. We watched—not wanting to, but no man turned away. Behind us, we could feel the entire town watching with us. Only the birds cried out and the squirrels and rabbits moved along the ground.

The human beings worked, or guarded, or watched in silence as death approached.

"When the salt blocks had been broken up, some more trucks arrived. These brought children and elderly men; the last one carried young girls. When I saw this, the whole meaning of Ritter's exercise became apparent. The women who had been digging suddenly began to cry out, and several stumbled toward the trucks, only to be struck down by the SS men. I could hear them pleading with the guards to spare their daughters, or husbands, or parents, who were being herded toward the mass grave. Then the killing began. People were pushed up to the edge of the pit and shot; when one side of the grave filled up, they were moved to another, and so on until the deed was complete. The SS men then forced the women who were watching to throw salt upon the corpses. I later learned that Ritter had remembered such a technique from his reading of Roman history. The sacking of Carthage and the salting of her fields was an episode that particularly appealed to him.

"That is the story of the Kupai massacre," Lev Veznarod said. He looked up at the Court with a solemn expression, his eyes searching their faces as though seeking some answer. "The Kupai massacre, where the mothers prepared the graves of their own families.

"The destruction did not stop there, of course. The brook in which the SS had bathed was dynamited; later those prisoners of war who were unfit for any labor where shot. But Ritter's main task had been accomplished: four hundred and thirty Russians had been executed for the deaths of forty-three SS soldiers, exactly as per orders."

Hans Kleemann rose and came before Veznarod.

"I must ask you only one question: are you certain that the man to whom Ritter reported to receive orders authorizing the reprisals was Adolf Hitler?"

"Yes, I am certain," Veznarod answered. "Not only did I recognize the voice, but Ritter referred to the Führer several times; when he spoke to him, it was by rank; when he dealt with Weber, by name."

"Thank you very much."

Hans Kleemann turned to the Court.

"I spoke before of the volume of words that have been written about the actions of the leaders of the Third Reich. But this is, to the best of my knowledge, the first time that we have incontrovertible proof, through testimony, that Adolf Hitler was personally responsible for the deaths of over four hundred persons—personally because the matter of retribution was referred to him directly from the field by an officer who was obviously close to him."

The prosecutor stepped over to his table and held up a sheaf of photostats.

"Accounts of the Kupai massacre may be found in the *Greater Soviet Encyclopedia* and the *Soviet Encyclopedia of Military Affairs*. It is also mentioned by Marshal Zhukov in his memoirs. In all three accounts the events that overtook Kupai that autumn day are described in a corroborative fashion. The death figures match with those offered by the witness.

"However, to be certain there could be no bias, I offer evidence from the Imperial War Archives of London. These documents, recently declassified, show that British sources confirmed reports of the massacre. Part of the confirmation involves the testimony of several SS men who were interrogated by the British at the conclusion of hostilities.

"I therefore submit that on the basis of Veznarod's testimony and the additional evidence, Adolf Hitler cannot deny his role in initiating this tragedy and, further, prescribing the exact form it was to take. His actions constituted a direct affront to the Hague Convention on Land Warfare of 1907 in which Article 23b reads:

" 'It is especially forbidden to kill or wound treacherously individuals belonging to the hostile nation or army.'

"And Article 23c:

" 'It is especially forbidden to kill or wound an enemy who, having laid down his arms, or no longer having a means of defense, has surrendered.'

"Yes," Hans Kleemann said softly. "So many words have been written outlawing brutality by men; yet was it not for the sake of brutality and death that the infamous extermination squads had been formed—to murder Jews, commissars and partisans already taken prisoner by the SS or Wehrmacht? Did not Adolf Hitler, in contravention of every civilized rule of warfare, deliberately set out to foster extermination? I can see where defense counsel might argue my questions meaningless without proper documentation. But for once we have the necessary evidence. We have it from the mouth of a survivor!

"I beg the indulgence of the Court," Kleemann said, his voice low and soft. "I would dearly love to bring into this court all others, all the millions, who have been brutalized by this man. Yet I cannot. I can only demand—yes, demand—that those four hundred and thirty lives, taken on a whim, be accounted for. There is no other way but to ask that the life of Adolf Hitler be given in return."

No sooner had Hans Kleemann concluded his statement than Helmut Toller requested a brief adjournment so that he might confer with his client. The prosecutor had no objection. Because he had so strong a witness, with authoritative sources to corroborate his words, the prosecutor hoped Toller would have to fall back completely on the accused. Kleemann would have the opportunity to cross-examine and, now that he had regained the upper hand in the trial, capitalize on his advantage.

"I warned you about this," Toller was saying. "Now it is very important that you *do* remember that incident!"

They were alone in the small conference room adjacent to the Assembly, and so no one witnessed the first instance when Helmut Toller had raised his voice against his master.

"Helmut, you must tell me why you are so upset about the testimony of one man," Hitler said languidly, sitting back in the chair, his good arm thrown, in a careless gesture, over the frame. "Especially when the man is a Slav and was a Communist. Probably still is. How can anything he says be of any value? Ach, we've been through this argument ever since you knew he would be testifying."

"It will be so unless I *prove* him a liar!" Toller said harshly. "Do you think Kleemann would have offered him up unless his testimony could be corroborated and his character beyond reproach? I have checked the records Kleemann referred to; there was indeed a Kupai, and the events there took place on September 4 as Veznarod stated."

Hitler was silent. He brought out his leather-bound note pad, carefully opened it to a fresh page and began to doodle in short, rapid strokes. The figure of a young man seated at a table was quickly emerging.

"I do remember it," Hitler said slowly, not taking his eyes off the page. "I remember being extremely upset over the incident. It is strange, is it not, Helmut, how a single event can make us forget the panoramic whole with which we are dealing in the same instant? When Ritter's call came through I was directing the greatest invasion the world has ever seen. The mightiest armies ever assembled, fortified with the most advanced technology, were marching to a conquest no one before me had succeeded in making final, the subjugation of the East."

He paused and stared at his counsel with a vaguely curious expression.

"And yet I choose to recall an event in itself so meaningless in terms of the whole yet at the same time charged with significance. I know I issued that order. I have no regrets, not even now, for having done so. Ritter, admittedly, was careless in allowing the Slav to operate the radio, but even that was more the fault of this Weber. You understand, as do all those hypocrites in there, that reprisal is a form of punishment—a version of Kleemann's treasured 'eye for an eye' philosophy. My elite troops had been butchered, and I simply took an appropriate course of action."

"There are mitigating circumstances here," Toller said, running his teeth across his lower lip, a gesture that irritated Adolf Hitler. "You told him to take ten lives for every German one; you did not authorize him to shoot women, children and old men, which is really what is at issue."

"I would not have expected him to do less!" Hitler snapped back at him. "I have told you: there are no excuses to be made for the actions of my men in the East. The East was to be destroyed and its population reduced to serve the needs of the German people. That is all!"

"And I cannot go before the court with such statements." Toller shook his head.

"In that case, if you are so much interested in absolving me of the responsibility, why do you not find *someone*, not something, who will refute the testimony?" Hitler suggested gently. "Don't tell me that knowing my views on Veznarod, you haven't pre-pared standby witnesses for us?"

"It is remarkable enough for Kleemann to have unearthed this one incident," Toller said. "There were only two men in the tent with Veznarod: Weber and Ritter. To find them would be extremely difficult, if they aren't already dead."

"Weber, yes; Ritter, no. He belonged to the SS, after all."

"And if he should corroborate Veznarod's account?"

Hitler looked upon him with disdain.

"You are, after so much, still an adolescent to have to ask that question."

And he turned his attention to the final details of his sketch.

Helmut Toller pivoted on his heel, thrust his hands deep into his trouser pockets and walked across to the windows, an angry, frustrated man whose authority had been usurped. Toller had never abided a client's interference or "suggestions" in his defense, and this cardinal rule had extended even to Adolf Hitler. Not that to this point Toller had had reason to admonish his charge. Hitler had provided him with supplementary information not found in the Nuremberg transcripts; he had made available a clear, concise account of his years in Emmaus; his answers to all of Toller's questions on material Toller believed the prosecution would use had been thoughtful and precise. In short, Hitler had not only cooperated, he had left Toller to do his work without playing the overseer.

Then why, Toller asked himself, did he choose this crucial point at which to become recalcitrant? The lawyer knew well enough that Hitler believed no apologies were necessary for his actions, that in his perspective they had all been necessary and right. But surely he could appreciate that a denial by Hitler of the charge would challenge the strength of Kleemann's entire argument! To Toller the potential benefit far outweighed a slight variation of the truth—that Hitler had indeed ordered the massacre.

Toller looked across at the old man carefully filling out his sketch. No, there was nothing Toller could say that would make Hitler change his mind. Querulous and stubborn, he had drawn a line of cooperation beyond which he would not step. And if such a stance damaged the defense . . .

"I have completed it," Hitler said. He raised the drawing for

Toller to view. It was an extraordinary likeness of the attorney in
profile.

"There are some things, like talent and principles, that one
does not lose," he said. "You might remember that."

As Hitler walked slowly to his seat be paused briefly by the side
of Kleemann's table and, smiling, shook his head. Kleemann
understood immediately: it was obvious Hitler would not be taking the stand. Although the prosecutor could challenge him to
refute Veznarod's testimony, Hitler would simply circumvent the
questions or plead a failed memory. To have the Court witness
such a charade would serve no purpose. The fact that *Toller*
wouldn't call his client as witness would damn Hitler sufficiently.

"I should like to put several questions to the witness," Toller
declared to the Court. Then, without waiting for permission to
continue, Toller turned to Veznarod.

"You mentioned that the prisoners of war were expecting to be
executed as a consequence of the vicious attack on German
troops. What happened to them?"

"Nothing was done to them that day," Veznarod replied. "I
later learned they had been given over to the execution squads
that were working their way east."

"Why do you say you learned of their fate 'later'?"

"Because the next day I managed to escape."

"Really. Would you tell me about that?"

"The remaining SS men seemed to have sated their blood appetite for the day, and Ritter did not replace the Wehrmacht
guards with his own as far as the prisoners were concerned. So
early the next morning a lieutenant came to the compound and
shook me out of my sleep. The horror of the previous day was
still with me. I remember it was very late, perhaps three or four
in the morning, before I had closed my eyes, out of sheer exhaustion. When I looked up at him, I thought they were finally coming
for us. But no, he wanted only me; there was a generator in the
town which the Wehrmacht needed repaired for their communications apparatus. Weber had ordered that I should fix it.

"There was no movement in Kupai as we walked through it.
Dawn had come into the streets, but its light fell on no one. All

the windows were covered, with curtains or shutters; or if those were missing, burlap sacks—anything at all to blot out the reality of what was happening outside. The lieutenant, a melancholy young man with the Knight's Cross for valor on his tunic, led me to the railroad station and, when we were inside, showed me the damaged generator that had once been used for transmission along the rail lines.

"Your people sabotaged it, so I assume you will be able to fix it," he said. He showed me where the tools were and left me to do the work.

"Two or three hours passed. No one interrupted me, and I was able to repair the damage without calling someone to fetch spare parts. After I finished I went out into the railroad yard to see whether the lieutenant or Weber was about. At that moment I saw a train preparing to leave. It was one of the old Russian freights, not very long, with a dozen short, squat cars pulled by a single locomotive. Perhaps because I saw no guards or perhaps because my instinct simply propelled me, I started running to the train. I dived under one of the last cars and hauled myself up to the floorboards, leaning against the axle for support. Only when the train began to move did I discover that the axle was grinding one of the wheels into the small of my back. Yet I couldn't move. I might fall off, or worse, be seen by someone looking at the cars from an angle. So I clung there, trying to obliterate the pain from my mind as the train left Kupai. After two hours I felt nothing in my back, the left side of it. Today that area remains desensitized. I shall carry the scar of the wheel into the grave."

"A moving account," Helmut Toller murmured. "I assume that at one point you were able to leave the train and join up with resistance forces?"

"We were traveling east, into territory that had just been captured. There came a point at which I knew I had to drop from the car; otherwise the journey would have killed me, for my wounds had torn open and I was bleeding profusely. At the first moment the train slowed I pushed myself away and was very lucky to fall in such a manner as to have the remaining cars pass overhead without touching me.

"God was looking after me, for it was the partisans, not the Germans, who found me."

"And did you tell those who rescued you that they had saved the life of a collaborator?" Toller demanded suddenly, his tone vicious.

"I must object to both counsel's unfounded accusation and his tone!" Kleemann cut in at once, coming to his feet. "We have seen such a spectacle before, with the witness Stephanus!"

"Very well, I shall rephrase," Toller countered immediately. "You did tell them, did you not, of your cooperation with the occupying forces, your willingness to act as radio operator and later as technician?"

"I will answer the accusation," Veznarod said calmly. "I have prepared myself for it."

He nodded in the direction of the prosecutor and motioned that he should sit, as one friend who is being unjustly attacked would gesture to another not to trouble himself to defend him.

"You are quite right," Veznarod said quietly. "I said nothing to the partisans about my activities in behalf of the Germans. It was my duty, as a soldier and a Russian, to deny the Germans anything they needed, which included whatever services I might be called upon to perform. Instead I had volunteered to help them, as you say. If you ask me today what part of my action was founded on cowardice, or on a will to live, or even on the insane hope that somewhere I might be of value to others, my own people, through what I did, that I cannot answer. But I do know that when I agreed to operate the transmitter for Weber, I never saw that as leading to my repairing the generator, which in turn afforded me the avenue of escape. All of which has brought me here today.

"Whatever it is I had to settle in my own conscience, I have, for better or worse. A man may be ashamed of certain acts he has committed, but he may always hope to expiate them in the future, to rise to the occasion another time, to have his failing in the past guide him along the correct path."

"Yet your correct path, as you put it, led you straight out of your native land!" Toller exclaimed. "Surely there must have been a great fear on your part that your collaboration would, at the end of the war, have been examined by the proper authorities."

"I fought with the partisans for two years and with the Red

Army another eighteen months, Herr Toller,'' Veznarod said gently. "I bear several medals for bravery—or what was seen to be bravery at the time. But toward the end, I knew all too well what awaited the homecoming soldiers. You must too, for it has been written about—how our returning armies went from the battlefield to the taiga, because Stalin believed them infected with Western ideas.''

"What went on in the Red Army after it pillaged Germany is of no concern to us," Toller retorted. "Only your testimony is important. Somehow I doubt the word of a collaborator and, in your own words, a coward.

"What the prosecution has offered us is the testimony of one man who may or may not have been in the tent, acting as radio operator when the alleged order from Adolf Hitler arrived. The documentation Dr. Kleemann has put forward makes no reference to a Veznarod at all. All we know for certain, from historical sources, is that a reprisal for the murder of German soldiers did take place.''

"I would like to point out to defense counsel that the Court does not understand his attempt to undermine the character of the witness," Thomas Worthington interrupted. "Furthermore, counsel has not chosen the simpler manner in which to rebut the charges made by the witness, and that is the countertestimony of the accused.

"Mr. Toller, the Court would very much like to know whether Adolf Hitler disputes the fact that he himself ordered Major Ritter to execute ten people of Kupai for every SS soldier ambushed.''

Toller was stung by the interjection. He turned on his heel and went over to Adolf Hitler.

"If you do not come forward now, everyone will accept Veznarod's words," he whispered. "This is our last chance to challenge him before I am compelled to seek an adjournment.''

Hitler was unmoved. He simply continued staring up at Toller with those fathomless eyes which neither assented nor refused. The attorney took a deep breath and faced the Court.

"The defense requests an adjournment in these proceedings," he said. "We have not had the opportunity of verifying the witness' testimony through a detailed search. I must ask for several days' grace in order that it be done.''

"You have had knowledge thirty days prior to this date—as stipulated—that this witness would be called," Morozov reminded him. "If that was insufficient, then how much grace are you asking of us?"

"I leave that to the wisdom of the Court," Toller answered in a neutral tone.

The members of the Bench deliberated among themselves, then decided to give the defense seventy-two hours in which to prepare a rebuttal. They also agreed to provide Lev Veznarod with protection as long as he remained in their jurisdiction.

Helmut Toller arrived in Munich very early the next morning. He went directly from the airport to his office and from there telephoned the detective who had been assigned to him in the first weeks of the investigation. They met one hour later, at a café the detective had named.

"I must contact Herr Bendt as quickly as possible," Toller told him. "There is a man we need to present to the court in New York, by the name of Ritter. He was an SS major on the Eastern Front and came to trial in Hamburg in 1956."

"I am familiar with the name," the detective said. "Wait here while I telephone."

The detective was gone for quite some time—by Toller's reckoning, half an hour. Upon returning he did not sit down again.

"Herr Bendt asks that you meet him on the Promenade Platz, near the Bayerischer Hof Hotel, in forty minutes. He will be in his car, a silver-gray Mercedes limousine. Now you will excuse me, for there are certain details that must be attended to—in terms of your request."

"That quickly. Your efficiency knows no bounds," Toller murmured. He rose and shook hands with the detective.

"We are very proud of the way in which you are defending the Führer," the detective said soberly. "You have a great deal of support among the people here and throughout Germany. I know; policemen always do."

Before Toller could thank him, the detective had turned away. Toller paid for their coffees and then began walking toward the center of the city.

He had to wait only a few minutes before Bendt's car came into view. The vehicle glided to a stop in front of him, the chauffeur stepped out and the next moment he was inside. It all happened in one smooth, silent motion.

"The cameras do not do you justice, Herr Toller. It must be that interesting plastic they are using to protect you."

Erik Bendt's voice was quite soft, unnaturally so, and it left one with the impression that he could not have spoken any louder even had he wished to. This hint of an infirmity contrasted strongly with Bendt's elegance and grace. Although he was a man in his sixties, Bendt's features were not marred by sagging flesh. The skin, which Toller thought must be perpetually tanned, was drawn smoothly and cleanly over the contours of the face, defining the nose, mouth and chin. It was only the eyes that detracted from the complete image of a tall, lean sportsman to whom the years meant nothing. These were withdrawn and meditative, perhaps even a little sad.

"It is a privilege to meet you again," Toller said. "I appreciate your having made the time."

"The privilege is mine, Herr Toller," Bendt replied crisply. "You have undoubtedly been too much preoccupied with the trial to appreciate what stature you have gained here in Germany—and abroad."

"The defense of Adolf Hitler is a tremendous responsibility. But thus far, I believe I have served him well."

"You are modest," noted Bendt. "But beneath it, I sense conviction and strength. I suggest you allow both to come to the fore. The exercise of power requires it."

Toller did not understand Bendt's reference and was about to admit as much when Bendt said, "The man about whom you inquired, a Major Karl Ritter, has been located. You are surprised that this should have happened so quickly? I surmised you might wish to speak with Ritter after Veznarod made those references to him. You must understand, Herr Toller, that there are few people in Germany who are *not* watching the trial."

"I am surprised at what you say—and very much pleased. As you know, I have no more than seventy-two hours to deal with this issue."

"It wasn't very difficult for me," Bendt remarked. "Ritter has been in contact with our people ever since the 1956 trial, when Veznarod helped convict him. After Ritter was released, we lent him financial aid to establish his furniture business in Hamburg. He is doing quite well, come to think of it. .... Herr Toller, tell me exactly why you seek the Major."

"Major Ritter carried out an order allegedly given him directly by Adolf Hitler. I wish to ascertain that this was the case."

"Herr Toller, I asked you to tell me *exactly* what you want of the Major," Bendt said evenly. "If I believed that to be your true motive, I would not have put the question to you."

"Very well. I had asked Adolf Hitler to take the stand and refute Veznarod's charges. He refused to do so, stating that he did in fact issue such an order. It was, therefore, impossible to have him testify. The best I can do under the circumstances is prevent the prosecution from insisting that he answer the charge, although silence on his part will be damaging. So to offset some of the harm, I must persuade Ritter to change his testimony."

"Have you read the transcript of the Ritter trial?"

"Yes, I have, although it was my intention to do so again as soon as I had arrived here. I am familiar with the '56 proceedings and recall that Ritter, in his defense at the time, stated that in the reprisals, he had been acting on higher authority. If he mentioned Adolf Hitler by name, then my position becomes even more difficult. Ritter would then be obliged to admit to perjury at the first trial, something the Court and prosecution would find difficult to believe, considering that Ritter was arguing for his life."

"Thank you for being frank with me," Bendt said. "I had to be absolutely certain of your intentions. Now, I have brought with me the relevant sections of the Ritter trial transcripts. It will not take you long to peruse them, but I suggest that there is a problem in regard to Ritter's having mentioned the Führer by name."

Bendt extracted from the center console a large leather-bound folder and passed it to Toller. The attorney opened the folder and began to read. By the time he was through, Bendt's driver had brought them to the outskirts of Munich and was heading for the countryside.

"Well, it appears that in his defense Ritter did implicate the Führer," Toller murmured. "I take it you have the complete transcript as well?"

Erik Bendt nodded. He was pleased that Toller trusted him but also wished to see for himself whether there were any other incriminating references to Adolf Hitler anywhere in those proceedings. Bendt respected thoroughness.

"The next step," Toller was saying, "would be to meet with Ritter and try to persuade him to remember the incident in another light."

"Forgive me, Herr Toller, but before that is done, there are several questions I wish to put to you, the first one being: do you understand what you are asking Ritter to do, and is his sacrifice so important to you?"

"To me the real importance lies in vindicating Adolf Hitler," Helmut Toller answered briskly. "To my client, it could well be the turning point.

"I have given this matter a great deal of thought, Herr Bendt. Under other circumstances, I would not seek perjury from a man. Yet I ask it on two counts: first, in spite of what I have achieved in court, the prosecution still has the upper hand. Kleemann, while building his case on sound legal grounds, never fails to introduce moral arguments. What do most people know, remember or care of Nuremberg, the Yamashita trial or the role of a head of state in conducting war? Nothing at all. But they are profoundly influenced, I believe, by the appeals to more abstract criteria such as justice, the nature of responsibility and so on.

The only manner in which I can undercut this attraction is to challenge Kleemann on every point in law, to make certain that he doesn't gain a single advantage other than those he already holds. Adolf Hitler's refusal to actively deny the charges already prejudices his case in the eyes of the world. But if Ritter testifies that the Führer issued no specific command—that, for example, there was a breakdown in transmission, or the reception was so poor he could not hear Hitler's voice and consequently acted on his own initiative—Veznarod's account would at least be damaged.

"Naturally, Ritter might face punishment for such an admission. Although he has served a sentence for other charges, Bonn might decide, because of public pressure, to drag him back into the dock and try him for his role in the reprisals. The question I have had to ask myself is which man should be spared: Hitler or Ritter? I concluded it should be Hitler.

"If Adolf Hitler is vindicated before a world tribunal, so much of our past history will have to be rewritten. The years of shame can be put behind us; our children need never be burdened with the stigma that it has been our lot to bear. To this end alone, I would ask for Ritter and his testimony."

"Am I, then, to assume that you have developed strong personal feelings for the philosophy of National Socialism?" Bendt asked him. "Or do your actions stem entirely from your concern for the person of the Führer?"

"Herr Bendt, I undertook the defense of Adolf Hitler because for many years I knew him only as Werner Busse. My education about the Nazi era of Germany truly began with my investigations in his behalf. Only then did I realize how terribly inadequate our system of education has been in this regard.

"Prior to this period, I came to have neutral feelings about Nazism. It wasn't an issue with me, political or otherwise. I was aware, of course, of the occasional clamors in the international press regarding war-crimes trials or the pursuit of wanted SS people, but as with most of my peers, such news was non-news; it had no relevance—none, at least, until the day I was told that a man I respected, admired and yes, even loved had been the leader of the Third Reich.

"I think we must all be students of history today. I became such a pupil the hour I accepted Adolf Hitler's request to represent him. In a very short time I learned a great deal about the Reich, and, Herr Bendt, I don't find that form of government wanting in many respects. It is no great pleasure to read about the excesses, particularly against the Jews, and of the fact that many notable figures in the arts and sciences either fled or were arrested; on the other hand, I can find far greater atrocities hiding in the pages of history. It is only the proximity of our time to that of Nazism which keeps the image of horror alive.

"I feel, Herr Bendt, that Adolf Hitler answered a tremendous need in Germany. I stand in awe of what he accomplished. Further, it is incredible to discover that the same man who led the Reich and could wage such battles could also live for twenty-five years in obscurity, going about his business, dealing with and helping his neighbors. In these years of his life in Emmaus, I believe I understand what National Socialism could have become had it reached fruition: a society conscious of its heritage, founded on struggle, but at last living in peace with itself."

"Do you see National Socialism as a potent force today?"

"From the little I know of the movement, no. The foundation remains the past glories, tarnished but nonetheless spectacular in memory. If National Socialism is to rise once more, it must, I believe, shed this close allegiance to the past which represents a rigid, uncompromising example. If the political philosophy is represented correctly, there is no reason why Germany, with its economic strength, cannot assume the leadership of such a rising sentiment. But it must rid itself of the bullyboy image."

Erik Bendt sat back in the soft leather seat. He glanced out the window, at the fleeting images of russet fields broken by trees whose leaves were turning color. It was the loveliest time of year in a land he considered more beautiful than any other.

"I have waited many years to hear such words from a man such as yourself," he said. "There were times when I believed I would never have the opportunity to do so. Today is a momentous occasion for both of us—or I should say, *all* of us. In a little while you will be meeting some of my associates. I think you will find that what we have to say is rather interesting."

The limousine turned off the highway and proceeded up a secondary road, lined on either side by trees whose branches curved to meet overhead, forming a leafy canopy. The sunlight and motion of the car threw dappled shadows across the two passengers, alternately illuminating and hiding their faces. The driver eased the car up a steep grade, twisting the wheel to avoid the potholes gouged out by the rain. After the last turn, the road became level and Helmut Toller saw a large stone house set in a glade of pines and firs.

"It is a private club, with an excellent restaurant, that I and my friends have established. Come, we will meet them first. Ritter will be brought to us a little later."

It was clear to Toller that however important Ritter might be to him, he was nonetheless excluded from higher councils.

Erik Bendt led the way, entering through a side door and passing along the hardwood-paneled hallway to a vast sunlit living room, appointed in the manner of a hunting lodge. The single concession to modern taste was the sunken rectangle in the center, lined with sofas whose rust-and-yellow fabric was set off by a black slate coffee table. Even though the weather was temperate, a fire was burning in the brick-lined grate.

As Bendt stepped down into the rectangle, six men entered from another room. They were all soberly dressed—three in midnight-blue pinstripes, three sporting conservative gray suits. All were in their sixties; all were endowed with the aura of power.

"I'm sure the introductions are a mere formality," Erik Bendt said. "You know everyone here."

Yes, Toller did. He shook the proffered hands and his mind supplied a note on each of the men behind them: Theodor Fritsch, head of a conglomerate that controlled radio and television interests across Europe and some in Asia; Maximilian Harden, newspaper magnate of the stature of a Hearst or Thompson; Gustav Klemm, chief German negotiator with the Arab world on oil matters and former representative of Krupp; Felix Kersten, currently the Minister of Defense and chairman of a dozen international arms companies; Oswald Pohl, right-hand man of General Gerhard Wessel, chief of West German intelligence, the BND. And finally, Toller's would-be client of days gone by, Hans Bayer Weiss, premier financier, whose case involving his daughter Toller had turned down.

"Welcome, Herr Toller," Weiss said, smiling expansively. "I somehow knew our paths would cross again. No hard feelings about the last time, eh?"

"None at all, Herr Weiss," Toller answered carefully.

"Gentlemen, time is rather important to Herr Toller," Bendt said. "I suggest we proceed."

The seven men, who, among them, carried enough influence to shape the political and economic conditions of Germany, took their seats. Erik Bendt, acknowledged spokesman, opened the discussion.

"You understand, Herr Toller, all of us here were and still are National Socialists. But this does not imply that we have remained fixed in our opinions as, you have so rightly pointed out, have many of the Führer's followers.

"Since our present organization is quite unknown to the general public, I will give you the background details—which, you appreciate, will remain confidential. This, I think, will help you in understanding our position and the proposal that will be put to you.

"The present-day National Socialist Party is far-flung, with major power centers in South America, Germany and Austria. Like any political group, the party has evolved a difference of opinion among its hierarchy, of which we are a substantial part. We therefore have a 'right' and a 'left' wing, and this is not as much of a contradiction as you might think.

"The right side may be called the 'old guard,' although many of its members are of our age, some even younger. These men, most of whom have lived, as a matter of necessity or choice, in South America for the last quarter century—or more—are the adherents of what they believe is the pure National Socialist philosophy—that is, the principles set down in *Mein Kampf*. It is necessary to understand that time and distance have had an effect in entrenching their outlook. South America, while a congenial place to live with a reasonable amount of security, is nonetheless five thousand miles from Germany. It is all too easy to live on memories rather than take into account the changing times. However, until a few years ago these men were the centers of power in our party. They had been responsible for the continuity of security in South America, the multiplication of our investments, recruitment and such. But in the last, I would say, half decade, the balance has shifted back to Germany, where we have come to take over many of the responsibilities once held by our South American colleagues.

"As the German Republic evolved, we found not only that our authority was expanding but that a new understanding of National Socialism was coming into being. You understand that the whole party has been very careful in dealing with a Germany where, even though our influence is great, we must tread somewhat carefully. But the upshot was that we agreed that a change, or rather, an evolution in our philosophy was what was needed. One had to replace the image of a monster or bullyboy, as you put it; to do away with the blind reliance upon dogma a half century old.

"Needless to say, there came a time of confrontation in which our Austrian colleagues, true to form, decided to sit on the fence. However, we in Germany slowly began to evolve our own program, regardless of the disapproval and, in some instances, out-right hostility of the South American wing. To date I am pleased to say we have attracted a great many people of high intellect and imagination, those who perceive the world much as you do and see National Socialism as a basis on which a new social order may be built. Matters were taking their course when, all at once, the Führer came back from the dead.''

"You can appreciate the tremendous impact this event had on us, all of us, in the party," Hans Bayer Weiss said, carrying on the deposition. "The generally quiet lines of communications between Europe and South America suddenly came alive as rumors gave way to frenzied plans, and men who had lived only on memories at once discovered that their dreams might finally be realized. All sorts of proposals were put forward: the Führer should be abducted and brought to South America to take his rightful place in the party; the party should use this revival by emerging from the shadows and show how broad its appeal was in Germany and Austria; someone even suggested a *coup d'état* against the German government. In short, euphoria overtook the party for several weeks.

"Such a mood gave way, as it must, to sobriety and, with it, a sense of caution. We were all quite awed by the Führer's reappearance; yet as world attention focused on him, so we too felt some of the glare of publicity. Too many people, primarily journalists and investigators, became interested in us; there was speculation as to how the party would react to such scrutiny. The South American wing came forward with the idea that we either act on this God-given opportunity or else retreat into silence. The choice was a difficult one, because while our emotions were with the Führer, pragmatically it was not expedient to act on them. It was at this point that I and my Continental colleagues gained the upper hand.

"Since the party was quite unable to come to a clear decision as to how to deal with the Führer's revival, this, we argued, was a clear indication that it had stagnated, on the theoretical level, to a point at which it was powerless to act. Such a situation had to be rectified at once. It was therefore put to the South American contingent to bring forth a plan of action or else allow us to make drastic policy changes. I shall not go into the details which can reduce all great ventures to pettiness. To put it simply, we, the Europeans, won out. The result of our victory was this: a unanimous decision that the Führer, although still the living embodiment of the movement, was no longer essential to it. The party had outgrown its creator."

"I see that such an admission shocks you," Oswald Pohl observed. "But consider, Herr Toller: does there not come a point at which a great man *must* be placed above the daily workings of his creation? When Stalin died, Stalinism was born; with the death of Che Guevara, a new cult around his figure emerged. So it should be with the Führer."

"But Adolf Hitler is not dead—and may not be for quite some time!" Toller objected.

"Hear us out, Toller," Weiss interjected. "We are not placing the Führer in the grave, only in perspective. Understand this: his emergence, and your involvement in this case—you because of your youth—have acted as weather balloons for the party—inadvertently, of course, but none the less effectively for that. The taboo has been broken. The people of Germany are talking of National Socialism once again. And may I tell you how they speak of it? With wonder and curiosity on the part of the young, which is most encouraging. I am not stating that all at once the party will reappear before the public; it is too early for that; but the acceptance of it is taking place. We are no longer condemned out of hand; instead, your generation, the one so burdened by the sins of the fathers, is taking stock of our principles. As for the reaction of older people, there appears to be relief among them, as though some burden, largely of guilt, had been lifted. Oh, it is nothing that might be equated with the euphoria of the 1930s, and it shouldn't be, yet the positive response is there; it is all that much stronger because it is so quiet, like the current you cannot hear, but rather feel around your feet when stepping into a stream.

"Since the hour of Kleemann's announcement that the Führer was alive, we in the German wing of the party have been monitoring public opinion most closely. Our conclusions are that while this is not the time for a rebirth of National Socialism as we, the veterans, understand it, we must pass on our mantle to the next generation—that which is reexamining our precepts and which will foster its own version of our philosophy based on the advances, as well as the errors, of the past."

"We are old men," Erik Bendt said gently. "Many of us are tired, some disillusioned, but all remain National Socialists. To give what is left for us to give would be the greatest joy of our lives. That is why I am honored to meet with you. For we believe that you should be, and will be, the spiritual heir to the Führer of the Third Reich."

His shock must have been evident, yet Toller saw no one smiling at his astonishment. The others regarded him levelly, with sober expressions, as though conferring upon him a responsibility they were satisfied he could bear but whose scope and implications he mightn't be aware of completely.

I am being offered the power, Toller thought. Its depths are opening before me. What began on the Walpurgis Night—no, even further back—is all coming to fruition.

Erik Bendt turned to Toller and took hold of his arm.

"Yes, Helmut: you are to replace Adolf Hitler. You are an excellent lawyer. In court, I have seen few with your skills and style. But you concentrate so much on the issues at hand that you do not step outside yourself and watch how you work, how it is you speak, the depth of passion in your words and gestures. You are brilliant! You must believe this, for in belief lies strength, and from strength a nation is reborn. You rose to a position of authority very quickly. The powerful and influential sought you out. For some you chose to work; others you turned away. Ultimately you elected to be not the servant, but the master, your own master. I am now saying to you: go, and be the leader of many."

"And how do you know I will not betray the trust you show in me?" Toller challenged him. "Are you so sure I would not refuse to lead? That I might not be content to live as an ordinary man?"

"Ah, it is always the mark of a leader to be tempted by humility," Hans Bayer Weiss declared. "But there are those who can look beyond it, who recognize the passion that burns behind humility, the will that comes forth only when a man is truly tested to the utmost of his genius, as you are being tested in your representation of the Führer. No, Helmut, to be great is in your blood; to strive and attain what other men can barely dream of:

that is your destiny; and I know—I can almost reach out and touch it—this force within you. The world does not yet realize that when it looks upon the Court in New York, it is seeing not only one great man, the Führer, but another, yourself. Those of us who, through experience, recognize the similarity can see in you the next generation of National Socialism. It is there, as surely as the characteristics of the father are visible in his son.

"But as with every responsibility, and surely you are heir to one of the heaviest, there are conditions to be fulfilled. The first is recognition of who one is and whether he is at all capable of assuming the task. This you have fulfilled by undertaking the Führer's defense and handling it in the manner we have all seen. There is another: you must be prepared to accept the idea of, and possibly engineer, the martyrdom of the Führer.

"We are willing to give you Ritter because his testimony will make for a stronger case. It is absolutely necessary to show that the Führer, although represented by the finest counsel, whose arguments were supplemented by testimony, lost the decision because the world could never have afforded to let him win from the beginning."

Helmut Toller turned on him. "But there is every chance I can succeed! If I have Ritter, then with the testimony of the other witnesses, I might place the Court in a position in which they would find it impossible to return a guilty verdict!"

"Oh, yes, that is quite conceivable. If I thought otherwise, I might not have spoken so frankly. As it is, I must tell you that the Führer cannot, for the sake of the Fourth Reich, of which you will become leader, emerge as victor. It is a fine line we have placed you upon: the man must die, yet he must do so a hero."

"You are asking me to engineer the loss of this case," Toller said softly. It was a statement, not a question. "To present a brilliant defense for all the world to see but one with intrinsic flaws, discernible only to me and Hans Kleemann, so that Adolf Hitler will be, inevitably, condemned."

"We realize what it is we are asking of you," Hans Bayer Weiss said softly. "You do not like to lose. It is natural for you to have reservations, especially in view of who your client is, the amount of effort you have devoted to saving him. But you must understand the concept of sacrifice."

Erik Bendt held up his hand.

"Gentlemen, time is pressing. If you feel that nothing else need be added to our conversation, then I propose that I introduce Helmut to Ritter. I believe he will then understand what we mean by 'sacrifice.'"

They all rose and once again shook hands with Toller. As he stepped up, Weiss said to him, "We believe in you, Helmut Toller. Nothing you ask for will be denied, remember that. For in you we have the living continuation of ourselves, our hopes, our ideals, our understanding of what the New Reich must be."

When the others had gone, Erik Bendt led Toller outside. "You see the man coming toward us?" Bendt pointed at the figure of a gentleman in hunting tweeds approaching the car, walking with a stiff military gait. Behind him, the attorney also recognized the detective with whom he had met that morning.

"He is Ritter. I shall leave you to speak with him. He will show you what I mean by sacrifice."

Ritter came up to them and snapped his heels together before Bendt.

"A privilege to meet with you again," he said crisply.

"This is Herr Toller," Bendt introduced him.

Ritter's handshake was hard, an extension of the manner in which he carried himself.

"Herr Toller, there are no words that suffice to show the gratitude I feel for what you are doing. In joining our cause, by fighting for the Führer, you are fighting for all of us."

"Herr Toller was apprehensive that you might have reservations about revising your testimony," Bendt said.

"None!" Ritter said immediately. "I place myself entirely at your disposal, Herr Toller. Unlike that scum Stephanus, I remember what a soldier's duty is: to serve his leader. The Führer remains my commanding officer. I am prepared to testify that he issued no such order and that I alone am responsible for ordering the executions at Kupai."

"You understand that by so doing you are leaving yourself open to subsequent prosecution by the Bonn Government?" Toller said.

"I am aware of it, yes. But that is of no consequence to me. I have a duty to perform, and I remain bound by my oath to the Führer."

Bendt looked at the defense counsel and said, "You understand now what it is I meant by sacrifice? The individual, no matter who, can never be more important than the whole."

"Would you give the court your full name and the military rank you held in September 1941," Helmut Toller said amicably.

"Karl Ritter, major, Fifth Corps, SS."

"You were present during the occupation of a town called Kupai on September 4, 1941?"

"I was."

"And on the morning of September 6 you discovered that a unit of SS soldiers had in fact been ambushed?"

"That is correct."

"Having had an opportunity to examine the witness Veznarod's testimony, do you dispute the fact that you took command of the situation following this attack?"

"No; it was my responsibility to do so."

"Having carefully read the testimony of Veznarod, do you feel the witness has accurately explained the circumstances that followed the massacre of the German troops?"

"Not at all."

"In what way is the testimony erroneous?"

"I remember the events as the witness has described them until the point at which he refers to the radio transmission between the front and the Eagle's Nest in Bavaria. I do not know how the witness could have construed that the order for the reprisals came directly from the Führer, since our link with Bavaria lasted only a few seconds. In fact, I recall being cut off almost as soon as I began speaking. I requested Berlin OKW, the High Command of the Wehrmacht, to reestablish the relay, but they said it was impossible."

"So in point of fact, Adolf Hitler could not have known of the tragedy at Kupai."

"No, not in the slightest detail. However, I did recount the incident to General Olden at OKW."

"Did *he* issue any directives?"

"No. The General stated he would inform the Führer and that I should have a complete report sent to Berlin as quickly as possible."

"Is this Court to understand, then, that you yourself ordered and arranged for the reprisal executions?"

"That is correct. The selection of hostages and the method of their execution was entirely my responsibility. I acted without any qualms, since I believed, and still do, that the execution of prisoners, civilian or military, in reprisal is a time-honored act of war. Had the killings of my soldiers never taken place, I should not have had to retaliate."

"I would ask you again, so that the Court and all who listen might not misinterpret what you have said: did the Führer, Adolf Hitler, explicitly order you to shoot four hundred and thirty civilians after the Kupai massacre?"

"No, he did not. I claim all responsibility for that action."

Helmut Toller addressed the Court:

"I am satisfied that the charge made by the witness Veznarod has been refuted and move that the second count of the indictment be dismissed."

"Does the prosecution wish to cross-examine the witness?" Sir Adrian Potter asked.

Hans Kleemann, who had been sitting listening very closely, stirred.

"Cross-examine?" he inquired softly. "Yes, there are in fact a few discrepancies I should like to have the witness set in order—discrepancies arising from his testimony in his own defense at the Hamburg trial of 1956. From a transcript of those proceedings I quote . . ."

Kleemann flipped through some pages and ran his finger down the lines until he found the passage.

" '*Question:* Did you receive orders to execute civilians in the subjugated territories of the East?

" '*Answer:* Yes.

" '*Question:* Who issued those orders?

" '*Answer:* SS General Maser.

" '*Question:* When were these orders issued?

" '*Answer:* In the final briefing before Operation Barbarossa.

" '*Question:* But did you not contact Maser again prior to ordering the executions of the hostages at Kupai?

" '*Answer:* Yes, but the communications with Berlin OKW were very poor. The reception was bad.

" '*Question:* Did OKW subsequently pass you through to Hitler in Bavaria?

" '*Answer:* Yes.

" '*Question:* Did you in fact speak directly with Hitler about the attack on your soldiers?

" '*Answer:* Yes.

" '*Question:* Did he give you a clear directive to begin reprisals?

" '*Answer:* He said that the reprisal should begin immediately. I did not consider the order odd, for it was known to all SS officers that any attacks upon their units were to be met with immediate reprisals. Although the ratio was not fixed, the figure of ten to one, hostages for our men, was the one I heard most often.

" '*Question:* From what you say, you took the initiative in determining just how many people you would murder?

" '*Answer:* No, that is not true! Do not put words into my mouth. The Führer commanded that the reprisals should begin at once. I have told you the ratio was generally ten to one. I only followed orders I knew to exist.' "

Hans Kleemann replaced the transcript pages and stepped over to the witness box. But although his questions were put to Ritter, his face was turned to the Bench.

"If you stand by your testimony now," he suggested quietly, "that means you perjured yourself in the Hamburg trial. Did you in fact commit perjury?"

Karl Ritter did not hesitate in answering.

"Yes, I did lie in the course of the trial."

"At that point in the transcript which I read out?"

"Yes."

"At any other time?"

"I cannot remember, but I do not think so."

"But there is the possibility you lied, as you put it, in other instances?"

"It is possible there were misinterpretations, things I might have clarified . . ."

"But you tell us now that in this case you lied—not misinterpreted, not forgot, nothing so indecisive—you lied!" the prosecutor kept on.

"Yes, yes, all right! I was fighting for my life then. I had to lie."

"Thank you for understanding your circumstances so lucidly. Perhaps you are unaware that in the case of perjury we will have to re-try you, and that the law for mass murder is still in effect, even though the Statute of Limitations did away with it in 1969— this because *your* trial was held prior to the passage of the Statute. Therefore, when you return to Germany, the prosecution, on the basis of your evidence here, will ask for the death penalty, quite appropriate for mass murder."

Hans Kleemann paused, looking into the steadily gazing, almost liquid eyes of the man on the stand.

He doesn't care, the prosecutor thought. He is like the *hashashin*—their minds polluted to the point of euphoria before they go forth to commit murder. He has been told to expect what I say to him, and he has received reassurances that the party will not abandon him. How can he be absolutely certain? He cannot. And here is the key. It doesn't matter if the party keeps or reneges on its word. He is convinced of his righteous position, of his adherence to the man sitting only a few feet away, his leader whom he is serving once again, to whom, before the world, he shall remain faithful to the end. He is willing to die for him—what greater immortality is there?

"Are you certain, Karl Ritter, that perhaps what you have recounted to the Court is not a misinterpretation, a slip of the memory, and that in fact your earlier account, in 1956, was the correct one?"

"I will not tolerate such an accusation!" Ritter lashed out. "I stand by my word. I did not speak to the Führer about the killings in Kupai, nor were the reprisals carried out on anyone's command other than my own!"

"I find it odd you should be so indignant," Hans Kleemann observed. "After all, you have perjured yourself once; what is to prevent your doing so again?"

"It is different now!"

"Oh? How is that?"

"I never said—ever!—that the Führer issued the orders for reprisals. I have come forward because he, the Führer, stands unjustly accused!"

"Unjustly accused, you say? How so? On this second count of

the indictment? Are you saying he never knew about the killings at Kupai?"

The barrage of questions forced Ritter to glance quickly at Toller, his expression one of panic.

"I must object!" Helmut Toller spoke up. "It is not permissible to badger the witness in such a shameful manner!"

"If such is the feeling of the witness, I shall put forward my last questions one by one, so that he may answer them fully." Kleemann offered.

"The witness clearly understands that he is under oath, and he has answered questions put to him without hesitation," Toller said coldly. "The last four were quite repetitive in their nature."

"Herr Toller, sit down," Dieter Wolff said quietly. "You overreach yourself in your concern for the witness' rights before the prosecution. I suggest you consider a more salient issue. Does the witness realize that if he stands on this testimony, he will be returned to Germany to face charges arising from the Kupai massacre?"

"He does," Toller said.

"I wish to hear the witness' own words," Wolff retorted.

Karl Ritter was barely aware of the question directed at him. Ritter shifted in the chair and caught sight of Adolf Hitler, staring at him. "He is the only one who matters," Ritter whispered, betrayed by his exhilaration. To serve once again, to rise to attention and salute his Führer . . . But Toller had warned him again and again about the danger of doing something like that. Such a gesture would not help the Führer and only antagonize the Court. So Ritter held back; but as a release for his anger, he turned on Hans Kleemann.

"I have nothing to add to or subtract from my testimony. I am sickened by what the prosecutor is doing to me and I seek the protection of the Court."

"That you shall have," Dieter Wolff said dryly. "You are remanded into the custody of the prosecutor's office until such time as formal charges have been filed."

"Before the witness is excused, I would like to propose a final motion to the Bench," Hans Kleemann said.

"Proceed."

"Given the nature of the witness' testimony, the prosecution believes it is unnecessary to challenge his character and credibility directly. His perjury speaks for itself. However, surely with such a direct and strong account, one that ostensibly exonerates Adolf Hitler of direct complicity in the Kupai massacre, the defense would now be willing to place the accused on the stand to corroborate Major Ritter's story. The prosecution therefore would like to have Adolf Hitler called to take the stand, with this witness to be held ready, still under oath.''

''The defense objects, naturally,'' Toller said. ''The testimony of Major Ritter is more than sufficient to exculpate the accused.''

''No, not at all. We are all aware that Major Ritter has a proclivity for changing his testimony. If the accused were to substantiate his story, then everything Major Ritter has told us might appear more credible.''

''The Court agrees with the prosecution,'' Sir Adrian said. ''Would the defense place its charge on the stand to confirm or deny this previous testimony?''

Helmut Toller stepped over to Hitler's side and whispered, ''Yes? Surely you see what we have to gain!''

''We have gained enough,'' Hitler said softly. ''You have done well.''

''As my client, you must listen to me!'' Toller answered fiercely. His voice was dry and choked with fury, and he tightened his grip over the head of the microphone to prevent its picking up their voices. ''Veznarod's testimony damaged our position—badly, but we made up for that with Ritter. A few words, that is all I ask of you, confirming what he has said. I will not allow Kleemann to mistreat you.''

Adolf Hitler did not rebuke Toller for his outburst. He was rather touched by it, and there stirred a feeling of gratitude within him for the concern Toller was showing.

''I will not say anything,'' he said distinctly.

''If not for yourself,'' Toller whispered viciously ''why not do it for him?''

In spite of himself, he flung out his arm at Ritter.

''He has obeyed his oath,'' Hitler said. ''He has served me to the last. I owe him nothing.''

Helmut Toller turned away from the table. He remembered Erik Bendt and thought how unwittingly Adolf Hitler was cooperating in his own sacrifice. It was almost pathetic.

"I'm sorry, I have no more questions," Toller said softly to Ritter.

Ritter nodded sharply, seemingly unconcerned, not taking his eyes from the Führer.

"I take it the accused will not come forward," Kleemann challenged him.

"My client wishes to abstain from commenting in any fashion on the testimony given by the witness."

"The prosecution will not insist that he do so," Kleemann said with finality. "His silence damns him enough."

As Toller wheeled about to retort, Karl Ritter rose and in one incredible motion flung out his right arm and saluted Adolf Hitler.

"Heil Hitler!"

For a moment, all motion within the world ceased. Toller, who had raised his hand and was about to hit the table out of frustration, froze his action in midair. Hans Kleemann stood a few feet away, head thrown back, stunned by Ritter's action. On the bench, each of the justices sat rigid; their common expression was one of incredulity.

Then Adolf Hitler rose and, facing Ritter, flicked up his right hand in the salute he had made famous and responded, "Heil!"

He remained standing until Sir Adrian's gavel came down to shatter the paralytic spell that Hitler had cast upon the Court.

Once again they were gathered at their private lodge in the Bavarian countryside.

Erik Bendt depressed a button on the console next to him, and the television picture faded into a single white dot, which then disappeared.

"Tenacious, isn't he?" Oswald Pohl, of BND intelligence, remarked. "I'm not reassured he has understood us."

Others of the seven men who had met with Toller nodded in agreement.

Bendt studied the skeptical faces and was about to reply, but it was Hans Bayer Weiss who spoke out.

"You refer to the fact that he is pursuing his defense of Hitler a little too diligently?"

"Precisely," Pohl said. "Even though he had his hand over the microphone it was obvious he was telling Hitler to say something in support of Ritter's testimony.''

"Undoubtedly," Weiss agreed. "But there is no need to be concerned. We have asked that he betray Adolf Hitler. Inherent in the man are personal sentiments Toller has for him. It is not the man or even client he must betray, but *his own feelings*. I submit to you that Toller's action is indicative of this. If he were a moral man, he would have *compelled* Hitler to testify. Obviously he feels deeply for Ritter and his contribution. But Toller did nothing, aside from giving rein to his feelings.

"Gentlemen, we are watching a man mold himself, not blindly accept what we want him to. Let him come to his own terms with what he is doing to Hitler and how. When the process is complete, we shall have a true leader, a man who understands betrayal, its necessity and how it is to be executed.''

There was no dissent.

A few hundred kilometers away, in the town of Emmaus, a light was suddenly extinguished in the window of a quiet house. Lillian Grubber lit yet one more cigarette and waved the smoke away. She too had been watching the trial proceedings, and had she heard the words of Hans Bayer Weiss, she would have agreed with him completely. But she would have added to them her feelings as a mother.

Lillian Grubber understood that she had lost her foster son the moment he had decided to represent Adolf Hitler. She had cried her tears of rage and helplessness; the catharsis had come, and a dull ache followed. But she would cry no more. There was only one act left to her in his behalf. She had considered it ever since speaking with Hans Kleemann in Emmaus. Now, as a last attempt to at least cripple the evil she saw infecting her foster son, Lillian Grubber would implement it.

Lillian rose and walked in the darkness to the telephone. She dialed the operator and asked for the number of Lufthansa airlines.

Hans Kleemann rose to his feet. It was a new day, but the words he would speak were old, ancient. He had uttered them so often in the past. Would it be different now?

"There was not one solution but many solutions. Each race and nationality—the Russians, Ukrainians and Slovaks, the Poles, Estonians and Lithuanians, the Magyars, Gypsies and Yugoslavs—for each of these, the Third Reich planned and, in most instances, was in the process of executing a predetermined end, consisting in extinction or enslavement. The final ignominy, which brought eternal shame upon the word 'solution,' was practiced upon the Jewish people, against whose fate we must measure all other suffering.

"In the course of the Nuremberg Trials, the world was offered precise details of atrocity proposals and extermination programs. We were all witness to the macabre spectacle of men, once leaders of various Reich factions, passing on the blame to one another: the Einsatzgruppen leader would say his order came from the RSHA, the Head Office for Reich Security of the SS; but an RHSA commander would immediately turn about and confront an official formerly in the Head Office for Administration and Economy. These were the same men, mind you, who in 1942 vied with one another to produce the highest death figures. But although they heaped and shifted responsibility, not one of these men—not one!—ever went so far as to place the ultimate responsibility on Adolf Hitler."

Hans Kleemann turned away from the Bench and looked out at the Assembly through the shield.

"We have arrived at the final count in the indictment, the charge of crimes against humanity," he said gently. "The previous charges were no less onerous to deal with, no less outrageous; yet it is impossible not to feel that in dealing with crimes against humanity we are faced with the most awesome responsibility. Awesome for this reason: unlike either the Nuremberg or Jerusalem courts, which had to rely on testimony from surviving Nazi officials, we have today the one man to whom all guilt on this count may be traced. We will not be obliged to concern ourselves with the argument of 'higher orders,' for there were none; we will not have to tolerate pleas of ignorance, since the initiator of an act may not employ such a subterfuge. We have gone beyond that.

"It would not have been difficult for the prosecution to arrange for witnesses—survivors—of Hitler's Holocaust to come forward. Each race and nationality could have been amply represented. But the world has already heard their testimonies many times over—in Nuremberg, Hamburg, Bonn, Jerusalem, Moscow. There is nothing to be added to their stories and accounts, nor is anything gained in having them again recount their personal tragedies.

"No, I will not call upon the victims to render testimony. Instead, the prosecution will ask Adolf Hitler to take the stand and, from there, tell all who listen why he undertook to bathe Europe in blood. The prosecution will represent the victims, all of them, and in the story of the Jews, it will ask the world to remember the fates of other nationalities who were brothers in suffering."

Hans Kleemann faced the defense desk and spoke out:

"I call upon the Führer of the Third Reich to come forward and, before speaking, remember that he is bound by the oath he has already sworn."

Slowly Adolf Hitler rose from his chair and limped across to the witness stand. Taking care, he installed himself in the box and sat down, head erect, eyes fixed on Hans Kleemann, proud, insolent and fearless.

"Would you admit that you held a particular antipathy toward the Jews, a hatred which you expounded in *Mein Kampf?*"

"Why should I deny it?" Hitler demanded. "Is not every man prejudiced against one breed of the human race?"

"But your prejudice went well beyond the boundaries of intolerance. It was transformed into a paranoia. Did you not in *Mein Kampf* write that 'the first task in the creation of a Germanic state is the elimination of the existing Jewish one?' "

"In my writings I state the obvious truth: the Jews are a homeless race and remain so even with the creation of Israel. But in the 1930s there was no Israel. The tribes of Judaism had been scattered throughout the earth. In Europe they were to be found in every land, and each country in its turn demonstrated its loathing for them: in France, there was the Dreyfus affair; in Russia, the systematic pogroms. In Germany we were developing our own method of dealing with this foreign element, methods put forward in *Mein Kampf.*

"I, however, insist that I acted only as the voice of the German conscience. For us, the Jew has always been the outsider; and worse, he has delighted in showing his difference. What can a race expect if its customs refuse to become part of the culture in which it lives? What need is satisfied by retaining strange dress habits and appearances; by adhering to a mystical faith which in its humility shows its pride and so demonstrates condescension to everything else around it? I have no answer to this; but I understood then, as I do now, that this *difference*, this insistence on remaining separate, was what repelled the German people.''

"It repelled them to the point at which you felt it necessary to include in your speech to the Reichstag of January 30, 1939, the following statement: 'There shall be a war which, with it, will bring the annihilation of the Jewish race in Europe'?''

"I was speaking as commander of the armed forces,'' Hitler answered coldly. "It is only natural for subversives to be warned of what might happen to them if they engage in sabotage or hinder the war effort.''

"You regarded Jews as subversives?'' Kleemann inquired thoughtfully. "How can you overlook the fact that of all European Jews, those living in Germany were by far the most assimilated; that they had, at great personal and emotional cost, loosened, if not altogether broken, their ties with Judaism; that they had embraced the German culture and enriched it, thinking it to be their own?'' he finished angrily.

"They were always outsiders!'' Hitler shouted back. "What loyalty had they but to their own kind? Do you think one could have trusted them as Germans, or Frenchmen, or Englishmen? I have always regarded Jews as I have Communists: traitors, a people with a greater allegiance to something other than the country in which they live. Of course traitors in wartime may expect to be punished!''

"You viewed Jews with the same contempt you held for mental and physical defectives?''

"Even more so. In time I came to look upon Jews as freaks of nature as well.''

"On September 1, 1939, did you send a written order to Reichsleiter Bouhler and Dr. Brandt, officials of the Führer's Chancellery responsible for euthanasia, which read in part: '. . . patients who are considered incurable according to the best available human judgment . . . may be granted mercy killing'?''

"Yes, I issued such an edict."

"By it, did you not condemn over one hundred thousand of your own countrymen to a premature death, since your sole concern was not the welfare of these unfortunates but rather the medicines and skills they required?"

"I do not deny that with the outbreak of war imminent, it was my duty as commander-in-chief to free as much medical equipment, supplies and personnel as possible so that all of it might be available to my soldiers. But what you are truly asking is whether I felt any compunction in so doing. I assure you I had none. You are making euthanasia out to be some heinous act because it suits your purposes to do so, because you feel the context in which it came into being was evil. But was it really? Have the healthy not always shunned the sick, and have you never felt or witnessed the revulsion of a healthy organism when confronted with a freak? Let us take pains to be honest: in many respects the alleviating of pain is just a placebo in societal terms; the removal of the unhealthy as a prophylactic measure is a responsible action. You cannot condemn me simply because I do not play the hypocrite."

"Even if I could accept your reasoning, that does not alter the direction of your acts or the inevitable results that ensued," Hans Kleemann said sorrowfully. "Philip Bouhler, who was responsible for the Führer's Chancellery, separate and distinct from the Reich and Party chancelleries, was also head of the 'secret decrees' section, was he not?"

"He was."

"And he was in charge of arranging *Aktion t 4*, as the euthanasia program was named?"

"That is correct."

"From *Aktion t 4* there evolved *Aktion 13 f 14*, the refinement of the same program but whose effects were extended to Jews, Communists and others with 'antistate tendencies'?"

"Bouhler had authority for the extension."

"Then *Aktion 13 f 14* was further refined, and the result was the directive Goering issued to Heydrich on January 31, 1941, mentioning a need to begin work on the final solution to the Jewish problem?"

"It is quite possible that Heydrich received such an order.

After all, Jews were being expelled from Germany at a tremendous rate, far too high for any kind of orderly resettlement.''

"You do not quarrel with Eichmann's statement at his trial in which he explicitly stated that Heydrich, in July of 1941, said to him: 'The Führer has ordered the physical extermination of the Jews'?''

"I do not recall issuing such an explicit order, but that is of no consequence.''

"Why is that?''

"Because Heydrich was one of my most trusted men. In 1939, when he realized the threat that Poland posed for us, he understood the need for swift, brutal action, not only against the military of that country but against the civilian population as well—especially the Jews.''

"Especially the Jews . . .'' Hans Kleemann murmured. "Against a defenseless population with no military tradition you turned loose such dogs as Heydrich, Frank, Mueller and Schongarth?''

"How sick your preaching makes me!'' Hitler shouted at him. "If Jews were such a precious commodity, why didn't anyone take them from me? Answer that! I did not want Jews in Germany; the German people did not want them. But when I placed nine hundred of them on a ship and it set sail, which country opened its arms to them? Not one! I told Himmler to sell them, cheaply if need be, only so that we might be rid of them, but there were no buyers; not even the fat, self-satisfied Jews of the United States, who did so many glorious things for their brethren *after* the war, came forward to claim their own people. So do not talk to *me* about a lack of mercy!''

"I have every right to bring those faces behind the Auschwitz wire before your eyes!'' Hans Kleemann raged at him. "You first made them stateless, then gathered them for expulsion; from there the 'resettlement' became internment, and from internment, death. Your contempt for all things human was so thorough that you did not have to issue distinct and separate orders; your slaves merely extended and purified your intentions—was that not it?''

"I was a military commander,'' Hitler said haughtily. "By 1941, because of growing incompetence on the part of my General

Staff, it was necessary for me to devote my time exclusively to the military campaigns. I could not have cared less about what was happening in the conquered territories, so long as it did not deter the war effort."

"But you knew of the death camps—their functions, their priorities; and most of all, *as a military commander,* you must have known of the tremendous burden they placed on your supplies and manpower?"

"Whatever Himmler needed he received; I did not interfere with his schedule."

"And his schedule concerned itself with the killing of people, did it not?—Jews, Slavs, Gypsies! This aspect of the war was far more important to you than the actual fighting. How can you tell us otherwise when you allowed hundreds of thousands of your own soldiers to die or be taken prisoner at Stalingrad when all the while the freight trains that might have saved them continued to run to and from the death camps?"

"Stalingrad was a mistake," Hitler said at once, his voice suddenly losing its force. "I lost so many fine men, needlessly. Stalingrad is my one regret; a battle I have pondered over and over again, with which I have not been able to come to terms. It should have been won; without question, we should have won it. . . .

"But I tell you also," he snapped, "that not all the locomotives and cars in the world would have helped my men in that hour. The General Staff had made a mess of the campaign; it was too late. . . ."

"So instead of creating your empire in the East, that 'living space' which you wanted for the German people, you turned the earth of Russia into a giant grave. Meanwhile, in Poland, the death camps kept on working, more furiously than ever before, even though you were losing the war."

"There was no time to think of those things. My loyalty was to my nation and my soldiers, and both were suffering."

"No time." Hans Kleemann turned on him, his eyes glistening with tears. "No time for the millions you made your victims. How profound your contempt for them must have been—and still is! You understand that this is the very essence of your crime: contempt. When we speak of crimes against humanity, we mean not only the acts of violence that are perpetrated by one man against his brothers; we concern ourselves with more than the executioners themselves. You surrounded yourself with and delegated the powers of life and death to men whose brutality and inhumanity were undisguised. You knew that you had only to voice a thought—that Slavs were subhuman, or that Jews must have their final solution—and that thought would be transmuted into action. After you had done this, you did not concern yourself with the consequences of these actions upon your own people, although you knew, in very specific terms, what they were: you had them accomplices in your crime."

"Who is the guiltier, I wonder?" Hitler demanded of him. "The engineer from I. G. Farben who designed the chambers and crematoria and who, as a result, understood the exact technical details of the killings, or I, who merely issued an edict that Jews be resettled and then that a final solution, as you call it, be found for them?

"You must understand that I never concerned myself with the details of deportation; I scarcely knew the names of all the camps that had been set up for enemies—*all* enemies—of the Reich! Yet now you wish to tell me that there was a single master plan for extermination and I was its sole originator. No, Prosecutor; had that been the case, then surely Europe would have had no Jews left at all! Even the Wannsee Conference over which Heydrich presided in 1942 failed to bring about a true direction to follow as far as the Jews were concerned. That they continued to be killed is true, but it wasn't until late 1942 and 1943 that Himmler succeeded in institutionalizing their liquidation."

"By then you knew what was being done to them?"

"I knew Jews were being put to work at Krupp; others were employed in sensitive defense industries. Whoever was of no use to us was, I presumed, being liquidated."

"And you had no remorse about any of this?"

"None. You are attempting, Prosecutor, to play the role of the moralist, the outraged 'good' man. I tell you, you are having little success. So your attempt to place guilt upon me must come to a futile end: this because there is too much guilt around us—then as now—right here in this Assembly—for you to portion out so much onto me. You know it was not the Germans who invented the modern-day concentration camp but the British in the Boer

War; it was not the Germans but the Russians, in the secrecy of
Siberia, who refined them, and who brought a new meaning to
the word 'genocide' for our age. Who remembers, Prosecutor,
the names of those eastern tribes Stalin had forcibly removed
from their Caspian homeland and sent off to the taiga? Do you?
Do I? No. How much did the world bleed for those peasants
Stalin systematically murdered in the 1930s? Does the conscience
of the world not function in precisely the way Stalin expounded:
one worker killed in a traffic accident is a tragedy; eleven million
dead is a statistic?

"Look around you, Prosecutor." Hitler swept his arm across,
as though displaying the delegates seated beyond the shield.

"How many of those honorable men and women represent
states that did not even exist during the last war? And how many
of them remain, for all their posture and feathers, simply sav-
ages? Why, I can see from here a black with tribal scars upon his
face! How will your refined arguments on justice and the nature
of guilt affect him, an animal who may turn and slay you in the
cruelest manner? Your civilization has given him the veneer of
culture; our great universities have shown him what it means to
be profound in spirit. But surely that is not what he cares about.
His concern is with arms merchants, military advisers and intelligence agencies. He seeks to bring his tribal skills of war into the
twentieth century so that answering to his innate bestiality, he
may slaughter more of his enemies than ever before. Do I have to
recount for you, Prosecutor, the massacres that have taken place
in Asia and Africa, in South America and the Middle East? Surely
I think it unnecessary.

"So you must tell me, Prosecutor, where it is my guilt lies!"
Hitler shouted suddenly. "You must tell me and the whole
world—because if you cannot, then surely you cannot convict
me."

"The world is an imperfect place," Kleemann said, staring out
into the Assembly, "and will remain so possibly forever. Yet
there comes an hour when the darkness must be pushed away; a
man must rise and say with clarity that this is enough, regardless
of what nightmare may be consuming his fellowmen. No, it is
true you are not the only tyrant alive today; there have been
greater and lesser men such as yourself in the past. But still you,

and you alone, because you exist and because the results of your deeds live on, must be punished."

Hans Kleemann turned on his heel, and his arm shot out at Adolf Hitler. Caught in the stark white lights, his hair askew and lips trembling, he cried out the final accusations in words born of unfathomable rage, his voice the clarion for all those who had waited a quarter century for their vindication.

"It is for the victims that I demand punishment! For them, so that they may be the last to suffer at your hands. We cannot bring them back, but at least we can ensure that no more will follow. And this will come to pass because we know that you are the evil which can no longer recognize anything other than itself, which has no conception of goodness, and so we know that we must banish you forever. We cannot leave you to judge yourself or to have you weave justification out of your twisted vision and logic. We do here only that which we hope others would have done for us had we been the victims—condemn you for our sorrows!"

He stood very still, as though frozen by the power of his words. Then slowly Hans Kleemann stepped back toward his table, his eyes still holding those of Adolf Hitler, who was getting to his feet, his fury about to break loose. It was at that moment that the door through which the justices entered and left the court was opened and a uniformed Marine stepped in. He marched smartly up to the podium and presented Dieter Wolff with a sealed envelope. The German jurist opened it, read the note and passed it around to the others. Etta Kirsch whispered the message to Sir Adrian, who nodded, then leaned toward his microphone.

"There will be a recess of a quarter of an hour," he announced.

Hans Kleemann immediately turned to Toller, who was looking at him. Each thought the other had arranged this interval as part of his strategy. But it was clear to both, from the expressions of suspicion and curiosity, that this wasn't the case.

The prosecutor sat back, forming a pyramid with his fingers, and waited for the outcome of this interruption. Before him lay the list of witnesses Toller would call when the proceedings resumed. These, the prosecutor knew, were several townspeople from Emmaus, selected by Toller to speak for Hitler, including the mayor, who would present that petition on behalf of the village to have Hitler released.

When he thought of the petition, Kleemann remembered Lillian Grubber, who hadn't signed. He wondered how she was faring now and regretted not having telephoned her before leaving Munich. What was it he had been afraid of? Her offer to help, or his reluctance to accept his own need for such a woman? Both seemed insignificant reasons for silence.

Perhaps, he thought, I should have accepted her help. Perhaps together we might have persuaded Toller to leave the case. If she had helped me, she would be close by now . . .

"Ah, this is so much foolishness," Kleemann muttered aloud, and was immediately aware that Toller had raised his head. He had forgotten the microphones.

Better for me, Kleemann thought, to concentrate on my job. What is past is past.

Yet as a lawyer, he reflected, he should have brought her to New York, it was the man who was all too aware of her suffering and had not wished to add to it. He felt Toller would make no impression with his witnesses, that he was playing on emotions and not rebutting points of law—a sign of weakness. However, if the witnesses proved strong, then Kleemann knew he would be tempted to ask for a recess and drag Lillian Grubber into the fray. It would be repellent to do so, but still more so if he allowed Hitler the slightest chance of exoneration.

The justices were returning, and when they were seated, Morozov motioned to Toller to begin. No reference was made to the interval.

"A monster! That is what the prosecution has been attempting to create throughout these proceedings."

Toller was standing behind his table staring malevolently at Hans Kleemann.

"To what end has this been done? What motive could the prosecution have for wanting, insisting on, dealing with Adolf Hitler as though he were evil incarnate rather than a man?

"I venture to offer the following answer: that the prosecution does not and never did have a true case in law against the accused. Time after time its arguments have degenerated into philosophical expositions instead of basing themselves on fact; allegations based on the hearsay testimony of one witness, Veznarod, have been taken as the gospel truth; the accused, who might very well have refused to participate in such a circus, nonetheless made himself available and for his cooperation has been repeatedly slandered.

"It is time," Toller said harshly, "to bring such a spectacle to an end. It is time for the prosecution and this Court to view Adolf Hitler as a man, not as some mythical entity; as a human being of flesh and blood and not some soulless vampire or beast of prey.

"Not once has the prosecution inquired into the kind of life Adolf Hitler has led since 1945. It has been of no interest to it. But I must challenge this silence: one cannot continue to focus on only a single decade of a man's life and blithely exclude the rest. To do a man justice, as is our responsibility here, we must examine his conduct in his postwar life as well. Surely the human personality retains its essential features regardless of circumstances.

"Because of the prosecution's stance," Toller went on, his voice dropping as though he were truly reluctant to say such things, "it has become necessary for the defense to bring forward witnesses to testify in behalf of Adolf Hitler. These men and women have journeyed to New York and will offer their testimony in person. Certainly the defense might have obtained sworn statements and presented them, without having to impose on the lives of those concerned. But it was felt that because of the object of the prosecution's attack, which was to discredit the accused, those who wished to speak in his behalf should do so in person, where all the world might hear *their* voices and watch *their* emotions in the presence of the man they speak for. Only in this way can we do away with the fantastic image, that of a mad barbarian, with which the prosecution has presented us."

Helmut Toller raised his hand in the direction of the Marine guard, who then opened the door to the right of the podium and admitted the first witness.

He was a tall man, dressed completely in black, with the pale, milky complexion of an undertaker. His bearing and slow, dignified gait accented this image, as did his voice, which was soft and somehow disembodied.

After the oath was administered, Toller asked him, "Would you tell the Court your name and occupation."

":My name is Franz Scheller, and I am the general manager and accountant of the Busse Nurseries, A.G."

"Who is the owner of these nurseries and your employer?"

"Herr Busse . . . that is to say, Herr Hitler."

"When did you learn that Werner Busse and Adolf Hitler were one and the same man?"

"When everyone else did: the day the announcement was made from Munich."

"That was the first time you knew this?"

"Of course. Everyone in Emmaus believed that Herr Busse . . . well, he was exactly that: Herr Busse, no one else."

"It was your decision to agree to testify. You could easily have refused. Can you tell us why you chose to come to New York?"

"If I may tell my story in my own words, perhaps, it will be easier," Scheller said, folding his bony hands in his lap.

"Please do so."

"You must understand that the news of Herr Busse's arrest, and his identification as Adolf Hitler, caused quite a shock in our town. For a time people refused to believe it; but then, as more reports came in and we heard about the trial, the mood changed from uncertainty to a desire to help. You see, there are few people in Emmaus who are not indebted, in one way or another, to Werner Busse. My story is rather typical.

"Immediately after the war there wasn't much of anything left in Emmaus—food, clothing, medicines; not even hope. Yet in 1946 and 1947 the town managed to survive. From somewhere supplies were procured, how and with what we had no idea. But it became obvious that we owed our salvation to two men: Werner Busse and Dr. Grubber. If something was needed, they were the ones to see. Oftentimes it wasn't a matter of food or money, but simply a need to speak with someone whose words would not make one despair, who might offer some kind of reassurance, even hope. I can honestly say that I do not know of one instance in which help was refused by these two men.

"I was still a young man in those days, who had been passed over by the conscription because of epilepsy. One day—I remember it was late fall, and the weather, on top of everything else, had been miserable—I came to Herr Busse and pleaded with him to give me something to do. It was a terrible thing to watch people live, day after day, without hope or commitment or a belief in the future. Despair—I cannot say this too strongly—was our most ravaging disease, and I felt myself becoming its victim.

"Before the war, I had been an apprentice engraver and had worked for my father, a stonemason who specialized in headstones. When Herr Busse heard that, he said—and I remember the words distinctly—'That is where we shall begin: to give people honor after death.'

"It seemed somehow poetic that out of death a new life should stir," Scheller said wistfully. "Yet it did. The cemetery, neglected for many years, was cleared and proper funerals arranged. I was in charge of organizing the carpenters and diggers; Herr Busse sent the women to collect flowers and from somewhere, one never knew, procured seeds so that we would not have to depend on the seasons. Very soon the first greenhouse was built, and I was in charge of that also.

"People began working with and for one another. When a villager passed on, all came out to pay final tribute. Aside from the work Herr Busse had us do, he instilled in us a sense of duty and continuity. The earth of the cemetery was *our* earth, where in time all of us would be placed by our friends, and just as we wanted that final dignity for ourselves, so we strove to accord it to others in their turn.

"It was not surprising, then, that in a short while the whole of the town was transformed. I remember Herr Busse working many hours a day—too many, really, for a man of his age and physical condition, but there was no stopping him. It was as though he would rebuild Emmaus with his own hands if he had to. But perhaps he received his energy from his commitment to the greenhouse and nursery he had had us build. In those days he lived in the nursery itself, and quite often I would see him tending the plants and bulbs in the evening, making certain everything was as it should be. . . .

"As the years went by, my duties became twofold: I was the chief undertaker for Emmaus, and I also managed the nursery as that business grew and expanded. In all this time I might say I was one of the few people who saw Werner Busse daily. I believe

I had not only his business but also his personal confidence, and there were many evenings that we would spend together discussing business or playing chess. I can tell this Court the only truth I know: that for the twenty-five years I have shared with Werner Busse, I have known him to be an exemplary human being, who spared no effort to help others when they needed him most. His caring did not change or lessen after the crisis period; even when all were prospering, Werner Busse did not grow away from the people."

"You say this, Herr Scheller, even though you now know that Werner Busse is Adolf Hitler," Toller asked him.

"I admit it was very difficult to believe he could be two men at once," Scheller said. "And I thought about this bizarre situation for a long time. But in the end, I concluded it made no difference. What we in Germany know of Adolf Hitler is not the truth. We did not know the man; we knew only a figure responsible for evil acts. Well, in Emmaus he is regarded as a human being of rare courage and compassion. I cannot believe that in 1945 all the qualities were suddenly bestowed upon him; they must have been there before—perhaps overshadowed by others, but they must have existed. Too much has been made of Adolf Hitler as a symbol; no one has spoken for the man."

"You have, Herr Scheller," Toller told him. "Very eloquently, and I thank you."

He turned to Hans Kleemann.

"Do you wish to put questions to the witness?"

The prosecutor looked up and shook his head.

"No questions."

"Your name is Ernestine Hassell?"

"It is."

"And you are employed as a housekeeper for Werner Busse?"

"Yes, I am."

Ernestine Hassell was a short, rotund woman of some fifty years. With her hair done up in a neat bun, and face devoid of any but the subtlest cosmetics, she appeared a motherly, compassionate figure and sat in the witness box much as one would have imagined her on a bus or tram car: purse held neatly in her lap with both hands covering the clasp.

"Can you tell us whether at any time in your service you knew or suspected Werner Busse to be Adolf Hitler?"

"No, never. I have worked for Herr Busse for over twenty years and I never believed he could be someone else. There was never any reason to even think such a thing."

"Why was that?"

Ernestine Hassell shifted in her seat and smiled benevolently at Toller.

"I was barely twenty-six in 1945," she began, "and pregnant with the child of a soldier whom I thought long dead. Gerd, my husband, had written to me often, and he had always said that if there wasn't another letter soon, I had best realize that he might be dead. He had no confidence in the army's informing the next of kin.

"At the end of the war, when he failed to return, I quietly gave up all hope and moved from Munich to Emmaus, which was my birthplace. I thought that if I were to survive anywhere, and the baby be born, it would be there. But not even I expected what was to come.

"When I arrived, the town was in a mess. Hunger and sickness were everywhere. Families, what was left of them, were intent on saving their own members, and there was little of anything left over for a woman alone and expecting a child. However, God's mercy prevailed, and Dr. Grubber took me in.

"Conditions at the inn, which served as the hospital then, were bad: so many wounded men, mutilated, crippled—it was all very horrible. Drugs were difficult to get. The pain—ah, I cannot describe to you what it was like to live in the midst of pain, knowing there was no relief for it.

"Dr. Grubber knew that my condition was worsening by the day. I was not a strong woman, and the tension around me was making me lose heart. We both understood that unless something happened, I would lose the baby. The will to fight on was leaving me.

"It was at this point that Herr Busse visited the hospital. I don't remember his calling on me—I was in pain and delirious a great deal of the time then—but one morning I woke up to find myself in a large bright room filled with plants and flowers. I recall so clearly my first thought: I must be in heaven! I had died and gone to heaven. The air actually smelled sweet; it was so delicious I wished I could taste it. Then Herr Busse arrived with Dr. Grubber and told me I was in his—Herr Busse's—home; that I would stay for as long as was necessary and shouldn't concern myself with anything but the birth of my child. For the first time in so many years, it seemed, I cried tears of joy.

"A fortnight later, Werner was born. Yes, I named my first and only child after the man who had given me shelter and found a place for one in his house and heart. Somehow I stayed on. After I had regained my strength, I insisted on working for Herr Busse, doing whatever I could to repay his kindness. I became his housekeeper and cook and later helped out a little with the accounts of his shop. Several times, when Werner was older, I offered to leave, thinking Herr Busse might not want a child in his home; but on each occasion, he insisted that I stay.

"It is difficult for a man to understand the concern a mother has for her child, and how, when kindness is shown to it, she seeks to repay with whatever she can. Werner Busse did not have to concern himself with my son; he had done enough, more so than even I would have imagined. But he did, and as a result the boy received not only the necessities of life—in the way of shelter, warmth and clothing—he was also made to feel a part of a home. It is for that, above all else, that I praise God."

"And, as you say, you stayed. . . ." Toller said gently, leading her on.

"Ah, yes, I did. Herr Busse was not a well man. There were days he needed someone to look after him, to relieve him of some of the responsibility concerning his business. I was there to help him. You see, I am a woman who counts her blessings. I suppose it would have been possible for me to remarry, but I was satisfied. I had my child by the man I had truly loved, and I had the companionship of a caring gentleman. I would not have traded places with any woman."

"Do you still feel this way, knowing who Werner Busse really is?"

"Am I supposed to tell my heart to change?" Ernestine Hassell asked him. "Am I to somehow erase—if that were possible—the years of kindness and contentment I have known in his house? I was never a woman who concerned herself with politics, Herr Toller. I do know what Adolf Hitler gave to Germany in those awful years after the First War. I know, for I saw the transformation in my father's house—how the bitterness and discontent melted away before the vision of a new day. But of war and its necessity, I know nothing. It took away my husband, but then . . .

"But today what I find horrible is the way in which Herr Busse—you must forgive me if I keep calling him that; habit is strong—is being treated. Why does everyone blame the war on him? Why do they not see that others, the foreigners, were equally guilty? I have always respected the Führer—but it was not the Führer, not as far as I knew, who took me in and saved my life. It was a man called Busse. Now that I am told the two are really one, am I to change my mind? You can ask many others—almost anyone in Emmaus—and they will tell you exactly the same story: Herr Busse never stopped giving of himself. He never refused to help where he could. Ask anyone; everyone you ask will repeat my words."

"I don't think that will be necessary," Helmut Toller said quietly. "You have said it as well as anyone.

"Your witness!"

Again Hans Kleemann shook his head and remained sitting, silently staring at the look of hatred with which Ernestine Hassell was regarding him. She still remembered him, from that time he had came to Emmaus.

"My name is Wilhelm Krause and I am the mayor of Emmaus."

He was a short, fat, stiffly dressed man whose shirt was too tight around the neck and whose vest was strapped around his chest like a corset. Perhaps that was why Krause was perspiring so heavily and constantly patting his forehead and balding crown with a sodden, stained handkerchief. Helmut Toller spoke to him from some distance, for he not only found Krause repulsive in appearance but was certain he smelled.

"Would you tell us how long and in what capacity you have known the accused."

"I have been mayor for seventeen years," Krause answered proudly. "It has been my privilege to know Herr Busse, both personally and professionally, for this period of time."

"Could you elaborate, please."

"Herr Busse has always conducted himself as a model citizen," Krause said gravely. "Not only has he contributed to the financial welfare of our community through his business venture—by offering employment and paying his taxes; he has also involved himself in benevolent projects and has generously given his time and counsel to our development committee which is planning the future of Emmaus."

"And there has been no discord in all of the seventeen years."

"Oh, nothing which could be called that at all!" Krause assured him. "I recall a difference of opinion about some bylaw, something to do with a new road that was being built by Herr Busse's property; however, we managed to resolve that issue quite amicably. Other than that, I can recall nothing which would detract from Herr Busse's excellent character."

Helmut Toller found the mayor a nauseous human being, so full of his own importance that the vanity fairly reeked through his pores. Yet his pomposity would serve its purpose.

"I would ask you to tell this Tribunal why you volunteered to come before it and testify in behalf of Adolf Hitler."

"Really, it was not my idea at all," Krause began modestly, but he immediately added, "although, of course, I encouraged it and eventually took charge.

"You see, when we, the people of Emmaus, first heard that Herr Busse was indeed the Führer and he had been arrested, we were shocked. Not by the dual identity—naturally, that was a surprise—but by the chorus of approval that followed from many countries around the world. We could not understand how the English or French or Americans could *congratulate* our government for handing over one of its citizens to be tried by foreigners. For many of us in Emmaus, such words brought back memories of Nuremberg, opened wounds best left to heal. Forgiveness has two sides; we too have not forgiven many things.

"For a time we were unable to decide exactly what might be done. Some people, it must be admitted, were reluctant to act at all when it became known that Werner Busse and the Führer were one and the same. Yet when we asked ourselves what it was we had to be ashamed of in standing by our former leader, we found no answer. After all, were we not the very people who had shared twenty-five years with him, on terms which I may call intimate and neighborly? Were we, those of us who spoke and dealt with him so often, not the truest and fairest judges of whether this was a good or bad man?

"I also admit we were in awe of all those distinguished names which became associated with the case. We asked ourselves whether there was any place for us in the proceedings, if we could affect them in any way. Well, I am proud to say that we did not back down from the challenge. Together with several others, I have drafted the following statement, signed by every citizen of Emmaus. You will find on it, no august names, no great figures or famous personalities . . . simply honest, hardworking men and women who felt it their duty and responsibility to rise to the occasion and speak for a fellow citizen.

"If I may, I should like to read the statement."

"By all means."

Wilhelm Krause brought out a single typewritten sheet from his jacket pocket and carefully unfolded it.

"The declaration is titled: 'The Voice of the Little People,' " he said solemnly.

" 'We, the citizens of the town of Emmaus, respectfully address this Tribunal and pray that our voice may remain with you in your deliberations.

" 'We are aware of the charges brought forth against the man we have known as Werner Busse but who has been proved to be the Führer of the Third Reich, Adolf Hitler. Nevertheless, we owe a debt to this man, and for this reason, before the Almighty, we wish to put forward our words in his behalf.

" 'Werner Busse, or Adolf Hitler—it matters not at all—was and remains an exemplary citizen of our community, a man who always gave more than he received in return. As a member of the commonweal, he never turned away the needy from his door or failed to intervene in behalf of those caught by misfortune. Although a modest and unassuming man, he held our great respect, and we welcomed his counsel.

" 'This man has lived among us for a quarter century. He has witnessed the birth and evolution of a new generation whose members wish it known that they too stand by him. Never did a word of evil pass through his lips, nor was an act of malice or injustice ever attributed to him. In his dealings with others he personified a Christian concern. Although he was not a member of any religious body, we devoutly believed him to be guided by the spirit of the Lord.

" 'The actions of this man as former leader of our people are of no concern to us. The great and the mighty rise, they come upon us to do what Fate had decreed they must do and they depart—often in glory, sometimes in shame, almost always in death. Adolf Hitler had been spared. Yet after so many years, he chose to confront the justice of the world and seek that it exonerate him. We join him in his brave and lonely crusade and beg the powers before whom he has laid himself naked to show mercy for his bravery, to accord him compassion for his achievements as a citizen, to grant him the reprieve of which he is richly deserving.

" 'As simple people, we have learned not to curry favor with the powerful but to look after our lot as best we can, helping one another in the spirit of brotherhood. Therefore we understand we must come forward and plead in behalf of our brother. We ask only that he be returned to us as he was when taken away. We shall care for him to the end of his days and see to it his hours are filled with joy, dignity and charity. Nothing less should be offered any man; no man should die alone and so far from the land he calls his own.

" 'Before God we pledge to honor our commitment to this man and pray that our words may intercede for him in this, his hour of greatest need.' "

Even when the echo of the last words had drifted away, the mayor of Emmaus continued to hold his script before him as though mesmerized by it. Toller, appearing visibly moved, came to his side and placed his hand on his shoulder, then looked across at the prosecutor. This time he did not ask whether there would be any questions; he waited.

Hans Kleemann made a motion to rise, but then thought better of it. He had listened to Krause's presentation with fascination, entranced by its likeness to a medieval plea, placed at the feet of a king by his subjects. At times pretentious, probably because Krause had laid his heavy hand upon it, the presentation had unmistakably been born in the heart, and it reduced the issue of justice to its simplest form: an understanding of possible guilt, based on a sense of man's imperfectibility, followed by the appeal for forgiveness without which life itself was impossible.

And, Kleemann thought, there was also a most ancient appeal in the words: the return of the native son to his homeland. In its spirit the address was tribal, seeking a reunification of the family.

Is this what we are, in the end, reduced to facing, he thought—the desire of a community to pass judgment on its own kind without thought for the wrongs a man might have committed beyond its boundaries?

This thought angered him, for he found it hypocritical and saw behind the words the cunning features of the peasant who understood how to tug at the heartstrings. At that moment it would have given him satisfaction to keep the mayor on the stand, badger him with questions and retorts, lead him into a simple trap. But that was not the issue, he reminded himself. He would let the "little people" have their say. In the end, this third count of the indictment, genocide and crimes against humanity, remained unassailable.

When Wilhelm Krause finally consented to be escorted from the court, Toller continued his rebuttal.

"Such a man is to be called a criminal against humanity?" he demanded, as though bewildered by the audacity of the thought. "I should like to put the following proposition before the Tribunal: that when a man is charged with crimes against humanity, his judges should consider the opposite side of the coin: what has this man *contributed* to humanity?

"I am not here to persuade anyone that Adolf Hitler's leadership was devoid of bloodletting; history tells us otherwise. But I must object when it is upon him and him alone that the burden of possibly criminal acts is placed, without any consideration of his subsequent actions. Nor do I insist that Adolf Hitler regarded the Jews and Slavs in any high esteem; on the contrary, he was clearly prejudiced against them. But are we to equate mere prejudice with a hatred of humanity—a contempt, as the prosecution characterizes it, so profound that it leads inevitably to mass criminal action? No, I think not.

"The very worst that may be said of Adolf Hitler is this: that because of his lack of interest in the fate of the Jews, he did not ask for and so did not receive reports from his subordinates as to exactly what the nature of the 'resettlement' program was, or in what manner the plan was being carried out by the SS. In this regard, we have two pieces of proof. The first, attributed by the Nuremberg authorities to Karl Klaus, Hitler's manservant of nine years' standing, is the following statement: 'Hitler lived in his own work and believed in the good in people rather than in the evil.' As the Tribunal will note, the statement was made in response to an interrogator's question as to whether or not Hitler could have known the results of Jewish deportations.

"The second testimony is that of Ribbentrop, who wrote: 'How things came to the destruction of the Jews I do not know. That Hitler ordered it I refuse to believe, because such an act would be wholly incompatible with the picture I always had of him.'

"I do not feel it necessary to adduce further opinions, particularly those of SS General Esslin, who believed Himmler to be the architect of the destruction, as to where the ultimate responsibility may lie. Enough has been written about the 'solutions,' as they are referred to, to completely do away with our conception of a master plan; there was nothing of the sort. Rather, it is clear from the fragmented and erratically organized conferences such as the one at Wannsee in 1942 that men such as Himmler, Heydrich and Kaltenbrunner seldom agreed on any unified answer as far as the deportations were concerned. At the same time it must be remembered that Adolf Hitler was, as his testimony indicates, engaged completely by his role as commander of the Armed Forces and was not present at any of these meetings.

"Therefore, as far as this aspect of the charge is concerned, I must demand that either the wording be changed so as to specify negligence as the prime wrongful factor or the charge be dismissed altogether."

Toller returned to his table and picked up a copy of the statement the mayor of Emmaus had read.

"It is called 'The Voice of the Little People,' " he said slowly, and turned to the Court. "We should not discount it, for if we do, we do so at our peril.

"The testimonies of the three witnesses offer us a distinct and unalterable picture: that of a decent human being who has in his dealings with his fellows received possibly their highest compliment: respect. This is a consideration of true merit. The people of Emmaus have nothing to gain or lose by offering it; yet once given, it remains forever.

"I have nothing more to add to their words. They remain eloquent in their simplicity and demonstrate that is impossible, no matter how much the prosecution might wish otherwise, to see a man, any man, as a totally evil entity. As I have said, unless this charge of crimes against humanity is rephrased, it cannot stand before such genuine feelings of love and gratitude as have been presented before this Tribunal.

"Whatever Adolf Hitler's oversights may have been in the war years, they pale before his achievements of the last quarter century, accomplishments that did not stir nations or bring him accolades and recognition, but that were initiated for the simple benefit of his community.

"Such actions are all the more remarkable from a man who once commanded vast power yet who came to find joy and satisfaction in the smallest human consideration, who gave without thought of return, yet who received, as we have all witnessed, a bountiful harvest because of his selflessness."

Both prosecution and defense counsel expected the day's proceedings to end when Toller concluded his statement. The final arguments would be heard tomorrow morning, after which the Tribunal would retire to consider its verdict. But this was not to be the case.

"The Tribunal has received an unusual request," Justice Dieter Wolff stated, holding up the envelope. "And while the Court has been inundated with petitions, we feel that this particular one is quite extraordinary and deserves consideration."

Helmut Toller quizzically looked over to the older man, but the prosecutor merely frowned and shrugged.

"Perhaps if I read this petition, the matter will clarify itself," Wolff said.

" 'On behalf of myself and in the memory of my uncle, the late Dr. Grubber, I beg the International Tribunal to consider my appeal.

" 'The Court will shortly be hearing from Wilhelm Krause, the mayor of Emmaus. Among other things, he will state that the citizens of my town have unanimously agreed, in writing, to ask that Adolf Hitler be exonerated of all charges against him and returned to them. I wish the Court to know that such a sentiment is *not* shared by all of us, and I have chosen to speak for the dissenters.

" 'I wish to make it clear that I have not approached Herr Doktor Kleemann with this petition, fearing others would believe he had prevailed upon me to appear before the Tribunal. Therefore I appeal to the Court itself and pray that they will allow one voice to be raised for all that remains good and decent in the German spirit.' "

Dieter Wolff looked down upon the puzzled countenances of the two attorneys and finished:

"The author of the petition is Lillian Grubber."

"What sort of travesty is this?" Toller demanded, slowly getting to his feet, his eyes traveling malevolently between the prosecutor and Dieter Wolff. Just as his anger threatened to spill over, Helmut Toller restrained himself, although shock had drained his face of color. His words came haltingly, in evident incomprehension.

"I cannot see how the Court would permit one relative to testify against another. That procedure is denied in most courtrooms under all but the most exceptional circumstances."

"The Bench has considered such an objection," Etta Kirsch said, her tone gentle, as though she felt pity for the younger man. "It would be only natural for you to raise it. However, you must concede, Herr Toller, that your foster mother's signature does not appear on the Emmaus petition presented to us. We checked very carefully a few minutes ago. And on her word that she believes her testimony is important enough for us to hear, the Court is agreed that she may speak."

"Could there have been an oversight on her part?" Toller challenged.

"If so, she may rectify it herself."

"No!"

"Are you suggesting that your foster mother is in any way incompetent to come before us?" Etta Kirsch demanded, her voice rising.

"No, but—"

"Then I take it you have no pertinent objections. Please bring the witness forward."

Toller stared at the Israeli justice, his face set in angry disbelief. He felt as though the ground beneath his feet had shifted, that he was helpless before some force he could neither understand nor control, yet which held him at its mercy. Slowly he sank into his seat and, calling upon the last of his discipline, told the Court, "I should like to know the prosecution's intentions as to this witness."

Hans Kleemann stirred and looked up at Toller.

"I did not ask her to come," he said softly. "Oh, I admit the temptation was there, after I heard of your intention to bring witnesses from Emmaus. But I could not find it in myself to subject her to such an ordeal, to have her confronted by the man she regards as her son. Still, now that she is here, it is only fair to allow her to speak."

"Then may her grief be on your heads!" Helmut Toller whispered.

Toller felt ashamed and bitter, as if he had been betrayed. Yet as he watched his foster mother enter the court, he realized that this was the moment he had feared ever since undertaking the defense of Adolf Hitler. He had deliberately closed himself off from Lillian Grubber in these past months, so as to avoid a confrontation. There was nothing he could say to her that would make her understand why he had agreed to accept the case; conversely, the thought of apologizing for his decision only repelled him.

But finally that moment was upon him, and he was powerless against it. He would be obliged to sit here and listen to her words, enduring the rebukes she had never spoken directly, watching as she tore at the love he still had for her and so creating a guilt that would separate them forever. The final price for defending Adolf Hitler, which he had put off paying for so long, which he had dreamed he might avoid altogether, was now presented to him, and there was no choice but to render the amount in full. He had known this time would come, known that first night when Hitler had called for him.

She walked into the court in the manner of a bereaved woman

following a coffin that bears the body of a lifelong friend. She entered with proud solemnity, her eyes carrying a distant gaze of remembrance tempered by strength, her movements reflecting certainty and decision. She was at once intimate with and removed from the Court; she had come to perform a specific act in this place, and it would be done in her own manner.

Kleemann rose and came over to her.

"I am glad you have come," he said gently. "I have no right to say this, because of the pain you must feel, but nonetheless, it is true."

Her green eyes held his, and a trace of a sad smile appeared on her lips.

"For him," she answered, looking at Helmut Toller, who in turn stared back, bewildered and angry, a man caught beyond his depth.

"I have no questions to put to you," Kleemann told her.

"I thought that might be the case," she said. "Nonetheless, it was necessary for me to come here."

Lillian Grubber took the stand and the oath was administered. Hans Kleemann turned to the Court and spoke out:

"The prosecution has no questions to put to Lillian Grubber. Given her relationship to the defense counsel, I thought it inadvisable to call upon her. However, this has not dissuaded her from coming forward, so I will ask the Tribunal to listen to her account as she herself presents it."

"The Court is prepared to do exactly that," Sir Adrian Potter said. "Fräulein Grubber, you may proceed."

"Thank you, your Honor."

Lillian Grubber took her seat and looked down calmly at the table where her foster son sat side by side with Adolf Hitler.

"I must first say that Wilhelm Krause was not very far from right in stating that the citizens of Emmaus were unanimous in their desire to have Adolf Hitler returned to them. There were very few opinions to the contrary, perhaps twenty or twenty-five out of a population of several hundred. Yet I believed that these voices should be heard and their protest be understood by the world, so that some respect might remain for the German people.

"But such a desire on my part is not the full reason I am here today. I would like to explain to the Tribunal exactly *why* Adolf

Hitler would be welcomed if he were permitted to return to Emmaus.

"Twenty-five years ago, my uncle, the late Dr. Grubber, and I were among the first people to have laid eyes on an injured Home Guard soldier whose papers identified him as Werner Busse. My uncle took him in and treated him, and after a long convalescence, this disfigured middle-aged man became part of our community. To many he appeared a good man, ready and willing to help, yet the truth behind such charitable intentions was yet to come to light.

"Among the medicines and equipment that my uncle found in the ambulance that brought Hitler to Emmaus was a case of gold bars. With the help of Brehm, the village blacksmith, those bars were moved to a hiding place. When Adolf Hitler recovered sufficiently, my uncle questioned him about the gold, but there was nothing he would say about it. So the obvious explanation was accepted: the SS lieutenant who had driven the ambulance had taken the gold with him as loot or to have a ready bribe.

"Both my uncle and the smith were concerned about the gold. It was an awful temptation. Lying there, the bars were valueless; they could not be used to ease the suffering and misery around us. Yet if they were taken to Switzerland and held as credit against loans, then food and medicines could be procured. The village would survive. I do not know what arguments went back and forth between them and Hitler; I was never present. In the end, on the pretext of traveling to Switzerland for medicines, my uncle helped Brehm move the gold to the Banque Skrip in Zurich, where the necessary credit arrangements were made. My uncle and Adolf Hitler were the only men who could authorize loans against that collateral, with the signature at the bank being Hitler's . . . or rather, Busse's.

"From the records left to me, it is clear that my uncle quickly relinquished his share of the control over the account. He was never a businessman to begin with, nor did he concern himself with finance. On the other hand, Adolf Hitler showed an aptitude for such management. At the time, no one thought it curious that this should be so; who knew?—perhaps Corporal Werner Busse had been an accountant before the war.

"In any case, it was he who arranged for moneys to be lent to those people who needed them. Very quickly, through word of mouth, it became known that if a man required capital to buy up surplus war matériel, this was where he could find it; a farmer who could purchase machinery at a cheap price would come to Hitler, and upon receipt of a written promise to pay in kind over a period of years or for a silent share in the enterprise, Hitler would arrange for financing. In short, for a period of two, perhaps three years, Adolf Hitler controlled, though never overtly, the economic life of Emmaus. No one knew where his money came from; no one, I believed, cared. With the beginning of the economic miracle, he was in a position to be regarded as the silent savior of our community. The townspeople were not about to jeopardize their good fortune by asking how all this came to pass."

Lillian Grubber paused and looked at her foster son keenly, as though trying to tell him something without the use of words.

"My uncle told me he had seen similar bars on a railway loading platform in transit from the concentration camp at Dachau. He recognized the gold, blood booty of the SS, as a temptation, yet he judged that he should use it, no matter how evil it was. In his hands it would become an instrument of salvation.

"But I have come to warn you; to show how—literally—a people's affection and respect may be bought and their indebtedness blind them to a man's true face.

"We must never forget—and to judge by the petition, we have forgotten—that our good fortune was built on the suffering of others. Nor is Emmaus alone in its evolution; a great deal of Germany's wealth may be traced back to the Third Reich. I believe that if we are to live with our conscience, we must admit to this and no longer foster it. For if we continue to believe that men such as Adolf Hitler are decent men simply because they have helped us, we will be lost. We will never be able to accept the profundity of the wrongs they have committed; we will never be free of their influence.

"No matter how generous his deeds may appear, Adolf Hitler has attained his own goal: the continuation of his influence and the survival of his adoration by our people. To come here to show this to you and to plead on behalf of those few of us, who will be branded traitors in our own home, has been my task.

"As a German, I am ashamed for my neighbors in Emmaus; as

a mother, I fear for my son, who sits before me, defending a creature he knows nothing of. God knows the ties of love and years are strong enough—but such sentiments cannot bind us to a continuation of evil; they must not!''

Lillian Grubber placed both hands on the edge of the witness box and leaned forward slightly, looking into the cold, impassive countenance of the man she regarded as her son.

''I am so very sorry, Helmut,'' she whispered. ''I beg of you, please, please do not turn your heart against me!''

Kleemann rose from behind his desk and looked out over the Assembly.

What, he wondered, can I tell them that they have not already heard? What words in what order can I speak that will help them understand all that has happened here?

At once he was seized by a violent feeling of doubt that he had done his work well enough. But, he asked himself, how long can I have them listen to me before my exposition becomes mundane? We have had equal time, equal opportunity—Toller and I—to present our arguments. It is out of our hands now.

But as he looked around the world behind the shield, passing each of the television cameras in turn, he realized that part of his fear lay in the knowledge that he would soon be denied this refuge; he would be expelled from the sanctuary behind the shield and once more be forced to confront his uncertain future. It was quite incredible that only seven days had passed; he wished the trial might endure a little while longer, for he did not know where it was he could go now or what place he might call home. The others—Toller, Hitler, the jurists and the witnesses, the millions who had listened to him—all had matters, important or insignificant, to deal with after today, or at the latest tomorrow, when the verdict would be returned. But he, where would *he* go? With whom, and toward what?

Hans Kleemann wondered if he mightn't try to answer these questions in his summing up. He glanced briefly at the Bench and saw that the justices were waiting for him.

''It has been an extraordinary journey for us,'' he began. ''All the more so for the fact that only seven days have elapsed since we embarked upon it. Yet I do not believe I exaggerate in saying that in such a short period of time, we the participants of this Court have been able to confront and grapple with one of the most powerful challenges with which any court has ever been presented. Now we must ask ourselves: where is it we go from here?

"As representative for the prosecution, I am convinced that the case against Adolf Hitler, put forward in the three counts of the indictment, has been presented with sufficient evidence to permit the Court to ascertain his guilt. It is not my concern here to speak of the crimes once again; the details have been heard and there is nothing to add. I wish to examine the nature of punishment.

"For we must punish. This is where the final aspect of the challenge lies. That we have brought Adolf Hitler before the world and tried him by civilized procedure is to our credit. Yet that credit will be diminished if we shirk our last responsibility and refuse to mete out a just sentence.

"As observer, as well as participator, in these proceedings, I note that for some the whole concept of punishment will be alien, for a variety of reasons ranging from the advanced age of the accused to what may be viewed as mitigating circumstances. The cry we have heard from the townspeople of Emmaus will go up from the mouths of others for a very lenient sentence, if not outright dismissal. I cannot but listen to it; yet equally, I may not be moved by it. For it is our duty today to pass sentence on both a man and a symbol. Our failure to do so only permits that which all civilized men abhor to continue to exist, untouched, free to work its evil upon us.

"It was noted in the Eichmann trial that there was a fundamental problem in perception: how could this insignificant, bespectacled man who spoke with a constantly faltering voice have been the architect of mass annihilation? But there were witnesses who came forth and, when faced with just such a discrepancy, reminded themselves and us by shouting, 'Ah, but you should have seen him in his uniform!'

"It is true: in many ways it is a stranger who has been on trial here, a stranger whose name we know as Busse, with a glowing personal history, one rich in friends prepared to defend him. But this man was and remains Adolf Hitler. Perhaps if Hitler had presented us with a man reborn, repentant and asking for mercy, our task of punishing him would have been that much more difficult. But in the course of this trial Adolf Hitler willingly came to the witness stand and spoke freely of his actions, none of which, by his own admission, had caused him any contrition over the last twenty-five years. He did not rationalize these actions, he regretted them only insofar as, in his view, they had been incomplete. He did not slough off responsibility for them on subordinates he could not control; he did not view them as anything but direct consequences of policies he had been advocating as far back as *Mein Kampf*.

"Usually, it is repentance which stirs our hearts toward mercy and compassion. But there is none. Here we are faced with a man who is devoid of remorse, who remains proud of his deeds, viewing them as tremendous historical achievements. And so they are—in the same manner that the pillage of Carthage was a great feat for the Romans, the devastation of Eastern Europe by Attila a triumph for the Mongols, the savagery of the Spanish Conquistadors in the New World a shining example of Iberia's holy heritage.

"What Hitler had left us in 1945 was a legacy, to be sure; what is incredible is that Hitler himself appears unable to acknowledge its evil.

"In the face of such adamant refusal to accept the nature of his acts and his own character, it is left to us to judge Adolf Hitler. We may not vacillate in our devotion to justice, for there is no room for pity here; we cannot say that in every man there is a little piece of Hitler's evil and so who are we to judge? This would be the greatest abdication of our responsibility: to choose between right and wrong. We cannot presume to share Hitler's guilt, for he alone holds all of it; he was, after all, *primus inter pares*. There is, in the end, nothing to be done but punish him, and we must be as firmly resolved to this end—the carriage of justice—as he was to his, that of universal destruction.

"Yet it is not enough to punish Adolf Hitler; we must understand *why* it is necessary to do so. In part, our motive must lie in our responsibility to the dead, to the victims of the final solution, to the soldiers of all nations who faced Hitler's onslaught, to the people who would have led decent lives had it not been for his intrusion. We owe these men, women and children a just end. In the West we do not believe that the spirits of the dead roam at night, unsatisfied for as long as their demise remains unavenged.

But I believe we have remembered them in our consciences. We must answer them now; after Hitler, there is no one whom we may call forth.

"We who dispense justice can ill afford indecision. Yet the effect of our actions will be diminished if they are not understood by the world at large. Every person who has viewed these proceedings must ask himself: would I have found the strength to pass sentence on this man?—or would I have taken an easier route, and simply dismissed the matter because it could not possibly concern me? I put these questions forward because I believe our second duty, as sacred as our duty to the victims, belongs to ourselves and, more, to our children.

"The laws we validate today will become the boundaries others live by tomorrow, boundaries that separate good from evil, the civilized world from the barbaric. All of us must ask ourselves whether our children would forgive us if we placed that which we prize so highly, the rule of law, in jeopardy because we were unable to wield its full force, unable or unwilling to carry out the final edict. We have only to look at the present generation in Germany, which *is* demanding, after a long period of silence on the part of its parents, answers to its questions on the Nazi era. History can be ignored, circumvented or tolerated as a mute embarrassment only for so long. We must look ahead and ask ourselves what respect for our judgment we will be leaving. Will it not appear natural for our offspring to shun our inadequacies or, worse, use them as an excuse to propagate exactly that evil we had hoped to eliminate?"

Hans Kleemann looked directly at Adolf Hitler and spoke to him:

"For your crimes, which still echo in the memory of mankind, for that part of human nature against which we must always stand vigilant and for our duty and self-respect as men who understand the meaning of justice, for all this which is so painfully inadequate as an expression against your monstrosity, I must demand the penalty of death."

"You are strangely silent for a man whose finest hour has arrived."

Hitler, with his hand over the microphone, had brought his face very close to Toller's. Although his breath repelled Toller— it smelled sour, like dung—he did not move.

"What is it you are waiting for?" Hitler demanded softly. "You have been sitting here like a cretin for two minutes!"

There was no response. What Hitler had said was true. The Court was waiting. So was the world. He would have to rise and speak, even though all words had deserted him and whatever thoughts came to his mind seemed to have no substance. Still he had to speak, present the last plea that would ever be heard in behalf of Adolf Hitler. After listening to Lillian Grubber, he no longer believed victory was possible. There had been a quality to her words that had made him see the impossibility of what he was trying to achieve.

It was a personal defeat, an affront to his brilliant legal career, to have failed in the defense of Adolf Hitler. Yet it was only now, after he had lived these five months, plotting and nurturing victory, that he could look back and admit that victory had always been a stillborn child, a falsehood, an illusion he had tried to coax to life. The reality lay only hours away, when Adolf Hitler would be condemned.

Yet as Helmut Toller thought of this, he at once realized that a cunning irony was at work here. Hans Kleemann would have his victory. He would, possibly forever, remain ignorant of the fact that this same death would be responsible for bringing forth a new claimant to the vacant throne. For behind Hitler stood Bendt, who, through the martyrdom of Hitler, would make way for him, Helmut Toller. On defeat was superimposed the plan of victory; in personal shame and ignominy were the seeds of far greater honors.

Without being conscious of it, Helmut Toller smiled. He had thought the circumstances through and perceived them as they truly were. He was certain that he was right and so there was nothing to fear. Everything satisfied him.

Helmut Toller came to his feet and addressed the court.

"Dr. Kleemann has spoken eloquently of responsibility and of duty," Helmut Toller said slowly. He came to the front of the desk, gently running his fingertips along its length.

"He spoke with passion and conviction, from a belief born of the heart. I applaud him; but at the same time I pity him, for there is no possible verdict the court may return other than one of innocence, on all counts.''

Helmut Toller gazed up at the justices on the podium above him.

''I do, however, agree with my colleague in one regard: the importance of this trial. And again, Herr Doktor Kleemann gave us the exact reason for this: it will establish, by the verdict it gives forth, the supremacy of the rule of law for future generations and hopefully rid us, once and for all, of the medieval mentality to which we have been subjected by the prosecution.

''The key here is the phrase 'rule of law.' We are not concerned with philosophic debates, as Herr Doktor Kleemann obviously is; we are not at liberty to debate the issues of good and evil as they apply in a universal sense; it is not our business to create or extend myths and conjure up monsters from flesh and blood. We, and this time I include the prosecution, have really only one goal: to decide whether Adolf Hitler is guilty or innocent on the counts with which he is charged in the indictment, such a decision being founded exclusively on the evidence brought forth before the Tribunal.

''I cannot state too strongly that if any considerations other than the rule of law are taken into account, the accused will have been cheated. For Adolf Hitler *voluntarily* placed himself at the disposal of the law, believing that he would be heard by those whose objectivity toward him was unquestioned, whose experience and understanding would be able to discern the point at which the prosecution's arguments strayed beyond the bounds created by the single issue of the trial: is Adolf Hitler guilty in law?

''The answer must, of course, be a resounding negative. Herr Kleemann states he is satisfied that the evidence is overwhelmingly in favor of a guilty verdict. I challenge him, not on the accuracy of his opinion, but rather on the premise upon which it is founded.

''Herr Kleemann has extended the province of this Court to suit himself. He believes that not only a man is on trial here but a symbol, a mentality, a piece of history. I am afraid such digressions make it all too easy to bring forth arguments which have no bearing on the central issue of these proceedings. If the prosecutor is satisfied that he has proved the existence of evil in the world, that is all well and good, but it does not concern us. If he feels he has delineated the lines of what morality is or ought to be, I commend him, but I must say such achievements are meaningless to this Court. I state unequivocally that it has been the defense and *only* the defense which has remained faithful to proving Hitler's innocence within the framework of the law. We have shown how Adolf Hitler may not be adjudged guilty on the count of planning and waging aggressive warfare; we have introduced substantial, not only reasonable, doubt on the charge of misconduct on the battlefield; we have offered unrefuted and virtually unchallenged testimony upon Hitler's character which speaks for itself. No, I am convinced by all that is right that there is absolutely no ground on which Adolf Hitler may be convicted—none!''

Helmut Toller scanned the faces of the justices and smiled.

"But there will be the temptation to condemn," he said softly. "Logic and reason will conflict with emotion, and which will triumph? The feeling for vengeance still runs deep. I should like to issue my own warning, just as the prosecutor felt it necessary to voice his particular concern, and it is this: if the Court should totally disregard the weight of the arguments put forth by the defense, if it should refuse to recognize that Adolf Hitler broke no international laws in existence at the time, then this Tribunal will have reduced its credibility to nothing. It will have acted in the basest spirit—that of vengeance—forever destroying the principle that a man is innocent until proved guilty, a cornerstone of civilized affairs.

"There is nothing more to be said in the cause of the defense. I am convinced in my heart that Adolf Hitler must leave this house a free and vindicated man; if he does not, then we are guilty of exactly that of which we have accused him."

V

Judgment

As HAD become their habit, they assembled in the conference suite of the Secretary-General's offices.

Etta Kirsch, standing in the corner by the floor-to-ceiling windows, watched the clear reflections of her confrères moving in the glass. Although it was only half past twelve, she saw that fatigue had burdened their faces and slowed their footsteps as they left the Assembly.

Thus far the cohesiveness of the group had not been tested. On the bench, they had looked after one another, making certain the defense attorney and Adolf Hitler did not challenge its legitimacy or impugn the character of any of the justices. She believed that they had been successful in this. After a day's proceedings they invariably returned to their suites at the Park Lane Hotel on Central Park. There had been two exceptions: once she had accepted Dieter Wolff's invitation to supper; on the second night the whole group had been the dinner guests of the Secretary-General of the United Nations. Naturally, no reference was made to the trial.

In spite of the respect and courtesy that underlined their relationships, Etta Kirsch was conscious of some element missing among them. They had been brought together too quickly, without an opportunity to become better acquainted. They were to decide a man's fate in unison, yet in the back of their minds lay the reminder that each of their governments was keenly waiting for the outcome, the verdict being as much a reflection of the body politic as of the jurist. They had one another as foils for legal opinions; but no one had turned to another for friendship.

Will the floodgates finally open now, during the deliberations? she asked herself. Is this where we will see all the prejudices and personalities emerge? Or will it all be over with in a few hours, the verdict decided and decision rendered?

Etta Kirsch noticed that Morozov had beckoned the others to his side. She had expected him to take charge, so casting aside her own reflections, she moved away from the cool windows.

"I have the following proposal to make," Morozov was saying. "We have the whole of the afternoon ahead of us. I suggest we debate the verdict now—not that too much debate is needed."

"Have you decided on your vote?" Wolff asked him.

"Undeniably guilty," Morozov answered simply. He had poured himself some vodka from the bar and now set the glass on the ceramic coffee table, carefully placing it on a square of red tile.

"We cannot afford indecision," he said somberly.

"Are we to deliberate the case on the basis of the facts presented, or shall we return the verdict everyone expects us to?" Worthington inquired.

Morozov glanced up at him, somewhat startled, and passed his fingers through his hair.

"That kind of thinking brings us back to the Nuremberg dilemma," he said impatiently. "Roosevelt and Churchill initially favored summary executions of the Nazi top echelon. Stalin agreed with that idea. Then somewhere in the discussions all three were proposing a trial. Thus the major dilemma of Nuremberg was born: that there would be a trial at all. Had we simply shot Goering, Kaltenbrunner and the rest *at once*, there would have been no argument about their guilt or lack of it."

"But must we not also be certain of the decision in our own minds?" Sir Adrian Potter remarked. "I feel that what you are proposing is a headlong plunge: we simply take a deep breath, pronounce a verdict of guilty with the appropriate sentence and pray to God we were right and can live with ourselves afterward."

Morozov walked over to the tall windows and stared out over the city, swathed in a blue-and-white light shot through with streaks of gray smog and exhaust fumes.

"There is a difference in our legal systems," he said slowly. "The due process of the West is often a mystery to the Russian, because it removes the personal element, the soul and conscience, from the proceedings. That is why, quite often, Russian justice is more merciful than your own; our notion of extenuating circumstances is more respected in the courts. Conversely, the sentence may be harsher when guilt is so evident."

He turned back to the company.

"We cannot afford mercy here," he said. "To even contemplate forgiveness of actions that were so vicious is to demean oneself. I care nothing for the twenty-five years Hitler has lived on this earth as a 'good man.' I would have enjoyed reducing those who came to speak for him to sniveling idiots, trying to explain where it was their remembrance of the horror had fled. True, we could pass a similar judgment on other heads of state; there is blood on many hands. But that is not our business here. We have only one man to deal with. If we dispatch swift, terrible justice, perhaps others in power will realize that for them too there may be a day of reckoning!"

"You would opt for an immediate verdict of guilty on all counts, with death as the penalty—is that it?" Worthington asked him.

"Oh, no." Morozov smiled, his eyes glacial. "Nothing quite so simple. Death is tempting but is too lenient a sentence for Hitler. I would suggest that the penalty be life imprisonment—without any option of parole, of course—in Spandau. Hitler can rot side by side with his lunatic friend Hess."

The barbaric nature of what the Russian proposed overwhelmed them all and silenced the conversation. Rudolf Hess, formerly Hitler's closest political adviser and onetime heir apparent, had, in May of 1941, stolen a Luftwaffe aircraft and flown to England intending to meet with Winston Churchill. Obviously mad, Hess believed he could persuade the British Prime Minister to throw in his country's lot with the Reich. At the conclusion of the war, Hess, along with other key Nazi leaders, had been incarcerated in the Berlin prison of Spandau, garrisoned by British,

French, American and Soviet troops. He had outlived all his fellow prisoners and now languished alone in the massive stone fortress. While the rest of the Allies would have gladly acted upon the appeals of the family to release the demented man into their custody, and save themselves two million dollars a year in his upkeep, the Soviets vetoed every such petition. To them, Hess was a living symbol of the destruction and evil they had suffered. No matter what the cost, as long as they had the power of veto Hess would serve out his full term—to the end of his natural life.

"Do you understand the enormity of what you are proposing to us?" Sir Adrian queried. "Surely you must see that to place Hitler in the midst of Germany is to have him a living memorial—no, a martyr—among his people."

"Perhaps that is precisely what they need," Morozov answered coolly. "After all, we have read about the demonstrations taking place in West Germany in behalf of the old Führer. I feel my method is instructive: we punish Hitler in a manner befitting him *and* remind those who are tempted by the Nazi cause as to what the penalty is."

"I cannot agree with that!" Etta Kirsch said vehemently. "As you well know, Ivan, I can understand the feelings you have, your country has, toward Hitler. But that isn't the way to express them. It would be a monstrous humiliation to the Germans to have Hitler placed on their soil, one that could lead to the very temptation we have seen expressed for Hess: give him back to us, he has suffered enough. The irony of your proposal is devastatingly simple: let those who spawned a Hitler now endure him and the shame he represents. But the gesture would cost too much. I could not support such punishment, causing, as it would, more harm than good."

"Dieter," Sir Adrian demanded. "Surely you have some comment to make."

The towering man sighed, breaking an unaccustomed silence.

"I'm sorry," he muttered. "It's not that I wasn't listening. This was delivered to my room this morning." He withdrew a vellum envelope from his breast pocket. "Brought by a personage no less than the German Ambassador's secretary. The note reads that at the conclusion of the trial, as soon as the verdict is handed down, the West German Government will ask the Tribunal to return Adolf Hitler to the custody of the authorities of his home country for carrying out of the sentence."

"Is this an official communication?" Morozov demanded.

"No. In fact, I thank my friendship with the Ambassador for having been forewarned. I would ask all of you to keep the confidence."

"Do you realize what is happening?" Morozov said angrily. "The Germans think that even if we render the death penalty we will add a proviso for a stay of execution! By using the phrase 'carrying out of the sentence' they are suggesting a lesser sentence than the death penalty, for Bonn would never ask for Hitler back only to execute him themselves."

"Not only that," Wolff said softly. "If we use your option, the Spandau internment, they would get around that. Spandau is not under the jurisdiction of the federal government but under Allied control. If a life sentence in Spandau were the case, can you imagine the uproar in Bonn? If Hitler were to be returned, they would demand full rights over him, no matter where he was taken. This, of course, assumes that sentence is incarceration rather than death."

"Is there any other interpretation?" Etta Kirsch asked him.

"An explanation more logical than Morozov put forward? I doubt it."

"But surely it would have been more to the point to make the request *prior* to the verdict's being handed down, and to do so publicly!"

"Ah, but that would have been construed as state interference in judicial proceedings," Worthington reminded her. "It wouldn't do, not at all."

"Then perhaps this note is a deliberate act of provocation," Morozov said bitterly. "To let Dieter Wolff know in advance what will be demanded—for as Etta rightly pointed out, there has been no public announcement—so that he might keep the consideration in mind while debating the verdict. Further, should this be the case, then whoever authorized the leak would have assumed that Wolff would share the information with us. I begin to detect the long hand of interference here. . . ."

Etta Kirsch could not have believed that within thirty minutes such a change could have overtaken the group. Ivan Morozov, calm, polite and reasonable, had suddenly shown his teeth, the dark underlying prejudice that characterizes the Russian, the unforgiving memory, the belief in punishment of one's enemies. Beside him, Dieter Wolff, for all his gruffness possibly the most sensitive of them all, was suddenly shamed by his government's maneuver, caught unaware and still at a loss as to what was to be done.

As for Thomas Worthington, she thought him an unknown quantity. Unlike Sir Adrian, who had voiced his growing conviction about Hitler's guilt, Worthington had said nothing at all that would indicate his thoughts on the subject. Etta Kirsch knew Worthington's reputation as a legalist who based himself on strict observance of procedure on the one hand and the necessity of a just decision on the other. She wondered if this second consideration mightn't be very complex for him to work out in this trial and if, of all of them, his wouldn't be the most surprising stance.

"We had better decide whether we should adjourn or sit down now and begin the debate," Etta Kirsch suggested. "I, for one, think a respite is in order."

"I beg to differ," Morozov answered her. "Obviously there is much too much to do. We should begin at once."

"A break would be of no value to me," Dieter Wolff said. "In fact, I'd rather we got this unexpected problem out of the way— if possible."

"I'm afraid I agree," Worthington joined in. "Suddenly affairs are getting out of hand."

"Then I suggest we make ourselves as comfortable as possible," Sir Adrian concluded. "We have a lengthy enterprise ahead of us."

Sir Adrian might have added grueling, and he would have been equally correct. Within the hour both Wolff and Thomas Worthington had taken off their jackets and ties, while Ivan Morozov, in an unprecedented gesture, unbuttoned his blazer. Only Sir Adrian seemed to take no notice of the growing tension in the room, preferring to leave his cravat and waistcoat as they were. Fine porcelain coffee cups, filled to various levels with strong black coffee or, in the cases of Etta Kirsch and Sir Adrian, tea, were to be found on the end tables or near the large urns that had been provided by the catering service. All the ashtrays were in use; some had already been filled and emptied. The result of all this activity was rather minor: an agreement as to the agenda they had before them, beginning with the situation of Dieter Wolff.

"Now that we are in agreement as to *what* is to be discussed, perhaps we may begin?" Morozov's rhetorical question was underlined by impatience.

"Has anyone further thoughts on Dieter Wolff's, ah, predicament?" he continued.

"Only that if the message was intentionally conveyed through the Ambassador, whether the Ambassador was a party to it or not, the ploy seems to be doing its work," Worthington commented.

"Dieter, are we certain this *could* be a deliberate ploy?" Etta Kirsch asked.

The German, who had been sitting on the edge of the couch, elbows on his knees, raised his great head.

"Let me put your question into perspective," he said slowly. "When Hans Kleemann elected to pursue the issue of an international tribunal against the express wishes of the Chancellor, who preferred that the issue be settled internally in a discreet fashion, he was stripped of his public position. Oh, it was obvious the Chancellor could not move against him openly, and therefore he remained the prosecutor for the trial. But Kleemann is nevertheless finished in West Germany, professionally and, I suspect, personally. The Chancellor can be a vicious man. It is conceivable, as Morozov so astutely observed a few moments ago, that his coterie dreamed up a scheme to permit the trial—which is costing them votes at home—but also to pull Hitler back in at the last moment. Therefore it is possible we are witnessing a ploy. Personally I do not believe the Ambassador is involved. If he had been, the message would have been delivered orally. Instead he has given me physical evidence—the note—of Bonn's plans. But even this isn't enough. If I were to challenge the Chancellor and cry interference to the press, the government would disavow the note and the Ambassador's career would be finished."

"What would Germany have to gain by such an act?" Sir Adrian inquired softly. "Surely international reaction would be most unfavorable."

"It isn't a question of gain so much as a question of loss," Wolff said. "There is a saying in Germany among those who fancy themselves mandarins: Six million dead Jews can't vote; a million former Nazis can and do, in every election."

"All right, we have a motive, but what about the end result?" Morozov asked. "What do they want us to do, knowing what we know?"

"I shall choose to accept it as a warning," Wolff said, looking up at the Russian. "The judgment should be unanimous. There are five of us, of course, to prevent a theoretical tie, but I think you will agree that no dissenting opinions are expected. Obviously if matters go awry and the majority of the Bench is leaning toward a judgment not in keeping with the wishes of the West German Government, I am to protest, both privately and then publicly. This after I have failed to dissuade you all from your positions."

"It would seem to me, then, that there are two choices—"

Wolff cut the Russian off harshly.

"Yes, I know: either state here and now that I shall not comply with what Bonn demands of me or resign from this Bench!"

"If you were to choose either, I think the result back home would be the same," Morozov suggested. "Like Kleemann, you would be finished. You must succeed in convincing us of the proper judgment or else all is lost."

"They would have to move the earth to get me off the German Federal Constitutional Court," Wolff said grimly. "Mine is a life appointment!"

"No, I don't think there is any question of your leaving this Tribunal," Etta Kirsch murmured. "Can you imagine the reaction of Toller and Hitler—how joyous they would be? Dissent on the Bench, resignation of one of the members! What sort of validity would *any* verdict we hand down have when our unity is gone?"

"It seems to me that every time we look for a solution further complications set in," Sir Adrian observed. "Dieter, can you tell us your opinion: guilty or not guilty?"

"In law, Hitler has nothing to call his own. That young bastard

Toller managed to present the facts in such a manner as to almost vindicate Hitler—almost, but not quite. If Hitler hadn't spoken for himself and had refused to answer certain questions, my own decision would have been made more difficult. But as it stands, there is only one verdict to be handed down: guilty on all counts."

"And the penalty you would suggest?"

"Death by hanging or firing squad."

Yes, Etta Kirsch thought, death for Hitler and your becoming a traitor in the eyes of your own people because you decided for punishment.

"Well, now, it seems to me that we might be overlooking a few things here," Thomas Worthington broke in. "Point one: this business, on the first count, about not being responsible for acts of state has validity in international law—that much my research has told me. Point two: as far as the Kupai massacre is concerned, we have conflicting testimony. I suggest we look at these elements before hasty decisions are made about guilt or innocence."

Whether by intention or not, Thomas Worthington had taken the group's attention from Dieter Wolff and focused it on himself.

"But surely you see how the defense has twisted these issues," Morozov said sharply.

"I do, I do." Worthington nodded. "My meaning is this: We cannot simply say Hitler is guilty and that's where the buck stops. If this trial is to remain in the memory of mankind, serve as a reminder for all those who come after us, we are obliged to explain the basis for our decision. We must take each point, deliberate upon it and present our verdict in such a way that it illuminates some of this morass in which we find ourselves. What was so wrong about the Eichmann trial was the sense of impaired justice that came out even before the verdict was handed down. Everyone knew that there was no possible way Eichmann would ever leave Jerusalem alive, if only because he was being tried in the court of the survivors. We cannot afford to repeat that. I am not suggesting that the spirit of retribution is wrong; we would be less than human if it were missing from our thoughts. But we cannot allow ourselves to use it as justification for our verdict."

"I would like to know exactly what it is you are having diffi-

culty with,'' Morozov said bluntly, his patience wearing thin.
"After the appearance by Stephanus, do you have any doubts
that Hitler hungered after the war? Are you suggesting that the
testimony of the fascist Ritter is as convincing, or more so, as
that of Veznarod? And the historical accounts of Kupai—don't
they merit consideration?''

"Whether the events at Kupai did or did not take place is
irrelevant to me," Worthington retorted. "The whole point of the
prosecution turns on one crucial point: did Hitler actually issue
an explicit order for the killings, as Veznarod suggests? That is
all I am concerned with, because the count in the indictment
refers specifically to battlefield conduct. If Hitler did in fact give
the order, then the question of innocence is moot. However, we
do have Ritter's sworn testimony to the effect that he undertook
the killings on his own initiative.''

"Holy Mother of God, aren't you overlooking the *character* of
Ritter?'' Morozov burst out. "How can you equate him with
Veznarod?''

"A fair question," Worthington admitted. "And one that is
responsible for my not disregarding Veznarod's testimony altogether. But I must look over that part of the transcript again.''

"When you do, keep in mind that Hitler refused to confirm
Ritter's statement," Morozov said viciously. "That would be
proof enough for anyone!''

"Not here," Worthington said softly. "That's not the way we
do things in America.''

Morozov was about to come back on that remark when Etta
Kirsch intervened.

"What about the first count in the indictment, Thomas, the
planning and execution of war?''

"I am satisfied with the documentation and Stephanus' testimony. There is no question that Hitler was totally responsible for
setting the wheels of war in motion. However, is the death penalty warranted on this charge?''

"Is it?'' she asked quietly.

"Toller's point was well taken: we did not execute certain war
criminals for reasons of expediency. They had become useful to
us. Is the case reversed here? Shall we execute Hitler simply
because it *is* expedient to do so?'' Ivan Morozov laughed cruelly.

"That is exactly what Toller wants! He doesn't truly believe we will acquit, but neither does he think that we will impose execution. After all, it is not good politics to send an elderly man to his death prematurely; better to condemn him and send him back to live with the eternal shame his fellows will cast upon him. Except that in this case there would be no shame! He would be welcomed as a hero!

"And on the issue of genocide, Thomas," he continued: "do you have reservations there as well?" Morozov challenged him.

Etta Kirsch was grateful someone else had raised the question. Otherwise it would have been her responsibility, as a member of the Jewish people, to do so, and there was always a reluctance in her to discover what others truly thought of the Holocaust. Now she found it odd that the Russian should have been the one to put it to Worthington. A curious little morality play they had created for themselves, she thought, wherein a Russian might speak for the thoughts in a Jew's heart and the Jew for the Russian. The rest of the world might learn something from all this.

Morozov was about to repeat the question when Worthington held up his hand.

"Do you remember the recent case of the Belgian art collector, Brug? Really didn't have that much of an impact internationally, but it is instructive in several respects.

"Brug was an art dealer as well as collector, with a very impressive collection valued somewhere around sixteen million dollars. However, it came to light that Brug had also been a member in good standing of the SS, had served in Holland and then was transferred to Treblinka as Stangl's deputy in 1943. It isn't known exactly how many deaths he has on his hands; the general figure is at least two hundred fifty thousand.

"Brug was tried in Belgium, which refused an extradition request from Poland, and was found guilty of crimes against humanity leading to genocide. His sentence was fifteen years.

"Now, what interested me particularly was the rationale of the Court. The justice who pronounced sentence stated that for his acts Brug deserved life imprisonment. But because of his age, sixty-one, and the fact that twenty-three years had passed, the justice believed fifteen years enough. The crux of the statement and the major influence on the decision was the passage of time.

The Bench believed that the temporal distance was important, that somehow it mitigated the ferocity of the crime, thus the sentence as well.

"I would be less than candid if I said I knew how this case applies to the present one—or even if it does at all. That Hitler is guilty of advocating and arranging for genocide is clear. But again I am faced with the issue of punishment."

"Isn't it odd," Sir Adrian murmured to Etta Kirsch, "how punishment is such a complex consideration when it's a question of genocide and Jews . . ."

"You delivered a paper on just that question at the conclusion of the Nuremberg Trials," Etta Kirsch said. "I remember it well, thinking how lucid and simple your reasoning was."

She touched the blind man's forearm and whispered, "Of all of us, only you remain silent, as though you have held the debate on sentence within yourself, have come to a decision which satisfies you."

"You are aware that a justice never makes only one decision on a specific case," Sir Adrian told her. "Each time he renders a verdict, he includes in that one pronouncement all the years of his experience. Perhaps he breaks new ground, but much more often he is simply rounding out, embellishing, decisions made in the past.

"All my judicial life, when I was obliged to render a verdict, I asked myself this question: will I, by my act, be contributing to the enlightenment of men, shoring up values and beliefs which they might otherwise allow to atrophy, protecting them against those who would infringe upon and debase liberty? As far as has been humanly possible, I have come to understand my personal prejudices and particular philosophy of law and exclude them from the deliberation. Thomas Worthington labors under his strict interpretationalism; Morozov answers to the hatred for the Nazi which permeates his blood; Dieter Wolff struggles to be a decent, humane man in the face of national pressure brought on by a still-lingering national shame; you, my dear Etta, fear what the Jews will inherit if the world chooses to see only them as the people who sat in judgment over Adolf Hitler. My experience on the bench has been greater than any of yours; I am unburdened by such considerations. I have listened to the defense evidence and must admit that oftentimes it was impressive—not only in delivery, although that tended to dramatics, but in substance. Had there been a less capable prosecutor than Hans Kleemann, my decision would have been made very difficult, but it was he who kept that fundamental question before my consideration: will the acquittal of Adolf Hitler not diminish the intrinsic liberty of men; will it not justify not only his acts, but those of others who hold power today, who wield it as ruthlessly, assured of impunity?

"To that, Etta, I must answer in the affirmative and therefore vote Adolf Hitler guilty."

Without their knowing it, evening had slid over the sky, and the shadows of the buildings lengthened, then disappeared altogether as the first of the city lights dotted the panoramic vista. At half past six, Ivan Morozov, wanting to stretch his legs, walked down to the kitchens and returned with a platter of sandwiches. The twenty-minute pause for food was the only respite the group allowed itself.

"You might have a look at these," Morozov said, passing around copies of *The New York Times*, *The Times* of London, *Le Monde*, *Pravda* and *The Washington Post*. "It appears we have more than one country interested in pleading Adolf Hitler's cause."

There was no need to even open the papers, since the stories were headline news.

" 'El Salvador States Hitler Refugee—Offers Asylum,' " Etta Kirsch read out from the *Post*.

" 'The President of Guatemala today reiterated his belief that Hitler may not be considered guilty of any so-called war crimes. He has extended an offer of sanctuary to the former German dictator'—this from *Le Monde*," Dieter Wolff said.

Similar offers were being made by African republics, some barely a fortnight in existence. Libya and Iraq both condemned the Tribunal in principle, stating that Hitler could never expect to receive a fair trial with a Jew on the Bench. *The Times* of London noted a resurgence of Nazi propaganda and parades throughout South America, particularly in the right-wing dictatorships of

Chile and Argentina. The trial also gave fuel to new rumors about
former Nazis still at large: Bormann was reputed to have held a
press conference in Paraguay, and Mengele, according to witnesses, had moved into the coastal town of Pierra, an interim
stop between the jungles of the Amazon and São Paulo.

"Lift the stone and see what crawls from under it," Morozov
muttered in disgust.

"Seems to add another dimension to our deliberations, doesn't
it?" Wolff commented.

"Such developments were inevitable, were they not?" Sir Adrian said rhetorically. "I somehow believe that Hans Kleemann
foresaw the fury he was letting loose—unleashing it deliberately
so that we might all recognize its existence and act."

"Well said," Morozov applauded him. "The only good that
will come out of this rubbish is that the Israelis might pinpoint the
bastards, send in the special teams. What do you say, my dear
Etta: won't your people go that route?"

"They may. There are still those who want vengeance."

"Don't you?"

"I desire justice. I think we had better return to that consideration."

"Justice and vengeance are two sides of the same coin," Morozov told her flatly. "It's merely a matter of interpretation."

"The issue of what is being reported is moot in any case," Sir
Adrian interrupted. "If sanctuary should become a factor, then
from what we've heard, West Germany takes precedence. I agree
with Etta: we should address ourselves to the matters at hand."

Three hours later the split in opinion was more pronounced
than before. Sir Adrian, Etta Kirsch and Ivan Morozov believed
Hitler guilty on all counts and were in favor of the death penalty.
Dieter Wolff, who had not taken a major role in the deliberations,
retired to a corner of the room, taking his coffee and cigars with
him, and sat down at the desk, doodling aimlessly on a pad,
sometimes scribbling down a few quick sentences, ending them
with a question mark. For him there was a decision of a different
nature to make. The most intense discussions, which sometimes
flared into shouting matches, took place between Ivan Morozov
and Thomas Worthington. Although the American justice was
convinced of Hitler's guilt on the first and third counts of the

indictment, the waging of war and genocide respectively, and agreed there was reasonable premise for the second, battlefield misconduct, he still could not embrace the death penalty as easily as his colleagues had.

"But there are no alternatives!" Morozov kept hammering away. "Everyone disagreed with me when I suggested the Spandau example; very well, I appreciate the arguments against it. To incarcerate him is to set up a living memorial and antagonize the Germans—even this point of view I can accept. But we can't give him away anywhere else. As Sir Adrian noted, West Germany has first option. Besides, if any of the South American or Arab countries took him in, he would be a free man as soon as his feet touched their soil. So for lack of any other feasible penalties, death it must be. Surely, Thomas, you can see that what it really comes down to is how we let him live, or whether we do away with him altogether. I'm sorry such a decision upsets your liberal conscience, but . . ."

That remark could have set off another vituperative exchange, but Worthington merely sat back and shook his head.

"God knows, it's not the liberal conscience," he said slowly. "No, Ivan, there is a sense of imperfect justice to all this, don't you see? It is ironic that the most severe penalty one human being may pronounce upon another—death—is still not enough to expiate, even acknowledge the enormity of the crime committed. To kill Adolf Hitler is merely to finalize an act which began in April of 1945. I desire something more. I want our sentence to reflect the fact that we have come to terms with this man; that we understand his nature, what he represents. We have the chance to instruct mankind on the meaning of justice, what it is that men live by. To execute him seems to me to be so . . . inadequate."

"Do you think that such thoughts—doubts, really—have not been considered by all of us?" Sir Adrian said gently. "We are to pronounce judgment on one of the greatest criminals in all of history. We try to grapple with the immensity of his evil; we attempt to reduce it so that it fits into our human scope, that we might deal with it as we do with other issues. Yet it is a futile attempt. We cannot apply ordinary rules and precedents to this case. We seek some expression for our inadequacy. We press our minds to prescribe a punishment that would be in keeping with the crime, but that is equally impossible: we are mortals; the possibilities open to us are, of necessity, limited. Evil is boundless, volatile in imagination and devastating in execution. Retribution—how can that recompense? It is my belief that no one man nor any body of men can even begin to approach, in justice, the feat Hitler created through crime. The idea of an eye for an eye does not work here. The lesson that you seek so desperately to ascribe to mankind, Thomas, is found not in the nature of the sentence, but in the fact that this trial ever took place, that a tyrant has been judged by those who fought and suffered under him. *The fact that justice endures* as a living entity in the minds of men and is not erased when the threat is past—that is our victory. I know you would like a more concrete manifestation of this; so would we all. But we must understand our limitations. We must declare the sentence with dignity, in unison, and you above all must believe that it will be recognized for what it is—an ultimate expression of faith in ourselves, our ability to distinguish good from evil and act accordingly."

The American jurist nodded soberly.

"A little more time," he murmured. "I need that to believe as you do.

"Perhaps," he continued, "we can settle Dieter's issues now."

Dieter Wolff looked around from his seat at the desk and, stubbing out his cigar, rose and came over to the group.

"I am very tired," he announced. "God in heaven, it's after midnight! But I have thought about my position. Further debate is useless. It is a *cul-de-sac*. Therefore I propose the following: my resignation from the Bench in return for West Germany's dropping of the proposed announcement."

"But the Chancellor is counting on your presence as leverage with us," Morozov protested.

"That is true. But if he does not accept my proposal I will tell him that word of his interference will reach the press immediately. Even if he disavows the Ambassador's communication, I would have stained his credibility by going public with it. There will be no end to the uproar and embarrassment, and finally the humiliation. It is an awful, tragic step to take, against my own people, but there is no other if this Bench is to preserve its integrity."

"I believe the German Government will go along with you," Etta Kirsch said. "After all, they can insinuate that your resignation came from inside pressure, from us who were unanimous."

"Undoubtedly there will be that. Also, as Etta mentioned, Hitler and Toller would be delighted, and feel at least partially vindicated."

"And is that what you want, Dieter?"

"No, I want Hitler dead!"

Etta Kirsch rose and came to his side. She looked at each of them in turn, her face set, the eyes suddenly very cold.

"I cannot accept this sacrifice on Dieter's part," she said. "Our unity mustn't be broken. Therefore, to forestall any interference on the part of West Germany, this is what I propose."

Quickly she outlined her intentions and concluded, "In return for these efforts, I would ask that you, Thomas, guarantee us your vote. I'm sorry. I know you feel you need more time. But there isn't any left. Not anymore."

It was clear that this diminutive woman had taken control of the debate, slicing through the issues, coming to the heart of the matter. Alone, unmoved, she gazed at Worthington, her eyes demanding his answer.

"You spoke of sacrifice," Worthington said. "Now you are offering one just as great. Perhaps that is what we have come here to decide: what kind of sacrifice it is that we all must make. Very well, I give you my pledge. We act as one."

"Then thank God it is over with," Etta Kirsch whispered, and quickly left the room before the others could see her tears.

The court reconvened at one o'clock in the afternoon.

Adolf Hitler examined the face of each justice as he or she stepped into the court, seeking out the telltale sign that might be the clue to what was to come. This time, Dieter Wolff came first, followed by Morozov; then came Etta Kirsch leading Sir Adrian Potter. Hitler was surprised at himself for such anticipation, and he did not altogether understand it. Yet the feeling had seized him that he *must* know the verdict before it was put forth.

Beside him, Helmut Toller lolled carelessly in his chair, one arm thrown over its back. As he watched the ceremonial procession, Toller, unlike the man he represented, exhibited only calm. It was a sensation he was familiar with, that came over him at this point in every trial he conducted. Born of resignation, an understanding that he could not add any more to the substance of the proceedings, it removed him from the role of participant into that of observer. He did not speculate as to whether he had won or lost; he made no attempt to bolster the confidence of his client. This moment was an end point for him—the quiet, blissful aftermath—and he savored it alone.

Across the room, Hans Kleemann stared out through sightless eyes as the justices assembled. The moment he had worked so hard to realize had come, and after this day he would be obliged to take his leave of this world within the shield and take his place among the lives of ordinary men. This frightened him. He no longer knew what he would do there; where he might pick up the thread of his previous existence; which was the way home and who would be there for him, to comfort him after this thankless task.

When the Court was seated, Dieter Wolff, chosen to read the verdict, cleared his throat and opened the session. Because of the angle at which the television lights were set, his face was invisible; only the powerful hands holding a few sheets of paper could be seen, and the voice that spoke out might have been disembodied.

"It is the responsibility of this Tribunal," Wolff said slowly, his voice like gathering thunder, "to examine and weigh the charges brought against the accused and to make known its judgment. The Tribunal is prepared to do so this day on the case before it.

"The accused will rise."

Both Hitler and Helmut Toller slowly came to their feet.

"Adolf Hitler, this Tribunal believes that the verdict and sentence we are about to hand down will withstand the test of time and historical judgment. Because of the magnitude and significance of this case we must render the verdict and not permit you, who are guilty, to judge yourself. As far as is humanly possible, it is our duty to do so. Yet in the sentence the verdict demands may be found the imperfectibility of justice, for no sentence, no matter how novel, could be just compensation for your crimes. We are only too much aware of this.

"It is our belief that precisely in your unwillingness to accept your acts as crimes lies the fundamental issue of this trial. And you are not alone in this; then, in the days of the Third Reich, as now, there were many who stood by you and shared your vision. It is the ultimate task of the Tribunal to pass judgment on that vision. We call it evil.

"It would have been easier to look upon you as a common murderer. In essence, that is all you are. Yet your acts have filled the imaginations of millions of people, polluting, distorting and ultimately destroying the good lives they might otherwise have led. Therefore it is also our task to banish you beyond the pale so that you may not infect more than those you have already touched with your terrible contempt for remorse and disgust for forgiveness.

"Adolf Hitler, you have outraged us long enough! To our shame, you have ingratiated yourself with your own people, whom you devastated only three decades ago, and obliged us, in ignorance, to have you present among us. But it is in our power to dispatch you from our presence, and this is what shall be done.

"Adolf Hitler, you stand accused of waging aggressive war, of crimes in battlefield conduct and of crimes against humanity. The Tribunal finds you guilty on all three counts and prescribes the sentence of death by shooting. Further, the Tribunal now asks whether the State of Israel would be willing to carry out the sentence."

"On behalf of the State of Israel I accept such a responsibility," Etta Kirsch said.

"Then the Tribunal places the condemned in the custody of the United States Marine Corps until such time as Israeli representatives relieve them of this responsibility. The execution shall take place within forty-eight hours of the conclusion of these proceedings."

Dieter Wolff paused, then challenged: "Have you anything to say?"

Adolf Hitler moved from behind the table and limped to the

center of the court, looking up, trying to see past the lights that
hid his accusers.

"I have come before you," he stated in a sharp, imperious
voice, "but you have not listened. You choose to hide behind
hypocritical ideals which only sicken me. You have judged me
with vengeance, and in turn vengeance will be done to you!"

He continued to stand there even as the gavel was brought
down and the justices stepped down from the podium. He
watched them leave, then turned to Hans Kleemann, who was
passing him by.

"You have lost, Prosecutor; you know that." Hitler smiled at
him.

"No, you are wrong," Kleemann answered. "We have taken
a chance, and the result will not be known for a long time yet.
We brought you here and exposed you because such was the
challenge with which you presented us. We have met it and
passed it on."

"It is cold comfort for you, Prosecutor." Hitler sneered. "It
will not sustain you very long."

"That is untrue," Hans Kleemann answered. "You have
brought great sorrow into my life; I will not deny that. Yet I did
what I had to do, and if I remember, in times when I think of my
loss, what has been done here today, I am satisfied. From this
satisfaction, I receive the strength to carry on."

Adolf Hitler laughed, and he was still laughing when Hans
Kleemann walked away from him—not in the direction the justices had taken, but straight up the center aisle of the Assembly.
For the shield had been raised and he had walked under it, a free
man.

The man who entered Chief of Staff General Dan Mendelssohn's
office that autumn dawn was weary and sick at heart. One could
read the symptoms from his swollen eyes, resting in hollows
tinged with red.

"They have accepted the proposition, Dan," he said, in a voice
cracked dry by too many cigarettes, worn raw by too much arguing.

General Mendelssohn butted his cigarette and came over to the windowsill, from which he took a large fresh orange. He peeled it quickly, broke apart the sections and handed them to the Justice Minister.

"Thank you, Dan."

The General watched his friend eat, sucking noisily for every drop of the fresh juice.

"What was the compromise?" Mendelssohn asked. He knew there had to be one—at least one. Otherwise the whole affair could have been settled well before this hour.

"He may not come anywhere near Israeli soil," the Justice Minister said. He looked keenly at the General. "There was nothing I could do about that."

Dan Mendelssohn nodded. He came to the window and viciously pushed it open. The cold air—still night air—felt very good on his face, and he thrust it forward, closing his eyes.

"Politicians—no offense intended—dislike having other people make decisions for them, yet they themselves think it their right to act in precisely the opposite fashion," he mused. "I'm very glad Etta Kirsch consulted no one."

"We wouldn't have gotten this far if she had," the Justice Minister said, chewing on the last slice of orange. "She virtually committed Israel to the carrying out of the sentence on Adolf Hitler."

He looked up at the General and asked, "What do you think made her do it?"

"You."

"I?"

"Of course. By taking responsibility then and there, she short-circuited the decision-making process, forced the issue before the Cabinet and gave you the opportunity to act as you would have liked to in the first instance. Etta Kirsch knew *you* wouldn't pass up the chance to deal with Hitler. She made things easier for you."

"Clever woman," the Justice Minister said gently. "And not without bravery either. She has incurred a great deal of political wrath from those who would rather we had had nothing to do with the execution of the sentence, who fear that only Jews will be blamed for Hitler's death."

"Forget it," Dan Mendelssohn advised him. "Whoever disagrees with us today will be proud tomorrow. It is only fitting that a Jew should deal with Hitler."

"Very well; then let's get under way before the Cabinet decides to have yet another vote on the matter. Where is Hitler now?"

"Five o'clock our time, then it's eleven in the evening in New York," Mendelssohn calculated. "He should be leaving any moment."

"Who is providing the transport and security?"

"A fellow I know by the name of Rokossovsky," Mendelssohn said blandly.

"I think you had better tell me how the Russians came to be involved."

"They're not. Rokossovsky heads a liaison intelligence agency with the acronym of ISIS out of Geneva, a sort of intermediary between the Americans and the Soviets. We've had dealings with him: highly reliable and absolutely discreet. Rokossovsky, by the way, is related to General Rokossovsky of Berlin fame."

"So no one government bears the onus in moving Hitler."

"Precisely."

"Go on."

"Hitler will arrive in Geneva on board Rokossovsky's private jet," Mendelssohn continued. "The security will disembark and our man will get on. Aside from himself and Hitler there will be only the pilot, copilot and navigator present. The plane will then leave for Location Delta in the Indian Ocean."

"Oh? And how have you managed to work this Location Delta into affairs?"

"When I heard of the ruckus in the Cabinet, an alternative site had to be arranged—neutral, distant and isolated," Mendelssohn said. "Rokossovsky was quite helpful there. He remembered an old British landing strip in the Indian Ocean. His representative was sent down to investigate the feasibility of using it for our needs; among other things, the runway would have had to be in reasonable shape for landing an aircraft. As it turned out, the location was ideal, from every standpoint."

"I see," the Justice Minister muttered. "Your efficiency knows no bounds."

"That is because I do not share your encumbrances."

"That was uncalled for. So how many people will know the final destination?"

"The pilot, copilot, navigator; Rokossovsky and his man who checked out the site; myself and the soldier. Seven in all."

"And I?"

"Do you want to know?"

The Justice Minister smiled at his friend and shook his head. "No, not really."

"This is the absolute minimum needed to bring the operation home. But I can assure you that the site will remain secret—forever."

"There mustn't be the slightest possibility of anyone's finding it, especially those who would turn it into a shrine."

"We have taken certain precautions against a possible accidental discovery," Dan Mendelssohn assured him.

"What about the man, then?"

"I waited for you to return before the selection."

The General picked up six bits of paper, each no bigger than his thumb, off his desk, held them above his cap and released them, watching the slips flutter to the cotton lining.

"Will you choose or shall I?"

"There are only numbers on the papers."

"Each corresponds to a name on the sheet." Dan Mendelssohn gestured with his cap. "The men have been chosen for their experience, past duty, specialization and so on. Each has been recalled from his unit to the vicinity of Tel Aviv, a medical reason being the usual excuse. I can have the chosen one here within the hour."

"And his name will never be revealed?"

"Never. Once here, he will be told of his mission and sworn to eternal secrecy. There will be no official listing of this mission, no commendation upon its execution, nothing at all."

"I suppose it doesn't matter who chooses," the Justice Minister murmured. "I might as well do it."

His eyes held those of General Mendelssohn as his fingers dipped into the hat, moved about through the papers and tightened on one slip.

"Number five," the Justice Minister said.

Dan Mendelssohn nodded. "How does it feel to have bestowed an anonymous immortality upon a man?" he asked lightly.

"I wouldn't have wished this kind of task on anyone," the Justice Minister said harshly.

"I know," Dan Mendelssohn answered him. "After all these years, it's as though we are sending a man out to execute a ghost."

The Israeli fighter, devoid of national markings, landed at the far end of the Geneva airport. It was still very early in the morning, and there were few passengers to witness this odd arrival. The fighter slowed and taxied close to where a Boeing 707 stood, poised on the edge of a runway.

From the rear cockpit of the fighter a figure emerged dressed in pilot's overalls, wearing a flight helmet whose visor obscured his face. He jumped down, holding a flight bag under his arm, and took a few steps toward the Boeing. As though on cue, another man appeared at the rear door of the 707.

They exchanged no words as the paratrooper trotted up the ramp and brushed by Rokossovsky's representative. Only when he was inside did the paratrooper remove his helmet and look down the aisle. Adolf Hitler was sitting in a window seat, the shade having been pulled down over the Plexiglas. The paratrooper turned back to see that the other had already descended onto the tarmac. He depressed a lever and the hydraulic gears folded the ramp neatly against the panels of the aircraft. By the time he had taken his seat, directly behind Hitler, the aircraft was rolling down the runway.

There was no fury or madness about him now as there had been in Berlin in 1945. He had no one to accompany him, which he found a relief. He was alone with his thoughts, and the idea that these were the last hours of his second life was held at bay by the particular sense of satisfaction of believing he had achieved his aim.

He remembered the final hour he had passed with Toller after the court adjourned. They had been taken to one of the conference rooms and there, at Hitler's request, had had a bottle of white wine sent up from the kitchens. The wine had been deliciously cold and invigorating, and throughout the conversation he had drunk most of it.

"Do you feel you have failed me?" he asked Toller.

"In a way," Toller replied. "I could have protested the choice of Israel to carry out the sentence. It is humiliating to think that you should be handled by Jews."

"Ironic, isn't it?" Hitler mused. "The 'chosen' people, whom *I chose* to exterminate, will now kill me. I always believed their craving for revenge would lead them to gross stupidity. In murdering me, the sons of Abraham will carry the stigma for the rest of their days. They will be branded as surely as Cain was, and one day others will seek them out and I shall be given my just retribution. No, let them bury themselves!"

"Where does that leave you? Would it not have been better, more worthwhile, to have lived, as a free man?" Toller paused, then asked, "Did you ever believe you would be vindicated?"

"For someone who uses words so deftly and with such precision, your question is sloppy," Hitler told him. "Yes, certainly I believed we would *win*. You were very good, brilliant—no one could have served me better. But the fact that victory was denied to us—in the sense that I must die—does not mean that I am not vindicated. On the contrary, my death will be the final stroke on the powerful portrait you have painted."

"Is that why you did not help me—especially on the question of Kupai?"

"You knew from the beginning that I wished to be judged on *my* truths, not anyone else's. I came forward not to deny acts, but to confirm them. I demanded to know whether others could sit in judgment upon me while guilty of all that they accuse me of. You were aware of these intentions, Helmut Toller; but being the attorney you are, you forgot them and became lost in your passion to set me free. This does not speak against you; it only shows the differences between us."

"And now you are satisfied: the world has heard from you and rests uneasy because of the verdict?"

"It is enough."

They were silent for a moment. Then Hitler asked, "You never mentioned if Bendt or any of the others called upon you."

Helmut Toller raised his eyes, unsettled by the statement.

"Yes, I met with Bendt in Munich," he said slowly. "He was the one who gave us Ritter. Do you know Bendt?"

"Personally, no. But I know a little of the movement. It is comforting to still have it out there . . . working for the future of National Socialism. . . ."

Adolf Hitler poured out the last of the wine and drank it down quickly. His hand was trembling, and his black eyes shifted around the room, reminding Toller of those of a cornered animal.

"What will you do now?" Hitler asked suddenly, then held up his hand. "No, do not answer me, for I know what you will say: 'I haven't decided,' or something to that effect."

Hitler pushed away his glass and leaned close to the young man.

"It was a sordid thing Kleemann did—bring your foster mother to the trial. But you must forget that—forget him and her and the foolishness they brought on your head. What do they understand of your motives and beliefs? They belong to an age that is rapidly passing away; it is left to you to guide your people into the future.

"Listen to me carefully, Helmut. You must have strength and resolution. Do not be afraid of the direction in which history is tending; instead, seize it with your hands and let it guide you. There were instances when I despaired—yes, truly despaired— at your lack of resolve. But I have come to believe that you understand me and my intentions as no other man has and, more, that you see them as being right. I ask for no promises; you are not in the correct state of mind to give them to me. But I believe, as surely as I am going to die, that you will be the one who will bring National Socialism glory. You are my hope! Remember for all time the words you spoke on Walpurgis Night: 'It is different this night!' "

Toller said nothing. He wanted to leave the room at once, to get away from the presence of this pitiful old man who was slowly coming to face the fact that he would have to die, yet who was trying to alleviate this realization by seeing Toller as his kin, a reincarnation not only of the man but of his beliefs as well.

He is not wrong, Toller thought. I am the inheritor of the mystery; the man who knows Hitler more intimately than anyone else; his confidant and protector; his rightful heir.

Suddenly he took Hitler's hands in his own and, staring back into the glazed black eyes, spoke with a voice terrible in its pride and conviction.

"I could not have defended you without faith in you or that which you represent. One day, I promise you, this verdict will be overturned and justice done . . . for I have the faith!"

Adolf Hitler pushed up the screen over his window and squinted against the brilliance of early-morning light. He swallowed several times in an effort to release the pressure on his ears.

That was how their conversation had ended. After he had said his words, Helmut Toller rose and left the room without turning back once, exactly as Hitler had believed he would do.

So, he thought, I have my disciple, and from him many others will spring. What fools they are, Kleemann and the others, to think that by killing me they also murder the faith! It will live to overwhelm them, and through it I will have attained immortality.

Drowsiness tempted the paratrooper, and several times he found his head nodding forward or slipping along the back of the seat toward the window. He pinched the skin on his neck, just above a central nerve, and shifted in his seat. Glancing at the window just ahead of him, the paratrooper saw the reflection of Adolf Hitler's face. He appeared to be sleeping, mouth open slightly, the scar along his cheek pulsing lightly as blood pounded beneath it. There was the beginning of a silvery-gray beard on the chin.

How odd it is, the paratrooper thought, that the condemned and the executioner should fall prey to such a human weakness at this time. And that was all the consideration he gave the matter, for he was not a poet, who might view such a situation with awe, or a philosopher, whose instinct would lead him to contemplation. The paratrooper was a manifestation of will, the tool which had only one task to perform. Because he was a veteran and long experienced at his craft, he removed all personal feelings from his mind. The significance of his work would flood his consciousness when it was safe, in the aftermath, the point at which what he was to do could not be changed or relived but only remembered.

Another two hours passed before the warning lights came on and the aircraft began its descent.

A hot, dry wind blew along the length of the runway, swirling bits of grass, bleached weed and sand around his boots. The paratrooper looked down the runway, at the jagged cracks that split the concrete into a senseless mosaic, and wondered how the pilot had managed to set his aircraft down without having the concrete buckle under him.

At the edge of the strip, a path had been cut into the tall sweet grass, and beyond it the paratrooper could see the first outcropping of rock. There was a rough spot of fresh red paint on one of the boulders, as though a child had walked up to it and slapped down a brush.

"You will have to help me."

The paratrooper swung around, startled by the voice. Adolf Hitler was standing at the edge of the platform that had been lowered from the plane door to the ground. But there were no handrails, and he was frightened to take the steps without support.

"I can't climb down this," he said. "There is nothing to hold on to."

The paratrooper placed his canvas bag on the concrete and, stepping over, held out one arm. Adolf Hitler grasped it, the bony fingers like claws on the other's flesh. Slowly, step by step, the paratrooper guided him down.

"So this is where I am supposed to die," Hitler said, his voice broken by a faint wheezing of his chest. "In this horrible, desolate place where, I am certain, no man lives. Didn't they know, whoever thought of this, that I hate the hot climates?"

The paratrooper said nothing but gestured with his arm in the direction of the path.

"Your orders are not to speak with me?" he inquired. He stopped walking and, as the Israeli came up to him and brushed his shoulder, he screamed at him, "I asked you a question! What kind of soldier are you?"

The paratrooper could feel drops of the old man's spittle on his cheek. Very deliberately he raised his arm, all the while keeping his eyes on Hitler, and struck him across the face. The momentum sent the old man sprawling into the grass.

The paratrooper squatted, undid the fastenings of his bag and brought out his machine gun. Having fitted the magazine, he then picked up a metal container, the size of a large coffee tin, and came to Hitler.

"*Raus!*" he said softly. When Hitler, curled up on the grass, did not move, the Israeli spoke again.

"It makes no difference to me if I shoot you here."

Adolf Hitler held out his hand for support, but the paratrooper did not move. Finally he managed to get to his feet and staggered back onto the path.

"This pleases you, doesn't it?" Hitler slurred his words through blood as he staggered along, his bad leg sliding along the grass. "You think you will deny me my dignity? You are a mongrel, from a race of parasites and whores; what do you know of human dignity?"

The paratrooper moved on steadily, eyes fixed on the back of Hitler's neck.

"Napoleon was exiled to Elba, but he returned!" Hitler was screaming. "They tried to kill him too, but it doesn't happen— not until Death is ready. And I am not ready!"

They had walked clear of the grass and stood on the edge of a shallow embankment, a gully that had been gouged out by the rains of the winter season but now lay dusty and dry, like an old grave that had gone unused.

"This?" Hitler demanded, confronting his executioner. "This is where you propose to bury me?"

Adolf Hitler stared incredulously at the paratrooper, his swollen face laden with sweat and blood. He remembered the way it had been in 1945, the fury and fires and death stalking the Reich. The terrible sounds of rockets bursting into the streets, of men screaming out as twelve years of vengeance poured back upon their heads; the hysteria of fear . . . it all came back to him. But here there was silence, broken only by the wind sweeping through the grass, and the only light was that of the sun which blazed down upon him and clouded his mind with its heat.

"Vengeance!" he croaked, the voice breaking up deep in his throat. "I shall have vengeance for this!"

At the sound of laughter, Hitler stared dementedly at the Israeli. But it was not he who had uttered the sound. The paratrooper was bringing up his gun, and at the same time, stepping back and behind him, Death rose from the grass and threw back its head laughing and nodding . . .

. . ."It is done," Etta Kirsch said.

Although it was three o'clock in the morning, when the human body is most vulnerable and susceptible to death, the justices were all gathered together in her suite. They were awaiting the telephone call which would inform them that the sentence had been carried out.

"But no one has told us—"

"Thomas, it *is* over," Etta Kirsch interrupted gently. "It's as though a goose had walked over my grave. I can feel it. Can't you? Something is different now."

The men looked at each other. Morozov shrugged and lit another cigarette; Dieter Wolff brought his great hands over his face, slowly massaging his eyes. Only Sir Adrian, the sightless man, did not move but seemed to cock his head to one side.

"She is right," he said finally.

A minute later the telephone rang. . . .

. . . In the hands of the paratrooper the weapon appeared puny. He gripped it hard, and so the gun did not buck. The first bullets streamed through the suddenly molten barrel, racing mindlessly at the old man who, with arm outflung as though to embrace them, was staggering into their path. . . .

. . ."Lillian, what time would it be?"

Lillian Grubber shook her head and stepped up to the porter who was pushing the cart with their bags. Impatiently he pointed to the overhead clock by the deserted lounge and continued on his way to the gate.

"A few minutes before three," she answered.

Hans Kleemann put a hand on her arm.

"What did you say?"

"A few minutes before . . . three."

The realization of what he was asking came over her, and she came to him and placed her arms around him.

"It is over," Kleemann murmured, holding her tightly. "Thank God it is over with at last."

She set her hands upon his chest and looked up at him.

"I don't want to go back," Lillian murmured. "Not now, not ever!"

"Just for a little while," Kleemann answered her. "Only a day or two so that you can set your things in order, and I mine. Then . . ."

"I don't want to see Helmut," she said. "I couldn't bear that."

"There is no need. You can stay at my home in the country. Just tell me what it is you want brought from Emmaus right now and I'll have someone do it. As for the house, well, you can decide on that later. But you never have to go back—never. . . ."

The porter who was responsible for their luggage had reached the gate and was looking back, staring and shaking his head at the strange sight of two people huddled together in the center of the all-but-deserted air terminal. . . .

. . . The bullets proved the stronger. They plunged deep into his body, spinning through the flesh, colliding with and breaking the bones to finally pass out. As Hitler was driven back, so the paratrooper advanced, taking care to fire directly at the torso. . . .

. . . "The Führer is dead; long live the Führer!"

"The Führer!"

Erik Bendt, who had arrived in New York several hours before, raised his glass and touched that of Helmut Toller. Together the two men drank the toast of champagne.

"It is the end and the beginning," Bendt said proudly. "As in all of nature, life comes from death."

Helmut Toller held his eyes steady and brought his glass up once more.

"To the new National Socialism," he said.

"To your leadership!" Bendt answered.

. . . Adolf Hitler was sprawled in the gully, his chest ripped away, one leg almost severed from his hip. The paratrooper stepped into the ditch and kicked the head so that it might face up. He brought out a miniature camera from a pocket and began taking pictures, careful to get the whole of the corpse in each frame. . . .

. . ."What is this—a memento?'' the director asked Kuzmin, who was scrutinizing the fresh copy of *The New York Times*.

"The picture on the left is that of Helmut Toller, the defense attorney.''

"Yes, I can see that.''

"Tomorrow I will request GRU intelligence to assemble a dossier on him,'' Kuzmin said.

"Oh, and why is that?''

"The next time, I do not wish to wait twenty-five years before killing an Adolf Hitler.''

"Call me.'' The director smiled and motioned toward his camera. "I'll have something on him by then.''

. . . When the photographs had been taken, the paratrooper replaced the camera and carefully opened the metal container. Taking note of the direction from which the wind was blowing, he stooped over the corpse and began to sprinkle light gray crystals over it. The substance was a highly toxic and corrosive compound which dissolved even steel. In a few minutes there would be nothing left of the body. The flesh, hair, even the bones would have been reduced to a dry powder. Nothing would remain, not even enough for the smallest predator.

The paratrooper emptied the tin and stepped out of the gully. The smell of decomposing flesh already filled his nostrils, and he picked up his gun and the can and slowly backed away. But he kept his eyes on the metamorphosis of the corpse as though he believed that any moment it might regain life.

He could not see that Death had swept by him and had already claimed Adolf Hitler for itself.

All Futura Books are available at your bookshop or newsagent, or can be ordered from the following address:
Futura Books, Cash Sales Department,
P.O. Box 11, Falmouth, Cornwall.

Please send cheque or postal order (no currency), and allow 25p for postage and packing for the first book plus 10p per copy for each additional book ordered up to a maximum charge of £1.05 in U.K.

Customers in Eire and B.F.P.O. please allow 25p for postage and packing for the first book plus 10p per copy for the next eight books, thereafter 5p per book.

Overseas customers please allow 40p for postage and packing for the first book and 12p per copy for each additional book.